Fully Involved
Amy Knupp

TORONTO • NEW YORK • LONDON
AMSTERDAM • PARIS • SYDNEY • HAMBURG
STOCKHOLM • ATHENS • TOKYO • MILAN • MADRID
PRAGUE • WARSAW • BUDAPEST • AUCKLAND

Recycling programs
for this product may
not exist in your area.

ISBN-13: 978-0-373-71658-6

FULLY INVOLVED

This edition published by arrangement with Harlequin Books S.A.

For questions and comments about the quality of this book
please contact us at Customer_eCare@Harlequin.ca.

® and TM are trademarks of the publisher. Trademarks indicated with ® are registered in the United States Patent and Trademark Office, the Canadian Trade Marks Office and in other countries.

www.eHarlequin.com

Printed in U.S.A.

ABOUT THE AUTHOR

Amy Knupp lives in Wisconsin with her husband, two sons and five (feline) beasts. She graduated from the University of Kansas with degrees in French and journalism and feels lucky to use very little of either one in her writing career. In her spare time she enjoys reading, college basketball, addictive computer games and watching big red fire trucks race by. She's currently fully involved in listening to the voices in her head and writing more books. To learn more about Amy and her stories, visit www.amyknupp.com.

Books by Amy Knupp

HARLEQUIN SUPERROMANCE

1342—UNEXPECTED COMPLICATION
1402—THE BOY NEXT DOOR
1463—DOCTOR IN HER HOUSE
1537—THE SECRET SHE KEPT
1646—PLAYING WITH FIRE*
1652—A LITTLE CONSEQUENCE*

*The Texas Firefighters

Don't miss any of our special offers. Write to us at the following address for information on our newest releases.

Harlequin Reader Service
U.S.: 3010 Walden Ave., P.O. Box 1325, Buffalo, NY 14269
Canadian: P.O. Box 609, Fort Erie, Ont. L2A 5X3

For being such a solitary craft, writing sure takes the support of a lot of patient people.

Many thanks to:

Kay Stockham, Jeannie Watt, Ellen Hartman and Kim Van Meter, my sisters in Superdom, who are there each day, from brainstorming to consoling and everything in between.

Extra thanks to Kay for all the time you took to critique this story in its earliest form.

Amy, Anna, Becky, Carol, Karen, Kristin and Mel... you're always there cheering me on, and this time the girls' weekend in the middle of the deadline was just what I needed to stay (mostly) sane.

Shawna Clawson, for the detailed information you provided on custody hearings, especially considering the last-minute nature of my plea.

The retired firefighter whom I nearly drowned in e-mail questions over the course of writing this series. I couldn't have written these stories without your generous input.

Justin, Camden, Colton, Mom and Dad, once again, for putting up with my many moods, fits and meltdowns (not to mention the messy house and the lack of home cooking).

CHAPTER ONE

CLAY MARLOW WONDERED for the hundredth time this week if he'd screwed up with his three-year-old daughter yet again. Wondered if she had, indeed, stopped crying as soon as he'd been out of sight, as his sister had sworn she would. Walking away from those tear-filled brown eyes nearly leveled him every single time. Every decision he made concerning his little girl made him doubt himself more.

He pulled into the small lot next to the Shell Shack, the beach bar owned by his friends Derek and Macey. Whipped too fast into the parking space next to Derek's red truck with his own extended-cab pickup.

And heard the cringe-inducing impact of his front bumper on the motorcycle a split second before he saw it.

Dammit. He needed more sleep. And a parenting manual.

He jumped out of the truck, adrenaline pumping, relieved there was no one in sight, which meant no one had been on the parked bike.

Wait a minute. He knew that bike. Knew exactly

who it belonged to. Andie Tyler, who, like him, was an attendant in Derek and Macey's upcoming wedding.

He didn't know Andie well, but he got the impression she wasn't particularly understanding or easy to get along with. Especially when someone crashed into her beloved Harley-Davidson.

He took the walkway to the nearest bar entrance. Macey had invited the four wedding attendants to a happy-hour get-together. All because Andie was to arrive in town today.

At the open doorway, he stopped. His eyes were drawn to Andie like a hummingbird to red. She sat on the outside of the small group, her stool a couple of feet from Derek's. She had a half smile on her face, while the others—Selena and her husband, Evan, were on Derek's other side and Macey was behind the bar—laughed without restraint at something Evan had said.

In spite of her rough edges, she was pretty, someone who'd caught his attention last summer when she'd spent a couple of months on San Amaro Island working behind the bar with Derek.

Pretty or not, she was going to be one pissed biker chick.

Enough stalling. Might as well get this over with. He forced himself to join the group, stepping between Andie and Derek.

ANDIE LOOKED UP TO find Clay Marlow standing inches away, taking all kinds of razzing from the others for being late.

"Andie, do you remember Clay?" Macey asked above the din.

Oh, she remembered Clay. You didn't forget someone who looked like *that*. Ever. Didn't matter that the people he hung out with were just as beautiful. He'd always stood out as the all-American guy who could do no wrong against Evan, the shameless flirt, and Derek, moody and unpredictable.

Biceps as thick as tree trunks bulged from a navy San Amaro Island Fire Department T-shirt stretched across Clay's shoulders. He had short almost-black hair, a cleanly shaved, stubborn-as-hell square jaw and…those eyes. Chocolate with flecks of gold. They'd made her nervous and fidgety when he turned them on her. They were filled with intense do-the-right-thing-ness and Andie sometimes did the wrong thing. Just because.

Clay laughed at whatever Evan said to him, then quietly said to Andie, "Your bike didn't happen to be parked out there beside Derek's truck, did it?"

His use of the past tense made Andie's skin prickle with foreboding. She narrowed her eyes. "Yes. Why?"

Clay shot a look at his buddies and rubbed the back of his neck. "I didn't see it," he said. "I hit it when I pulled in. I'm s—"

"My *bike?*" Andie was off the stool and out of the bar before he could finish speaking.

She saw it as soon as she cleared the doorway. The motorcycle lay on its side on the pavement, several feet from the front of a dark blue truck. The motorcycle's front wheel was bent and lying at an abnormal angle.

The handlebars were also crooked, and her formerly shiny bike was generally scratched up, dented and no longer pretty by any stretch of the imagination. She had the urge to yell but held herself to muttering under her breath.

For the first time since she'd arrived on the island this afternoon, she noticed how hot it was. The sun beat down on her and she felt as if she was burning up. She clamped her teeth down on the inside of her lip, tears pricking her eyes.

All of her belongings in the world had been strapped to the back and were now scattered on the pavement. She knelt and hurriedly picked them up.

Heat burned her cheeks as she scrambled to pack everything away. Nothing quite like having your meager life on display for anyone who wandered past.

"I'm really sorry." Clay came up behind her and bent to gather her toiletries. As he tucked them into one of her duffel bags, the sun glinted off the metal of her handgun. The thirty-eight she took everywhere with her caught Clay's eye, too, judging by the way he froze for a heartbeat.

"I've got it." She took the bag from him and zipped it shut.

"I'll take care of the repairs." Clay picked up the book about technology and the environment she was currently reading, and she snatched it away from him.

"Yeah." She coached herself to take a deep breath and calm the hell down. Likely his insurance company would do the taking care of, but whatever. "That'd be good."

Without his or his insurance company's "taking care of it" there was no way she could get her bike road-worthy again. She didn't have insurance, and though she had a puny emergency fund saved up, she was spending a lot of it on Macey's wedding.

Her bike was the only possession besides her gun that mattered to her. It was her freedom, her lifestyle. Her way off the island when she needed to escape. She would undoubtedly have to go without it for several days, minimum, and that made her sick to her stomach. Glancing at the tangle of metal she wanted to cry or, better yet, beat the crap out of something. Or someone.

"What *happened?*" Macey asked as she appeared on the scene. Evan walked out more slowly behind her.

"I didn't see it," Clay said. "I was preoccupied and this is where I normally park. The motorcycle was in the way."

"How could you miss that, man?" Evan leaned

against the front of Derek's truck. "That's not some kid's tricycle that you can't see under the wheel."

Andie seconded that. How the hell did a guy miss a dark red Harley Sportster?

Clay shrugged, clearly aggravated. "I'll take care of everything."

Andie slowly hefted the motorcycle upright. "The exhaust is busted up. Handlebars. Brake pedal."

Her control faltered and she clenched her teeth. She glanced around at Clay's bully of a pickup truck. How deeply satisfying it would feel to kick the crap out of it and punch dents into the sides.

"Andie." Macey employed her calm but firm voice, the one she'd used plenty on Derek when he'd been so messed up last year. "Let's take your bags inside. You can eat and we'll figure this out."

"I'll treat," Clay said. He stuck his hands in his jeans pockets and let them go inside ahead of him.

"I'll buy my own dinner," Andie told Clay after she put her bags in the back room.

Derek was behind the bar covering for Macey, and Clay took the seat between Andie and Selena. Macey rejoined her fiancé and explained what had happened to him and Selena as she topped off Andie's lemonade.

"Know anyplace that fixes Harleys?" Andie asked Derek.

"Not off the top of my head, but Gus might. I'll ask him tonight. Want something to eat? A burger?"

Andie shook her head. "Just some nachos, please."

"Get out," Macey told Derek, gesturing over her shoulder. "I've got it covered. You're off today."

"Bossy thing. Lucky you're so cute." He pressed a quick kiss to Macey's cheek, came around the counter and sat on Andie's right side.

"So where are you staying?" Macey asked. "Did you find a place yet?"

"I came here first. I need something cheap and temporary."

"I used to love cheap and temporary," Evan quipped. The other two men laughed but he earned a slap on the arm from a very pregnant Selena, whom Andie had just met this afternoon. "Where'd you live last summer when you were here?"

"In my tent. Closest campground is on the mainland about ten miles north. Works great as long as you have transportation." She couldn't help glancing at Clay.

"I said I'm sorry." He smiled sheepishly, making Andie forgive him a little bit.

"I told you you can stay with us," Macey said.

"Third wheel on the soon-to-be bride and groom's couch? Thanks, but I don't think so." Andie shuddered. "Might as well go with you on your honeymoon."

"No way," Derek said. "You promised you'd help run things here so Macey will actually stop worrying and enjoy herself."

Andie smiled and nodded, doubting Macey would have any trouble at all losing herself in her sexy fireman husband.

"Do you smoke?" Clay asked abruptly.

"No." She tried to figure out how that related to running the bar.

"Have wild parties?"

She stared at him. "Only when properly inspired."

"If you can keep it uninspired, I have a place you can rent," he said.

"Thank God. I was going to suggest it, Clay, but I didn't want to presume," Macey said. "Clay has a duplex over on Seagull Lane. He doesn't really need a tenant but I've been telling him he has the space so why not make the extra income?"

"I'm sure it's over my budget," Andie said honestly. Taking advantage of opportunities had become her way of life, vital when you traveled with no permanent address. When you never knew where your next meal or room would come from, it paid to not rule things out. But her budget was definitely closer to campground than duplex.

"I might be convinced to negotiate," Clay said. "To make up for wrecking your bike."

Now he was talking her language. "*I* might be convinced to check it out." She forced herself to be warmer than she'd been with him so far.

"Let's go now," he said. "I'll even give you a ride."

"Big of you," she said, grabbing a handful of her chips and shoving a couple in her mouth. "On the drive over you can start thinking about your 'I destroyed her livelihood' discount."

CLAY FOLLOWED ANDIE OUT to his truck and couldn't help watching the way her hips swayed and her worn jeans hugged her curves. The snug burgundy T-shirt fit her slender body as if she'd been born in it. Her usually straight brown hair hung just past her shoulders, tousled and tangled, he assumed, from her helmet and ride into town.

She had a hint of mystery about her, never one to talk about herself as far as he'd seen. Restless. According to Macey, she drifted around the country, never settling in any one place for more than a few weeks at a time.

Clay was well acquainted with that kind of restlessness, or had been in a past life. He'd never given in to it like Andie did, but he'd felt it. Let it get him into plenty of trouble as a teen. He knew what *he'd* been trying to get away from. What, he wondered, haunted this woman?

She stopped beside her motorcycle and Clay frowned.

"Let's get it loaded in the truck and I'll find a place to take it in the next day or so."

She nodded sadly as if she'd lost her best friend, her feistiness gone.

He opened the tailgate and pulled out a ramp,

then they turned the bike around and tried to roll it toward the back of the truck. The damage made it difficult.

When they got to the ramp, they inched it along until, finally, it was loaded.

Clay secured the bike in the bed of the truck, brushed his hands on his jeans and went to the passenger side to open her door. He checked his instinct to help her up, clenching his fist. He went around and climbed in his side.

"Bike means a lot to you, huh?" he said as he started the truck.

She snapped her head toward him, her eyes narrowed. "It and the three bags you knocked off the back of it... That's pretty much everything I own."

"Takes guts to live like that."

She stared at him. "Maybe," she said finally. "Or maybe it's a lack of guts."

He studied her in his peripheral vision.

Though it probably wasn't wise, he was drawn to her. Lured by the need to know more about her, to figure her out. What made her doubt herself?

What made her run?

ANDIE EXHALED HER RELIEF when Clay pulled up at his place. She could normally hold her own with anyone but riding in the truck with him made her clam up. He'd seemed to fill up the whole space with muscles and testosterone, and she'd been hyperaware of everything about him.

The duplex looked fine from the outside. It was a narrow, sand-colored, three-story building built on stilts and a carport. Instead of side by side units, they were stacked on top of each other. Clay lived in the top two floors, he explained.

They climbed the flight of stairs to the main door on the side of the lower unit. He unlocked it for her.

The place had more than enough room for her, though she imagined most people would consider it small. The living room was to her left when she walked in, and a compact kitchen was to the right. The rooms were semifurnished.

"Love the vintage look," she said, running her hand over a circa seventies Formica dinette with an olive-green plastic chair at each end. There was a futon in the living room, mismatched coffee and end tables, and a low shelf on cement blocks that could act as a TV stand.

"It serves the purpose," he said, almost apologetically.

"Oh, I was serious. It's perfect for the space."

"There's an in-ground pool in the back you can use when you want."

Andie went to the other door and looked out at a tiny balcony. Below, she could see blue. Not bad.

She wandered farther in and poked her head into a narrow bathroom—as long as it had running water, she couldn't care less.

Across from the bathroom was the bedroom. She

flipped on the light. A full-size bed and a night-stand were the only furniture that could fit in the room, leaving about a foot between the bed and each wall.

"Closet's decent," Clay said.

She glanced at it but wasn't worried. Her bag of clothes would fit just about anywhere.

What she was more worried about was the man standing inches behind her, looking over her shoulder. His scent, a mix of subtle spice and male, made her step away. Unfortunately, there wasn't far to step.

"How much per week?" she asked, her jaw stiff.

"Despite what Macy said, I had put some thought into renting this out—except I was going to lease by the month. A thousand."

"I can't pay that much," she said, banking on the suspicion that he was at least a little desperate for money if he planned to rent.

He studied her too closely, unblinking, making her squirm. Finally he nodded. "That discount you mentioned…for you, I'll go down to eight hundred."

Andie crossed her arms and inched forward. Eight hundred would be as far as she could stretch. "I have to pay by the week but I'll be here for four."

He stared down at her with those disarming eyes but she held her ground. "Two hundred a week. And one other thing…unload the gun."

"What?"

"I don't want a loaded firearm in my house."

"Your house is upstairs."

"I won't bend on it."

She sized him up. She could take the ammo out while he watched if that would make him happy. And then she could put it right back in once he left. What was he going to do—a nightly inspection?

Bad choice of words, she thought, as she pictured him in her bedroom at lights-out.

She closed her eyes briefly. Ultimately she wouldn't bend either but she could fake it. She doubted she could find another rental this size, this close to work, for as low a price. She didn't have wheels to get around to look at a bunch of places, anyway.

Andie was about to offer her hand to seal the deal when the door in the other room squeaked open slowly. She figured the wind had caught it—until she heard the small, unsure voice.

"Daddy?"

CHAPTER TWO

ANDIE WAS ABOUT TO suggest that the girl was lost when Clay cleared his throat.

"Payton, honey, I'm in here."

He left the bedroom and Andie tried to process this new information.

Daddy?

Clay was a father?

How had she not known? When she'd lived here last year, he'd spent plenty of late nights at the bar with Evan and Derek. As far as she knew, he hadn't been married then, either. She really hoped that wasn't his idea of being a good dad—not that she knew from experience what one was.

"Who's here?" the little girl said, drawing Andie out of the bedroom.

"This is Miss Andie," Clay told her. "She's going to be our neighbor for a few weeks. This is my daughter, Payton."

A tiny girl hugged Clay's leg, hiding halfway behind him. Brown wavy hair hung past her shoulders and framed her angelic face. Andie could see immediately that Payton had inherited her father's beautiful eyes. She was dressed in a plain cotton-candy-pink leotard, saggy tights and dark pink Crocs.

"Hi, Payton," Andie said, walking closer. "You remind me of a little girl I know in Illinois. I bet you're about the same age."

Payton leaned out a few inches farther. "I'm three." She had the same trouble pronouncing the letter *r* that Andie's cousin's daughter did.

"Three? That makes you a big girl then," Andie said.

Shyly, the child came out of hiding. "I go to San Amaro Dance School."

"How lucky for you."

"My birthday's coming soon."

"And then you'll be four? That's exciting, Payton."

Clay crossed his arms and took a step back, looking from his daughter to Andie.

"You have pretty hair," Payton said to Andie.

"Thank you. You do, too."

"My daddy doesn't know how to put my hair like a ballerina's."

Andie glanced over at Clay and she couldn't help cracking a grin. "There are certain things that boys just don't get."

"Can you make a ballerina hairdo?" Payton asked.

Girl or not, Andie wasn't even sure what a "ballerina hairdo" was. "Do you have a picture of one?"

Payton nodded emphatically. "In my ballerina book."

"Maybe if you show your dad he'll be able to figure it out."

She seemed doubtful. "I showed him already."

A young woman, maybe in her early twenties at the most, poked her head in the door then. "There you are! You scared me to death."

Andie wondered if this was Payton's mother. If so, Clay was a cradle robber. The girl was attractive, with thick brown hair that hung down her back and big brown eyes. She was small. Much smaller than Clay.

The child threw her arms around the brunette's legs, giggling.

"You can't run off like that, girly. When Bridget's in charge, you have to stay with her so she doesn't think you're lost." Clay's voice was soothing and gentle.

Payton craned to meet Bridget's gaze. "Sorry."

Bridget picked her up, kissed her forehead loudly and supported her on her hip. "We'll leave you alone," she said to Clay.

"Miss Andie's going to live here," Payton said.

"We're just finishing up." Clay opened the door for them.

"No problemo. We'll let you get back to business. We're going to have a snack, right, Pay?"

The girl nodded reluctantly and stared at Clay.

She wound her hair around her finger and her lower lip trembled.

"I'll be home in a few minutes." Clay kissed his daughter's forehead. He held out his hand and waited for her to give him five. She did, finally, with the hand that wasn't tangled in her hair. "How 'bout the other side, too?"

She hesitated but finally unwound her finger and touched that hand to Clay's. He grasped it and nibbled her fingers, eliciting a giggle from her.

"Don't take too long," Bridget said to Clay as she carried Payton out.

Andie watched the two leave, digesting the whole scene.

"No tears," Clay mumbled. "Progress."

"Was that Payton's mom?" she asked.

"What? No, Bridget's my baby sister. She watches Payton for me."

"Nice of her to help you out." She guessed that was what typical families did. Help each other. Andie didn't have a sister and she didn't have a functional family, so this was about as close as she'd ever get to one.

"I just got temporary custody of Payton," Clay explained as he pulled a copy of an apartment lease out of a kitchen drawer. Clearly he was *much* more prepared to be a landlord than Macy thought. "My ex isn't a shining example of parenthood. She's in rehab."

She struggled not to show her surprise that Mr.

Got-It-Together would've been involved with some-one less than ideal. "How long will you have her?"

"Forever, I hope. Just need to get a judge to see things my way. It's an uphill battle for a single father. Her mother has a vicious lawyer and they'll use any-thing against me, but I'm doing whatever I can to argue my case."

"What could they possibly use against you?" Andie asked. Even compared to his friends, he seemed more stable, organized…serious.

"Let's see, my past, my career, even the apart-ment I shared with Evan. That's one of the reasons I bought this place. That and Evan felt the need to get married."

"Wow. I see your point about the lawyer being vicious." Andie leaned her shoulder against the wall, hands in her back pockets, while Clay filled in the document. "You're good with her."

He frowned and shook his head. "It's like I'm holding on to the edge of a cliff by my fingernails. She's having a tough time with all the changes."

"She seemed well-adjusted. Comfortable with you."

"I tried to spend as much time with her over the years as I could." His face tightened and Andie could see how much being separated from his daughter upset him. "The bigger challenge we're facing right now is when I leave her, no matter how briefly. Tran-sitions are hard. I think she's afraid she'll get taken to yet another home."

"Understandable," Andie said. "That didn't seem so bad just now."

"No, she was much better. Didn't cry. Maybe you put her at ease. She seemed to like you."

"I'm flattered," Andie said. "I like kids."

His eyebrows shot up as he pushed the lease in front of her. "You? I wouldn't have guessed."

"Kids are cool. What you see is what you get. You know where you stand with them."

"Pretty hair's big in Payton's book." Clay went over the lease terms quickly and pointed out the lines for her to initial and sign.

"Maybe I'll try to do her hair sometime…although I'm not sure I'll measure up," Andie said, scribbling her name. "I haven't had little girls to practice on."

"I've been surrounded by girls my whole life and I still fail miserably, as you heard. I have four sisters."

"A big happy family."

"Some days." A frown crossed his face for a split second. "We have our problems. Same as any other family."

"So…when can I move in?"

"When do you want to?"

"That depends on whether I have to walk back to the bar to get my stuff. Assuming this place is ready now."

"It's ready," Clay said. He took the lease. With the gentlest, shudder-inducing touch on her cheek, he brushed Andie's hair back. "I suppose in addition to paying for repairs and giving you a discount on rent, you want me to give you a ride to the Shack."

"You're perceptive." She did her best to ignore his effect on her, but heat climbed up her neck. "Think of it as penance."

"You're not going to let me live this down anytime soon, are you, biker girl?"

"Not a chance."

ANDIE WAS OFFICIALLY MOVED in by 6:39 p.m. She'd insisted on Clay dropping her off at the Shell Shack and stayed for a couple of hours helping out in the kitchen. When Macey finished her shift, Andie caught a ride with her to Clay's. They carried her belongings upstairs in one trip.

"You sure you won't come back with me for dinner?" Macey asked after they'd tossed the three bags on the bed. "We're cooking Thai chicken."

"I better not. You and Derek might kill me with all your domestic bliss." She set the biggest bag, still fully packed, on the floor of the closet, preferring to dig things out as she needed them.

Macey laughed. "I'd apologize, but…"

"I'm happy for you guys. I just don't do third-wheelness very well.".

"Someday you'll find the man who will make you itch to be domestic."

Andie put the second bag, which held all her bathroom stuff and her gun, around the corner in the bathroom. "Macey. You know me better than that."

Still smiling, Macey continued her crazy talk. "Settling down isn't as bad as you think."

"Maybe not for normal people, but I've never pretended to be normal."

"No, I wouldn't call you normal."

"I'd miss traveling. Riding. Doing whatever the hell I want to when I want to." Which was true, even if it wasn't the whole truth.

"Well, if you decide you want to eat with us, come on over," Macey said. "Dinner will be ready in less than an hour."

"Thanks for the offer and for helping me lug my stuff up."

"Everyone should be as easy to help move as you are. See you at work tomorrow."

Andie went to the door with Macey and saw her out. "Night. Enjoy your bliss."

She shut the door and registered the silence. Living on the road, sleeping in campgrounds, crappy motels, hostels—what-have-yous—she was used to not having a lot of personal space, used to having plenty of surrounding noise. She'd become accustomed to being alone in the middle of a crowd, frankly, and now, without the crowd, her ears rang. She paced.

She went back into the bedroom and put away the contents of the third bag—paperbacks, a crossword puzzle book, a reading light, her tie-dyed teddy bear, Lyle, that went everywhere with her. In the bathroom, she unpacked the toiletries she used daily and took the gun to the bedroom. She set it under the pillow, still loaded.

Andie went to the kitchen and considered the empty cabinets. By her standards, there was tons of space. What did people do with all this room? Buy groceries. Stock up. Feed a family.

Not since Trevor had she gone to the trouble of grocery shopping for more than one meal at a time. When you didn't have a fridge, there was no point in stocking up. Even back when she'd still lived with her dad, it'd been a fend-for-yourself situation for as long as she could remember. Her dad had excelled at filling the liquor cabinet and the beer fridge, but not so much the kitchen.

She wandered aimlessly into the living room. It was early, and usually she'd get on her bike and ride when she was bored or unsettled. Her second choice was to lose herself in a book, but she was too restless to sit still and wasn't in the mood for the book she'd been reading. She needed to find a way to get to the library on the mainland. She'd used it a lot last summer but then the library had been right between her campground and work.

As she stared at the off-white walls, the sound of her cell phone—her one regular monthly expense— reached her from the bedroom. Puzzled, she followed the sound. She rarely received incoming calls. She kept the phone for emergencies.

Caller ID showed her a number she knew well, even though she rarely used it.

"Hey, Jonas. What's up?" she asked her cousin.

"Where the hell have you been, woman? I've been trying to call you all day."

Andie chuckled. "Riding. Moving in. I didn't think to check my messages." She didn't often *have* messages.

"Andie, you need to check them."

Something in his tone wiped the smile off her face. "What's going on?"

"Just got news today. Trevor's out on parole."

The bottom dropped out of Andie's gut and she sank heavily to the bed. "Already?"

"Apparently he's been a good boy. Found religion. Blah blah blah."

Just like that, Andie fell back through memory to the horrific time three years ago when Trevor had used her as a punching bag. Nauseous, she broke out into a cold sweat.

"What do I do, Jonas?"

"Andie, honey, you're panicking. You don't need to panic. You're not the same girl. And you're hundreds of miles away."

She sucked in air and nodded, repeating Jonas's words to herself silently. "Right. You're right. God, I hate feeling like that."

She *wasn't* the same person. She'd made absolute certain of that. By learning to defend herself, for starters. By becoming completely independent. Accountable to no one. But the very news that her ex was free brought back the fear and doubt, the hopelessness, that had once been as much a part of her as her straight stringy hair.

"Calm down. He's not going to find you anytime soon. We don't have any proof that he'll try to track you down."

"Maybe he won't," Andie said, sitting up. "Right?"

"It's been a long time. You've moved on. Hopefully he has, too. Just relax."

Relax. Yeah. "Thanks, Jonas. Keep me posted."

"Check your damn messages."

They disconnected and Andie curled into a ball on her side.

God, she hoped Trevor had better things to do than dig up the past.

But she remembered all too well his promise to her the last time they'd seen each other, in court. He'd sworn he would love her forever. That they'd be together again someday. Trevor would do everything in his power to make that come true.

CHAPTER THREE

IT WAS A LAME EXCUSE, Clay fully acknowledged.

But Andie needed a copy of her lease eventually. Why not tonight? She was alone one floor below—he'd seen her arrive with Macey out his bedroom window. Not too long after, Macey had left. He wanted to see Andie again.

Payton was in bed now and his sister Bridget and her boyfriend, Reid, had come over to swim. When they came upstairs afterward, Clay asked them to stay for a few extra minutes and then went down.

After three knocks on Andie's door, there was still no response. "Andie, it's Clay."

An eternity later, the door opened a crack, still chained. Was she afraid of something? Someone? Surely not him.

"I brought your copy of the lease," he said, holding up the papers.

After hesitation, Andie closed the door, undid the chain and opened it wide enough for him to come in the entrance. However, she still barricaded him from getting any farther with her body.

"Did I wake you up?" he asked, though he didn't

think that was the case. Her hair had been brushed and fell to her shoulders like a silk curtain. It didn't look as if she'd been tossing around on a pillow.

Andie shook her head. It seemed as if she was two hundred miles away, distracted and…disturbed. Her eyes were glassy.

"Are you all right?" He touched her upper arm.

She swallowed and looked up at him. He could see when she came to and realized she was revealing too much.

"I'm fine. Just tired."

"That didn't look like tired."

"What did it look like?" She backed away with an insincere smile.

"Fear."

Her smile vanished and she met his eyes. "I'm okay, really."

"You don't like having anyone concerned about you, do you?"

She tilted her head a degree. "I'm a big girl. I do fine on my own."

"Coming from you, that sounds almost like a challenge." He took another step toward her, and she didn't retreat. He brushed her hair off her cheek. "I like a challenge."

"Yeah? Is that why you're here?"

Clay's mind went blank, sidetracked by her mouth, so close, and he couldn't remember *why* he was here. Ah, the lease in his left hand. He held it up. "I'm here to deliver your copy."

"That's service," Andie said, taking the pages from him. "And here I thought you'd come to beg for forgiveness for crushing my Harley." She placed the copies on the kitchen counter, and Clay sauntered after her.

"I'm new at the whole landlord gig," Clay said, ignoring the topic of her motorcycle. "Making an impression is important."

When she turned to face him, he was directly behind her. Startled, she put her hand on his chest and dropped her eyes toward his lips for a heartbeat.

"An impression," she repeated, her voice low and sexy. "I'd say you're good at making an impression."

"At Chez Marlow, we want to welcome you to the neighborhood." He grinned then closed the final few inches between them and touched his lips to hers. Lightly, waiting for her acquiescence.

"I'm feeling very welcomed." She ran her hand up his chest and twisted it in his T-shirt.

Their mouths met again, more insistently.

ANDIE MOVED INTO CLAY'S hard body, relishing the feel of his hands on her. His kiss was amazing, turning her inside out. He was somehow gentle and demanding at once, tender and yet assertive. Like no one she'd been with before.

The kiss shot heat clear down to her toes. Their urgency increased as their tongues met. He trailed his palms up her sides and then cradled her jaw with one hand. The gesture was surprisingly intimate. Andie opened her eyes and met his gaze. The sincerity in his eyes knocked the breath out of her and she pressed her lips to his again, hoping to lose herself in physical sensations.

It was too good. And though it was extremely difficult, after a few more seconds she ended the kiss because, when you got down to it, it was too scary.

Her reaction to this man was more than just physical. She had no idea what that even meant or if she was imagining more than there was, but...

She bowed her head and put some space between them. "Where's your daughter?"

"Payton?" He seemed momentarily confused. "Upstairs. In bed."

"By herself?"

"Of course not. My sister and her boyfriend are there."

She nodded, touching her lips.

"You're going to be here for a month?" Clay said, even though he knew that from the lease she'd signed. "We could have a lot of fun in a month."

Something clicked in her like an alarm going off. A month of fun with this man sounded way too tempting. Judging by the way he'd made her feel after just a few minutes of kissing, there was a real danger that she'd care too much.

She was *not* up for that. She'd promised herself she wouldn't ever fall that deeply under a man's spell again, wouldn't let herself get so caught up that she lost herself.

Andie met Clay's playful gaze with a serious one. "That's not a good idea."

He straightened, studying her.

"Your daughter," Andie said, grasping for something that would get through to him. Scare him away. "You said they'll use anything against you for your custody case."

He nodded slowly, narrowing his eyes, all hint of amusement erased.

"They'd have a heyday with me as a bad influence, Clay. Not only do I look the part with my tattoos and piercings but..." She swallowed hard and closed her eyes. "I have a police record."

His look was chillier now, as he worked through what she'd just confessed to.

"What'd you get picked up for?" he asked quietly after several seconds had passed.

"Which time?" She threw it out there as flippantly as she could.

"Pick your favorite," he said without missing a beat.

"Not my favorite, but the most memorable was assault charges against my ex."

His eyes widened just enough for her to notice.

"They were dropped. Big of them, really, since I hit him in the midst of having several of my bones broken by him."

She hated that she watched so closely for his

reaction. Hated admitting any of her past to him. His face changed as he absorbed what she'd said. Disbelief became something akin to pity.

"Andie…" He took a step toward her but she put out a hand.

"It's in the past, Clay, but yeah. That's the kind of past I have. Not pretty. Easy to dig up. Other incidents that weren't dropped. Nightmare in a custody case. So while tonight was…*fun,* it's probably best that we don't let it happen again. For Payton's sake."

CLAY STARED AT ANDIE, still reeling.

She was one hundred percent correct.

Andie Tyler was the last person he should associate himself with if he wanted to win custody. Getting permanent custody of Payton was paramount, as necessary as oxygen. His little girl had been through too much trauma already.

"Thank you," he said quietly, "for being honest. Payton means too much to me to jeopardize—"

"It's probably best that you go now."

The tough girl was back, solid as stone. He couldn't resist closing the gap between them one last time and pressing his lips to hers, gently.

"I'll see you around," he said.

"Thanks for the personalized landlord service."

"Anytime."

The truth hung between them, though, and they

both knew his remark was empty. He couldn't afford to flirt with her or get any more personal.

And yet…he was shaking inside.

CHAPTER FOUR

CLAY WISHED HE SHARED his daughter's enthusiasm for visiting Grandma and Grandpa's house.

At the end of the two-hour drive Friday evening, he pulled the truck up along the curb in front of the home he'd grown up in, and Payton shot out of the backseat. She ran around to the backyard where the rest of the family were likely already relaxing. If Clay had his way, they'd take their time getting there.

Towering oak trees that were older than Clay shaded the entire sprawling yard. A multilevel deck offered an ideal setting for entertaining, which the Marlows used frequently for social and business functions. For family gatherings, they tended to congregate on the stone terrace next to the grill and outdoor kitchen, so that Clay's mother, Della, could remain involved in all the action and conversations.

Clay's father, Vince, sat in his favorite Adirondack chair. Bridget and Reid shared a double bench to his right and Laurel, the oldest Marlow sibling, and her husband were to the left. Laurel and Charles's three boys played a high-contact version of keep-away toward the back of the lawn.

"Grandma!" Payton ran directly to Clay's mother. The woman was in her realm—the gourmet outdoor kitchen her husband had built for her several years back, as the family expanded with marriages and births. When she heard her granddaughter's voice, she set down her utensils and wiped her hands on her apron.

"How's my girl?" Della said, wrapping her arms around Payton.

"I'm fine!" She said it with so much enthusiasm that everyone laughed.

"Don't you go giving all your hugs to your grandma," Clay's dad said.

Payton giggled and skipped over to him. As the only granddaughter in the family so far, and the youngest of the grandchildren, she'd become plenty spoiled in the few times Clay had been able to bring her to the weekly family dinner.

Clay kissed his mom, then took a seat next to Bridget. Laurel, Bridget and Reid were engaged in conversation, but Charles said hello. Clay's dad merely nodded and Clay did the same in return.

"It sounds like an interesting project," Laurel, the family's surgical prodigy, was saying to Bridget.

"The more we learn about motivating teenagers…" Bridget said, "I'd like to think that could lead to better learning solutions for kids who don't get straight As, underachievers, those with discipline issues."

"The kind of kids who cause explosions in

the chemistry lab, for instance?" Laurel finally acknowledged Clay with smug amusement.

"Exactly that kind of kid." Bridget relaxed against the back of the wooden bench she shared with Reid and grinned at Clay.

"Really?" Clay said, trying to smile at Laurel and act like this wasn't a sore spot. "You're going to bring that up *again?*"

"How can we not?" Laurel said. "It's such a classic."

"I don't think I've heard this one before," Bridget's boyfriend said.

"You really don't want to," Clay said.

"It was Clay's junior year in high school," Laurel began, almost as if she was reading a script. She'd told the story that many times.

"Clay wasn't exactly a motivated student," Bridget added.

"You were too young to even understand what motivated meant." Clay leaned back in his lawn chair and rubbed his eyebrows with his index finger and thumb.

"He and a buddy couldn't be bothered to study for their chemistry class," Laurel continued, "but that didn't stop them from breaking into the lab after school one day to mix up some gun powder, thinking they'd concoct their own fireworks."

"No way," Reid said. "You didn't."

"Turns out they made something more powerful

than they thought." Laurel could barely get the story out, she was laughing so hard.

"They blew up a couple of beakers, ruined some equipment and set off the sprinkler system throughout the school," Bridget said. "Our boy got himself suspended for ten days."

"All that ambition and only a *D* in chemistry." Laurel shook her head.

Clay happened to glance at his father at that moment, when everyone else around the circle was in hysterics. The disappointment Clay was so well acquainted with made only a brief appearance.

Yep, that was him. Dad's major letdown.

He looked back at his sisters and their significant others, who'd all gotten a kick out of the rehashing of the story. He forced himself to laugh with them, though he found nothing amusing about being the one who'd always caused trouble, always embarrassed his father. The chemistry lab story was just one of many examples that his high-IQ sisters liked to tease him about.

Not only was he the nonacademic of the family, but he'd regularly gotten picked up by the cops. Back then, he couldn't have cared less.

He'd grown up in a heartbeat when he'd learned he was a father, though. He'd dramatically changed his lifestyle, but his family still saw him as the black sheep.

Payton edged over to Clay and climbed up on his

lap, as if she sensed he was uncomfortable. He kissed the top of her head and smiled to reassure her.

Clay wrapped one arm around Payton and used the other to run his fingers through her soft, little-girl hair. In truth, she brought him as much comfort as he tried to give her. He caught snippets of the conversation that carried on here and there: Laurel's life-saving surgery, Bridget's studies as she worked toward a doctorate degree in psychology. Their mother filled them in on the other two siblings' successes as well— Gwen, the software developer who lived in Seattle, and Izzie, the biology professor and researcher, who'd taken a job on the East Coast a year ago.

Clay loved his sisters, but he'd never been close to any of them except Bridget. He was too different from them—always had been, and it went beyond gender. His new closeness to Bridget had been brought about because they both lived on the island. He'd always been the misfit, the lone blue-collar guy in a circle of brainiacs.

After several minutes of sitting quietly, Payton started squirming. Clay welcomed the excuse to escape. He challenged her to race him to the tire swing, making a show of trying his best to keep up with her, then lifting her over his shoulder and tickling her when he finally did.

"WHAT HAPPENED TO THE big happy dad who was chasing his daughter around like an overgrown kid?" Bridget asked Clay after dinner.

He was leaning his elbows on the stone wall at the very back of the parklike yard, gazing over at the trickle of water in the ravine that bordered the property.

"Got a phone call with big ugly news," he said, not looking at her.

Bridget copied his stance at the wall. "What news, Clay?"

He shook his head.

"You can't tell me you got bad news and then not explain," Bridget said. "Is somebody sick? Is it Payton?"

"It's the custody hearing. My lawyer called to tell me they changed the judge." He straightened and watched a pair of birds chase each other in a nearby tree. "Apparently the one we got has a rep for being tough on single fathers. Believes a mother is the better option for a kid."

"But it's obvious Robin isn't. She's addicted to some hardcore drugs."

"We're worried she'll see the rehab stay as Robin's valiant effort to be the best mom she can be."

Bridget nodded. "I guess it could be, if you disregard the way she's treated Payton for the past three years. Your lawyer's good. He'll fight this."

Clay nodded unenthusiastically. He'd been confident before the first custody hearing back when Payton was a baby. It was painfully obvious to him that Robin was not cut out to be a mom. But that had been twisted and buried by Robin's lawyer, her uncle.

Now Clay knew it was an uphill battle even with a fair judge.

"Is this why you were so quiet at dinner?" Bridget asked.

"Guess so."

"Why didn't you tell us right away, Clay? We're your family. We're on your side."

"You think so?"

She faced him. "How can you doubt me?"

"I don't doubt you, Bridge. But the others…you know how things are between Dad and me. He's said before a child needs her mother."

"When?"

He shrugged. "Couple years ago. Before the second hearing."

"He actually said that?"

"Yes."

She was quiet for a couple of minutes, lost in thought. "His opinion has probably changed. He's seen you with Payton. How could he ever think Robin would be better for her?"

"It's not so much that Robin's good. He just doubts I'm the best solution."

"I think you're wrong, Clay."

"There's no love lost, Bridge. He doesn't talk to me, can barely say hello. It's awkward as hell coming over here but I want Payton to get acquainted with her family. She deserves their love."

"She does," Bridget agreed. "So do you. And you both have it."

He checked his watch. "I need to get Payton home and to bed. See you Sunday morning?"

She nodded, not able to hide her concern.

"I'm fine, Bridget. I don't need his approval."

His dad's approval would be nice—unimaginable—but he could live without it. He had for years now. The only person he had to do right by was Payton. He worried, night and day, that he'd do the wrong thing for her. But he would move mountains to figure this parenting thing out. Whatever it took.

Somehow, he and the lawyer needed to figure out a way to make the judge see that Payton would be better off living with him than with her half-there, drug-addict mother.

CHAPTER FIVE

A MOSTLY PRIVATE POOL was a new treat for Andie and one she could get used to fast. Clay had given her a key to the wrought-iron gate he'd installed to keep Payton safe.

Hot sun, cool water, a padded lounge chair that was more comfortable than most of the beds she'd slept in and a pile of new books. Life didn't get much better than this.

Andie lay on her stomach with a biography of a local zoologist and founder of Turtle Town, a rescue center for endangered sea turtles at the north end of town. Not something that would've caught her attention necessarily, but the bookstore owner had recommended it and had gone on about the turtle project. Three chapters in and Andie was hooked and determined to visit the turtles.

The gate to her left creaked and she saw Payton out of the corner of her eye. She waited to see what the girl would do.

"Hi, Miss Andie."

"Hey, kiddo." Andie used the store receipt as a bookmark and put the book down. "What's up?"

Payton looked to the sky and shrugged, making Andie laugh.

"What are you doing?" Payton asked.

"Reading about the Turtle Lady."

"Turtle Lady?"

Andie nodded. The turtle rescue center would be a great place for Clay to take his daughter. "She started a reserve called Turtle Town here on the island."

"What's Turtle Town?"

"It's where they rescue sick sea turtles and try to heal them. You can go and look at the big turtles."

"How big?"

"As big as you," Andie said, grinning until she saw the child's frown. "But they're nice turtles. In big tanks. They can't get out, but you can watch them swim."

"Do we hafta?"

"You don't have to. Only if you want to. And if your daddy will take you."

"Why do you have all those butterflies on your back?" Payton asked, moving to the side of her chair.

"It's a tattoo."

Tattoos, actually. What had started as a single butterfly on her shoulder blade had grown into a flock. Each time Andie visited her cousin Jonas in Illinois, she had his tattoo artist friend add to it.

"Mr. Evan and Mr. Derek have tattubes but not a butterfly."

"What about your dad?" Andie asked, slightly

ashamed of prying Clay's personal information from his daughter.

"He doesn't have any at all." Payton stared at Andie's upper arm. The tattoo covered a fourth of her back, swirled up to her shoulder and down a couple inches on her arm. "I like butterflies."

"Me, too. You know why?"

"Uh-uh."

"Not only are they really pretty but they're free to fly wherever they want."

Payton studied her thoughtfully. "Yeah."

"That's why I got one on my back."

"Can I get one on my back?"

"Not till you're a grown-up. Tattoos hurt."

Payton considered what she said then shook her head. "I don't want a tattube."

"Then you never have to get one," Andie said, chuckling at Payton's very sound logic.

"I have a butterfly book," Payton said, abandoning her serious tone of five seconds ago. "Wanna see it?"

"Okay."

"I'll go get it."

"I'll be here."

CLAY STEPPED BACK OUT OF sight on the middle landing of the outdoor stairway, where he'd been watching Payton and Andie. He couldn't get over how open and easygoing his hard-edged renter was with his daughter. Not to mention how accepting Payton was of Andie.

She'd broken a rule, though, and he couldn't let it go unmentioned.

"Payton," he said quietly but firmly when she was two feet away from him, oblivious as she sang something about butterflies.

"Hi, Daddy." She gave him a look that said she knew she was busted and was waiting to see what he would do. "I'm getting my butterfly book."

"You went downstairs without me." He kneeled to her level.

Payton nodded slowly, nailing him with those brown eyes.

"That's against the rules, honey."

"Sorry, Daddy."

"Come here," he said and lifted her into his arms. He took her upstairs as he explained. "You always have to have an adult with you in the backyard. It's dangerous to go near the swimming pool alone. You could get hurt badly, girly."

"Miss Andie's a adult."

So she was. "But she's not the adult in charge of you. You have to have Daddy or Aunt Bridget or Miss Macey or Miss Selena…"

"Or Mr. Evan?"

"Yes."

"And Mr. Derek?"

"Exactly. Those are the adults who take care of you."

"Miss Andie has tattubes, just like Mr. Evan and Mr. Derek," she said as they went inside. "Hers has a butterfly."

He gave his imagination free rein as to where it might be located. Shaking his head and grinning, he realized Payton had just successfully distracted him from disciplining her, even if it was innocent on her part.

"Payton, I need you to be clear on this. When can you go to the backyard?"

"When there's a adult." She proceeded to list the appropriate names again, adding her grandparents to the list.

"And nobody else."

She shook her head dramatically, eyes big.

"Not Miss Andie."

"I like Miss Andie."

"I like her, too, girly, but she's just our neighbor. In a few weeks she'll move away."

Clay hadn't let Payton out of his sight for more than two minutes and she'd escaped down nearly forty steps. He'd caught up in time to see her wander through the gate and had stopped his full-speed pursuit when he saw Andie there, interested in how she would handle his daughter when he wasn't around. But that didn't mean he wanted to make a habit of running into her.

She'd handled his daughter's never-ending questions well and had seemed to take the girl seriously instead of dismissing her.

Points for the biker girl, if he was keeping score. But it was his daughter's life, not a game. And he couldn't afford to like anything about the Harley-riding woman too much.

Once in their place, Payton went up to the top floor, a small, low-ceilinged attic room he'd hired Selena to cover with murals of fairies and butterflies and rainbows. She returned a few seconds later carrying one of her favorite books, *Blue Butterfly,* under one arm as she made her careful way down the stairs to him.

"Come on, Daddy."

"Come on what?"

"We hafta show Miss Andie my book."

"You weren't supposed to go down there in the first place, Payton."

She craned her neck to look up at him. "I promised her."

Clay held in a grin, realizing Payton had picked up the phrase from him.

"I'll take you down this time, but if I ever catch you in the backyard without one of your adults, I'll have to take your butterfly book away for a few days."

"Put it in time out?"

"A long time out. Let's go show Miss Andie your book and then we'll make lunch." He wanted to check out the tattoo, anyway.

Going down to see Andie was a mistake, Clay thought as soon as they opened the gate. From upstairs, his view had been blocked by the bushes and foliage along the fence. The eyeful he got now wasn't something he would forget anytime soon.

She wore a red-and-black string bikini and was stretched out on her stomach. His eyes were drawn to the firm curves of her barely covered ass and her long, slender legs, then up to her narrow waist. Her skin was lightly tanned and looked as smooth as ice cream and just as mouthwatering. And that was a completely inappropriate thought, especially when you were holding the hand of your three-year-old daughter.

"See?" Payton said, touching the tattoo on Andie's upper back without hesitation.

Andie jerked her head around and Clay suspected she'd dozed off in the sun.

"Payton, don't touch. Not good manners." There was no way not to see the giant tattoo. Somehow, though, it wasn't obnoxious, as he'd expect something that size to be. Instead he found it intriguing. Fitting. Andie-ish. He wanted to lean closer and inspect the detailed scrolling, the designs in the butterflies' wings and the flowers.

"It's okay," Andie said. "Did you bring your book, Miss Payton?"

"See?" She held the book out and Andie sat up, lowering her feet to the pavement, providing Clay with an excellent view of her cleavage.

Andie opened the book in front of her and Payton wormed her way between Andie's knees, facing the pages. As she usually did, Payton began narrating the pictures on the pages, making up her own story to go with the images.

"Once upon a time, there was a garden full of flowers…"

Clay wandered to the opposite end of the pool to check the water temperature and the skimmer. They didn't need to be checked but he was grasping for any damn thing that would distract him from the view.

That all worked fine until Andie and Payton were done flipping through the book and his daughter called out to him.

"Can I go swimming, Daddy?"

"I thought you wanted lunch, girly." He had to get her into some swim lessons so he wouldn't worry about her around the pool this much.

She shook her head. "Swimming. Please?"

"We'll go get your suit in a minute. I need to talk to Miss Andie."

"Am I in trouble?" Andie said, grinning as if she knew that, in that bikini, she was all *kinds* of trouble.

"Payton is. She's not supposed to come down here without me. I hate to ask but if she does it again while you're out here, would you let me know right away?"

"Sure, but she was no problem. She's a great kid."

"Payton, wait for me," he called out. She was half-way up to Andie's landing. "Thanks. I agree. But she's not your responsibility," he said to Andie, more harshly than he'd meant to.

Andie sized him up. "You don't want me to be seen with her. Probably smart. This yard isn't very private."

"Nothing personal."

Their eyes met and neither spoke for several seconds. "Of course," she finally said. And the truth was that it was, indeed, very personal.

She nodded as she gathered her book and drink. "I'll get out of your way so you can enjoy your pool."

"You don't have to—"

"I do, but it's okay. It's best this way."

She stood and picked up her towel, her smile regretful…or was that wishful thinking on his part?

It was going to be hard enough keeping Payton away from Andie and as detached as possible. The more pressing challenge, it appeared, could be to keep himself detached.

CHAPTER SIX

CLAY WATCHED EVERY tantalizing step of Andie's departure until his view was blocked by his sister.

Bridget hugged Payton then looked questioningly at Andie, who gestured toward Clay. As Andie went upstairs, Bridget and Payton walked toward the pool, where Clay still sat like a guilty kid caught eyeing the cookie jar.

"To what do we owe the pleasure?" he said, hoping to cover his thoughts of thirty seconds earlier.

"Gorgeous day," she said cheerfully. "This girl needs some fun in the sun."

"We were just going to change into swimsuits, weren't we, girly?"

"Yes!" Payton jumped up and down and dragged Bridget by the hand back toward the stairs.

"I'll come up with you," Bridget said.

The three of them left the pool area and Clay closed the gate behind him. Payton scurried to the stairs and started up, while he and Bridget took their time.

"So," Bridget said heavily, once they'd passed

Andie's landing. "What's going on with *her?*" She pointed toward Andie's door.

"Not a thing."

Bridget stared hard at him when they got to his landing.

"What?" he said. "What do you think is going on with her?" Might as well let her get it out in the open, whatever she suspected.

"You sound defensive."

"You sound offensive."

Bridget laughed as they went inside. Payton was already coming down from her room wearing her pink-and-purple swimsuit.

"Don't forget your towel," Clay said, and Payton went back upstairs. When she was out of earshot again, he added, "Andie's a renter. For a month. That's all."

"You were drooling, Clay."

"What man wouldn't drool at a woman who looks like that in a bikini?"

"A man who's trying to fight a nasty custody battle, maybe? Look, Clay, I don't know this Andie chick but from my objective viewpoint over here, maybe you shouldn't mess around with just anyone right now. Unless you have wedding bells in mind, it'd be smart to be a good boy until after the hearing."

As if he wasn't already aware of that. "Got it under control, Bridge," he said, fighting to keep his tone level. "I'm going to change."

When he returned, Bridget had helped herself to a glass of apple juice.

"No coffee?" he asked, checking the pot he'd brewed earlier. It was still half full, so he poured some into a travel mug.

"Giving it up, actually."

"Let's go!" Payton said, rushing between them and grabbing their free hands.

"Lead the way, girly. What's up with no more coffee?" Clay asked as they trooped down the stairs again. He made a concerted effort not to so much as glance at Andie's door as they went by.

"Well…" Bridget took her cover-up off to reveal her simple bright blue one-piece suit. Pointing at her abdomen, she said, "This bulge? Is not due to fat." She grinned widely, glancing toward Payton to make sure she was otherwise occupied.

It took several seconds for what she'd said to get through to Clay. He stopped as he was about to jump into the water and looked at her belly again—which, yes, was slightly swollen—and then at her face. Her eyes were full of excitement. "Bridget?"

She laughed and nodded. "I'm pregnant."

If people could glow, she definitely was.

"Congratulations," he said, studying her. "I take it you and Reid are happy about this?"

She nodded enthusiastically. "Very. He'll be such a good father."

A month ago Clay would've heartily agreed. Now-adays, he found himself wondering what the heck a good father was. Fatherhood seemed to consist of constantly walking a fine line—between friend and disciplinarian, between protecting and letting a kid breathe.

"Reid's a decent guy. If anyone can find his way on this twisted path, he can."

"Thanks for the overwhelming support," Bridget said, then added as if it just occurred to her, "you'll find your way, too."

"Hope it's before my daughter turns thirty," he said with a grin. He glanced around at Payton, who had wandered over to the turtle-shaped sandbox in the corner of the yard. She was intent on shoveling sand into her pail. "When are you two getting hitched?"

She tested the water with her toes. "We aren't."

"You're not." Clay sat on the edge of the pool and dipped his legs in.

"No."

"You love each other."

"Of course we do."

"You're having a baby."

"Right again." She lowered herself to the ladder, submerging to the waist as she sat on the top rung and bracing herself against the cool water. "We don't need a marriage certificate to verify our relationship."

"You're going to be parents, though."

"Yes. We live together, Clay. We love each other. We'll raise the baby together. Just like if we were married."

"So why not get married?"

She stared at him for several seconds, head tilted. "I thought you'd be the one to understand."

"Why? Because I have a kid and I'm not married? Bridget, that's entirely different. I don't love Payton's mother."

"Did you ever?"

He hesitated. "I thought I did. Before she got pregnant."

"Well, I love Reid. He loves me. That's all we need."

"You two are lucky, Bridge. Why won't you take that final step for the sake of your child?"

"Marriage isn't what we want."

"Why not?"

"Why? Because everyone else does?"

"Yeah, actually. It's the thing to do."

Bridget shook her head, her forehead wrinkling in disgust.

"Mom and Dad aren't going to be okay with this."

"If so, it's my problem. Not yours."

Clay chuckled humorlessly. "I wish that were true. They're going to blame me for being a bad influence on you."

"Clay."

"They will. I set the bad example for my little sister."

"That's ridiculous."

"I know it, and you know it, but they love to see me as the bad guy."

"So you were the rebel boy growing up. You've changed. The minute you found out you had a child, you cleaned up. Enough of the doom and gloom 'I'm the bad guy' crap. No one in the family still believes that."

"Parenting is…hard, Bridge. I don't get why you'd want to be single…."

"Not single. There will be two of us." Bridget launched from the ladder into a leisurely side stroke. She grabbed the wall next to Clay. "I get that you're scared. Getting custody so suddenly would make anyone's head spin."

"I've been trying for this for so damn long…now that I have her, all I can think of is what if I screw up?"

"You're doing absolutely right by her," Bridget said quietly. "Trust yourself."

"This was supposed to be about you," he grumbled, not liking how easily she'd hit on his Achilles' heel. "Not me."

He studied his little sister. There was no denying the joy in Bridget's eyes.

Who was he to scold her? He had as much as he could handle with Payton…and then some.

The princess in question pranced toward them then, spilling sand with every step. She burrowed into his side for a hug. Clay picked her up and set her on his lap, squeezing her tightly, and kissed the tip of her nose. "Hey, girly."

"Hey, Daddy."

He held her close, wondering whether his sister was right. Was he doing okay? He was doing the best he could, dammit.

And yet he would always worry it wasn't good enough.

How could a man who battled fires and handled every kind of emergency imaginable be felled by three and a half feet of toddler?

"REALLY? YOU'RE GOING TO a baby shower?" Andie said as she climbed into the backseat of Macey's Corolla that evening. Derek frowned as he backed the car out of Clay's driveway.

"Not a shower," Derek said. "I've been assured this is just a party."

"It's a party to celebrate the impending birth of Evan and Selena's baby," Macey clarified from the passenger seat.

"You invited boys," Andie remarked.

"Lots of 'em. Lots of firefighters, several of them single." Macey turned enough to raise her brows suggestively at Andie.

"Also lots of beer," Derek said. "Which is the only way to get lots of firefighters to a baby party."

"This should be interesting," Andie said.

"Yeah," Derek said. "Who will be most out of place? The men? Or you? Female or not, you don't really seem the shower type."

"You'd be correct with that assessment," Andie

muttered, leaning back in the seat and wondering how early she could cut out for the evening.

The party was at the home of Pilar and Curt Silver, who lived on the mainland, just a couple of miles past the bridge. Curt was a firefighter on the island. Andie remembered meeting Pilar a couple of times at the Shell Shack last summer—she worked in administration at the fire station and socialized a lot with the firefighters. With everyone, actually.

Andie stood at the edge of the large backyard when they arrived, watching the hostess make her rounds, cracking jokes with the guys, hugging the women, making sure everyone had something to drink.

Might as well be on another planet, Andie thought.

Macey was in the kitchen with the caterers. Good thing she was used to being an outsider.

"Miss Andie, I'm sure glad you came back to San Amaro to see me," Gus said, hobbling up to her. Derek's uncle—the only other person Andie knew in the whole place—wore a shirt with a wild chili pepper print on it and a tight belt to keep his khaki pants on his scrawny body. As always, his light blue bucket hat was perched on his head of wispy hair.

"You're looking fine, too, Gus," Andie said, genuinely happy to see him. "Are you going to introduce me?"

By his side was a woman who looked even older than his eighty or so years, with snow-white hair, cheekbones that jutted out from her thin face but must've been beautiful years ago, and a vibrant energy about her that said Gus would have to work to keep up with her.

"This is the love of my life, Thelma Ballard."

"Nice to meet you," Andie said, holding her hand out.

The woman ignored her hand and instead pulled Andie into a surprisingly robust hug. "Come here, sweetie. Pleasure to meet you. How did you meet my Gus?"

"She's a barmaid at the Shell Shack," Gus said. "Helps Macey keep my nephew in line."

"That's quite a chore." Thelma winked. "To have to keep a big handsome man like him in line. If I didn't have Gus, I'd be shopping around for one of these firefighters here tonight."

Andie chuckled. She had no doubt.

"Look, there's one. You can tell by the muscles," Thelma said, motioning to the gate. "A lonely one."

Clay stood there by himself, taking in the scene, nodding to people as they said hello.

"You talk too much, woman," Gus said to Thelma. "Let's go dance." He winked at Andie and pulled Thelma onto the flagstone terrace at the back of the yard where several others had already started dancing. They were, by several decades, the oldest ones out there, but you could argue that they were having the most fun, too.

"Crazy old man," Clay said from behind her. "I hope I'm half as alive as he is when I turn eighty."

"Hope I'm *getting* half as much," Andie said. "There goes living proof that sex doesn't have to end with senior-citizen-hood."

The warmth of Clay's smile caught her off guard. She looked into his eyes, which were focusing all that sexy maleness on her, sending a shiver clear through her.

"Where's your daughter tonight?" she asked, in search of something—*anything*—innocent to say.

"Staying with Bridget. Had a hard time convincing her she'd have more fun with her aunt than coming to a baby party with me."

"She has no idea how lucky she is," Andie said.

"What made you show up?"

Andie shrugged. "I like Evan. Selena, too. Guess I'm trying to play nice with others."

"My theory is as long as there's decent food and drink, I can persevere. Speaking of which, can I get you a drink?" he asked.

"No, thanks. I can get one myself."

"Prickly woman," Clay said with a shake of his head.

"I prefer self-sufficient." She said it over her shoulder as she walked toward the patio to coolers overflowing with soft drinks and bottled alcoholic drinks. The keg was in the back corner of the yard. She was surprised to find Clay behind her when she bent to choose a drink. "Following me?"

"Since you didn't offer to get *me* a drink."

"I'm inconsiderate that way."

"I've noticed."

"Do you know everyone here?" Andie asked, gesturing to the expanse of the yard with her can of lemonade. The place was crowded, with probably fifty or sixty people.

Clay followed her gaze. "Lots of them. Firefighters, wives, office staff, friends. Have you met Evan's twin sister?" He held out his arm to the nearest woman. Andie shook her head.

"Melanie, this is Andie Tyler. Melanie helped Macey and Pilar organize this bash."

"Nice job. Lots of people," Andie said, immediately seeing the resemblance between Evan and his sister in their blue eyes and the shape of their faces.

"Where's your little man tonight?" Clay asked.

"We got a sitter for him. He would've loved being Mr. Social but I'd be too preoccupied with him here."

"Payton still talks about playing with 'the baby.' We'll have to get them together again soon."

"Absolutely. I'm sure they'll spend some prime playtime together next weekend at the wedding."

While the two of them discussed babysitting options for Macey and Derek's wedding, Andie took the opportunity to escape back to her place along the perimeter, away from Clay's clean-cut good looks and everyone else's small talk.

She glanced at her watch and tried to hide her disappointment. Dinner hadn't even been served. They were heating up the grills now but it'd be an eternity before she could leave. Even if she could beg off, she had no way home until Macey and Derek were ready to leave.

It was going to be a long, painful night.

CHAPTER SEVEN

"Guys, find a woman!" Pilar bellowed from the top of one of the patio tables a couple of hours later. "Partner up, people!"

Clay watched as everyone, pretty well liquored up, did as she said.

"This is high stakes," Pilar continued as if she were born to direct drunks in party games. "The winning team will get two prizes—the king of all Super Soaker water guns for the guy and a gift certificate for a sixty-minute massage for the lady. You know you want it, folks. When you have your partner, line up at that end of the yard."

"Get a woman, Clay," Evan said, Selena's arm through his. "I feel the need to defeat you. That prize is mine."

Clay had to give Pilar credit—she'd done her research. Almost all of the guys from the station collected super-powered water guns for the periodic water fights that broke out during slow times. If anything would motivate this group to get into a ridiculous baby shower game, it was the biggest, toughest water gun. That and a bunch of booze.

Clay was no exception, even though he was stone-cold sober. The better to take down these lushes.

He spotted a group of three women eyeing him. He knew at least one of them was an E.R. nurse. Two were pretty and one was downright hot. Any of the three could make this game more bearable.

What the heck…he was itching to leave Evan in the dust.

As he took a couple of steps toward the trio, he noticed Andie standing by the fence alone. At the last second, he nodded, said, "Ladies" and walked past them. They'd have no trouble finding other partners.

Andie was sending off a strong people-repellent as only she could do, but Clay didn't let that deter him. If he had to get involved in this charade, no reason she should be allowed to sit it out. Besides, if he went strictly by competitive instinct, the biker chick would be more of an asset than the softer, sweeter nurse types anyway.

"Come on," he said to her, holding out his hand. "I need a partner. Have to put Evan in his place."

"No, thanks," Andie said. "There's plenty of women on your tail tonight. Pick one of them."

"I'm picking you. Have you ever had a professional massage?"

"Define professional," she said.

"Come on, Andie. I can only stay for a little longer. Join me on the social side. You'll have more fun if you're not squeezed up against the fence trying to escape."

She glanced around and he discerned something he'd never expected from her—self-consciousness. "I'll play if you'll take me with you when you leave," she said. "You're going soon?"

He studied this woman who was so different from all the others he knew. Unlike everyone else, who'd dressed summer casual, Andie wore torn black jeans that hugged her long legs, a plain gray tank top and her black biker boots. The tank didn't quite meet the jeans, showing off a navel piercing and the very top of a tattoo. Besides the belly-button ring, her only jewelry was a collection of small silver hoops that went up the edge of her ear. She was tough-looking, unconventional and she stuck out in this crowd. But until he'd seen that hint of insecurity, he would've believed she dressed that way purposely, emphatically. With a thumb of the nose.

"Everybody ready?" Pilar called out. "Come on, people, we're going to start. Get to the fence and I'll explain the rules."

Andie stared at Clay, waiting for his answer but making no move to join the others.

"It's a deal," he said. "I'll take you home with me."

ANDIE FROWNED WHEN PILAR explained the rules of the don't-drop-the-baby game. She'd never played party games as a kid, never been invited to parties then. To be thrown into them now, with this group of happy-go-lucky people… Maybe she needed to take up drinking after all to get into the spirit because right now she wasn't feeling it.

The first game was a race, down the length of the huge yard and back. Each couple had a water balloon—their "baby"—and they had to support it between their abdomens without using their hands. If your balloon burst or fell, you were out. If you touched it with your hands, you were out. According to Clay "I Play for Blood" Marlow, *out* was not an option.

"Clay, you finally get to touch a woman," Evan called to a chorus of laughs.

"Keep talking, Evan. You're going down."

"I don't think so. My wife has a built-in shelf." Evan set the balloon on top of Selena's very swollen belly and moved in close with his body.

"Respect the belly," Selena said, and Andie chuckled in spite of herself.

Then she sobered because Clay was suddenly inches away from her pressing their "baby" gently against her and holding on to her waist. The scent of him enveloped her and sent her blood pumping without her permission. His hands on the bare skin at her sides made her want to fidget—either closer to him or far, far away.

"Here's our strategy," he said in a low, intimate voice so no one else could hear. He leaned so close she could feel his breath on her skin and she fought the sudden urge to taste him. She was pretty sure *that* was not the strategy.

She backed away a couple of inches because what she was feeling was ridiculous. To him, this was a party game, and he was in the middle of the place he belonged, was obviously well liked and among good friends. She was an outsider who would never fit in. Getting bothered over Clay Marlow was futile and embarrassing.

"I'm going to hold your hips so we can keep just the right amount of pressure on the balloon," he said. "I'll go backward. You watch my back."

Hold her hips. *Great.* "Terrific strategizing, chief. You do realize those water guns aren't that expensive," Andie said, attempting to distract herself from his closeness. "I bet if you saved your pennies for a couple of weeks you could buy one yourself."

"Here's a little something you women just don't get. The sweetness of that gun will be quadrupled when I beat out Evan and everyone else for it."

"Ah. Got it."

"Good. Get ready for that professional rubdown, then."

She could think of a rubdown she'd prefer, but that wasn't going to happen.

They moved to the starting line with the other couples and it took some time for Pilar to shut everyone up enough that they could hear the signal to go.

True to his word, Clay didn't take his hands off her

hips once and in spite of her best attempt to worry about the balloon, Andie couldn't drag her attention from his strong hands and how they felt on her flesh. Dammit. His hands were large enough he could wrap them almost all the way around her waist. The way they encircled her so easily…it did things to her. Made her think thoughts better left unformed, unuttered, un-anything.

At the end of the yard, as they went around a chair to head back, she and Clay were actually in the lead. All the guys—and some of the women—were trash-talking as they went, yelling taunts and insults, howling whenever a couple got disqualified.

"Hey, Evan, you better slow down," Clay said. "Don't want Selena to go into labor."

"Keep talking, man. We're gaining on you."

Clay sped up, so Andie followed, grabbing his sides. They were close to the finish line—less than a third of the yard to go—when Clay sealed their fate. He tripped over a rock and went down. Andie lost her balance, too, and landed on top of him.

Just what she needed—becoming the center of attention when she already felt like a misfit. She reached for the ground to push herself up.

Clay's arms came around her and he laughed. "Don't run away. At least try to pretend it's not terrible to fall on top of me."

It wasn't terrible. It was so not terrible that her heart was hammering. Which was exactly why she needed to move.

Andie scrambled up, not worrying about how that made Clay look, but rather the way he made her *feel*.

She belatedly realized the balloon had burst and a cool liquid seeped into her jeans. Clay swore good-naturedly, of course, because wasn't he just a good guy all around, even when his clothes were soaked and he landed on the ground in front of everyone. He hopped up and brushed himself off, then touched Andie's waist. Unable to take another second of close contact, she inched away.

"Yes! The mother of all soakers is mine!" Derek's voice rose over the noise as everyone else who hadn't been disqualified earlier hit the finish line.

"Sorry about that," Clay said to Andie. "I take full blame."

"Somehow I'll make it," Andie said drily, smiling and relaxing a little when she realized attention was now on the winning couple.

Clay high-fived Derek and Macey. "Glad you two beat Daddy Drake over there. He'll get enough loot tonight as it is."

"What happened?" Macey asked. "You were ahead of all of us."

"There's a rock jutting from the ground out there," Clay said, pointing. "Likely planted by Evan."

Pilar's husband, Curt, delivered the coveted gun and an envelope with the gift certificate.

"Yesss," Macey said. "I'm going to need this in the next week. My hero." She hugged her fiancée.

Derek took his prize and, after kissing his partner long and hard, went to find a hose. Macey and Andie shook their heads as Pilar announced the next game.

Andie was aware that Clay had sidled next to her before she turned her head. Before he spoke.

"Biker girl, you going to be my partner again?"

"Not a chance. You'll have to find someone else." Without checking his reaction, she wished Macey luck and hurried off to her corner to wait for her ride home—as far removed from Clay's world as possible.

"READY TO GO?" CLAY growled later.

Andie turned toward him, laughing. Macey had dragged her into the middle of the action and begged her to write down all the gifts and who they were from. Her reasoning had been that Andie was one of the sober few, but she suspected Macey was just trying to fit a square peg into a round hole. It hadn't been bad, she had to admit—everybody did their best to put her at ease—but she was more than ready to go home. Being sociable took a toll on her.

Andie said her goodbyes and followed Clay out.

He'd parked a block away and didn't utter a single word to her as they walked. She would've been fine with the silence except it was so unlike Mr. Upbeat. Once they were driving away, she snuck a look at him. His jaw was tight, mouth downcast in a frown.

His gaze pointed forward, on the road, but he was somewhere else.

"What's wrong with you?" she asked as he turned onto a busy street toward the bridge to the island. "Someone piss you off?"

He shook his head minutely. "Did you need to get home right away or did you just want out of the party?"

"What do you think?"

Instead of answering, he flicked his turn signal and pulled unexpectedly into a dark, bayside park.

A few feet from the water's edge, he killed the engine and got out. Andie sat there weighing her options, sensing the storm beneath Clay's quiet facade, wondering if she'd somehow upset him. No, scratch that. Old habits died hard. She wasn't responsible for Clay's mood—she hadn't even been near him since the moronic party games.

She got out and followed him to a bench by the shore.

"What happened, Clay?"

She saw his eyes narrow in the near-darkness and waited. Another minute.

She shrugged and had decided she wasn't going to drag it out of him when he finally said something.

"Watching Evan and Selena tonight," he said, then hesitated. "Seeing them open their gifts, looking forward to adding everything to the nursery, talking about who the baby might look like... That got to me."

She leaned against the concrete back, sensing there was more.

"I missed all that."

"With Payton," she said unnecessarily.

"I missed the entire pregnancy, her birth, the first three months of her life."

Andie had stayed with her cousin Jonas and his wife shortly after their daughter was born. The first few weeks had been stressful but also vital for bonding. She remembered getting up one night very late and seeing Jonas, mostly asleep in the recliner, feeding the baby. She couldn't imagine a father missing that. "Was it by choice?"

He laughed, a bitter, humorless sound. "Choice. Women talk about having a choice all the time but I had none. I had no idea I was a father until Robin decided it'd be worthwhile to get money out of me."

"Did it work?"

"Did she get money out of me? Hell, yes, it worked. I'd just found out I had a kid." He started to say more but cut himself off.

Andie watched him, at a loss. She could feel how upset he was—it was as if there was a third person sitting there between them on the bench. And yet she had no idea what to say or do. For the first time, she saw past the image of the perfect guy. Realized maybe his life wasn't as easy and happy as she liked to blame him for.

"I'm sorry," she said quietly. "That sucks. All of it."

He shook his head slightly, closed his eyes for a beat. "No, I'm sorry. This isn't your problem."

"It's good to think about someone else's problems for a change," she said, affected more than she wanted to be, more than she should be. "A judge actually granted this woman custody?"

"There are apparently plenty of them out there who tend to think just like my father—a baby's better off with its mom."

"Your father?"

"He's a different long story that I don't intend to tell tonight, but yes, he actually said to me, after I first found out about Payton, that she might be better off with her mother."

"I take it you don't get along well with him." Maybe they had something in common after all.

"I'm his greatest disappointment." He said it matter-of-factly, as if he'd accepted it years ago.

Andie frowned as she looked Clay over. What the hell about this man could be disappointing? "You have a police record or something?" she asked, grinning.

"Only as a juvenile."

Andie tilted her head in surprise.

"Minor stuff. But in the small town where I grew up, everyone found out. My dad was convinced I was out to ruin his career as a Texas senator."

"Were you?"

"I didn't care one way or the other about it. I was a selfish kid, just out to enjoy myself."

"That sounds halfway normal to me."

Clay leaned forward, running his hands through his short hair. "I said I wasn't going to talk about my dad," he said tersely. "Subject closed."

"Will Payton be asleep yet?"

"I wish. She's a night owl, no matter what I try. Why?"

Andie stood. "You shouldn't go home while you're upset. Let's go on a junk food run."

"What do you have in mind?" he asked.

"We can do lots of damage at the convenience store. They have all the vital food groups."

"Let me guess. Chocolate, donuts, pizza and beer." He leaned his elbows on his knees.

"Something like that. You in?" She knew firsthand how it felt to have anger unfairly taken out on you. Especially when you were a kid and didn't understand that adults could be mad about one thing and yell at someone else who had nothing to do with it. Of course, chances were decent that Clay handled his emotions better than her dad ever had.

He stared at her as he also stood, a flicker of interest in his eyes. Heat? "You might be able to tempt me with a little sugar." He moved closer.

He stopped mere inches from her and Andie's breath hitched.

"We probably shouldn't kiss," he said in a slow, husky near-whisper.

"Probably not. If we want to stick to our

agreement..." She wasn't sure how she made her voice work.

His mouth was so close she could feel his breath on her skin. He closed his eyes and took a step back. Finally he gestured for her to precede him back to the truck and Andie tried to ignore the humming of her blood through her veins.

"OKAY," ANDIE SAID AS they made their way up and down the aisles at the brightly lit convenience store. "Chocolate, check. Donuts, check. Pizza, check. Lemonade, check."

"Got all the groups except beer," Clay said, amused by her enthusiasm over such a simple thing. He hadn't seen this lighthearted, easygoing side of her before. Maybe she was trying to distract him. If so, it was starting to work.

"I'll leave that up to you. I don't drink it," she said as she went toward the line of refrigerators against the back wall. "Popsicles, on the other hand..."

"You don't drink beer, or you don't drink?"

"Yes." She pulled out a box of double popsicles and added them to the week's worth of food they were already lugging around.

"Huh," he said to himself and picked up a pint of vanilla ice cream with chocolate bunnies in it that he thought Payton would like.

"What's 'huh'?" she asked, pausing in the aisle for him to catch up.

"You told me you throw parties, have a police record and yet…no alcohol?"

"Stereotyping much?" She set the items she was carrying on the front counter. "Oh, and I lied about the parties. In case you couldn't tell tonight, I'm allergic to them."

He chuckled and shook his head, seeing her a little differently. Not so…okay, stereotypically.

"Try living with my father for a day and you'll decide you can do without alcohol, too."

"Does he have a drinking problem?" Clay asked.

"Among many others. Do we have everything we need?"

"You could use some laundry detergent," he said, glancing down at her jeans. She had a grass stain on her knee from their fall during the relay game.

Andie inspected her jeans, grinned and shrugged. "Are you sure you want to be seen with such a disreputable biker chick?"

He thought she was joking but he wasn't entirely sure.

"I think my reputation is strong enough to handle a little tarnishing."

They split the cost of everything, Andie lifted the bag and they turned to leave.

"I'll take that," Clay said, reaching over to grab the bag from her. His arm brushed against her breast and in an instant he was hyperalert to everything about her—the way she didn't move away from him, the berry scent of her hair, the surprise in her eyes. His pulse kicked up as if she was standing there naked in front of him.

"What a small world."

Clay abruptly turned toward the speaker at the door.

"Got to be kidding me," Clay mumbled so only Andie could hear.

Morris Lipp, his ex-girlfriend's uncle and, more significantly, her shark attorney, breezed into the store.

"Nice to see you enjoying the night life, Clay." The asshole looked every last inch of Andie over as if he was selecting a steak for his dinner.

"What are you doing on the island, Lipp?" Clay asked, striving to keep his tone indifferent.

"Enjoying a relaxing weekend." The man's chin went up an inch and he grinned as he looked at Andie again. "It's pretty late…where's Payton?"

"That's none of your business," Clay said automatically.

Morris held out his hand to Andie. "I don't believe we've met. I'm Morris Lipp."

"Pleasure," Andie said. When she didn't reciprocate with her name, Clay wanted to throw his arms around her and hug her.

"Catch you later, Lipp," he said as he ushered Andie outside.

"What was *that?*" Andie asked as soon as they got in the truck and closed the doors.

He wanted to collapse against the head rest, but Lipp was still in there and he refused to show any sign of weakness. "That was Payton's mother's lawyer."

Andie's eyes widened and she looked down at her grungy biker attire. "Oh, no. That's not good, is it?"

"Nothing about that bastard is good."

"He won't use this against you will he? Or me? That we were shopping for food together?"

Clay had no doubt Lipp would dig until he found out who Andie was and then dig some more, into her past, her business, anything that would show what an irresponsible father Clay was. "You were smart not giving him your name." It would slow him down a little, at least. Make him work.

Andie closed her eyes and swore. "I'm sorry, Clay. This is why we're not supposed to be together."

They'd been in public for less than ten minutes. Morris Lipp didn't even live on the island, though Clay had run into him once before, a couple of years ago. What were the damn odds?

"Nothing we can do now but eat some junk food and hope for a sugar coma." He tried to keep his tone light.

If Lipp used her past against him in the custody case, Clay had no one but himself to blame.

Some things never changed.

ANDIE SAT ALONE ON THE futon in her living room, shoving powdered donuts into her mouth. She'd ended up dividing the food between her and Clay and sending him on his way. She'd done enough damage for one night.

The thought that she might have harmed Clay's custody case was too much. She didn't know a lot about the situation, and what she did know was from Clay's perspective, but she felt certain Payton's mom was bad news and the wrong option for Payton. Such a sweet girl deserved the best…not a mom who was coked up or drunk all the time. Regardless of whatever trouble Clay had had as a teenager, he seemed like a dedicated, honorable man now.

How many lives would be changed if all parents were like him? How different would Andie be today if she'd had someone as decent as Clay for a dad?

And because of her, because of her past, really, since she hadn't broken any laws for some time, a child's future could be messed up.

Andie wasn't proud of her teen years when she'd have done—did do—just about anything to stay away from her father. And then there was her gargantuan mistake, Trevor. She'd made bad decisions and gotten into a terrible position, one she'd felt like she couldn't get out of. And she was still paying for it today in so many ways.

But dammit, who was that lawyer to use her mistakes as a way to ruin a child's life?

Andie tossed the donut box on the cushion beside her and propelled herself off the couch. She wasn't the same person she used to be and the new post-

Trevor Andie was a woman who refused to let others make her feel bad about herself. She'd had enough of that for a lifetime.

She hadn't done a damn thing wrong tonight. She'd been trying to do something right.

She pulled the door to the tiny balcony back harder than she should have, and it slammed into the wall. Ignoring it, she went out into the steamy, quiet night. Breathed in the humid air. Closed her eyes and focused on the insect noises, the hum of the air conditioner when it came on.

That smarmy lawyer had somehow made her feel like dirt in the two minutes they'd been in contact with him. Clay had, too, to an extent, even though he'd tried to act like everything would be okay.

Andie could keep her distance from Clay and Payton, that was no problem. But she would not keep beating herself up for a past she couldn't change. She wouldn't give anyone that kind of power over her again.

CHAPTER EIGHT

"Is that our newest recruit?" Derek asked as Clay ushered Payton into the fire station two days later.

"Doesn't quite meet the height requirements yet," Clay said, glancing down at his daughter. She carried his San Amaro Island Fire Department hat against her chest like a teddy bear and had twisted her hair around her fingers. "My sister's sick. Can't watch her today. I'm hoping like crazy your fiancée has the day off."

"Macey has to open the bar, actually. Works till six or seven tonight."

Clay held in some choice swear words and picked up Payton. He kissed her cheek and held out his hand for her to unwind her hair and give him a high five.

"Maybe Selena's available," Clay said, pulling out his cell phone and scrolling through his contacts.

"Good luck with that. She's finishing up the last mural before the festival this weekend. Evan says she's transformed into a ranting madwoman."

Well, wasn't he just screwed. Before he had time to comment out loud, Derek was on his own cell phone.

Payton began to squirm and Clay let her down. She pranced along behind them as they moved toward the locker room, her pink shoes clicking down the tile floor.

"Mace," Derek said into his phone. "Got a favor to ask." He explained Clay's predicament and asked if she would watch Payton until she had to go to work. She apparently answered in the affirmative, and then Derek asked. "Is Andie scheduled today?"

"No." Clay gestured to him, trying not to let Payton know how strongly he was against it.

Derek was off the phone within seconds. "She said you need to call Andie yourself."

"I'm not calling Andie."

"Who are you going to call? Dial-a-nanny? Andie's fine."

"I hardly know her. I can't ask her to babysit for a twenty-four-hour shift."

"If the price is right…"

"Who's not working today? There's got to be someone from the department who can watch my kid."

Derek put his hands up. "Whatever. It's none of my business but if it was my kid, I'd trust Andie." He went into the locker room.

Clay leaned against the wall outside the room, watching his daughter meander, completely wrapped up in the photos of fire trucks and fires on the walls.

"Payton, you like Miss Andie, don't you?" he

asked, looking for any kind of hesitation from her which would signal a big no-go to him.

"Yeah! I like Miss Andie. I want to see the Turtle Lady with her."

He had no idea what the Turtle Lady was but there wasn't anything he could remotely interpret as doubt on his daughter's part. And, hell, he'd seen how good Andie was with Payton. That wasn't in question.

What was in question was whether any harm would be done by letting Andie get close to his daughter. What if Lipp sent someone sniffing around?

Of course, if Morris Lipp was going to bring up Andie's questionable past during the hearing, he likely already had all the ammo he needed.

Dammit.

They didn't need to make it easy for him, though, by being seen together regularly, by putting themselves in the position where a witness might testify they were "close." However, today, he didn't have many other options.

Clay poked his head into the locker room and motioned to Derek. "What's her number?"

"Payton, you're playing with the big girls now," Macey said, watching the child in her rearview mirror. "You up for a girls-only brunch?"

Andie turned sideways in Macey's passenger seat. Payton was peering back at the fire station uncertainly, as if they were ripping her away from her daddy forever. She'd broken into tears when they left but that hadn't lasted long. "It's okay, sweetie." She reached back to pat Payton's leg.

"What's brunch?" Payton asked, sniffling once.

"It's the *br* from *breakfast* and the *unch* from *lunch. Brunch.* The meal you eat in between breakfast and lunch," Macey explained.

"Is there milkshakes?"

Andie met Macey's gaze and they held in a laugh. "You like milkshakes?" she asked.

"Yes. I like strawberry and chocolate and banilla and marshmallow."

"We could probably make milkshakes part of the deal," Macey said. "Too bad Selena's not with us. Ice cream is about fifty percent of her diet."

"Is my daddy going to eat brunch, too?"

"He has to be a firefighter today, honey," Macey said. "Normally Aunt Bridget would come to your house to take care of you but she doesn't feel well. The good news is that you've got the two coolest girls ever to entertain you."

She could tell Payton still wasn't convinced and her heart went out to her. "Later on, after Miss Macey goes to work, we can try to do your hair like a ballerina," Andie said.

"Can we play beauty salon?"

"Sure." Andie had never in her life played beauty salon, and spent as little time and money in them as she could, but if it helped stop those sad gazes back toward the station, she'd do her best.

Macey snickered and pursed her lips together. "Do you even have the supplies?"

"I'm hoping she does," Andie said quietly, uneasy about the prospect of entertaining this child for an entire day. She'd stayed with Jonas's daughter before for an hour or two at a time, but had never pulled a three-meal shift.

"After brunch we can stop by my place and pick up some girly hair essentials." Macey pulled into the parking lot of a bagel shop.

"Is this the place where they have milkshakes?" Payton asked from the backseat.

"Yes, ma'am, they do." Macey turned off the car. "They even have chocolate chip. Let's go."

The three of them got out, and Payton ran along the sidewalk to the door.

"I'm dying to know," Macey said as they caught up.

Andie looked at her questioningly and held the door open.

"How in the world did Clay get you to agree to babysit for twenty-four hours?"

"What do you mean?" Andie asked innocently, turning her attention to the menu board behind the counter. Payton wandered a few feet away, checking out the pastries behind the glass counter.

Macey chuckled. "While you do have a good heart buried deep in there somewhere, twenty-four hours is a long time for someone you've just met. What'd he bribe you with?"

"Nothing much," Andie said. "Just a loaner Harley while mine's in the shop."

ANDIE WOULD NEVER ADMIT it to Clay but she'd definitely gotten the better end of the deal. Not only did she have transportation while her bike was in the hospital—or she would have as soon as Clay took her back to Bud's for one of the bikes he rented out—but hanging out with Payton was a lot of fun.

The girl was a fan of all things, well, girly—ballerinas, hair, butterflies, rainbows, princesses. Things that had escaped Andie completely during her childhood, as she'd been more apt to make a secret hideaway in an evergreen tree or an obstacle course in the woods behind her house.

They'd borrowed Macey's curling iron and Andie had turned Payton's long waves into curls tied back in pink and purple ribbons. Cute, but definite over-kill. Andie couldn't bring herself to mention that to Payton, though, who'd been spinning and check-ing the mirror ever since. Life should be so simple, truly.

They'd made it through the morning just fine, even after Macey left them to open the bar. Andie had cooked mac and cheese for lunch. They'd spent the afternoon in the front yard, covering the driveway with sidewalk chalk art, reading the butterfly book (several times), coloring a princess poster and now they were inspecting wildflowers, picking them from the flower bed to study or put in their hair.

"This one's for you," Payton said, yanking a bright pink bloom from its stem and handing it to Andie. "It goes in your hair."

Andie sat on a boulder in the garden while the child secured the stem behind Andie's ear with her clumsy little fingers.

"There," Payton said with a nod and a shake of the flowing, unevenly hemmed princess skirt she'd insisted on wearing over her pink leotard. "You're pretty now."

"Why thank you, princess," Andie said, laughing. "How about if we—"

She was interrupted by Payton's screaming.

"Sweetie, what's wrong? Can you tell me so I can help you?" Frantically, she turned the crying girl around, looking for blood, bruises—God, she had no idea what she was looking for but something was causing shudder-inducing screams.

She picked the girl up and carried her to the steps, but looking up at all those stairs changed her mind. Instead, Andie sat on the second step and hugged her.

"Shh, it's okay. Show me where it hurts, sweetie."

Finally Payton pointed to the back of her leg, behind her knee.

Bee sting. *Stings.* There were two large red spots swelling up, one of them with a stinger in it.

"Aww, Payton, that hurts, doesn't it? We'll put some mud on them and that will help soothe the sting." Payton quieted a couple of notches as Andie sat her on the step and got up to take some dirt from the flower bed. She'd been stung lots when she was a kid. When she was really young, she remembered crying to her mom, who put the innards of an unlit cigarette on the area. Mud worked nearly as well.

She glanced over at Payton as she bent to scoop up some dirt.

Something wasn't right.

Payton had lain down across the step and Andie couldn't put her finger on why she looked *off*, but she did. Then she saw the girl's skinny forearms—there were red marks popping up all over.

Forgetting the mud, Andie ran to her. "Are you okay?"

Payton looked at her but didn't answer. She'd stopped crying and when she inhaled, Andie heard a rasp. Oh, God. She knew that sound. She was having a reaction.

Andie pulled out her cell phone, shaking so badly she could barely dial 911. She'd watched a woman at a campground go through this, had been sitting right next to her when her symptoms started.

Minutes later Andie heard a siren and she rushed, blinded by tears, with Payton in her arms to meet the paramedics.

CHAPTER NINE

THE MEDICAL ALARM sounded throughout the station and Clay's heart started thundering at the mention of a child in distress. When he heard his own address from the speaker, he lost his mind.

"That's my kid!" He sprinted to the truck, yelling the whole way, not sure what he was even saying.

The firefighters on San Amaro Island routinely went on medical calls with the ambulance and vice versa. This time the ambulance was coming from a different location than the station. Clay had no recollection from where and frankly didn't give a shit as long as they got to his house in about ten seconds flat and did whatever they needed to do for his daughter.

"Let's go! Get your ass on the truck!" It seemed like the others were moving through molasses.

He shut up once the four of them were ready to go, all his energy focused on getting to Payton. Hopefully the damn ambulance was closer than they were. If this thing didn't start rolling in about five seconds, he was going to jump out and run for his little girl.

Derek was riding backward next to him, looking

gravely at him. "We'll get there. She'll be all right, Clay."

He should never have come to work today. All his trusted babysitters were unavailable, so he should've been the one to stay home with Payton. That was his responsibility now. She was his priority. What the hell had he been thinking?

God, let her be okay, please. He'd never leave her with anyone again if she could just be okay right now. He twisted around and urged Evan to move it.

The ninety seconds it took them to drive there seemed more like ten minutes, too much precious time ticking by. When the truck finally stopped, he jumped out, relieved that the ambulance was already there. Scott and Blake were on the grass bent over Payton—he was sure of it even though he couldn't see her clearly. Andie knelt next to her but he couldn't waste a millisecond deciding if she was to blame. He had to be with his daughter.

"Payton." He bent down next to Scott. "What's happening? How is she?" He could see she was conscious but she didn't say anything to him, just looked at him with those scared eyes. She was dazed.

"Just gave her epinephrine and she's starting to respond. She called right away," Scott said, indicating Andie with a nod. "Fast reaction. Makes all the difference."

"Payton, Daddy's here," he said, afraid to take his eyes off her, as if in looking away something could go seriously wrong. He took her little hand in both of his and summoned up an everything's-going-to-be-fine facade.

He moved around to his daughter's head, next to where Andie crouched over her, robotically brushing Payton's hair back from her face again and again.

Scott handed him the equipment to prep the oxygen and Clay realized his hands were shaking so badly he could hardly function.

The guys, who normally stayed out of the way until they were needed during medical calls, had crowded around to see how Payton was and if they could do anything. Evan leaned over Clay from beside him. "You all right, man? Want me to do that?"

"I got it."

Once the oxygen was hooked up and Scott was checking her blood pressure again, Clay bent over Payton and pressed his lips to her forehead. "It's okay, girly. We're going to make you all better."

As he continued to talk to Payton, reassuring her, trying to keep her calm and relaxed, he noticed Andie had walked away and was sitting on the bottom step. She leaned over her knees and held her head with both hands, her hair draped over her face.

Somewhere in his mind it registered that she was scared to death, too, that she needed someone to comfort her. But Clay couldn't be that person. His concern was his daughter. It wasn't his place to worry about Andie.

"She's stabilizing," Scott said at last. "Blood pressure is improving. Let's take her in."

Clay felt as if he was breathing for the first time since the alarm had come in and he'd heard his address blasted out over the speaker at the station.

Blake had grabbed the stretcher from the ambulance and he and Evan lifted Payton onto it. The sight of her little body on the large sterile equipment, which was such an everyday part of his job, twisted him up inside. The two weren't supposed to be together. *She* wasn't ever supposed to be the one lying there helplessly.

He held Payton's hand and walked beside her to the ambulance. Andie was suddenly keeping pace with him.

"Can I ride with you?" she asked. "I know you don't want me around but I don't have any other way to get there."

At the back end of the ambulance, he stared down at her, at the anguish on her face, the tears in her eyes. It was more emotion than he'd seen from her in all the time he'd known her.

"I'm going, Clay. To the hospital. One way or another."

He nodded. "I'm riding in back," he told Scott. "She's coming with me."

CLAY WAS NEVER LETTING Payton outside again. He'd lock her in the house and let her out when she turned thirty. Maybe.

The terror of the day had receded—she'd just received the okay to go home and now they were waiting on the formalities—but he'd aged a good couple of decades in the past few hours.

Payton was asleep on the exam table, curled up on her side beneath a thin hospital blanket, still wearing her leotard and skirt. Her expression seemed peaceful now. Clay repeated the mantra of gratitude he'd been saying to himself all evening and slumped in the uncomfortable chair next to her bed.

"Here's the prescription for the EpiPen she'll need to have with her at all times," Joanna, one of the nurses he'd refused to play with at Evan and Selena's party, said softly when she came back in. "Still waiting on Dr. Milton to sign off and finish the paperwork but it shouldn't be long. Isn't the tall brunette in the lobby with you?"

Clay frowned. "Andie? Is she still here?"

"If she's not with you, I'm not sure who she's here for. Think she was with you at the Drakes' party. Straight, dark hair past her shoulders, skinny. Wearing some god-awful boots?"

That was Andie. His pulse picked up speed. He'd assumed she'd left hours ago.

He watched Payton sleep, thankful for every rise and fall of her little body. He couldn't leave her now.

"I can bring her back here," Joanna said. "She doesn't look like she's doing too well herself."

Clay nodded, telling himself the only thing he felt for Andie right now, the only thing he *could* feel, was gratitude. "Thank you."

After all, he'd fallen for Payton's mother. That mistake, that lapse in judgment, was still hurting the people he loved today—Payton, his family. He knew his mom worried about her granddaughter all the time, wishing for more normal circumstances for her. Payton had paid with more than three years of God knew what from her mother.

Andie was a drifter. She was used to watching out for herself and would do what she had to for number one.

She carried everything she owned on the back of a motorcycle, and yet…she seemed to have more baggage than a loaded cruise liner.

THEY SHOULD PUT COTS IN the E.R. waiting area, Andie thought as she turned to her side on one of those uncomfortable double chairs with no arm rest between them. Her legs were draped over the arm rest that separated this double chair from the next one. Pain shot through her hip—these damn things had virtually no cushioning.

She could've gotten up and walked home at any time. Called a taxi, even. But she had to know that Payton was going to be all right. Had to see with her own eyes that she'd recovered.

She knew waiting to see Payton meant she'd have a run-in with Clay, too. That could be ugly. She'd seen his animosity when he'd arrived on the scene to find his daughter laid out in the front yard. His fury had been directed at Andie—rightly so.

She'd been responsible for Payton and the girl had almost died.

Nausea rose in her throat for the hundredth time today. What if she *had* died? Andie would never have been able to live with herself.

"Are you with Clay Marlow?" A nurse had come out from the back without Andie noticing.

Andie sat up. "Um, I guess so."

"I can show you to where he is."

She stood and followed the woman—a blonde wearing scrubs with penguins all over them.

"Is Payton okay?" Andie choked out, exhausted and starving. She hadn't grabbed her purse or anything else when they'd left.

"She's going to be just fine, thank goodness," the nurse said.

Andie let out a long breath and nodded.

"Here you go," the nurse said, pushing the door of the exam room open a few more inches.

Andie noticed Clay in her peripheral vision but she zoomed in on the bed, on Payton. She took a couple of steps forward, not feeling as if she had the right to get too close, and drank in the sight of the girl. Her coloring was much better and the fear that had torn Andie up was gone from her angelic face. Her body rose and fell in even, non-raspy breaths. Payton was really okay.

Andie's eyes filled with tears.

"She's going to be fine," Clay whispered. He stood a foot away, smiling.

Smiling?

"Clay…" Andie began in a low voice. "I'm so damn sorry. I should never have agreed to watch her for you. I don't have a lot of experience with kids or emergencies or bees or anything. I was so focused on getting a temporary bike, I didn't really think about it and I almost—"

"Shh." Clay took her by the elbow and directed her to the far corner of the room. He leaned against the counter and pulled Andie in front of him, their thighs touching. "Everything's fine." His voice was just above a whisper, still soothing and lacking any trace of the anger she expected. He brushed his fingers under her chin, forcing her to make eye contact with him.

The gentle action from this bulk of a man was such a contradiction that all she could do was stare at him. Take in his features, the warmth in his eyes, the insistent set of his chin, the alluring stubble.

"You were mad at me," she said.

"I owe you an apology, Andie. I can't tell you how terrifying it was to hear my own address on the speaker at the station. I was out of my mind when we got there. My anger wasn't directed at you…or it shouldn't have been."

Andie hadn't known Clay would respond to the alarm, hadn't given it any thought.

"I admit I hesitated to call you this morning. If I hadn't, though, she might not be alive right now."

His voice was rough, ragged. "I don't know how to thank you for reacting so fast."

She started to shake her head but he grasped her wrist and gave her a stern look.

"It made a difference. She could've been so much worse off if you hadn't called immediately."

The terror from earlier bubbled up and nearly suffocated her. Her tears finally overflowed and ran down her cheeks.

"It's not adequate," he said, "but thank you."

She saw such sincerity in his eyes, through her damnable tears, that she could've collapsed in relief. "I'm..." Her voice wasn't working right. She cleared her throat. "So glad she's okay."

Saying the words out loud released the last of her pent-up fear and she did the worst thing she could do at that moment. She started crying in earnest. Not just little sniffs and sharp inhales. Oh, no. Her shoulders shook and all the emotions came out in ugly sobs.

Clay pulled her to him, wrapping those mammoth arms around her. She buried her head in his shoulder and fought for control to avoid waking up Payton. He was the last person she wanted to break down in front of but apparently that didn't make a difference.

He pressed his lips to her hair and made comforting sounds in her ear. Andie kept her face down, taking long, unsteady breaths, trying to fight through the emotions that had blindsided her. As she gradually calmed down, she became more aware of the man who held her. He caressed her back with long, slow strokes, up and down. His chin rested on the top of her head. The chest beneath her face was solid, reassuring. Sculpted. Alluring.

She stirred, suddenly overly conscious of the heat where her body aligned with his—her abdomen and thighs were pressed into him. Even though he wore long pants and a fire department T-shirt, she could feel the muscle, the ins and outs of his body, as if he were unclothed.

Bad line of thinking, she realized, as her body reacted.

Andie reached between them to wipe her eyes. When she looked at him, his gaze bore down on her. Before she could school herself and do the smart thing, he glanced at her lips and she was a goner. She wanted his mouth on hers again. Couldn't have walked away from it if the building had been in flames.

Except…apparently he could, because he raised his chin then looked beyond her to his daughter. Andie backed away, feeling like an idiot for wanting so badly what he just passed up with no problem. Again.

The nurse who'd shown Andie to the room breezed in. Clay turned to her while Andie tried to shake off his effect on her.

"All set to go," the nurse said. "Dr. Milton signed everything. We just need to review Payton's care instructions with you." She set down a stack of papers next to Clay.

Andie half listened as the nurse gave him directions.

Payton stirred while the nurse was still talking, and Andie was surprised when the girl reached out for her and asked her to pick her up. When Andie lifted her, Payton threw her skinny arms around her neck and hugged her tight.

"When we get home," Andie said quietly, "I have something for you to borrow."

"What's borrow?"

"It means you can use it for a few days and then give it back to me when you don't need it."

"What is it?" Payton asked, lighting up despite exhaustion.

"His name is Lyle. He's a teddy bear who loves to get hugs." She rested her forehead on Payton's. "Interested?"

"Lyle?" Payton giggled. "Okay!"

"Okay, then." Andie closed her eyes and breathed in the baby shampoo of the girl's hair, never once before having guessed that hugging a child could be so…comforting.

When she opened her eyes, she caught Clay's gaze on her but couldn't read his thoughts. His arms were crossed and he rubbed his chin with one hand—a capable, strong hand that captured Andie's attention like it hadn't before.

The nurse left and Andie carried Payton over to Clay. His daughter tried to spring toward him, making her difficult to hold on to until Clay stepped in. Andie's body brushed his as she handed Payton over, and she was overwhelmed by the idea of the three of them.

Andie quickly relinquished the little girl, weak and nauseous at the direction of her thoughts. Once Clay had Payton, she flipped her arm over so she could see the long white scar there. The scar—one of them—caused by Trevor. It was a reminder, whenever she needed it, of what could happen when you trusted someone.

She was leaving in three weeks. Because she *wanted to*. Leaving these two people, both Payton and Clay, wouldn't be easy, but it would be necessary.

She rubbed the raised scar, over and over.

CHAPTER TEN

"DADDY, WE HAVE TO GET LYLE."

"Who is Lyle?" Clay asked as they approached Andie's landing.

"He's the bear I promised to loan Payton," Andie explained. She opened the door to her place.

"You didn't lock your door?" He followed her inside, shifting Payton to his left arm.

"Uh, no. I left in a hurry?"

Of course. In the ambulance. "I'll check all the rooms."

"For what?" She was unsuccessfully trying not to laugh at him.

"Freaks. Crazies. Axe—"

"What are crazies, Daddy?"

"Big hairy bugs," Andie said, glancing into the bathroom and bedroom. "And there are none here."

A cell phone blared in the quiet of the apartment and Andie dug it out of her pocket. She checked the display and her entire demeanor changed. Tensed.

"Hey, Jonas." Her voice was tight.

Who the hell was Jonas and why was she afraid of him? Clay held on to Payton and paced.

She listened for a while to the Jonas guy. His voice carried but Clay couldn't make out his words.

"So you talked to him yourself?" Andie asked, her tone conveying how upset she was. "Yeah. Okay." She ran her hand through her hair. "You're right."

Clay looked down at Payton. She was also paying rapt attention to Andie's end of the conversation.

"You're tired tonight, aren't you?" he asked, trying to distract her. That didn't prevent him from hearing what Andie said next.

"Still over two weeks before I can leave. After that I can go wherever I want. That'll help." She glanced at Clay. "I need to go, Jonas. Thanks for the call."

"Good friend of yours?" Clay asked when she ended the call.

She avoided eye contact and stuck the phone back in her pocket. "My cousin."

"Everything okay?"

"Just fine. Let's get that bear so you can go to bed, sweetie." She held her arms out to Payton.

Clay let her down, clenching his teeth. He had questions, but not in front of his daughter.

While the girls went into Andie's bedroom, he paced to the balcony door and peered out into the darkness, his mind spinning. Andie's business was certainly not his, but he couldn't help wanting to get involved. He was the kind of guy who tended to jump in whenever someone was in trouble. Didn't make any difference if it was his sexy renter or an old woman on the street.

Payton giggled and he relaxed marginally. He went to the doorway of the bedroom and leaned against it, watching her hug the tie-dyed bear while Andie told her Lyle's favorite foods.

"You didn't mention we'd have to feed the bear," Clay said.

Andie grinned and came around the bed toward him. "He likes his green beans cooked just right, too."

"He's in trouble then. I've been known to burn them."

"Is this real?" Payton asked, making both of them turn back to her.

"Payton!" Andie leaped the few feet to her at the sight of the one hundred percent real gun she held in one hand. "Don't move!"

Clay froze, knowing in an instant she had never unloaded it, as he'd insisted when she moved in. Flooded with adrenaline, it was all he could do not to tackle Andie and grab the gun.

"Payton, point it toward that wall over there and slowly hand it to Andie." His heart hammered out of control and he didn't breathe until Andie had it securely in her hand.

"Come here, girly," he said, sitting on the bed and stretching his arms out. Payton crawled over the mattress and flung herself at him, as if she sensed how terrifying that moment had truly been. He wrapped her in a tight hug, squeezed his eyes closed and thought he might throw up.

Andie unloaded the thirty-eight. Clay sat there quietly, watching her.

"I'm sorry," Andie finally said, turning her back to him and putting the gun in the drawer of the nightstand. "I screwed up."

He'd screwed up worse. He'd been stupid enough not to make damn sure she'd unloaded the gun.

Who the hell was this woman who lived so dangerously close to his three-year-old daughter? What was she afraid of?

His jaw locked, he narrowed his eyes, unable to speak and unwilling to have Payton hear what he might say to Andie anyway.

He stood, not about to let go of Payton. "Time for bed," he said softly into her ear. He walked out of her unit without a word.

His next tenant would go through one hell of a background check. And he would never take someone at their word again.

Bridget had said he'd changed, left his screwing-up tendencies behind him but obviously she was wrong. And this time he'd put his daughter's life in jeopardy. He had to do better before someone got hurt again because of him.

TWO DAYS LATER THE NEED to talk to Clay, to apologize again, ate away at Andie.

She'd knocked on his door three different times since Payton had found her gun but he hadn't answered. Now he sat across from her at a picnic table, but they were surrounded by a crowd. Clay, Evan and Payton, who'd set Lyle the bear on the table next to her, were across from her and Macey. Hundreds had gathered for the recognition ceremony of San Amaro Island's twenty-fifth birthday party.

Andie vowed to corner him somehow so they could talk privately. So far he'd done a fine job of ignoring her.

"That is *not* your dinner," Andie said to Macey, trying to distract herself. "There's a child present."

Macey laughed and licked her fingers, gripping the battered and fried candy bar on a stick tightly with her other hand. "Payton knows better than to follow my example, don't you, hon?"

"Daddy said if I eat my taco all gone, I can have my own one of those."

Tables were scattered throughout the courtyard of the fire station, and a small stage had been set up close to the main entrance. Most of the benches were filling with families who'd grabbed their dinners from the huge variety of fundraising booths along the street.

"Ladies and gentlemen…" A man spoke into a microphone, setting off ear-piercing feedback. He introduced himself as the mayor and received polite applause. "Welcome to the twenty-fifth anniversary celebration of San Amaro Island!"

Andie half listened as she picked at her pork tamale. She wasn't particularly interested in the goings-on. Except, of course, she wanted to see Selena recognized for her gorgeous murals. Besides, when she'd found out Clay would be here, she'd decided to see how far he'd go to avoid her.

"When's Selena's thing?" she asked Evan.

"Should be pretty soon, right after they get through all the volunteers," Evan said. He'd turned backward on the picnic table bench so he had a direct view of his wife when she had her big moment. "Should've done the pregnant lady first."

"She does look about to pop, doesn't she?" Macey said, still licking her fingers. "Don't you dare tell her I said that. She'll take it the wrong way."

Evan chuckled. "Lately she takes just about everything the wrong way. Except ice cream."

"How many more weeks?" Andie asked.

"Three and a half. Then life as we know it…" He gestured with his hand across his neck.

"And you'll be insanely in love with your new baby," Macey said.

The whole table quieted as the person on the stage—some committee chairperson—praised Selena's art and gushed about how wonderful she was to work with.

When a very large-bellied Selena finally approached the podium to accept a plaque and the final payment for her services, their table made a noisy show of supporting her. Andie chuckled at Evan, clearly so proud of his wife he was about to explode. What a case. A happy one, to be sure, but if someone had told her last year that the tall, charming playboy would fall so hard so soon, she would've laughed them off the island.

"Thank you," Selena said into the microphone. "This was a dream project for me—every artist wants to see her work bigger than life and…" She gestured to the mural that had been ceremoniously uncovered minutes ago. "This is definitely larger than life." She looked pointedly at her abdomen. "I can kind of relate." Laughter broke out through the courtyard.

"On a more serious note, I'd like to thank the city of San Amaro Island for offering me the opportunity. And most importantly, thank you to Evan Drake, who has supported me from the beginning." She scoped him out in the crowd and met his gaze. "He's my husband now, so it looks like his evil plan worked."

The audience stood and clapped. Some of the firefighters on duty, including Derek, lined the wall of the station and several of them hollered at Evan.

"Thanks again." Selena made her way down the three stairs and through the tables to her husband. He welcomed her with open arms and an R-rated kiss, which generated more reaction from his coworkers and an elbow from Clay.

"Kids here," he said. "No public displays."

They all sat down and listened restlessly to the last part of the presentation. Finally the mayor let them get on with their evening. Most of the crowd headed to the beach, where there was an outdoor concert starting.

"Now can I have my candy?" Payton asked Clay.

"You ate that whole taco?" he asked her, patting her belly. "Are you sure you have room for a candy bar in there?"

Payton grinned and nodded shyly as everyone at the table looked at her.

"I promised you, didn't I?" Clay said. "I'll take you as soon as I finish my last dog."

"I'll take her," Macey said. "I need to wash my hands anyway."

"You want to go with Miss Macey?" Clay asked.

Payton nodded again and skipped around the table, carrying the tie-dyed bear with her.

"You have to be a fried-candy-bar expert to order them right," Macey told Clay, standing.

"I think we're heading out," Evan said. "Right?" he asked Selena.

"So right. My ankles must be triple-sized. I need air-conditioning. Now."

Everyone said their goodbyes, Macey and Payton headed toward the concession stands, and Clay and Andie were finally alone. In the middle of the crowd.

Andie stood and Clay didn't so much as glance at her. She walked around the table and sat right back down again. Next to him.

"So," she said. "I've been trying to track you."

"I've been busy," he said, then stuffed the last third of his hot dog into his mouth.

"Clay, I'm really sorry about the gun."

He nodded once and grunted.

"It's unloaded now." She swallowed hard, her chest tightening painfully at the memory of Payton waving the thirty-eight, one wrong move away from tragedy. "It'll stay that way until I leave."

She didn't like it, didn't like the thought of not having that security under her pillow, but a repeat of Payton finding it was unthinkable.

Clay watched her as he finished chewing. "Tell me, biker girl. What the hell are you so scared of?"

That wasn't what she wanted to talk about, particularly, but she had to open up. He'd leveled with her the other night by the bay. If she shut him down now, there was no chance of his forgiveness.

For some reason, that mattered to her.

"Is it your dad? You said he's a drinker," Clay prodded. "Are you running from him?"

"My dad is dead."

"I'm sorry."

"I'm not. He drank himself to death, which is exactly what he deserved. No," she said, narrowing her eyes. "I take that back. He deserved to have someone beat the hell out of him. Regularly. He deserved to live in fear…." She forced herself to meet his eyes.

He didn't say anything, didn't ask prying questions, thank God. But she could see in those brown eyes he understood what she'd just admitted to indirectly.

She fidgeted and rubbed her thumbs together in a

nervous circular pattern. "My ex recently got out of prison back in Illinois," she said.

"You're scared of him?" he asked, his head close to hers so no one could eavesdrop.

"I...guess you could say that."

"Does he know where you are?"

"No." He was looking for her, though. Asking around. He'd asked Jonas, who'd been friends with Trevor's brother for years. As far as she knew, though, Trevor had no clue she was in Texas.

CLAY BELIEVED WHAT ANDIE was telling him, and maybe that was him being stupid. But he didn't think so. What reason did she have to lie about any of it?

"Tell me something else," he said. "You said you have more than one hit on your police record. Besides the run-in with your scumbag ex-boyfriend, what are we talking here? Bank robberies? Mugging old ladies?"

She looked as if she wasn't going to tell him, which wouldn't surprise him. But he needed to understand better what kind of woman he had living downstairs from him. From Payton.

"Trespassing. And I got in a fight a couple of years ago," Andie said quietly after several seconds. She studied the table in front of her. "I'm not proud of any of this, Clay. I want you to know that."

"I have some unproud moments in my past," he said. "I get that."

"I left home when I was sixteen," she said. "I had

no friends at the time, nowhere to go, but anywhere was better than enduring another episode with my father."

Clay became so engrossed in what she was saying that he filtered out all the people around him, felt as if they were alone. "What did he do to you, Andie?"

"Standard stuff. Beat me up." She glanced at him nervously. "Nothing sexual if that's what you're thinking."

"So you left," he said, trying not to dwell on her piece-of-shit dad.

"I left. Spent the next few years taking whatever job I could get, living wherever I could find a place, no matter how temporary. One winter I got really sick. Flu or something, it was horrible. Lost my job because I couldn't show up for work, and got kicked out of the place I was living. I had nowhere to go. Didn't care where I was as long as I could sleep. I snuck into an old house I thought was abandoned."

"I take it it wasn't?"

"It wasn't. The owner found me and called the cops." She ran her hands up and down her arms, even though it was hot and humid. "I didn't even care. I just wanted to sleep. In jail I could do that."

Clay couldn't help comparing his teen years to hers. He'd been a troublemaker, a cliché rebel without a cause. He'd left home a couple of times himself, a week here, few days there. But looking back, it was one of the dumbest things he'd done. He'd had a good home, a family that loved him.

Unlike Andie.

"Was that the only time?" he asked, resisting the urge to touch her. Comfort her.

She shook her head. "There were two others. Same kind of deal except I wasn't sick. Just cold."

"These were after you turned eighteen?"

She nodded. "I'm not the same person anymore, Clay. My life...I've changed my life. Even though I still move around, it's by choice now. Not because I don't have anywhere else to go."

"And the fight you mentioned?"

"A guy in a bar wouldn't leave me alone. I punched him."

"You fought a guy?"

"Technically, no. Only one punch. He pressed charges. Ever since Trevor, I take defending myself very seriously."

"I understand that."

"But the gun is unloaded."

He nodded slowly. "I've heard too many tragic stories about kids—"

"You can check it every night if it will make you feel better."

A deep-seated need to protect her evoked images of him keeping her safe. In his bed. "That won't be necessary."

He hoped. Was he making a mistake to trust her again? On the same issue? Maybe he'd check once or twice after all...

It was a big deal for her to reveal to him everything

she had. He was certain of that. His gut told him he could believe she would keep the weapon unloaded. Unfortunately, he didn't often trust his gut.

"Daddy!"

Clay looked up to see Payton and Macey making their way back to the table. Payton walked slowly, carrying her candy bar/sugar conglomeration as carefully as if it were a bowl of boiling water she didn't want to spill. A self-satisfied grin split her face in two. Macey held Lyle the Bear between her elbow and torso and carried another plate.

"Are you really going to eat that thing, girly?" Clay asked, his stomach turning.

Payton walked around the table to him and burrowed her way onto the bench between him and Andie.

"If you get a tummy ache, just remember it's Miss Macey's fault," Andie said.

"I won't get a tummy ache," Payton said, sitting up straight and surveying her treat.

"You got another one?" Clay asked Macey in awe.

Macey laughed. "It's a present for Derek."

"Didn't realize he liked junk food so much."

"He doesn't. It's kind of an ongoing joke between us. I'm sure someone else at the station will end up eating it. Back soon."

Payton finally stuck the end of the bar in her mouth and took a dainty bite. "Yummy."

Clay chuckled. "Don't talk with your mouth full, Pay."

Andie stood and extricated herself from the picnic bench. She picked up her paper plate of half-eaten dinner to throw away and grabbed Clay's, as well.

"You don't have to do that."

"I know," she said. "I usually wouldn't." She carried them to a nearby trashcan and returned to the table.

"We need to pick up that bike for you," Clay said, holding the stick for Payton while she nibbled like an enthusiastic mouse.

"Anytime. I have tomorrow off."

"I do, too."

"Tomorrow is my birthday party!" Payton hollered, craning her neck to see Andie's face.

"No way! You're turning four already?" Andie said, once again surprising him.

Payton nodded, chewing, and then turned to Clay. "Can Miss Andie come to my party, Daddy? Please?"

"Andie probably has other things to do," he told his daughter, sputtering, searching his brain for a graceful way out of this.

"Do you, Miss Andie? Can you come?"

"I'd love to," Andie said, looking amused at his obvious discomfort, "but only if your dad says it's okay."

Those big brown eyes were one hell of a weapon. When Payton pegged him with them, he struggled.

He could imagine how having Andie as a guest at their family dinner would go over, especially with his dad.

"My mommy can't come," Payton told Andie very seriously.

"I'm sorry to hear that," Andie said.

"Okay," Clay said, aware that his buttons were being pushed, however unintentionally, but unable to deny this one little thing for his daughter's special day. "If Miss Andie wants to come, she can come."

"Yay!" Payton clapped her chocolate-covered hands and made a bigger mess, causing him and Andie to laugh.

"Five o'clock, on the beach in front of the Shell Shack. We're having a cookout. Bring a lawn chair or blanket to sit on."

"Got it. And the bike?"

"My sister's taking Payton to a matinee tomorrow. We could do it then."

They discussed a time and Andie went off to find Macey. Clay listened to his daughter's chatter and prayed, yet again, he hadn't just done something he'd regret.

CHAPTER ELEVEN

THE NEXT DAY, CLAY and Payton made their way down the stairs to Andie's. Bridget was due to pick Payton up in a few minutes for their movie, a princess-y one, Clay had been reassured. And he'd been forbidden to join them. It was a girls' day, and he wasn't invited.

Payton carried Lyle in one hand and the dainty butterfly purse Clay had given her for her birthday, over her shoulder. She'd thrown in some play makeup, a notebook and pen and her plastic cell phone—everything a girl could need.

When they got to Andie's landing, however, the big girl facade fell away.

"You can go watch for butterflies if you want," Clay told her as he knocked on Andie's door.

Payton glued herself to his side and shook her head. He looked down at her, puzzled, as Andie opened the door.

"Hi," he said, then put one finger up and bent down to Payton. "What is it, girly? You don't want to hunt for butterflies?"

Payton shook her head and Clay picked her up. "Why not? You love butterflies."

She squeezed the teddy bear and leaned on Clay's shoulder. He looked in the front yard to see if someone was there. No one.

"Bees," Andie said, studying his daughter. "Are you scared of getting stung again, sweetie?"

Payton nodded slowly, and Clay ached for her. What could he say, though? The thought of her getting stung again filled him with dread, too. Yet he couldn't encourage her to become a hermit.

"I'm right here. I can watch you the whole time. Remember we have your EpiPen to keep you safe if anything happens." Clay held up the pink mini knapsack he'd bought especially for that purpose.

Her lower lip threatened to pop out as she pursed her lips and shook her head.

"You can stay with me until Aunt Bridget shows up." He kissed her temple and tightened his hold on her.

"Oh, just a second. Got something for you," Andie said.

She was inside for less than a minute. Bridget pulled up by the curb and Payton squirmed to get down as Andie reappeared.

"Hey, birthday girl, here you go." Andie handed Payton an envelope. "Take it with you."

Payton smiled widely.

"Tell Miss Andie thank you," Clay reminded her.

"Thank you."

Andie hugged Payton. "Happy Birthday. I'll see you at your party."

"YOU'RE LUCKY TO HAVE such a generous sister," Andie said when Bridget and Payton were out of earshot. "Is the rest of your family like that?"

"They might be if I let them. I try not to rely on them too much. I don't want to burden them with my responsibilities. Been there, done that. You ready to get a motorcycle?"

"Like you wouldn't believe. Walking is for the birds."

"Birds actually fly."

She stopped and looked at him. "Funny. Didn't realize you had it in you."

"I'm a very funny guy if you get to know me." They walked down the stairs side by side.

"I'm very specifically not *supposed* to get to know you. Remember?"

"Touché."

"So how much will this bike rental cost you?" she asked as they climbed into the truck.

"Enough that you should be nice to me."

"I'm always nice to you."

He chuckled. "Yeah. Nice like a scorpion."

TENSION CRACKLED BETWEEN THEM in the truck. It might be an extended cab but Clay always managed to make it feel cramped and too small just by virtue of sitting his long, muscled frame in the driver's seat.

Andie crossed her arms and turned her head away to watch the scenery out her window and ignore him, ignore the undercurrents.

She couldn't wait to get her bike so she could stop relying on others. She wasn't used to asking for favors and had tried to walk wherever she needed to go while hers was in the shop, but the times she needed to go to the mainland she'd had to bum a ride.

Then there was the restlessness. The need to be out on the road, without a month-long lease or a promise to a friend weighing her down. Just her, the endless pavement and a 1200cc engine between her legs.

The first couple of days without her motorcycle had nearly driven her over the edge. She felt penned in. Trapped. She'd started walking to Turtle Town whenever she could. Her mind stayed occupied at Turtle Town, unlike the duplex where it wandered, wondering what her sexy landlord was doing at every creak or thump. Without her daily turtle trips, she'd swear to God she was in prison.

They turned down the alley and Andie spotted Bud's wooden sign. She watched Clay out of the corner of her eye while he maneuvered the truck into a parking space. As usual, she couldn't remain indifferent to the sight. His square jaw was shadowed by the beginning of rough stubble. Dark glasses hid his eyes but she knew the milk chocolate with gold flecks by heart anyway. She studied his profile, thinking for the thousandth time he'd been blessed with symmetry and perfection, marred only by the scar on the right side of his face, near his hair line. This time, though, there was no lingering resentment. She felt only the lure of him. How could she not, after getting to know him better?

She climbed down from the high seat, uneasy at that realization.

Bud greeted them as he came out of one of the bays, wiping his hands on a towel. "Waitin' on a part but I've got her lookin' a lot better," he told Andie.

He took them inside and pointed toward her mostly intact motorcycle. Andie circled it, as if she'd be able to see if something was off. The urge to jump on it and ride away was overpowering and she recognized it was partly because of the firefighter who'd driven her here.

"It's starting to look like my bike," she said. "How long will the part take to come in?"

"Still tryin' to locate one, so I can't say. Got a lead on a possibility, though. Understand you're wantin' a loaner today."

Andie glanced at Clay, who stood outside, browsing a couple of used Harleys for sale.

"How much is this going cost him?" she asked quietly.

"Loaner? Seventy a day plus insurance."

Andie tried not to flinch. "And…how long do you think it'll be before mine's done?"

"No more than a couple weeks."

"Lot of money." She said it more to herself than him, but he apparently picked up on it.

"Cheap, actually. Lot of places charge a hundred, hundred and fifty a day. I'm not making a profit on it, just covering costs."

She nodded. "What kind of bike would it be?"

He rattled off the model as he led her to the other side of the garage, but she didn't pay much attention. It didn't really matter what kind, did it? She glanced at Clay again.

He was the one who'd suggested renting a motorcycle. She hadn't asked for it. He knew how much it would cost. They'd made a deal. So why should she not go through with it?

For one thing, it would be a tangible tie between them, one that his ex's attorney could track down and present in court as proof of…something between them.

Beyond that, though, Andie could no longer consider taking advantage of Clay's offer. He was a hard-working guy busting his ass to do right by his daughter. She was sure he could use the money for her somehow.

CHAPTER TWELVE

CLAY SAT WAITING FOR ANDIE on the bottom step outside their duplex, still trying to figure that woman out.

They'd argued in Bud's lot over renting the motor-cycle. Clay had thought she was feeling guilty again since Payton had gotten stung on her watch.

Andie had told him, in the end, he could throw away as much money as he wanted on a "stupid rental" but she wouldn't ride it if he paid her.

That was the stubborn woman he was familiar with, and the one he eventually decided to listen to.

The door behind him opened and he stood.

She wore light blue jeans that hugged her but yet weren't so tight or worn that his parents would think the wrong thing. On top, she had a white short-sleeved shirt mostly unbuttoned and a jade-green tank beneath it. The only signs of the Harley girl were the boots and the numerous earrings. Even her tattoos were pretty much hidden.

"You clean up well," he said as she descended the stairway.

"Go ahead and say it, I can hear what you're thinking."

"Say what?"

"I clean up well *for a biker girl*."

He tried not to stare at the alluring way her shirt opened just right so he could catch a glimpse of the curve of her breasts above the tank.

"I didn't think that," he said. "Well, not much."

"You said your family would be there. I do have the sense to try to dress appropriately."

It was more than appropriately. It was…*she* was hot, and it was hard to forget that as he followed her out to the carport.

"You didn't have to buy her a gift," Clay said, gesturing toward the box Andie carried.

"Are you kidding? I can't show up at a four-year-old's party without a present."

"You're good to her," he said, moved more than he wanted to be by the gesture. "Thank you."

This was a very bad idea…bringing Andie to the family party when all he wanted to do was sneak her away and peel those appropriate clothes right off of her.

But Payton was ecstatic that Miss Andie was coming, along with Miss Macey, who'd be working at the bar but had promised she would come out and join them on the beach as often as she could.

They parked outside the Shell Shack, in the same place Clay had when he knocked over Andie's bike, and unloaded all the necessities he'd packed while

Andie had changed clothes. They set up the minigrill close to the sea wall below the Shack and put the two large coolers—one full of meat and the other with drinks—in the shade. A few more trips and they'd brought bags of chips and grocery-store side dishes, the presents from Clay and Andie, lawn chairs and a beach blanket. Macey had stowed the rainbow-and-butterfly, pink-frosted cake in the bar's kitchen earlier.

Clay tensed as his parents came down the concrete steps to the beach.

"Hey, Mom," he said as she hugged him. His dad gave him his usual nod.

"Where's the birthday girl?" Vince asked, glancing around and setting down two camp chairs. He looked right over Andie in the process and that set Clay on edge.

"Bridget took her to that princess movie that's out. They should be here any minute." He relieved his mom of the presents she carried and set them with the others on the blanket. "Mom, Dad, this is Andie Tyler. She's renting the lower unit from us and has become friends with Payton."

"It's nice to meet you, dear," his mom said warmly, shaking Andie's hand. "She's a special little girl, isn't she?"

"Yes, ma'am. She teaches me some of the frillier, girlier points I missed as a child."

Clay saw his dad subtly inspect Andie. Andie either missed it or wasn't bothered by it.

"Mr. Marlow," she said, offering her hand. "You have good taste in baseball teams." She glanced up at his Cubs hat approvingly.

Clay couldn't have planned that better. If there was a way to his dad's heart it was baseball.

"You a fan?" he said, his gruff voice soft around the edges.

"I am." She launched into a rehash of last night's game, impressing both Clay and his dad. He wouldn't have figured she could follow sports very well the way she traveled so much.

Clay and his mother moved to the grill to warm it up just as the birthday girl herself came bouncing down the steps at full speed.

"Grandma! Grandpa!" Payton ran to each of them and threw her arms around their legs.

"Sorry we're late," Bridget said, following at a more normal pace.

After hugging her grandpa, Payton grabbed Andie's hand and told her all about the princess movie. To Andie's credit, she nodded as if she'd been dying to hear all about it.

"Payton, what's that on your arm?" Clay asked, removing his sunglasses to get a better view. She wore her brand-new orange-and-white-striped dress with cap sleeves and white sandals. It was tough to miss the large black blob on her upper arm.

"It's a tattube, Daddy. Three butterflies. Like Miss Andie's."

"Where'd you get that?"

"In the birthday card from Miss Andie."

"I picked up a book of temporary butterfly tats at the fair last night," Andie explained. "I thought Payton would like them."

He groaned to himself. What would his parents think? A tattoo...

"We need to wash that off, Payton," he said sternly. "You're too young for tattoos."

"Aunt Bridget said it was okay. She has one, too."

Clay's sister held up her ankle sheepishly, showing off the outline of a flower.

"Didn't know it would be a problem, big guy. Sorry."

"How do those come off?" Clay asked Andie, rubbing his daughter's arm with his thumb.

"No idea," Andie replied. "Mine *don't* come off."

The artwork didn't so much as smear at his touch.

"Oh, let her have a little fun, Clay. Your sisters used to love tattoos." His mom inspected it more closely. "It is a pretty design, Payton."

His mom disapproved of him trying to clean his daughter up. He suspected if he'd ignored the tattoo, his dad would disapprove of the way he raised Payton. Clay closed his eyes. He could never win.

"What do you need body art for, pumpkin?" his dad said, strolling over. "You're perfect without it."

"Miss Andie has tattubes, Grandpa." She pointed at Andie and Clay cringed. "Lots of 'em."

"What's so special about this Miss Andie?" his dad asked. "Besides that she cheers for the right team."

"She saved me."

No. She did not just say that.

"What do you mean, she saved you, honey?" his mom asked, bending down to Payton's level.

"She called the am-blu-lance to take me to the hospital."

His mom looked up in alarm at him. "Clay?"

"Yeah. Uh, Payton got stung by a couple of bees. Turns out she's allergic to bee stings. Andie was babysitting her and called 911 right away." He couldn't help smiling gratefully at Andie yet again.

"Bee stings? My lord, Payton." His mom hugged the child to her. "Clay, why on earth didn't you call us?"

"I didn't want to worry you. By the time I could get to a phone, she was okay."

And there was the part about him not wanting to hear how he might've handled things better, or how he could've avoided the problem, or what he'd done wrong. There was always that.

"So what happens with a bee-sting allergy?" his mom asked, studying Payton's face as if to make sure she showed no signs of lingering problems.

"Her airway started closing up," Clay said gravely.

"Payton's fine. Let's talk about happier things. It's her big day."

His mom wasn't ready to let it rest yet, though. She hugged Payton close. "I'm so glad you're okay, honey."

Clay's dad ambled closer to Andie. "Must've been quite the experience," he said to her. "How'd you know what was happening?"

Was it Clay's imagination or did his dad doubt Andie's heroism?

"Scared the…scared me to death," she said nervously. "I'd seen a similar reaction once before in someone else."

Vince merely nodded and rubbed Payton's head affectionately.

"I've got happy news," Bridget said, and Clay instantly realized where she was going. Couldn't she wait for another time? One that wasn't supposed to be his daughter's big day?

"Reid wanted to be here for this but he had to work tonight."

"What's going on, Bridget?" his mom asked.

His sister looked around the circle at all of them. "We're expecting a baby."

Their mom squealed and hugged Bridget while their dad gauged Clay's reaction.

"She told me earlier," Clay confirmed.

Bridget looked at their dad expectantly.

"When are you getting married?" he asked.

Clay listened while Bridget went through the

same spiel she'd given him a week ago, relieved, at least, that Payton wasn't paying attention. Andie extracted herself from the intimate group and joined his daughter.

Not surprisingly, their father shook his head.

"This isn't like my situation, Dad," Clay said, feeling the need to try to help his sister out. "Bridget and Reid chose this. They'll be in it together."

"You think it's okay?" his dad asked in disbelief.

"I think they'll be fine." It wasn't a lie, even if it was dodging the true question.

"Clay chewed me out when I told him," Bridget said. "He thinks we should get married. He said you'd blame him for this, but Clay has nothing to do with it."

Vince paced away, shaking his head some more.

"He'll come around, honey," their mother said. "He'll love that grandbaby and forget everything else, just like he does Payton."

"He doesn't forget everything else," Clay said without thinking.

"I must confess, I don't understand why someone would choose this, Bridget. But another grandchild…" Their mom rubbed her hands together and smiled widely. "Why don't we go set things up. We have a lot of celebrating to do tonight."

"Come on, Miss Andie," Payton said, dragging Andie to the group and taking her grandma's hand on the other side. Bridget hung back with Clay at the grill.

"Thanks for trying to stick up for me," she said.

"Just trying to keep the peace on my daughter's birthday," Clay grunted.

"Suddenly Andie's her best friend," Bridget said in a low voice. "Do you think that's wise?"

Clay set the charcoal briquettes just so and held a lighter to them. After several seconds, satisfied the fire was started, he stood.

"No, Bridge. I don't think it's wise. But I don't know what the hell to do about it. She put me on the spot. Asked if Andie could come in front of Andie."

"She needs friends her age."

"I know that," he snapped. "I don't know where to come up with them."

"Relax, Clay. I'm not accusing you of anything. Just made a comment. Maybe we could set up a play-date with one of the girls from her dance class. I think Diana lives on the island. They seem to get along."

"Good idea. I need all the good ideas I can get. Payton's mom called this morning to wish her a happy birthday. She ended the call by threatening me."

"About?"

"She doesn't want Payton exposed to Andie." Clay said it with a scoff. "The queen addict is passing judgment."

"What in the world does she know about Andie?"

Clay told her about the run-in with Robin's lawyer at the convenience store.

"So what's the threat?" Bridget asked.

"Let's just say Andie's past isn't pristine."

"Well…neither is yours."

"Thanks for the reminder. She's got a police record and no permanent address."

"Yikes." Bridget turned her attention to the biker in question. "She's a little rough around the edges but she's pretty. Especially when she doesn't try to look all tough."

Clay grinned in agreement. Wisely or not.

"That doesn't mean I think you should get involved with her."

Ignoring her—it was either that or snarl at her—Clay went to the meat cooler and pulled out the hot-dogs and burgers he'd packed.

He was the only one who seemed to notice that Andie was more than the bad girl front she put up. That she had a bigger heart than she would probably ever admit to herself.

Or was he just seeing what he wanted to see?

BY THE TIME THEY'D EATEN dinner and cake and Payton had ripped open her many packages, the sun was low in the sky. Macey had joined them long enough to shove down a hotdog and watch Payton unwrap the bead set she'd given her. The evening's weather was perfect, which meant the beach bar was filled to capacity, and now she was back tending bar.

"Well, Miss Payton," Clay's dad said, "I believe it's time for your grandma and grandpa to go. We've got a long drive home. Did you have a good birthday, pumpkin?"

"The best birthday ever!" Payton moved from present to present, inspecting each one more closely now that all the wrapping paper was removed. She carried the plush turtle Andie had given her.

Bridget had left a few minutes before to meet Reid when he got off work. Andie stretched out on the beach blanket next to Payton, while Clay sat on Payton's other side. He and his parents stood to start packing up their belongings.

"Thanks for coming all this way," Clay said as they stuffed the shredded wrapping paper into a trash bag.

"We wouldn't miss it for anything. We've got lots of time to make up for with our granddaughter."

Coming from his mom, Clay knew that wasn't a shot, but he felt bad about the missed time anyway. For all their sakes.

"Come tell your grandparents goodbye, Payton," Clay said. He folded his mom's chair while his dad folded the other one.

"Bye, Grandma." Payton hugged her with a lot less energy than the embrace when they'd first arrived. Clay needed to get her home to bed.

"You be easy on your dad, pumpkin, you hear?" Clay's father said.

Maybe he meant nothing by it but his words grated on Clay anyway. Knowing his dad, it was a veiled insult. He'd never believed Clay could handle being a single father. Clay let it go, though. He'd given up battling his dad years ago.

"Let's get this stuff loaded," he said, ready to send them on their way. "Where'd you park?"

"Right next to your truck." His mom picked up her purse and a bag of leftover supplies and the three of them went up the stairs, across the crowded Shell Shack patio to the lot. At the trunk of their car, Clay hugged his mom.

"Thanks for coming. Payton was glad you were here," he said to his dad.

"Take care of her, Clay."

When he got back to the beach, Andie and Payton were stretched out on their backs, side by side on the blanket. Payton hugged the turtle, staring up. Clay gazed up to see what he was missing.

"We're watching for the first star so we can make a wish," Andie explained.

Clay lay on the opposite side of Payton and joined their search of the purple-blue sky. The beach, previously packed, had emptied as the sun fell. The muffled conversations of well-fed customers filtered over them from the bar, but the roar of the waves covered most of it. To the far west, streaks of pink and orange still lightened the sky, but above them it deepened to dark blue.

Several minutes passed without any of them saying a word. Clay was as content as he'd been for a long time, next to his daughter, in the peace of dusk. He wouldn't let himself consider how the woman on the other side of Payton contributed to his mood.

"There," Andie whispered just loud enough to be heard over the waves. She pointed and after several seconds, Clay saw the faint twinkling. He turned to gauge Payton's reaction and chuckled, meeting Andie's gaze over the sleeping child. "It's been a big day."

Clay tucked his daughter closer and looked back at the star. He didn't, however, make a wish. In his state of mind tonight, that was liable to get him in trouble.

CHAPTER THIRTEEN

CLAY ROLLED OVER IN bed, suddenly aware that something had woken him up. He peered into the darkness, looking for Payton, although she rarely got up in the middle of the night. Especially not after a busy day like they'd just had.

At the sound of light tapping on the front door he realized it wasn't the first time someone had knocked. Sitting up, he checked the clock. 4:57. His adrenaline started to pump and he rushed to the door without a thought to his undressed state, wearing sweat shorts and nothing else.

He checked the peephole and though it was dark, difficult to see, he could swear that was Andie. He swung the door open.

Sweet Mary, that was Andie all right.

"What's wrong?" he asked, looking for an injury or a sign of alarm. But she just looked…sleepy. Bed-rumpled. Sexy as hell in a white camisole, which did little to hide her breasts, and satiny pink boxers. Nothing on her feet but dark toenail polish and a modest tattoo at her ankle. Her hair, normally smooth and brushed flat, was tangled, mussed. He itched to touch it, run his fingers through it. Mess it up more.

"I think the smoke alarm is broken," she said. "Keeps beeping. It's maddening."

If this was a joke, she was keeping a perfectly straight face. "The smoke alarm is beeping," he repeated.

"Every thirty seconds. I counted. I checked to make sure there was no smoke."

He leaned against the jamb. "You woke me up at five in the morning."

"I don't know how to fix it," she said. "I've never had a smoke detector before. I didn't figure you'd like it if I threw my boot at it until it shut up."

Clay tried to hold the laugh in. He looked down at her bare feet and could imagine all too well the sight of her nailing the smoke detector with those ass-kicking boots. Eventually he gave up the effort and his shoulders shook.

She scowled at him. "You're no help. Boot it is." She started down the stairs.

"Biker girl, wait. The thing just needs batteries. Give me thirty seconds." He went inside and jogged up the stairs to Payton's attic room. She was sound asleep when he kissed her forehead. He stopped by his room on the way out and pulled a T-shirt over his head. Locking Payton in, he went back outside. Andie sat on the top step, hunched over her legs against the breeze, which made her camisole crawl up and afforded him a nice view of her smooth, tanned lower back. Tattooed, of course.

"Let's go," he said speeding past her, ignoring the sight, the hair. The desire.

Mostly.

"You put a shirt on," she said, sounding…disappointed?

"You're observant in the middle of the night."

"I liked you better without it." The sleepy huskiness of her voice was a turn-on, dammit.

Ignore.

She followed him down the stairs and into her unit.

"Which one is it?" he asked, walking into the darkness.

"Bedroom."

"Keep the door open. I don't like leaving Payton up there alone."

The detector beeped, right above his head.

"Yep. Battery's dying."

He flipped on the light and squinted his eyes against the brightness. Her bed was front, center, left and right, taking up the entire room and impossible to ignore. The covers were twisted and he could clearly make out where her body had lain in the very middle of the mattress. Guess she wasn't in the habit of sharing with someone. But then neither was he.

Back to fire safety.

"You really didn't know that?" he asked, turning

to face her where she stood in the doorway. "Or are you messing with me?"

She looked genuinely surprised at the accusation. "How was I supposed to know? Not a homeowner here."

"Apartments have them. Hotels, motels, hell, even McDonald's has to have a smoke detector."

"I've seen them. I've never had one beep at me."

"Not even growing up?" he ventured.

"Let's just say my dad wasn't the Safety Sam type."

"I don't suppose you have a nine-volt handy?" he asked, swearing at himself for not yet replacing his after using the last one in his living room detector a few days ago. Normally he was vigilant about such things.

"I don't have a nine-volt handy. It's no big deal, Clay. It can wait till morning if you can just make it shut up."

He shook his head. "Sorry. Not going to take a chance."

"It's five o'clock."

"Believe me, I'm aware of that."

"What do you want me to do, walk to the nearest store and buy a stinking battery?"

"I want you to stay with Payton upstairs while I get one."

"You're serious, aren't you? There's not going to be a fire tonight."

"Hope not. Still replacing the battery."

"I'll be on your couch."

He'd rather have her in his bed, frankly, but they had an agreement about that. In the middle of the night, with her looking like that, he couldn't quite remember why.

A LIGHT BLARED INTO THE darkness of Clay's living room, abruptly waking Andie. She opened her eyes to find it was the kitchen light. He hadn't turned on the one over her head as she'd initially suspected, but still… It was easier to sleep in a tent next to the freaking highway than it was in this building tonight.

She pulled the comforter she'd taken from his bed around her chin and curled back into the couch, wondering what he was doing now but not caring quite enough to brave the harsh chilled air.

Seconds later, she sensed his presence and opened her eyes again. Sure enough, there he stood, looming over her. He still wore the plain dark gray T-shirt but she had no trouble recalling how he'd looked without it—like a tantalizing, sex-filled ad for a gym. Sign her up, please.

"What?" she asked.

"Make yourself at home." He indicated the comforter.

"You keep it refrigerator cold in here. This is all I could find. Want it back?"

"I'm up for the day. Have to work in an hour and a half."

Crap. She'd forgotten. "I'm sorry." She sat up, wrapping the thick blanket around her shoulders.

"Want breakfast? I stopped for coffee and bagels."

"I don't normally eat at this hour, but it seems like I was not meant to sleep tonight."

"Seems that way. I got cinnamon raisin, double chocolate and sesame. And some Puerto Rican blend."

"Yes to food. No to the man coffee. Who wants to stay awake at this hour?" She had every intention of heading back to her place to sleep for a couple more hours before she had to be at the Shell Shack. "Let me just put this back."

Andie shivered as she took the comforter into his room, allowing herself one more chance to breathe in Clay's scent, which had permeated it, before she spread it out over his double bed. She joined him at the kitchen counter, picking up a sesame bagel and slathering cream cheese on it. As she took her first bite, she turned and leaned against the counter.

Clay perused her, up and down, reminding her she was slightly indecent, especially now that the cold room was doing a number on her nipples. Heat simmered in his eyes when he dragged them back to her gaze, and then she was quite sure the temperature of the room was no longer responsible for her body's reaction.

"So," she said, crossing her arms over her chest. "Is your sister watching Payton today?"

Clay nodded, frowning. "Guess this is what they mean about a firefighter trying to be a single father. It's tough leaving her for twenty-four hours at a time."

"It evens out to a person with a regular job, though, doesn't it?"

He rubbed the back of his neck. "In theory. I just hope it's not making the whole transition from her mother even harder on her. I don't want to do anything to make her life worse…."

Andie set her bagel on a napkin and moved closer, facing him, demanding eye contact. "Clay. You're a wonderful father."

He scoffed. "Not wonderful."

"Why would you think that? Compared to her addict mother? You think you're not good for her?"

He thought about that for a few seconds. "When you put it that way, I know this is a better place than her mother's. But I've got my family around and they eternally judge me, watching for mistakes."

She thought about the people she'd met last night. "They don't seem like that to me."

"You've known them how long?" he said curtly.

"Sometimes an outside perspective is more accurate. They care a lot about both Payton and you. That much was evident."

"I live in constant fear of doing the wrong thing with her."

She took his coffee from him and set it on the counter behind him so she could grab his arms without making him spill. "Don't you see? That right there proves to me you're a good father. Sucky fathers don't give a thought to whether they're doing the 'wrong thing.' Believe me on this one."

He met her gaze and took her hands, weaving their fingers together. "From what you've said, your dad was the worst of the worst."

He pulled her closer, until their bodies touched. Andie's mind temporarily stopped working as her heart revved up. She was close enough to see the gold flecks in his eyes, the shallow laugh lines, every last bit of stubble that had grown overnight. The subtle sheen of moisture on those lips…

"I definitely don't want to talk about my dad right now," she said softly. "Trust yourself, Clay."

"Trust myself."

Andie nodded, sensing the subject they were discussing had changed. She reached up to touch his face, grazing her fingers over his sandpapery cheek. He moved his hands to her lower back, beneath her camisole.

Andie's blood pulsed hard through her veins as she waited to see if he would push her away as he had more than once before. His eyes darted toward her lips and she decided the hell with waiting.

Their lips met and there was no gentle, unsure moment when they tested each other out. The attraction they'd been fighting for days had been ignited like a match tossed into a puddle of gasoline. His tongue plunged into her mouth. She matched his intensity, needing to knock him off his feet the same way he was doing to her.

Clay drew her into him, his hands roving over her body, making her crave more of him. Lots more.

Andie pushed his shirt up to touch the amazing chest she'd gotten too brief a glimpse of earlier. The hard ridges of muscle, the sprinkling of hair…she didn't think she could get sick of this body in a hundred years. She pulled his T-shirt over his head and discarded it behind her.

CLAY COULDN'T GET ENOUGH of her.

He wanted her naked, now, wanted his shorts off. Wanted to carry her into his bedroom and spend days exploring her body and making her scream. He slid his hands beneath her pajama shorts and moaned at the feel of the smooth skin of her ass.

He trailed his lips to her neck, kissing beneath her ear, lower, down to her shoulder. When she let out a sexy moan, he opened his eyes to see her face. His attention was drawn to the intricate body art on the skin he'd been kissing.

As he inspected it, remembering the first time he'd seen it out by the pool, he caught a glimpse of the eight-by-ten photo on the wall of Payton in her sequined dance costume. He fought with himself for several seconds, wanting to kiss Andie more, see where it led, but… *She had a police record.*

No matter what he thought of her, that record was in black-and-white, a fact, something that could and would be used against him in court if he was involved with her.

Clay was wildly attracted to this woman—there was no way to deny that. But could he honestly stand before a judge and swear that Andie's influence on Payton was completely positive? Part of him thought so. But was that the part he could rely on or the part that had steered him wrong in the past? His judgment had been skewed before. Who was to say he knew any better now?

He closed his eyes, full of regret for what he had to do. He had to stop. He kissed her temple, held her close, savoring a few last seconds. Then he ran his hands down her arms, trying to be more brisk and businesslike.

Andie looked up at him with lust-hazed eyes, which only shot more heat through him. Damn, this trying to do the right thing idea stunk.

He glanced at Payton's photo again. He couldn't lose her.

"Aaand, just like that, we're done," Andie said, taking a step back.

"You make me lose my damn mind, biker girl."

"Apparently not completely," she said with a hollow smile.

"You know why—"

Andie nodded. "I know why." She stood straighter, adjusted her camisole, her eyes becoming clear. "It's good you stopped before either one of us did something we'd regret."

"Right." He was going to keep telling himself that all day.

"I'm going back to bed while you go off and do noble things."

He smiled at what she'd said, but even more, at the image of her in her tangled sheets.

Before he realized what she was doing, Andie stood on her toes and nibbled him briefly beneath his ear.

"Have a good day at the office, dear," she said, then snuck out the door just before the sun started rising.

He walked off to take a cold shower, wondering if he was the dumbest man on the planet.

CHAPTER FOURTEEN

ANDIE WANTED NOTHING more than to go home and get naked.

It was hot enough to melt flesh today, a couple hundred degrees in the shade. She'd been working since ten this morning, after very little sleep (thanks to dreams of a certain landlord that were a hot of an altogether different nature.) Her clothes were sticking to her, her skin felt grimy from sweat, spilled beer, grease, you name it.

Most days, the walk home was pleasant, helped her come down from rushing around waiting on demanding, thirsty customers. This evening, it made her head throb and her boots pinch. At last, just after seven o'clock, she climbed the flight of stairs, fantasizing about the cool air from the window AC unit blowing over her flesh till she got goose bumps….

And apparently someone had helped themselves to her apartment, judging by the half-open door and the pounding noise coming from within. What the…

She stopped just outside the door, not scared exactly, because whoever was in there wasn't being sneaky in the least. Then she saw a familiar thick biceps.

"Hi, honey, I'm home," she called.

Something crashed, he mumbled to himself, and then the door opened wider.

"Hey," Clay said. He bent and picked up the hammer he'd dropped. "I was trying to finish before you got here."

"Finish what?" Andie walked into the living room, out of the scorching sun.

"Maintenance."

"Hi, Miss Andie," Payton said from the floor by the balcony door. She was stretched out on her belly, knees bent, feet in the air, with a giant box of crayons on the floor in front of her.

"Hey, Pay, what's up?"

"I got a new coloring book. I'm making you a picture."

"Oooh," Andie said, stepping closer to look. "Looking good so far." She ruffled the girl's hair then stood back up.

Andie inspected the backside of the main door where Clay had been working. "A dead bolt?"

"You got it."

"For me?" She couldn't help smiling.

"For now. When you move on, it'll be for someone else."

Ouch. "Thank you," Andie said, her tone more formal.

"I hope it makes it easier to keep up your end of the agreement."

"It's still empty," she said of the gun. "I can show you."

He looked like he was about to say yes, then shook his head.

"Are you almost done?" Andie asked, lifting her tank out from her stomach where it stuck to her skin.

"Not exactly."

"Daddy said a bad word when you weren't here," Payton explained.

Andie raised her eyebrows and looked at Clay.

"Didn't have everything I needed. Had to go back to the hardware store a second time. I've barely started." He pointed to a second lock still in the package on the floor. "Plan to put one on the balcony door, too."

She nodded, too exhausted to express her gratitude.

"Miss Andie, want to color with me?"

"Tell you what," Andie said. "You let me take a quick shower and then we'll do whatever you want until your daddy's done. Deal?"

"Deal!"

"Maybe we can even have a popsicle if he says it's okay."

Payton nodded thoughtfully, glancing at her dad. But he was back at work, getting ready to use his drill.

"Give me ten," Andie said to Payton. "All right with you?" She aimed the question at Clay.

He nodded. "Thanks. She's been so patient today."

She took the few steps to her bedroom to pick out clean clothes then locked herself in the bathroom.

Flowers and candy wouldn't mean half as much to Andie as a couple of sturdy deadbolts.

She found herself smiling as she pulled the plastic shower curtain closed around her and stepped into the blessedly lukewarm stream of water.

Then she stopped in her tracks and swore.

Since when did she let herself be appeased by a man doing something nice for her? Not since Trevor had she shown that kind of weakness, that lack of self-sufficiency.

Desperately, her heart thundering in a panic, she ran her fingers over the scar on her arm and closed her eyes.

She'd trusted two men in her life. Trevor and her father. In the end, they'd nearly ruined her sense of self. They'd hurt her so thoroughly—physically, yes, but even worse, emotionally and mentally—that she'd had hours she hadn't been sure she wanted to live through.

Andie would never let herself fall to such depths of despair again. She'd sworn to rely on no one else, to never let her happiness or her will to live depend on another human being.

That Clay was different held no bearing. Her

promise to herself hadn't been to become fiercely self dependent *unless a seemingly nice, sexy man happened along*.

Her attraction to Clay was undeniable. Scary as hell, truly. She wanted him like she hadn't wanted anyone for years, if ever. Who could blame her?

She could accept the chemistry between them. Wasn't dumb enough to try to go through life without a physical involvement here and there. But that's where it had to end: with the physical. Lust and only lust. With Clay, there was something more, an underlying current that went beyond wanting his very fine, very muscular body on top of hers. And that *something* made Clay dangerous.

She rinsed off the soap and got out of the shower. She pulled on short denim cutoffs and a thin-strapped white tank. Instead of drying her hair, she tied it in a bandanna to keep the damp strands off her face. She couldn't stand the thought of putting anything back on her feet and she kicked her boots to the corner of the bathroom. Then she headed out to entertain Payton…and resist the girl's daddy.

"WE'LL BE OUTSIDE," Andie said, ignoring Clay's shoulder muscles as he bent over the holes he'd drilled in her door.

He straightened and raised his eyebrows.

"Only just to the top of the steps," Payton clarified with big, serious eyes. She held up both halves of a grape double popsicle. "So our popsicles don't drip and you don't get mad at Miss Andie and make her buy new carpet."

Clay grinned. "Smart plan, girly. Have fun."

Andie took the bag with Payton's EpiPen. Clay let them by and then pushed the door most of the way closed.

Andie and Payton discussed important topics such as sparkles on hair ribbons and what butterfly wings were made of as they sat side by side on the top step of Andie's landing. The sun had dropped behind the building next door, making the temperature more bearable.

Andie finished her popsicle quickly, successfully avoiding dripping bright red melted ice on her white shirt. Payton, however, was another story. By the time she'd licked down to the wooden sticks, she and the landing were wearing more purple than she'd consumed. Laughing, Andie ran inside for a handful of wet paper towels. Payton waited for her as close to the door as she could get.

It took an eternity to remove all the purple that would come off—and there was plenty that wouldn't.

"How about if we go down to the front yard and draw with sidewalk chalk?" Andie suggested.

"Um, I don't wanna."

"What?" They'd spent hours drawing pictures when Andie had stayed with her before. "Bees," she said. "You're really afraid of them, aren't you, sweetie?"

Payton's shame and sadness as she nodded made Andie's chest constrict. "Oh, Payton, come here."

The girl watched her warily for several long seconds as Andie wondered if she'd decide to trust her. Andie squatted and held her arms out. Finally, Payton moved toward her and wrapped her arms tightly around Andie's neck. She didn't let go even after several seconds. Andie backed up to lean against the outer wall, next to the door, taking Payton with her.

"Let's sit down," Andie said. "You can climb on my lap."

Payton loosened her grasp and Andie sat, pulling the child on to her legs.

"Getting stung and going to the hospital was pretty scary, huh?" Andie asked.

She felt Payton's nod against her collar bone.

"The thing is, sweetie, you're okay now and we have the medicine you need if you ever get stung again. Right here with us." Andie pointed to it. "You know that's what it's for, right? To make sure you'll be okay?"

Payton nodded again.

"How many times have you ever been stung by a bee?" Andie continued. "Just that one time, right?"

"There was lots of bees, though. They all got me."

Andie tightened her hug. "That was unfair of them, wasn't it?"

"Bees are mean."

"Not all bees," Andie said. "Out of the millions and millions of bees in the world, only two of them decided to sting you. The rest...they might be nice bees."

Payton giggled. "Bees aren't nice."

Andie tucked Payton's head under her chin. "How many times have you been outside before and had no bees sting you?"

Payton was silent for a moment. "I dunno."

"Every single time but one, right?"

Payton shrugged and wouldn't agree. So much for logic.

Didn't matter how much she liked kids, Andie was out of her element trying to cure a four-year-old girl of her deepest, darkest, justified fear.

After a few minutes of thought, Andie tried again. "You know everybody is afraid of something, right?"

Payton straightened in her lap and met her eyes. "Are you?"

"Of course. Even your dad is."

"What are you afraid of?" Payton asked, ignoring Andie's attempt at diverting attention from her to Clay.

"My fears..." What the heck was she getting herself into? "I'm afraid of..." What could she say that a child could relate to? She had to tell her something, and she didn't figure "my ex-boyfriend" was appropriate. Ditto "trusting people."

"Bullies," she finally blurted. That was Trevor, so

it was totally valid and yet, she hoped, not something that would worry Payton.

"What's bullies?"

Andie filtered out all the swear words that cluttered her mind when she considered Trevor. "A bully is a mean person."

Payton looked thoughtful for a moment, then frowned. "I'm scared of bullies, too."

"Hopefully you won't run into any bullies for a very long time." Or love one, or trust one…

She hoped she hadn't created a new fear for Payton. This childcare thing required a stinking doctorate degree. "So about the bees. And fears. You can't let the mean bees keep you inside your whole life, Payton."

"Why not?"

"Because you love being outside. Remember how much fun we had that day before you got stung? Picking flowers and drawing rainbows on the driveway?"

"The bees ruined it all."

Okay, good point. "What if we went downstairs, took your EpiPen and played only on the driveway, where there aren't any bees? They'll all be busy in the flowers getting a drink."

Payton leaned out to survey the yard below, obviously interested.

"We could draw more rainbows and flowers and maybe a few butterflies."

Still no answer.

"You can stay close to me and if we see any bees on the driveway, we can run back inside."

Payton stood, straining to see the driveway.

"Yeah?" Andie asked, getting up, as well.

"I guess so."

Payton made Andie carry her along the flower-lined walkway to the drive. Once they got to the wide slab of pavement, though, she wiggled down and pulled Andie to a bin in the carport where Clay stored a bucket of colored chalk.

Andie set the bucket down on the side of the driveway farthest from the flowerbeds, and they both selected a piece of chalk. As Andie sketched a lopsided, top-heavy butterfly, Payton kept a wary eye on her surroundings. Anytime an insect flew close, she ran to Andie's side, but there were no bee sightings.

By the time Clay came down, more than a half an hour later, Payton was thoroughly engrossed in coloring the figures Andie drew.

"Hey, girls," he said as he walked around the front corner of the duplex.

"Hi, Daddy!" She sprinted to him and jumped into his arms.

"She's outside," he said, his voice laced with surprise. "In the front yard."

"Andie carried me past the mean bees."

"We decided it wouldn't be fair to let the mean bees force her to stay inside," Andie explained simply.

He set Payton down and she galloped off to finish coloring the last rainbow.

"You're amazing," he said so his daughter couldn't hear. "I overheard your conversation with her up there."

"Eavesdropper," Andie said, uncomfortable with his praise.

"I've tried a dozen times in the past week to get her out here."

Andie shrugged. "I was winging it. We brought her EpiPen just in case." She pointed to it at the base of the steps, but Clay's eyes remained fixed on her.

"Thank you."

There was so much gratitude behind those two little words that she squirmed. She was counting the days until she could leave the island and ride away from this tempting man for good.

Eleven. More. Days.

CHAPTER FIFTEEN

"YOU DON'T LOOK SO HOT," Andie said to Selena the next day. "Are you okay?"

They were on the patio at the Shell Shack four days before Macey's wedding, assembling favors. Selena was painting "Derek and Macey," along with the wedding date, on the sides of miniature tin buckets, while Andie filled the buckets with fire-helmet-shaped chocolates and tied on dark red ribbons that would match the bridesmaid dresses.

Selena held on to the side of her belly and winced. "Braxton Hicks is all. False labor I think they call it but I'm here to tell you, if this is false, I don't have any interest in seeing what true labor is like."

"How do you know it's false?" Andie asked skeptically.

"It's been going on for over a week. I've been to the hospital twice thinking this is it. But no. It's practice."

"A week? That's cruel."

"Tell me about it. I'm just praying I can make it through the wedding without my water breaking or something equally embarrassing."

"Isn't this a little early for the baby to show up?"

"Three weeks. So yes, early, but not dangerously so. I hope. I'm ready to get rid of these ankles." Selena held up one foot for Andie to see. "My legs look like elephant legs. Not really how you want to feel as a newlywed."

Andie laughed. "From what I've seen, Evan loves you so much you could turn purple and sprout horns and he wouldn't blink an eye."

Selena's expression said she felt the same way. "Everything's happened so fast. Last year at this time, I was still on the East Coast. Single. My biggest worry was my brother, who'd been hurt in Iraq. When I came down here, I never planned to stay forever. More of an extended getaway. Now I'm married, own a business and am decorating a nursery."

"I've always been of the belief that the most interesting things come along when you don't make detailed plans. Who am I kidding? *Any* plans."

"It was true for me. Maybe next year at this time, you'll be knocked up and married, too."

"Let's not go that far," Andie said. "You'll make me hyperventilate." She was so *not* going anywhere near there.

"How's it coming, ladies?" Macey's mom, Cheryl, who'd been working with Kathy, Derek's mom, on centerpieces, wandered up to their table and pulled out a chair. Both women, plus Derek's father, had come into town yesterday to help with last-minute details.

"Making progress, as long as the paint girl doesn't go into labor before she's done with her job." Andie glanced at Selena again to make sure she was okay.

"You poor thing," Derek's mom said as she joined them. "I remember those last few weeks of pregnancy well."

She told them how Derek had gotten the hiccups several times a day during her last month. That prompted Macey's mom to add her own late-pregnancy stories.

Andie kept working as she listened. How completely bizarre to sit here chatting with a bunch of women, about such domestic topics as babies and pregnancy—and to not be bored out of her skull. And tying ribbons on little tin buckets? If anyone who really knew her saw her now, they'd think she'd lost her sweet mind.

Of course, there wasn't a single person she could think of who *really* knew her.

Her cell phone buzzed on the table in front of her, and, okay, her cousin Jonas knew her as well as any. Maybe her thoughts had conjured him up.

"Hey, Jonas, what's going on?" She set down the ribbon she'd been working with and stood.

"Nothing good. He's MIA, Andie. No one's seen him for a week. I think he blew town."

Her heart stopped and she turned away from the

table. Without a word, she walked to the stairs leading to the beach.

"Andie?"

"I'm here," she rasped out. She walked along the sand, unseeing. Reeling.

"You're hundreds of miles away. He has no idea where."

"As far as you know."

"No one else knows your whereabouts, do they? He may have asked around, but there's no one who could tell him. You need to be alert, but, Andie, I'm assuming he's not supposed to leave the state."

"He wasn't supposed to beat the crap out of the woman he claimed to love either," she said as she slid her back down the sea wall and settled on the sand a couple hundred feet up the beach from the bar. "He doesn't put too much stock in what he is or isn't supposed to do."

"Like I said, be alert. I'll keep my ears open."

"What if he finds me?" It was as if no time had passed and yet again she had to spend every waking moment figuring out how to navigate Trevor's moods so she didn't set him off. Her body was a ball of tension, her muscles already aching with it, cold with fear.

"What's he going to do, Andie? You can hold your own now, physically. Remember what I taught you. You've got distance. You won't be sucked in again. Right?"

Her most painful years were with Trevor. Growing

up with an abusive father had nothing on falling in love with and trusting a man, as an adult, who should've been the best part of her life. She'd learned young that her father veered toward inhuman anytime he drank, which, after her mother died, was most of the time. She'd figured out to avoid him as much as possible. With Trevor, she'd *chosen* to trust him. She'd been old enough she should've seen a sign of the trauma that was to come....

"Andie. Quit it, honey. He doesn't have any power over you now."

She opened her eyes and focused on the incoming waves, a reminder she was far, far away, both geographically and mentally, from where she'd been when Trevor had hurt her. "This is what I'm afraid of, Jonas. Just the mention of him and I lose my freaking mind, turn into this scared mouse. Makes me sick to my stomach."

"Well, get over it. There's no way in hell he could ever do the same thing to you again. Would he track you down to hurt you?"

She'd thought about this often, especially lately, ever since Trevor's possible release from prison. "I don't know. All-out force was never the way it started. But he has such a temper.... I'm just not sure." It could get ugly. He'd proven he had no qualms about hurting her.

"The good news is you have a door. With a lock. You're out of that goddamn tent."

"For now." Thank God for her new deadbolts. Nothing would make her relax completely but they would help.

"Andie, I know it makes you crazy to stay put but maybe that's the best place for you. At least for a while."

"Maybe. Look, I gotta go, Jonas. Keep me posted."

"Yep."

He disconnected and Andie felt all alone on a beach full of people. She sat there for several minutes. When she finally stood, she was pissed. Bottle-crushing, plate-throwing pissed. Fortunately, there were no bottles or plates in sight so she had nothing to shatter or draw attention to herself with. She kicked at the sand several times, jaws and fists clenched, swearing to herself. After a few minutes, she worked at calming herself down so she could head back to the patio to help Selena.

As she approached, she was relieved to see that Selena looked better, not as pale, and engrossed in painting. Andie commented on the improvements when she sat back down in her chair.

"Yeah, they're gone for now," Selena said. "What happened to you, though, Andie? You look really upset."

Andie forced a smile. "If it's false labor then I'm in trouble."

Unfortunately, she didn't believe there was anything false about the possibility of Trevor trying to track her down. She could have weeks before he caught up to her…but maybe not. And the only damn thing she could do about it was keep an eye out for trouble.

CHAPTER SIXTEEN

ANDIE WAS GOING TO BE the death of him.

After her breakthrough with Payton, Clay had forced himself to stay away. He'd successfully avoided her for days, with the exception of the wedding rehearsal and dinner last night.

As they'd gone through the ceremony details, they'd been cordial but distant. It'd been as if they both sensed something had changed, though Clay didn't know what or when. They'd made a point of not touching during the practice recessional as they walked out together. He'd steeled himself to be immune to her today.

Lot of godforsaken good that had done.

The women had gotten ready for the wedding at Derek and Macey's place and had shown up at the Shell Shack—the ceremony was on the beach below the bar just as Payton's birthday dinner had been—about half an hour ago. Clay wouldn't forget anytime soon the moment he'd spotted Andie.

The female half of the wedding party had emerged from the limo that Macey's mom had insisted on hiring and his eyes had popped out of his head.

Andie—tomboy, biker chick, blue-jeans-wearing Andie—belonged on a New York runway. She, like the other women, wore a long, silky dress in a dramatic deep red, the color of a velvet-soft rose. The sleeveless gown emphasized Andie's tall, slender body in all the right places. It was snug beneath her breasts, cinching in at her narrow waist, and flowed over her hips in a column to the floor. When she'd gotten out of the car, Clay had caught a glimpse of her black stiletto heels through the thigh-high slits in the dress, and oddly that had put him on edge. He'd never been a man who appreciated a woman's shoes, but when one who normally cloaked herself in clunky boots showed up in those strappy, sexy things… *Yeah.*

And that bloodred color… With her dark hair and smooth, tanned skin, Andie was stunning. In the past thirty minutes, he'd had no less than several dozen fantasies of sliding the silken material off her body….

"Clay, get your ass over here, man." Evan gestured impatiently and Clay realized the rest of the wedding party was gathered for pictures before the ceremony began.

The photographer lined them up—Derek and Macey in the middle, Evan and Selena on one side and Clay and Andie on the other. Together, of course. Close. Hands on her waist, standing slightly behind her, with her back warm and soft against him. He couldn't avoid her intoxicating scent and didn't try to.

"You two on the left, relax," the peppy female photographer said to them. "This isn't a firing squad, it's a wedding! Fun! Happy! True love! Act like you're enjoying yourselves."

"Macey, what the hell?" Clay said quietly through his forced smile.

The bride laughed. "Shh. Do what she says, Clay."

The photographer clicked a couple photos and then looked up from her camera again. "Groomsman on the left, much better. Bridesmaid? Is it Andie? Honey, you have to relax."

Clay squeezed her side gently, trying to get her to lighten up. She was so stiff she flinched.

He pointed his index finger in the air and smiled at the photographer. "Can you give us a minute? I'll loosen her up."

"Please."

He turned Andie toward him, and she moved almost robotically. "Biker girl?"

"What are you doing, Clay?" She looked at him with one hundred percent distrust, as she should at that moment.

"This is for the greater good."

Before she could respond, he took her face in his hands and leaned down to kiss her with all the pent-up attraction he'd been trying to deny for days. It took a good three seconds for her to yield and open to him. As soon as she did, he deepened the kiss, but instead of controlling the moment as he'd intended, he nearly forgot where he was and who might be watching. The howls from the rest of the wedding party were a distant racket. He dropped one hand and pulled Andie's slender waist into his rock hard body, devouring her, losing his ever-loving mind.

Andie broke the contact abruptly. "Clay."

He gathered his wits and flashed her what must have been a dopey grin. "That was just getting good."

"Clay and Andie," Evan drawled. "Who saw that coming?"

"About time," Macey said.

"Little eyes all around, including your daughter," Andie whispered. She looked like she was having as much trouble breathing as he was.

He glanced around and spotted Payton on the bar's patio above them. Her attention was on Evan's sister, Melanie, who would be taking care of her during the ceremony. "She missed it. And you're more relaxed."

"This isn't relaxed." The heat in her eyes spoke of the same burning tension that threatened to lay him flat out. "Sorry, everyone. Nothing to see here. The man temporarily lost his marbles." She turned back to her position for the photos.

"You're right. Maybe not relaxed," he said in her ear.

Derek's mom rushed out from behind the photographer. "Wait! Lipstick emergency."

She handed a napkin to Clay and indicated a spot of Andie's color at the edge of his mouth, then carefully applied a new coat to Andie's lips while he wiped his face. She scurried off just as quickly, and the three couples settled back into their spots, the others cracking jokes here and there that Clay didn't really hear. He was too wrapped up in wanting Andie.

BY MIDWAY THROUGH THE reception, Clay had driven Andie to a pathetic state. He wore a tux like no one she'd ever seen before, with those broad shoulders, the handsome, tanned face, the muscular thighs.

She stood against the concrete wall of the patio, her back to the crashing waves. She was doing her best to concentrate on the stories Derek's parents and Macey's mom were regaling her with, detailing the longstanding friendship of the bride and groom. Normally Andie would love to hear about such a normal childhood, love stories or not, but her attention was stuck on Clay, across the patio in a huddle of robust, dripping-with-testosterone firefighters. The group as a whole was a big pile of brawn but all Andie could see was the one man.

"We're needed in the restroom," Selena said to Andie as she walked by.

Thelma Severson giggled like a woman who'd had

one too many cocktails. "Pee time for the bride, I suspect."

Andie raised her brows in disbelief as she set off.

"Wedding dress maneuvering is a three-woman job, minimum," Macey's mom called out to her, as tipsy as her cohort. Andie heard Derek's dad excuse himself as the two women began retelling memories of their own wedding days.

Clay met her gaze as she went past his group and she swore silently at her traitorous body's thrill.

As soon as she entered the restroom, she heard the snickers and swear words coming from the handicapped stall.

"Uh, need help?" Andie asked, afraid of Macey and Selena's answer, unable to concoct a visual in her mind of what she was about to walk in on.

"A crane would do the trick," Macey said.

"Maybe you should've just succumbed to a diaper for the evening," Selena suggested.

"Whoever invented wedding dresses never thought about how the heck a person might be able to relieve herself."

"Obviously invented by a man."

The stall door was open and Andie made her way to it, full of trepidation. When she peeked in, she couldn't help laughing at the sight of them digging their way through layers of dress and slip.

"I need a camera," she said, stepping into the white fray.

"You'd be a dead woman."

Macey's veil was long gone, and tendrils of hair curled around her temples. She still looked gorgeous, and the juxtaposition of the beautiful bride in her satin next to the cold, hard toilet made Andie laugh so hard tears fell.

Macey soon joined her, and then Selena.

It took a good ten minutes for them to compose themselves enough to figure out the logistics of peeing in a wedding gown. Mission accomplished at long last. And then they had to put the bride back together.

"You lucked out," Macey said to Selena as they straightened her full slip. "You missed this experience with your short and sweet wedding. You, on the other hand…" She pointed to Andie. "You're going to pay one of these days."

"Good luck with that, Mace. I won't be donning the white in this lifetime." Andie said it with certainty and, okay, a little smugness.

Selena snorted in response.

"What?" Andie asked, narrowing her eyes.

"Oh, girl." Macey wasn't tanked, but sober wasn't a word Andie would use to describe her, either. "I'd bet money that you're going down next."

"Instead of *if,* we should start a pool for *when* it's going to happen," Selena added.

"What are you two going on about?" Andie asked as she straightened the back of Macey's gown.

"If there was any more electricity between you

and Clay tonight, the whole island would surge and blow up," Macey said.

Andie glanced at Selena, who nodded emphatically. "It's beyond Chemistry 101. You two are at the nine-hundred level."

"Because we kissed? During pictures?" Andie did her best to look baffled, knowing full well there was no way they could've hidden the strength of their attraction.

Macey sighed dreamily. "The way you kissed, the way you danced. The way you've spent most of the night with one eye on him even when he's a hundred feet away."

"And he's done the same," Selena said. "So what's the lowdown? And why are we having to beg you for it?" She moved to the counter and reapplied her lip gloss.

Andie stepped away from the mirror and the bright lights, feeling exposed enough without them adding to it. She picked at some imaginary lint on the front of her gown. "There's nothing going on."

"If that's the truth, there's a serious *yet* at the end of it," Macey said, her cheeks red and her eyes bright.

Andie shook her head. "Not going to happen, girls." Even as she said it, she felt the heat radiating off her.

"That's like saying the waves of the Gulf are going to stop," Macey told her. "Strictly from an outsider's perspective, it looks like it'd take an act of God to keep you two apart."

"An act of God or a four-year-old." Andie shook her head when Selena offered to let her borrow her makeup.

"Isn't it convenient that said four-year-old is already tucked away in a hotel room with Melanie and Brad?" Selena raised her chin knowingly and Andie desperately wanted to be mad at her but she couldn't. She couldn't hold in a smile, in fact. Then she half-heartedly shook her head.

"Mace?" Derek's voice came in through the screen door of the restroom. "Got a problem."

Macey frowned and headed outside. Andie and Selena followed.

"What's going on?" Macey asked.

"Ice machine is on the fritz. We're down to several scoops. It's not even ten o'clock."

Her eyes widened. "Fritz? Is this a joke?"

He kissed her. "I wouldn't do that to you. At least not tonight. It's really broken and I can't fix it."

"We have to go buy ice, then. Mass quantities," Macey said. "Do you have your phone?"

He fished it out of his tux and handed it to her. Clay wandered over to Derek and asked what was up, catching Andie's eye momentarily. He'd taken his jacket off long ago and rolled up the sleeves of his shirt. His tie was missing, and the top half of his shirt was unbuttoned. Derek explained the situation to him.

"You can't leave your own wedding. I'll go get it."

"You sober?" Derek asked.

"Not entirely, but I know someone who is." He smiled at Andie, and her heart stopped. "You game?"

She was game for just about anything when he zeroed that beautiful smile in on her.

"You're going to let me drive your truck?" she asked, trying to play it cool.

Macey hung up and rattled off a distributor just over the bridge on the mainland that would sell her a truckload of ice for next to nothing. "A little out of the way but they have plenty and they'll bill the bar."

Clay dug his keys from his pocket and held them out to Andie. When he surrendered them, he held her hand for an extra second. Or three. The electricity Macey had mentioned pulsed through the air between them.

Without glancing at anyone around them—knowing the looks the girls would give her—Andie headed inside the Shell Shack to get the tiny evening purse Macey had loaned her, all too aware of Clay's presence half a step behind her on the way.

CHAPTER SEVENTEEN

NEITHER OF THEM SPOKE A WORD on the drive. The tension in the air was so thick it would strangle a lesser man than Clay. He couldn't remember the last time a woman had affected him like this.

He stared openly at Andie as she pulled into the parking lot. Somehow he managed to follow her into the place and help the guy load bag after bag of ice into the bed of the truck. They threw pads on top for insulation, thanked the man and signed the invoice.

Instead of going around to the passenger side, Clay followed Andie to the driver's door and opened it for her.

She looked shyly at him. "Trying to kiss up?"

"I don't know about *up*," he said. He pressed her into the side of the truck with his body. "You're stunning in that dress, biker girl."

Her smile faded and her eyes dropped to his mouth. "You're not so bad yourself."

He kissed her, all the need that'd been building up for the past four torturous hours—hell, the past few days—surfacing. Demanding. He'd long passed the point where gentle was an option, but Andie didn't appear to mind. She wove her fingers into his hair and pulled him closer.

"Clay," she uttered into his mouth, arching into him, setting off all kinds of friction that burned through every last layer of clothing that separated them.

His reply was more a groan than a word. He wasn't sure he could speak if he wanted to.

She pulled away when a car full of teenagers went by, the group of boys howling and hollering at them through open windows.

"Clay." Her voice was firm. "Get in the truck."

She was breathing hard. They stared at each other for several heartbeats, and he saw the need in her eyes, matching his own. With half a nod, he sucked it up and stepped away from her, the loss of contact like no loss he'd ever felt before.

By the time he closed his door, she had the engine running and had thrown the truck into Reverse. He had no idea what her intentions were—he'd thought when she told him to get in the truck that finding the nearest motel was a possibility—but she drove with remarkable control, not an tick above the speed limit. When she reached out to punch on the radio power, though, he could swear her hand shook.

When she turned off into a small park along the bay—the one he'd stopped at after the baby party— his hope soared. She pulled all the way to the far end of the parking lot, in a private corner without light, and killed the engine. Before he could say a word, she climbed over to his seat and straddled him.

"Hi," she said in a low, sexy voice.

"Hello." His voice wasn't working right, but then neither was his brain. "Andie, what are you doing?"

She laughed, the sound seductive as hell. With a whisper of a kiss on his lips, she said, "You're smart." She nibbled at the corner of his mouth. "Capable." Ran her tongue over his upper lip. "I imagine you can figure it out."

"We've talked about this…"

"It's time to get it out of our systems. Let it happen. No one will see us here."

Those were points he couldn't begin to argue with.

He closed his eyes and pulled her closer. "I'm shocked." He grazed his lips over hers. "Scandalized."

She laughed again, the sound turning needy as his hands roved over her.

"This isn't a good place," he whispered.

"Why not?"

"We're like teenagers. Stealing away. I want you stretched out beneath me. In a bed."

"Play your cards right and you might be able to have me there, too."

"Andie…"

"This isn't a honeymoon, Clay. We don't need satin sheets." Her mouth caught his and wore him down, which took exactly two-thirds of a second. "But I can drive you back to the reception if you want."

He laughed and yanked her to him. "I don't think so."

ANDIE'S DRESS HAD INCHED up her thighs when she'd climbed onto Clay's lap. She felt his hand sliding over her leg, beneath the material, leaving a trail of fire wherever he touched. Then he was touching her everywhere, with his mouth, his hands. She was drowning in the sensations.

She made it her mission to explore every accessible inch of his body. Yeah, the truck cab was a little cramped but that wasn't going to keep her from Clay. It became their private, steamy world and Andie couldn't make herself care about anything else—the reception, what the girls would say, what might happen between her and Clay afterward. She couldn't even process afterward…. She was fully absorbed in the right now, aching for him to fulfill her longing and yet never wanting the moment to end.

He lifted the dress over her head and tossed it on the driver's seat, revealing her black, lacy slip. He drew both straps of the slip down her arms, baring her, and took her breast in his mouth. His tongue alone drove her to a fever. She arched her lower body into the very distinct hardness that bulged between his legs, her breath shallow. She pulled at the still-buttoned lower half of his shirt and ripped it open with both hands, craving the feel of his skin.

The buttons flew, one of them clinking against the window.

"Didn't need that shirt anyway," Clay said, eliciting a shaky laugh from her.

He pulled her into his chest and the heat of skin on skin had her promising herself they would wind up in a bed, soon, where they could stretch out naked and have nothing but friction between them. For now this was working just fine, thank you. She smiled.

"What's the grin for?" Clay asked, his voice rough with need. "You could give a guy a complex, you know."

"Like you're short on confidence," she whispered into his ear. From what she could feel, he wasn't short on anything. She rubbed her hands over his chest, relishing the hard ridges and the dips beneath her fingertips. As her fingers trailed lower, down to where their bodies were separated by too many layers of material, she tasted him, running her tongue over him, kissing and nibbling at his muscled chest. When she undid his pants, slid them down a few inches and grasped him, he leaned his head back and let out a sexy, groan from deep in his throat.

He was granite-hard and bigger than she could've imagined even as she'd straddled him over his clothes. She needed him inside her more than she needed her next breath. Her slip was now around her hips so the only thing between them was her panties.

"My turn," Clay said, and in an instant her ripped panties were a wad in his hand.

Andie reached for her purse on the console between the seats.

"What are you doing?" Clay asked, trying to pull her back to him.

"Condom." She unzipped the purse and dug to the bottom.

"I've got one," Clay said, grabbing his wallet, also from the console.

"Aren't we just a corner drugstore," Andie said, still fumbling to find hers.

"We can use mine."

"Here," she said, finally locating the packet and dragging it out.

"Got it," he said, ripping his open.

"What's wrong with mine?" she said, truly not caring what they used as long as she didn't wind up pregnant.

"I know mine's not expired." He unrolled it along his length as she watched, biting her lower lip. After a second, his words sank in.

"I can't decide if that's an insult or not."

"Take it however you want." Clay grasped her hips.

"You know," she said, fighting his effect on her, trying to keep her voice steady. "It's not the best time to get on my bad side." She touched her forehead to his and gazed into his eyes.

"You going to put your panties back on and drive off?" The grin on his face was wicked.

She slid him inside her and couldn't help moaning.

She ground her hips to take him in farther, her head falling back, body arching into his. "Not…just…yet." Her words came out as barely more than a whisper.

"Was hoping you'd say that." He tried to shift in the seat but got nowhere. "Good thing I bought the biggest truck on the lot."

His large hands dwarfed her waist as they guided her body. Their rhythm quickly became urgent. Clay wrapped his arms around her and pulled her tightly to him so their skin, damp with sweat, was in full contact.

Andie buried her head into the side of his neck and nibbled at him relentlessly until she could barely breathe. She had no concept of the minutes that ticked by, only that she hoped this never ever ended. Because later…

No. No thinking about later. Only now.

As he drove her higher, she threw her head back and called out his name repeatedly. Maybe she was being too loud but then he wasn't exactly quiet and besides, who was going to hear? He took her higher, made her crazy. Then he drove her to the sweet, mind-blowing release she'd been aching for and followed her over.

Andie melted into him as he trailed his lips along her neck and caressed her back. Her heart thundered in her chest. And maybe she could feel Clay's, too. She noticed for the first time the windows had fogged up in the humid night, granting them even more privacy. As if she'd been worried about *that* ten minutes ago.

"Damn," Clay said, his breath still ragged. "You do amazing things to me, biker girl."

She laughed, low and lazy, totally sated. "Might have to start calling you truck boy, for more than one reason."

"Might have to take this elsewhere for an encore so you don't have reason to call me truck boy."

The thought of doing this again made Andie shiver. Yet again she pictured him stretched out on top of her in her bed…

"Ow. Ow. Ouch." She slid off him quickly, un-ceremoniously, and pushed her dress off the driver's seat as she fell into it.

"What the hell?" Clay asked.

Andie started laughing. Hard. "Cramp. In my leg. Too small in here."

Clay's low laughter joined hers as she massaged the muscle that had sent her through the roof. "Come here," he said. "I'll rub it for you."

"Not in here. You're not rubbing anything until I can stretch out all my parts completely." She leaned across the console between them and met him for a long, unhurried kiss. "It's getting better," she said, still rubbing at the tight spot.

The sound of her cell phone ringing made her jolt upright as if they were high school kids getting busted in a car. Which, except for their age, they pretty much were. Andie scrambled to find her phone, holding her dress over her near-nakedness in a panic.

"Got a video camera on your phone or something?" Clay asked, grinning and reaching out to help her with her slip straps as she answered the call.

"Hello?" She tried hard not to sound breathless or…like she'd just had amazing truck sex.

"I don't want to know where you are or what you're doing," Macey said, "but it's hot and we have thirsty people."

Andie glanced over to see Clay putting himself back together, buttoning his shirt with the two buttons that remained.

"On our way. There was a crowd…."

Macey laughed wholeheartedly. "Stop, Andie. Just bring the ice. Drive safely."

"Yes, Mom."

"Later, I'll want to hear all about it."

CHAPTER EIGHTEEN

"Is EVERYTHING PUT back together?" Andie whispered to Clay when they'd climbed out of the truck back at the bar. She ran her hands down her gown, checking for the fortieth time that it wasn't caught somewhere—though there wasn't much it could get caught on since Clay had ruined her underwear.

"You look amazing," he said, then pressed a light, intimate kiss just below her ear.

Andie shivered and touched her hair. "No bed head?"

He laughed quietly. "How would you get bed head when there was no bed involved?"

"About time you two showed up," Evan said out of the darkness. "The masses are demanding ice."

Andie could only smile and mutter that she was off to find Macey. For the first time in her life, she understood what people meant when they said they were floating on air.

She floated around the perimeter of the party, searching for Macey's white dress, thinking it was even more crowded than when they'd left for ice. The wedding guests who'd been on the beach must have migrated up to the patio to be closer to food and drink.

As she made her way along the wall between the patio and the beach, toward the bar itself, she wondered if maybe she'd missed out on another bathroom run because she couldn't see Macey anywhere. What she did see, however, stopped her cold.

Across the way, just off the bar's property and close to the hotel on the other side, a man stood in the shadows. Watching her. She could see his outline from the streetlights and she'd recognize him anywhere, even though it'd been three years.

Trevor.

She froze—long enough for him to know she'd seen him. But he didn't move, didn't acknowledge her. Forgetting her search for Macey, Andie moved into the relative shelter of the bar. It was closed to the public tonight and full of wedding guests, and Kevin was at the counter filling orders for mixed drinks. No one was in the kitchen, though, since the caterers had set up on the patio.

Andie slipped behind the counter, nodding at Kevin as he mixed a cocktail, and disappeared into the kitchen. She turned the light off and moved to the door that looked out where she'd spotted her ex.

He stood in the same place, leaning against a wall, arms crossed. Andie's mouth went dry and she couldn't swallow. How had he found her? Why was he here?

He wasn't looking toward Andie's window so she

had plenty of time to stare. She'd give anything to be wrong about who it was, but no. He looked mostly the same, maybe a few pounds lighter, hair a little longer, but undoubtedly the man who'd hurt her so badly.

She had to get out of here.

He's seen her outside, and he'd probably be watching for her to leave so he could catch her alone. Whether he intended to hurt her or not, she couldn't handle the thought of being by herself with him. Talking to him. Hearing that voice…. Not tonight. Maybe not ever.

Her dress would make it damn hard but she'd escape to the restroom first, then into the darkness on the other side of the building. There was another tall hotel on that side of the patio and once she got around it, she'd be out of sight from the reception. Glancing around, she searched for any extra clothing Macey—or anyone—might have left lying around. Nothing.

She'd leave a message on Macey's phone—which she knew for a fact Macey didn't have on her—that she'd begun to feel sick as soon as she and Clay had returned.

Clay. God, how had her night gone from him to this? Not that she and Clay had any kind of chance at long-term anything, but couldn't the high she'd been on have lasted longer than fifteen minutes?

Andie avoided Clay and everyone else on her way to the restroom.

Once there, she waited in one of the stalls till the room was empty, and then she left and went the opposite direction from the party. The duplex was the other way, but she couldn't walk by out in the open. Like a criminal, she crept around the hotel in the shadows, on the side nearest the street, heart pounding out of control, and dammit, it pissed her off that Trevor forced her to do this on Macey's big night.

She went two blocks out of her way to the west and then angled south toward home. As far as she knew, no one had seen her and she didn't have a tail. She'd never been so glad to see the house she shared with Clay and Payton, never been so relieved to have, as Jonas had mentioned, a door with a lock.

Heart still pounding, she let herself inside, closed the door quietly but firmly and locked it with a reassuring click. Leaving the lights off, she slid to the floor and hugged her knees to her chest, trembling like a little girl.

CLAY KNOCKED ON ANDIE'S door again.

Where the hell had that woman gone? Had sex in the truck really flipped her out so much she had to disappear? He'd never kidded himself that she was a stable influence, but he'd thought she could handle some mutually consensual fun. Especially since she'd initiated it.

Mother of God, it had driven him wild to see her hike up her dress and climb on top of him.

"Andie!" He pounded on the door one more time, at a loss where to search for her next.

He was about to walk away when he heard movement inside.

"Andie, it's me. Open up." He spoke more quietly now, bowing his head next to the door. She was right on the other side. He could practically hear her debating with herself whether to open it or not. "Don't be a damn coward."

The door opened.

He wasn't sure what he'd expected when he finally laid eyes on her but it wasn't to have her search left and then right to make sure the coast was clear.

"What are you looking for?" he said, stepping inside.

"What are you doing here?" she whispered.

It dawned on him there was no light in the room behind her. "Were you sleeping?"

She closed the door softly and the lock clicked home.

"Can we turn on a light?" he asked, so confused that he forgot he was annoyed at her.

"It's too late. What's up, Clay?"

"Why don't *you* tell *me?* Where the hell did you go?"

"I…felt sick."

He could hear it in her voice she wasn't being honest. She sounded…scared.

"Did you hear from your ex or something?" he asked. He'd heard what she'd said about bullies to

Payton the other day and couldn't help but wonder if he was the only one and what exactly he'd done to her, what she'd gone through.

Andie tensed. "My ex?" She shook her head, distracted. "No. He hasn't contacted me."

He wasn't altogether convinced.

There was enough light coming in from the balcony door that he could see her outline and he reached for her hand. Led her over to the futon and pulled her down next to him. When he drew her into his side, she didn't resist. Clay pressed his lips to her temple and tried to ignore the rush of lust.

"Why'd you really take off?" he asked. "Wedding party isn't supposed to leave until everyone else is gone."

"So it's over now?" Andie asked.

"Not quite. Winding down though."

"Then why'd you leave if the wedding party isn't supposed to?"

"Because we were concerned about you. No one saw you leave. Macey was ready to send out a search party when you didn't answer your phone."

"I didn't want to worry her on her wedding night. Just… needed to get out of there. Too many people."

"So you weren't running away from me?"

ANDIE SAT UP AND SEARCHED Clay's chiseled face in the near-darkness. The insane, overwhelming panic that seeing Trevor had caused was dissipating as she became more attuned to Clay and the present moment. "Why would I run away from you?"

He shrugged. "You don't seem like the type who sticks around for cuddling and conversations if you can help it."

Andie laughed, not sure she liked the picture he was painting of her... But then, he wasn't far off the mark. "I've been known to do both," she said. "Though at the very least I would require room to stretch out, for cuddling."

Clay laughed. "I haven't been compelled to do anything like we did tonight for years."

"So I'm not just a notch in your dashboard?"

"Nope. The truck needed to be christened."

He smiled his killer smile, then cupped her cheek in his palm and leaned in, pressing a gentle kiss to her lips. He looked into her eyes questioningly.

She'd have to be superhuman or three-quarters dead to turn this man away. Selfishly, she wanted that chance to be with him again, unhurried, uncramped. Now that she'd had a sample, she wanted more. That it would serve as a distraction from the rest of her life was just icing on the cake.

Andie took his hand and stood. "The sheets here are cotton, not satin, but they, too, need to be christened. If you're up for the job."

"I've always been one to rise to the occasion." He got up from the futon and wrapped his arms around her, lifting her. She wound her legs around him, and he carried her to the bedroom.

ANDIE OPENED ONE EYE, enough to get her bearings. Excellent bearings they were, too—Clay slept naked, facing her, inches away, his arm draped across her middle. Enough light came in the window above the head of the bed for her to see the shadow of hair on his jaw and the peaceful look on his beautiful face. And that body. It was perfect. She could stare at it for days.

Over the course of the night, he'd shown her what that body could do. He was an unselfish lover, definitely well versed in satisfying a woman. Over and over and over again.

"Clay," she whispered. "You should go soon. The sun's coming up."

He didn't stir. She ran her fingers down his solid chest, biting her lip against the urge to follow her hand with her tongue. Before she realized he was awake, his arm tightened around her. He rolled onto his back, pulling her on top of him.

She was toast. She had to have him one more time. Because after this, once he walked out that door, she was done.

He kissed her till she couldn't breathe, ran his strong hands all over her, making her feel feminine, sexy. As if he couldn't get through the next minutes without her.

He rolled her to her back in a sudden movement and wedged himself between her legs, then proceeded to lavish her with attention from his mouth and hands.

"Clay, please…"

He made his way up her body. "Want to make sure you start your day right, biker girl."

"Um, yeah." She caught her breath and arched into him. "Anyone ever call you an overachiever?"

His laugh was gravelly and sexy. "Like to cover my bases."

"If we're going the baseball route, it's time for a home run. Bases are loaded."

Clay made a growling sound in his throat as he took his sweet time with her, teasing her, driving her into a frenzy. When she thought she was going to burn up and disintegrate, he leaned to the side and reached for the night stand. They'd made their way through a portion of the box of condoms last night—after Andie had proven to him they weren't expired.

He sheathed himself and returned to her within a few seconds but it seemed too long. She looked up at him through lust-heavy half-closed eyes and was surprised to find him staring at her with…tenderness? Not something she'd had a lot of experience with. It warmed her clear through and, if she was honest, scared her.

Clay brushed a rogue strand of hair off her face.

"You're shaking," she said softly. "What's wrong?"

"Nothing's wrong, Andie. This is what you do to me."

Without another word, he buried himself in her,

her name on his lips. She liked the way he called her just *Andie*. Not Miss Andie. Not biker girl. For some reason, that affected her almost as much as what he was doing to her body.

After, as they lay together sated and quiet, she rested her head on his chest and listened to his heart pound. His arms were still wrapped tightly around her, her head tucked under his chin. She didn't remember ever feeling so content. So safe, protected.

But safe and protected, because of someone else, was not what she was looking for.

She only had a week left on the island. Why should Andie deny herself...*this* or whatever little bit of this Clay might be willing to give her?

The custody issue wouldn't go away until after the hearing later this week, and Andie wouldn't push him. She wanted Payton to live with Clay about as much as Clay did. But she would no longer fight her attraction for this man. She could keep it casual for seven days.

Andie's cell phone started to ring in the living room, but she didn't move. It was probably Jonas. She'd left him a frantic message last night after sneaking out of the wedding reception.

"You going to get that?" Clay asked, propping himself up on his arm.

She shook her head and ran her finger across his chest distractedly. The urgency to talk to her cousin had disappeared. Having Clay here had calmed her down, allowed her to think about something besides her ex. She wasn't ready to step back into that stress yet.

Ignoring her touch, Clay sat up and turned to put his feet on the floor. He picked up his tuxedo pants and boxers from the floor and pulled them on. It took Andie a few seconds to realize he wasn't happy. His movements were quick, staccato. Jaw clenched.

"What are you doing?" she asked.

"I need to pick up Payton." He didn't bother with the dress shirt that was missing most of its buttons, just grabbed it along with his shoes and stood. "I can let myself out."

Obviously that incredible bond they'd just been sharing had come to an abrupt end. She guessed he knew something was bothering her—hiding it when he'd arrived last night had been impossible—but it was *her* business.

She kicked the covers out of her way and headed for the shower, more upset than she wanted to be that Clay might not be around as much as she'd thought for the next week after all.

CHAPTER NINETEEN

"YOU SURE WENT MIA last night after the reception,"
Evan said to Clay as they finished their third treadmill mile of the afternoon. They were the only two in
the fire station's workout room at the moment. "Anything to do with our favorite dark-haired Harley rider,
who, coincidentally, also seemed to be missing?"

Clay stopped the treadmill, wiped the sweat from
his face with a towel and took a long drink from his
water bottle.

"Thought we were doing four today," Evan said,
still running.

Shaking his head, Clay went over to the weight
machine. He started his upper body workout without
a word.

Evan ran for another five minutes. Clay threw
himself into another set of reps, blocking out all
thoughts of Andie.

The noise of the treadmill stopped and Evan came
over to the weights. He situated himself on the bench
press after making adjustments to the machine. "I'm
going to take a wild guess and say this black mood
of yours has to do with Andie."

Clay counted ten reps and then slowly released the weights. He swigged some more water and readjusted the machine again to work a different muscle. Evan still lay flat on his back on the bench, not lifting, just watching Clay expectantly.

Dammit. Clay blew out a breath and looked at the ceiling. Eyed the punching bag hanging across the room. "I screwed up, man."

He stretched his arms up and put his hands on the back of his head, closed his eyes and beat himself up yet again.

"Screwed up how?"

"With Andie."

Evan finally started benching and Clay moved over to the free weights.

"What'd you do to her?" Evan asked when he paused between sets.

"Nothing." Well, last night sure as hell wasn't *nothing*. "I've known since I met her I shouldn't get involved."

"So what's wrong with a little fun for one night?"

Clay tried a set of biceps curls and stopped when he lost count.

Evan stared at him in the mirror.

"Ah, man," Evan said, then switched his gaze from the mirror to look directly at Clay. "You're in deep."

Clay did his best to keep his expression unreadable. "It was one night, Drake."

"You don't do a lot of 'one nights.' "

"Just because I'm not a man ho like you used to be doesn't mean I don't know what I'm doing."

"So what *are* you doing?"

Clay blew out what breath he had. "Playing with fire."

"You care about her?"

"Hell, yeah, I care about her. Some of us don't sleep with a woman unless we care about her."

Evan grinned. "Roger."

"But…she's not telling me something."

He explained about the gun, the disappearance last night, the lack of a straight answer. "She was involved with some jackass who beat her. You don't just walk away from something like that and pick back up with a normal life."

"See your point. But you're falling for her."

"I've been down this road before. Nothing good can come of it."

"You mean with Robin? You think Andie's like your ex?"

Clay considered the question. The two women were nothing alike. Except… "Andie's used to being alone, being accountable to nobody. She doesn't trust me."

"Have you confronted her about what she's hiding?"

Clay nodded. "She won't open up and bare all."

"Sounds like she bared enough."

"Aren't you supposed to grow the hell up once you get married and have kids?"

"I sincerely hope not," Evan said.

"Then there's the way Andie lives, drifting all over the country. That's not normal, is it?"

"No, man. I'd advise a little caution. Before you get too involved."

"You think I should stay away from her? Derek trusts her."

"Derek isn't sleeping with her. Derek doesn't have a kid, either. You have to put your daughter's safety first."

"I know that," Clay said, annoyed not only because Evan was acting as if Clay was an idiot, but because he'd had these thoughts already himself. If it was just him, and Andie presented some kind of mystery, he wouldn't let it bother him much. She was only on the island for another week or so. They could see each other and he didn't have to know everything she was hiding.

He went over to the punching bag and pummeled it repeatedly with both fists.

"So what, we got the big *L* word here?" Evan asked.

"It wasn't just sex."

Evan nodded. "Happens to the best of us. Does she know?"

Clay shook his head. "We made an agreement when she came to town. I was worried about the custody hearing. She's the one who figured out a judge could use her against me."

"When's the hearing?"

"Thursday."

"What about after that? You'll have your answer for Payton, for better or worse, but there's no more danger of what being with Andie could cause."

"Then she leaves."

"You okay with that? Just letting her go?"

The thought of not seeing her again made it difficult to breathe. Even before last night, he'd gotten used to knowing she was close by whenever he walked down the stairs, past her door to the ground level. He couldn't imagine anyone else living in her half of the duplex.

"She's still Andie," he said. "The woman who'd rather hop on her bike and ride away than plant any roots."

"Then you might have to let her go."

He just might, and that brought him right back to where he started. Screwed.

THERE WERE ADVANTAGES TO the presence of a chattering four-year-old, Clay thought as he pulled into Bud's parking lot on Tuesday morning.

Payton, who'd insisted on tying her hair back with a bandanna just as she'd seen Andie do, had allowed him and Andie to avoid an awkward silence by grilling Andie. She'd been fascinated to learn that girls could ride motorcycles, too, and their discussion had turned into Andie's "girls can do anything" speech. Another message Payton's mother had apparently never thought to deliver to her daughter.

Clay parked the truck and his eyes met Andie's. Andie had been cordial when she'd knocked on his door to tell him her bike was ready for them to pick up. When he'd first seen her, the urge to pull her close and kiss her had overwhelmed him, but he'd held back.

Clay helped his daughter down to the pavement. Andie hurried ahead of them like an excited child herself, carrying her helmet, and Clay smiled.

The hard-edged woman squealed like a girl when Bud rolled her dark red Harley out of the garage. She showed more emotion for that hunk of metal than anything else on God's green earth. Clay shook his head, not sure if he was amused or insulted.

"It's cool!" Payton said, jumping up and down beside Clay.

Andie turned and held her hand out to Payton.

"You should give it a tattube of a butterfly right here." Payton pointed.

"I like that idea, Pay." Andie circled the motorcycle slowly, inspecting every inch, then put her helmet on. "I'm going to take it around the block. See how it rides."

Bud nodded.

"Can I come?" Payton asked.

"I don't have a helmet for you," Andie said.

"Got a kid-size one you can borrow," Bud said,

walking toward a work table that held several large parts and an assortment of helmets.

"I don't think that's a good idea," Clay said.

Andie met his gaze. "Tell you what." She leaned down to Payton's level. "If you can convince your dad, maybe we can ride up and down the alley one time where there's not much traffic. A slow ride."

"Please, Daddy?"

"I'd be careful," Andie said.

He didn't have a chance when the two of them ganged up on him. "No more than fifteen miles per hour?"

"If it'll go that slow," Andie said.

"Forget—"

"Kidding, Clay."

It was only the alley. "You hold on to Andie at all times," he said finally.

Payton cheered and ran up to Bud to get the smaller white helmet he offered.

Clay went out to the edge of Bud's lot to watch the ride, up one way, a slow turn around at the end, and back down to the opposite end. When they rode by, Payton waved, a wide grin on her face. As they approached the lot at the end of the ride, he went inside the garage to settle up, secure in the knowledge that Payton had survived her first motorcycle ride.

Bud handed him a detailed slip showing what his insurance had covered and how much he owed for the deductible. Clay handed him a credit card and strolled back to the open doorway of the garage to check on the girls.

Andie removed her helmet and hung it from the handlebars, then ran her fingers through her hair. She climbed off, lifted Payton down, talking to his daughter the whole time though Clay was too far away to make out what she said. Then she pulled off Payton's helmet, as well.

Clay was about to turn around and finish paying when Payton threw her arms around Andie's legs, full of pure, four-year-old joy. Andie laughed as she picked her up, swung her around and then hugged her. Something in Clay's chest shifted as he watched them.

He was rooted to the spot because of the realization that struck him.

Andie was the *right* woman for him. For them.

He'd been so caught up in his own self-doubt all these weeks, his inability to trust his instincts, that he'd looked for all the ways she *wasn't* right. Most of what he'd come up with was irrelevant. Tattoos. Motorcycle. Past mistakes.

Heck, if you went by past mistakes, Clay wasn't the right guy to raise Payton. But his daughter didn't see his screw-ups from years ago. It made no difference to Payton's well-being that Clay had gotten caught drinking or racing on the highway or staying out all night years ago. Just as it didn't matter that Andie had been in desperate circumstances and done the wrong thing when she was younger. All that mattered was the kind of people they were now.

There were so many ways Andie could be right. She was giving and considerate once you dug down through a couple of layers of defensiveness. She may not be traditional in any way, but she was responsible, practical, down-to-earth.

She loved Payton, would do just about anything for her, and was one hell of a positive influence on his little girl's life. Andie treated Payton like a person, not an inconvenience. She shared herself with Payton, tattoos, bandannas and all, shared her time.

He'd fallen in love with her nonconforming ways and refusal to bend to anyone's idea of what she should be or do. The very traits he'd told himself were reasons to stay away were the ones that had drawn him in.

And she'd been spot-on when she'd told him he needed to trust himself.

He tore his eyes away from this beautiful woman and his daughter to quickly finish the transaction with Bud.

"Biker girl," he called as he exited the garage.

Both Andie and Payton turned to him, and Payton ran over, telling him all about the ride, as if he'd missed the whole thing. He picked her up and carried her to the truck, feeling lighter than he had in weeks.

"Climb in and get your seatbelt on," he told her. He shut the door and faced Andie. "She loved it."

"Hope so. Maybe next time we can inch up to eighteen miles per hour."

He barely registered her joke, his mind spinning.

"The custody hearing's the day after tomorrow," he said. "I was wondering if you would go with me."

"Uh, Clay? It's me, Andie. We agreed I wouldn't do your case any good."

"This isn't about helping or hurting the case. You're important to me, Andie. You're the one I want sitting there with me."

She studied him, confused. "I don't want to cause you and Payton problems. If I cost you custody of her, I couldn't live with myself."

"If Lipp wants to use you against me, he's already got everything he needs. He's had plenty of time to investigate you, find all your skeletons. He can bring those up if he wants to but I intend to fight every last negative thing he says about you. And I'd like to do it with you by my side."

"Why?"

He moved closer to her, lowered his voice. "I happen to care about you. Beyond the other night, beyond the mind-blowing chemistry we share. You're important to both of us."

"Likewise," she said shyly.

"Thursday's huge for us. If we win, I want to celebrate with you. If we lose…" It would crush him.

Andie nodded. "I'll be there if you're sure I won't do any harm."

He grasped her hand, dying to kiss her. But Payton watched them from inside the truck and he wasn't sure enough about where they were heading to let her witness that. Not yet.

"Thank you," he said. "Starts at ten o'clock."

She smiled and walked to her bike. Clay watched her the whole way, his body reacting to the sway of her hips as always. But it went beyond physical now, and he finally recognized that, embraced it.

Now the question was, could he get her to level with him about whatever she was afraid of? And just as importantly, could he get her to stay?

CHAPTER TWENTY

D-DAY WAS HERE.

Clay jammed his hand into the pocket of his suit jacket and wrenched it, pacing the floor outside of the courtroom. He was painfully early but he hadn't been able to sit with Payton this morning, trying to act normal. He'd called Bridget and begged her to come immediately.

He couldn't help glancing around every few minutes in search of Andie. He didn't doubt that she'd show—Andie did what she said she would. It was more that he'd be able to settle once she got here.

A woman's shoes clicked rhythmically on the tile floor and Clay whipped around. Instead of Andie, though, it was Robin, her mother and Morris Lipp. Robin had dressed in what was, for her, a costume—a respectable pair of brown tailored pants and a nondescript white, button-down blouse. Modest two-inch pumps, light makeup and neatly brushed hair completed the disguise.

Clay had hoped to avoid them. He had nothing to say to any of them and it was all he could do to keep his nerves under control.

"How's my daughter?" she asked.

He grasped his keys in his pocket so hard they cut into his skin. "*Our* daughter is doing very well. How's rehab?"

"Almost over. I'll be out in another week. I'll be back home for Payton then."

"We'll see what the judge says." Clay wished he was half as confident as he acted. When he'd talked to Robert Davis, his lawyer, two days ago, they'd run through all the possible speed bumps that might arise during the hearing. Not a lot had changed since the last time Clay had appealed, only that Robin had gone into rehab. Robert had explained before that that could actually count in her favor. Her lawyer would do everything he could to position it as her overwhelming dedication to changing her life for the better and doing whatever it took to be a better mom.

Total crock, and Clay had faith that Robert would do everything he could to show that.

"We will, at that," Lipp said, doing very little to hide his smugness. The bastard was doing his best to intimidate him.

The party of three moved down to a bench on the other side of the main atrium of the courthouse.

"Clay." Robert approached, holding his hand out. "You ready?"

They shook hands. "Ready as I'll ever be."

Instead of his usual gravity, the balding fiftysomthing lawyer actually smiled and Clay would even say there was a sparkle in the man's eye.

"What's going on, Robert?" Clay asked suspiciously.

"Big arrest last night," he said. "Remember that character I told you about, Lewis Tober?"

"The guy Robin kept calling from rehab?"

"That's the one. Suspected dealer." Robert paused for effect. "He went down last night."

Clay felt a sliver of new-found hope. "What does this mean, exactly? Spell it out for me."

"It doesn't prove anything about Robin outright, but it'll help us paint her as an unfit mother. Inject some doubt into the judge's mind about whether this woman is really making all the sacrifices and great efforts to change that we know she's going to claim."

Clay nodded, afraid to hope too much, but encouraged. "Excellent. Sounds promising."

"I'm going to go do a final prep down the hall where it's quiet. I'll see you in a few minutes."

Clay nodded and looked nervously at his watch. Twenty-five minutes till ten. He needed to set eyes on Andie. As Robert strode off, Clay scanned the people around him.

He did a double take.

"Mom? Dad? What are you doing here?"

His mom reached him first and hugged him. "We wanted to be here for you, Clay."

They'd never come to a hearing before. Of course,

previous ones had been up in Corpus so it would have been an even longer drive for them.

"How'd you know when the hearing was?"

"Your sister told us," his dad said. "Since you never mentioned it." His old man's face actually hinted at humor.

"Sorry," Clay said. "I didn't figure—"

"I'd like to speak to you," his dad said. "In private."

Clay went instantly on alert. They hadn't spoken in private in years. The atrium and hallway of the courthouse had gotten more crowded. He pointed down the hall to a door that led outside. "That might be our best bet."

"I'll wait here for you," Clay's mom said, lowering herself to a granite bench along the wall.

Clay and his dad walked down the long hall in silence. Once they were outside, they stood side by side, awkwardly, hands in their pockets, watching the traffic drive past.

His dad cleared his throat. "I just wanted to tell you I'm proud of you, son."

Clay stared at his father.

The older man swallowed. "You're doing a good job with Payton. Better than I ever would have guessed."

Unexpected emotion clogged Clay's throat, making it difficult to speak.

"There were times when I wondered if you'd ever pull your head out."

Clay nodded. "I never meant to hurt you or the rest of the family, though I'm sure that was hard to tell."

"Hard to tell. Yes." His dad cleared his throat. "You've grown up. As soon as you found out you had a daughter, it seemed like something finally clicked inside of you. You've become one heck of a father."

"Thank you, Dad," Clay managed to say, reeling.

"She's an amazing child, isn't she?"

Clay nodded, picturing Payton in the yellow tutu she'd been dancing around in this morning. "That she is. She blows my mind every single day. I just hope she'll be okay."

"What's your lawyer think about your chances today?"

Clay told him about the latest discovery and they discussed how the hearing might play out. At a quarter to ten, Clay suggested they head inside. As he turned toward the door, he spotted Evan's truck pulling up alongside the curb a hundred feet or so away. What was he doing here? Clay paused, watching.

A familiar, beautiful brunette head emerged from the back of the extended cab and Clay's heart pounded. His dad followed his line of sight.

Clay locked his jaw to keep from gaping. Andie looked…amazing. Conservative. Her hair was pulled up on the back of her head, with delicate strands hanging at her temples. She wore black tailored pants with open-toed heels that showed off her long legs and a mint-green sweater with a scarf at her neck. All Clay could do was stare as she hugged Selena then made her way down the sidewalk toward them.

"Wow," his dad said.

"Yeah." Wow was an understatement. "While we're being so open, Dad, you should probably know that I'm in love with her."

His dad's gaze shifted to Clay, who waited tensely for his dad's verdict.

"She may not be your idea of conventional wife material, but she's the one for me."

His dad turned his attention back to Andie. "She know this yet?"

"Not exactly. We have a few things to work out first."

His dad nodded slowly. "She's the one who called 911 so quickly, right?"

"She's the one."

"I imagine she's all right."

"Hell, all that's left is to convince *her*."

Which he'd do tonight, regardless of the outcome of the hearing. So much on the line, all in one day. He inhaled nervously and waited for the woman he loved to notice them standing there.

ANDIE CHECKED TO MAKE sure her hair wasn't falling out of the clip Selena had loaned her and moistened her lips. Her hands were sweating and her stomach was tied in a knot. Not only was she worried about the hearing and especially about whether she should be there or not, but Selena's water had broken minutes before they'd left her and Evan's beach house. Andie had been ready to call a taxi instead of having the Drakes drop her off, but Selena insisted it would be hours before the baby was born. The courthouse was just blocks from the hospital on the mainland, so she'd finally given in.

Selena, bless her heart, had offered to give Andie full access to her pre-pregnancy wardrobe so she could look presentable at the hearing. Thank God they were almost the same size. Fortunately, Selena had also lent Andie her fashion expertise because Andie had zero on that front.

Clay stood about twenty feet in front of her, next to the door. Sinfully gorgeous in a black suit. Her mouth went dry as she approached him.

"Hello," he said, smiling. "You look incredible."

"I feel like an imposter."

"You remember my father?" Clay gestured. Andie hadn't even noticed the man. She'd been too busy staring at Clay.

"Hi, Mr. Marlow. I didn't realize you'd be here."

"I didn't, either," Clay said. His demeanor toward his dad was upbeat, almost…warm. A one-eighty from Payton's birthday.

"Want to be there when my son's awarded custody."

Was this an alternate reality?

Andie glanced at Clay, and he nodded minutely.

"I'm going to check on your mother," Mr. Marlow said.

"We'll be there in five minutes," Clay said, opening the door for his dad.

"What *happened?*" Andie asked as soon as the older Marlow was out of earshot.

Clay leaned against the stone wall as if he'd been bowled over. "He and my mom showed up out of nowhere." In disbelief, he told her about the conversation they'd finished just before Andie arrived.

She'd never been a hug person but she couldn't help stepping closer and wrapping her arms around his neck. "I'm so happy for you, Clay. I know how much that's weighed on you."

She backed out of the hug quickly because feeling his hands on her sides did things to her, made her think things that shouldn't be thought in such an official, public place.

"Let's head to the courtroom," he said, peering down at her.

As they went inside, he took her hand in his as if it was the most natural thing in the world. He leaned close to her. "You really do look amazing," he said just loud enough for her to hear. "But you know what?"

"What?"

"I'll take you in your jeans and tank any day."

That one little sentence warmed her insides, clear down to her toes.

No matter what happened after this or how hard it would be when she left, Andie was glad she'd come.

CHAPTER TWENTY-ONE

AT THE JUDGE'S LATE-AFTERNOON statement awarding Clay full custody of Payton, Clay's shoulders sagged and he closed his eyes, letting the ruling sink in.

The judge had been tough, as he'd been warned, but the news concerning the busted drug dealer and Robin's ties to him had been pivotal in swaying him, making him doubt her dedication to staying clean.

Robert shook his hand, and the next thing Clay knew, he was surrounded. His mother threw her arms around him wordlessly, tears running down her face. His dad hugged him awkwardly, the first time they'd hugged since Clay had reached puberty. His dad clapped him on the back and told him how happy he was for him.

Clay released him and turned to find Andie, who hung back a couple of feet, as if she thought she didn't belong. As soon as their eyes met, though, she lunged into his arms and held on tight.

"I'm so, so happy for you and Payton," she said directly into his ear so he could hear her over the surrounding noise.

He kissed the side of her neck and thanked her. "We're picking her up and going out to celebrate. The whole family. You in?"

"If you want me there," she said uncertainly.

"Damn straight. And then afterward, maybe you and I can have some time alone."

Andie smiled. "Are you sure we can't just skip the whole family deal?"

"You tempt me, woman." He kissed her and put space between them. "Later. Right now I need to get my daughter and tell her the news."

CLAY NEVER THOUGHT LIFE could be this good.

He looked around the Italian restaurant's large circular table at his family.

Bridget and Reid to his left. His mother. Dad. Laurel, Charles and their three boys. Andie at his right. Payton smack in the center of his lap. Even his other two sisters had called to wish him and Payton well.

Everyone listened to Bridget telling a story about middle-of-the-night cravings for Pop-Tarts and Reid going to the store to get some. Inane topics. Happy topics. Exactly what this evening called for.

The waitress came around and collected empty plates, filled coffee mugs, offered dessert.

"Heck, yeah, we need dessert," Clay said. "What's everyone want?"

Everybody placed an order except for Andie, and he studied her, the woman he loved, her eyes on his sister as she returned to her story. She was with-drawn, quiet, probably a little overwhelmed by his family.

She didn't quite look right to him without all the earrings, but she was beautiful, even in her play-nice-for-the-judge persona. He couldn't wait to get her alone and tell her how much he loved her. How much he wanted them to be a family. He felt confident he could convince her to level with him…that was the only thing left standing in their way.

THE PROMISE OF SPENDING TIME with Clay was all that kept Andie going that evening.

After dinner, they'd driven to the hospital to visit Selena and Evan and their brand-new baby, Christian. Despite Selena's vow this morning that it would be aeons before he was born, he'd shown up just an hour after they'd checked into the delivery room. Payton had been in quiet awe of the tiny baby and even Andie had to admit that holding someone so new and help-less had been an incredible experience.

Clay and Payton waited in the truck while Andie went inside the Shell Shack to check in before head-ing home for the night. Kevin, Sean and Charlotte were closing and they usually handled everything well but Andie had to make sure they didn't need anything or have any problems, just to put her mind at ease. She used the side door by the patio, survey-ing the crowd at the outdoor tables as she passed by.

That's when she spotted him, sitting along the wall by the beach, alone at a table.

Trevor.

He was looking the other direction, so Andie hurried inside, heart pounding, hoping he hadn't seen her.

Kevin was working the register nearest the door and nodded when he saw her, too occupied with a line of customers to speak. Her vision swimming, she rushed to the back room. Sean was prepping food and greeted her cheerfully but all Andie could do was search for a place to sit down and get her bearings.

She settled for an old milk crate on end against the padlocked door.

"Aren't you all fancy," Sean said as he worked.

Andie put her head down on her hands and concentrated on getting air into her lungs. She'd never passed out in her life but figured this must be what it felt like just before you did. She didn't care for the sensation.

"What's wrong with you?" Sean said.

She shook her head, still grasping it in her hands. "Overheated."

The room gradually stopped spinning and breathing became a little easier. The next thing she knew Sean was holding an icy lemonade in front of her.

"Thanks." Andie took the drink from him and sipped it.

"You okay?" he asked, going back to the grill to flip the burgers.

"Yeah." Thank God this was Sean, the densest of the dense males who worked at the Shack. Kevin would've called an ambulance. "I'm fine now. Just get the food out."

Sean shrugged and carried on and Andie was able to lean against the door. She willed her heart to slow down. Practiced the deep breathing exercises a woman had taught her at a hostel a few years back.

Finally, she stood and eased herself to the doorway between the kitchen and the main bar.

"Everything okay tonight?" she asked Kevin when he moved to the drink prep area.

"Insanely busy but yeah."

"Need anything?" She couldn't help glancing out where she'd seen Trevor.

"We're low on a bunch of things but we'll make it to closing."

She nodded, relieved. "Call me if you need me. Otherwise, see you tomorrow."

"See you."

Andie made her way slowly to the door, checking for Trevor from the safety of the building before venturing out onto the patio again.

The table he'd been sitting at was now empty. She searched the area for him but didn't see him anywhere. Thank God. But then…it was almost worse knowing he was out there somewhere but not knowing where.

She scanned the parking lot and the shadows, not wanting to lead Trevor to Clay or Payton or the house they all lived in. When she'd convinced herself there was no one hiding in the dark corners, she hurried for the truck, attempting to look like nothing had just scared the wits out of her.

ANDIE WAS STILL RATTLED at ten forty-five that night. As they'd planned, Clay had waited until Payton fell asleep and then he'd called Andie to come upstairs. They'd figured Payton would drift off faster if Andie wasn't around.

She dug out a hoodie to throw over her tank and jeans, remembering how cold Clay kept his place. Earlier, she'd washed off her makeup and let her hair down. She glanced in the mirror, not really worried about how she looked. This was her, and Clay knew that.

When he opened his door, she sank into his offered arms, pushing her ex from her mind and trying only to savor the man who held her. She must've held on too long, though, because he asked, "Everything okay?"

"Fine." She pulled away and sat on the couch.

He studied her and she sat up straighter, doing her best to smile.

"I thought we could go out on the balcony. Enjoy the night. It's perfect now."

"Sure."

Clay opened the door for her. He left it open so he could hear if Payton awoke.

Andie stood at the railing looking down into the

dark backyard…and into all the yards around them. It hit her how visible they were here.

"Could we turn the light off?" she asked, gesturing toward the single bulb by the door.

He switched it off, making it a lot darker, though the lamp in the living room still illuminated them more than Andie wanted. She wanted to believe she was just being paranoid, but Trevor had tracked her down from Illinois to the southern tip of Texas. He must have figured out she worked at the Shell Shack because she'd seen him there twice. It wasn't a stretch that he might've figured out where she was staying.

Clay came up behind her and slid his arms around her, tucking his chin on her shoulder. She closed her eyes and fought to forget their potential for an audience. She breathed in the smell of him, relishing his strong arms around her. They stayed that way for several minutes and Andie was almost able to convince herself everything was as it should be.

Clay nipped and kissed her ear and neck, then turned her around to kiss her lips. That was all it took to get Andie's full attention… All her thoughts slid away.

"You know," he said huskily, "this is a lot of fun but we should probably talk first."

His tone was too serious. Talking in situations like this was never a good idea. She tried to distract him by kissing him again, which worked for about thirty seconds.

"Andie."

"Clay."

"Today's been unbelievable. Not only did I finally get custody of Payton, but my dad came around. How often does all that happen?"

She smiled, genuinely thrilled for him on both counts. "Maybe you should buy a lottery ticket."

He brushed her hair back from her face and stared into her eyes. "Actually I had a different gamble in mind and I'm hoping the odds are better."

"Yeah?" Her nerves stretched taut as she guessed where he was going next.

"Yeah." Her heart felt like it might hammer right out of her chest. "I love you, Andie. I know you've been hurt in the past and you have a hard time trusting people…"

"Uh-huh," she said, swallowing hard around the lump in her throat. *He loved her.* "Clay—"

"Something's bothering you, scaring you. You can tell me anything. It won't change the way I feel about you."

"I'm leaving in a couple days."

He pressed his forehead to hers. "You could stay. But…you have to let me in completely for this to work. Let yourself get fully involved."

Andie wanted to. So badly. Tell him about Trevor, that he was on the island, that he was fixated on her enough to track her down. But then she'd have to tell him all the other stuff, too. Their history. Her stupidity. Naïveté. Gullibility. Whatever you wanted to call it. The fact was she couldn't talk about it.

Couldn't let anyone else know the parts of her life that still shamed her so completely. Because sharing that would expose her, make her vulnerable. Trusting Clay that much, telling him everything…no. He only thought he loved her enough.

"It's not going to work, Clay." She blinked away tears that had suddenly appeared.

"Why don't you trust me?"

"I don't trust anyone." She lowered her gaze to the floor when she said it.

He let go of her and turned away, obviously frustrated.

"I'm sorry, Clay. I…care about you. A lot." She couldn't say *love*. Whether she did or not—and maybe she did—it was a moot point. Because she couldn't trust. Wouldn't let herself.

Abruptly he went inside and began picking up the huge pile of crayons Payton had left on the floor. One by one, he threw them into the box, his back to Andie.

She sat on the arm of the couch. "I never wanted this to happen. It's why I tried to scare you off that first night, when you kissed me."

He didn't say anything, just kept throwing crayons. When the mess was cleaned up, he set the box on the stairs to Payton's room. Slowly he turned to stare at her.

"You're scared," he said in a quiet, measured voice. "I understand that. But at some point you have to take a chance on somebody, Andie. Otherwise you're going to be alone."

"That's my plan," she said. "It may suck to be alone, but it beats the hell out of being hurt."

"I'd never hurt you on purpose. I'm not the guy who hit you."

"I know that, Clay. I don't mean you would hurt me physically. Maybe you wouldn't hurt me at all… but I can't take that chance."

He studied her for several more seconds. "Then I guess there's nothing else to say."

Andie nodded, struggling to keep every hint of emotion off her face. She took in a shaky breath, turned and walked out the door.

CLAY FELL INTO THE BEANBAG chair in front of the TV and turned on a video game. His jaw was clenched so tight it throbbed. He settled back with the most mindless, violent game he owned.

He was in the mood to kill things.

He'd known Andie would be tough to crack. Had known from the beginning, thanks to her frankness, that she had layers of issues to overcome before she could be in a relationship.

He was an idiot, plain and simple. He'd thought it was good enough between them that she'd want to try.

Obviously, he'd been a thousand percent wrong.

She'd told him he needed to learn to trust himself. Well, he'd proven he was better off *not*.

He should be happy, over the freaking moon, be-cause today had been a big deal of a day. His daugh-ter. His dad.

But he wanted more.

He wanted it all.

Two out of three was damn hard to swallow.

CHAPTER TWENTY-TWO

THE MOMENT ANDIE HAD been dreading for four years came at 9:47 p.m. Friday.

She'd stumbled through the past twenty-four hours in the funk to beat all funks. Missing Clay. Feeling terrible when she recalled the hurt in his eyes before she'd walked out. Suffering the worst kind of regret that she wasn't the woman for him, wasn't able to be what he wanted.

Her shift was almost over…the last shift she was scheduled to work. Macey and Derek would be back in town tomorrow. Then Andie would be free.

She'd gone into the back room to open a box of napkins when her cell phone rang in her purse. Her first mistake was answering it, but if she was honest, some part of her had hoped it was Clay. He had no reason to call her, of course, but that's what went through her head. That's what made her stop what she was doing and dig out her phone.

"Hello?"

"Andie." The rough male voice was familiar.

A chill went through her even though it'd topped one hundred degrees outside today. She made a beeline for the door, away from Sean, who was at the grill, away from the crowd, out into the muggy evening.

"Hello? I know you're there, Angel."

Bile burned her throat at the pet name he'd always called her.

"What do you want, Trevor?" she choked out, walking blindly away from the bar and everything that might give her comfort. This was her hell and she'd handle it by herself.

"After all this time, that's the greeting I get?"

She could hear a smile in his voice. She picked up a rock and nailed the side of the hotel's Dumpster with it. Her hand shook out of control—actually, her whole body shook.

"Get to your point or I'm hanging up."

"I need to see you."

Andie could swear her heart stopped. She fell to her knees in the sand.

"Andie? I didn't scare you off, did I?"

She couldn't let him know how much he scared her. "No."

"We have unfinished business." He paused and she squeezed her eyes shut. "Please."

"We don't have any business, Trevor. Ancient history."

That wasn't altogether true, though. She had to face up to him one last time. Had to show herself she could do it. If she didn't, he'd keep bothering her. She'd have to keep eluding him.

"I won't hurt you, Andie. We can meet in public."

She bent forward over her knees, resting her head on the ground.

"You still there?"

"I'm here," she said, her voice hoarse. "When and where?"

"Tomorrow. Noon. There's an outdoor bar at the Casa Del Mar."

"Fine." She pushed End and sat up, staring off at the outline of the waves in the moonlight. Fought the nausea by taking in long, cleansing breaths.

By the time she'd stopped shaking and thought she could hide the tempest inside her, it was after ten and her shift was over. She made her way back to the Shack to tell Sean and Kevin goodbye. After she met with Trevor tomorrow, she was leaving.

For the first time in her life, she didn't yet have an idea where she'd be going.

TWELVE HOURS LATER, Andie hadn't been home yet. She hadn't slept or eaten. Couldn't have done either if she'd tried.

What she had done was walk. Miles. Down the beach all the way to the jetty. Around to the bay side. Up past the bridge to the mainland. All the way north on the island to Turtle Town.

One of the turtle caretakers had pulled up at seven and found Andie at the fence, peering in at the viewing windows of the biggest outdoor turtle tanks.

The workers all knew Andie by name from when her bike was in the shop. Yolanda had let her come in this morning and help with the chores. Feeding the turtles was calming. Watching them swim around their tanks, soothing.

But after helping for two and a half hours, she figured she better leave before anyone started wondering why she was hanging out for so long.

With every step she took away from Turtle Town, her fear came back in nauseating Technicolor.

She absolutely had to face Trevor. But she didn't have to face him alone. Did she?

It wasn't that she was afraid he would hurt her physically. As he'd said, they were meeting in public, and Andie knew enough self-defense now that he would never overpower her like he had in the past. That and she'd have her gun with her. Loaded.

While she was confident of her physical capabilities, though, she was terrified he would cut through her mental ones. Why had she ever stayed with him after the first time he'd knocked her around? She'd loved him once. Would seeing him again negate all the progress she'd made toward getting her confidence and her self-esteem back?

She'd concluded at some point in the night that she couldn't see him alone. Clay was the only one besides Jonas who knew anything about Trevor. Of course, he was the last person she wanted to ask, and he'd probably tell her exactly where she could go.

When she returned to the duplex, she packed her bags and got everything ready to go. The last thing she did was load her gun and put it into the small backpack she used instead of a purse. Then she went upstairs, empty-handed.

She knocked on the door, heart pounding.

No one answered and her nerve slipped a little.

She knocked again. Two times. A third. Tried the doorknob but it was locked.

Now what? She didn't have a plan B yet.

She went down both sets of stairs toward her bike, not sure where she was heading or where to look for Clay but not ready to concede yet that he wouldn't accompany her. Her shoulders sagged.

As she went to the garage for her Harley, noting the truck parked there and wondering where Clay and Payton could've gone on foot, she heard a noise in the distance. Another Harley coming down the main road. Turning onto Seagull. Toward her. She turned to see what it was that approached—something older than hers, but bigger, she could tell by the sound.

A bright blue Fat Boy came around the corner, carrying two people. It looked maybe ten years old, but was in good condition. The sound of the engine was like a lullaby.

Belatedly, she took note of the riders. A man and

a girl, both wearing helmets. Her hope soared as she realized who it was.

Clay pulled up on the driveway and stopped close to the garage, on the opposite side from her.

"Miss Andie!" Payton squealed. "Look at us!" She yelled it over the sound of the engine before Clay turned it off.

"Hey, Pay." She perused the motorcycle. "You got a bike," she said stupidly, now focusing more on the people than the machine.

Clay nodded, eyebrows raised, clearly wondering what she wanted.

"I didn't even know you could ride."

"Part of my dark and troubled past," he said.

Payton squirmed to get down and Andie helped her off. The little girl took her helmet off and ran to the garage to put it away.

"Do you have a minute?" she asked, scuffing her feet on the driveway.

He took several seconds to answer. "I suppose I do. What do you need?"

His tone toward her was different now. Less personal. Colder. Even though she'd been the one to walk away, it made her sad.

"Do you want to go upstairs?" She looked down the street, feeling exposed out here.

Clay shrugged. "Payton's getting the sidewalk chalk. Down here's fine." He climbed off the bike and ambled to the back of the truck. He released the tailgate and sat on it. Andie wouldn't let herself watch the way he moved or remember how that body felt. She'd given that up and thinking about it now would only cause physical pain.

Clay stole a careful look at Andie while she studied the ground. She looked like hell. Black jeans, the usual boots, black body-hugging T-shirt and the same gray hoodie she'd been wearing the other night tied around her waist. Her hair looked stringy and tangled. Shadows under her eyes told him she'd slept about like he had last night and, hell, the night before, too.

She could roll through the dirt and get in a fist fight and he'd still want nothing more than to pull her to him and never let her go.

Dammit.

"What do you want, Andie?"

She looked up at him, startled.

"Is something wrong?"

She hesitated, then leaned against the tailgate. "You know the ex I told you about?"

He made sure Payton was far enough she wouldn't overhear this conversation. "The bastard who hurt you?"

"That's the one." Andie folded her arms across her chest. "He's on the island. I'm supposed to meet him today."

"What the hell for?" He clenched his hands into fists.

"No idea. But I need to do it. For…closure, or something…"

Nothing good could come of that, but he didn't air his opinion. It was no longer his right. Hadn't ever been, come to think of it.

"So I decided to do it, but…I don't want to go alone." She rushed through the last words so that he could barely make out what she said.

"If you're looking for my opinion, you should take a SWAT team and have them take him out. Do the world a favor."

The corner of her lips that he could see from this angle curved upward slightly.

"No one else knows about him here."

"You haven't told Macey and Selena?"

She shook her head. "It's…embarrassing."

He didn't want to care about her, didn't want to worry about her, but he did and he would. He couldn't just shut that off. "I'll go with you."

She looked at him. "You will?"

"Isn't that why you're here?"

Andie nodded. "I didn't think you'd say yes, though."

He fought not to touch her, to try to comfort her, to soothe away her fear. He stood and turned her toward him. "You may frustrate me until I want to shake you, Andie, but I meant what I said. I love you. I'm not about to let anyone hurt you in any way."

When she finally looked up at him, tears filled her eyes. "Thank you."

He must be a glutton for punishment because he pulled her to him and held on.

CHAPTER TWENTY-THREE

ANDIE AND CLAY DIDN'T speak as they waited at a high table at the outdoor bar. He ordered a beer and Andie sipped on a lemonade, mostly for something to occupy her. She'd seated herself so that both entrances to the place were in her view, wanting to spot Trevor before he saw her.

At ten minutes after twelve, when Clay had said for the dozenth time they should leave since the bastard couldn't see fit to show up on time, Trevor walked in from the hotel.

"There he is," she said.

Clay followed her gaze but didn't say anything. Just took a swig from his bottle.

Trevor zeroed in on her and headed her way. He looked…good. He always had, with his blond hair and rough edges. He'd put on some muscles and slimmed down in prison. Andie waited for the old emotions, any of them, to hit her.

She exhaled quietly in relief.

When he got to the table, he glanced at Clay before turning to her.

"Andie. You look great."

Clay tensed and she put a hand on his thigh under the table.

"Trevor, this is Clay Marlow, a friend of mine."

He nodded at Clay. "I hoped we could talk privately."

"Anything you have to tell me you can say in front of Clay."

Trevor seemed to consider that and finally nodded. He slid onto the empty stool.

Their waiter came by and took Trevor's drink order.

"What do you want?" Andie said as soon as the waiter left. "Why have you been stalking me?"

"I knew you saw me at the wedding," he said, taking a handful of peanuts from the bowl on the table and shoving a few in his mouth.

"After we got ice?" Clay asked her, as if finally figuring out why she'd left early.

Andie nodded, distracted. "You were at the Shell Shack again Thursday night."

Trevor tilted his head. "You weren't. Though I've seen you there before. Working."

"Why the hell have you been spying on me?" The idea that he'd been watching her without her knowledge gave her the willies and made her want to slam a heavy object into his head.

"I've been trying to work up the courage to talk to you."

Andie narrowed her eyes. "Like hell."

The waiter delivered Trevor's iced tea and Andie realized it was strange for him not to order a beer. He'd always drunk beer.

Trevor took a drink and set the glass down. "I know you're not going to believe me, Andie, but I've changed."

She scoffed automatically.

"I'm not here to ask you to take me back."

"What are you here for? Cut to the punch line," Andie said. "I've got better things to do."

"The reason I wanted to talk to you is so that I could apologize. I caused you so much pain.... All kinds of pain. I realize you can't forgive me, but I needed to face up to you and say I'm sorry."

Andie looked at Clay and he took her hand, still on his leg, and twined their fingers together.

"Is this for real?" she asked Trevor.

"Why else would I do it? I drove all the way from Illinois, Andie."

She nodded, not sure what to think.

"I won't lie and say it's selfless. Facing up to you is for me."

"So now you've faced me. You've said sorry. You can go." She couldn't begin to process what he was saying, what was happening, because it was so far off from anything she'd ever imagined.

He stood and dug into the pocket of his jeans. "One last thing. I have something that belongs to you. My brother found it in the kitchen."

The kitchen where he'd taken a corkscrew to the inside of her arm and knocked her around until he'd broken three of her bones. The memory made her dizzy, lightheaded.

"Andie?" Clay squeezed her hand as he said her name.

She nodded. "I'm fine."

Trevor held out his hand. "Your necklace. I remember it was important to you."

Andie sucked in her breath and took it from him. "My butterfly necklace."

"The chain was broken. I put a new one on it."

She let it dangle from her fingers, then clasped her fist around it to keep it safe. "Thank you for returning it."

"You couldn't have mailed that to her?" Clay asked.

"I told you, I needed to face her. Apologize."

"Are you supposed to travel out of state?"

"My parole officer knows where I am, in case it's any of your business."

"Then he'll be thrilled to hear you're on your way back home. Thank you for giving Andie her necklace. Don't ever contact her again."

Trevor glanced between Clay and Andie, then nodded.

Andie opened her hand and held the silver charm in her fingers, surveying the etched detail of the butterfly's wings. Remembering. She'd found the necklace on the sidewalk in Chicago not long after she'd left her father's house. It had given her purpose.

"You ready to leave?" Clay asked her.

Andie nodded. "Like he said, don't call me or search for me again," she told Trevor. She was shocked to realize she had trouble summoning any real anger toward him. She couldn't seem to feel anything toward him at all. As if he didn't exist.

"Let's go," Clay said.

She took one last look at Trevor, then grasped Clay's hand. They walked to the parking lot, to Clay's motorcycle.

"You doing okay?" he asked as they put on their helmets.

Andie nodded. "Yeah, actually. That wasn't nearly as bad as I thought it would be. Weird."

They climbed on the bike.

"Home?" he asked over his shoulder.

Andie nodded and frowned, thinking that it wasn't her home anymore. That it was time to leave.

That she didn't want to leave.

ANDIE'S BAGS WERE BY the door, ready to go. She'd been sitting on the futon, staring at them for ten minutes, working up her courage.

Clay didn't know she was planning to take off this afternoon. When they'd gotten back from meeting Trevor, he'd muttered a casual goodbye as he'd hurried up the stairs to Payton, anxious to relieve Bridget since she'd agreed to come over without notice.

Andie heard Bridget descend the stairs. Now was her chance.

She ran her fingers over the butterfly charm she held in one hand, reassuring herself that she wasn't about to make a mistake or a wrong decision. This was the biggest decision of her life and her heart pounded hummingbird fast.

Slowly, she nodded. Closed her eyes. Then popped up off the futon.

She grabbed her small knapsack, jogged up the steps to Clay's door and knocked.

"Hi," she said when he opened it.

"Hi?"

"I was wondering if you could do me a favor."

"Another one?"

"Yes. Two in one day. I'll owe you."

He glanced behind him and Andie spotted Payton sitting in front of the coffee table, rolling out a ball of Play-Doh.

"What do you need?" he asked, stepping outside but keeping the door wide open.

"Could you fasten this necklace around my neck? I've been trying ever since we got home."

His forehead creased but he said, "Turn around."

She turned and held her hair out of the way. She

could feel the heat of him along her back and longed to have him even closer.

He clasped the chain for her and she raised her hand to the charm. She leaned her back against the railing.

"I found this necklace a couple of weeks after I left home," she said.

Clay checked Payton behind him again and stepped out onto the wood planking of the landing next to Andie.

"I was enthralled by the butterfly," Andie continued. "I remember thinking about how a butterfly was so beautiful and delicate-looking and yet…so free. I decided the necklace would be my reminder to be free, to live my life the way I wanted to."

"I like that," Clay said. "A little New Age, but it's a good message."

Andie nodded. "Worked well for me. Until Trevor. I don't know how or when but I stopped living the way I wanted to. I let him control me." She closed her eyes, ashamed at the admission.

Clay touched her arm. "You don't have to talk about this."

"I do. Bear with me." She took a slow breath and continued. "When I met him, I was twenty years old. I'd been on my own for four years. Mostly alone. I'd had roommates and coworkers and guys I stayed with, but no ties. Trevor was the first."

Clay sat on the top step and gestured for her to sit next to him.

Once seated, she continued. "I fell hard for him. He seemed to care so much, did all the right things. Bought me gifts, took me out."

"When did it start getting bad?"

"We'd been living together for almost a year," she said. "A guy I worked with had called one evening while I was out picking up dinner, wanting me to take his hours. Trevor thought he called because there was something going on between us. We fought. He slapped me." She ran her fingers over her eyes. "I forgave him."

Clay took her hand in his.

"It happened infrequently at first. A few weeks would pass without incident. Then he'd get so mad he'd hurt me again."

Clay's jaw was tight and she could see a muscle twitching in his cheek.

"You don't need all the details," she said. "Just that I didn't find the courage to leave him for three more years. And it took a trip to the emergency room even then."

Andie pulled her hand away from him. "I was so stupid. After everything with my dad, I should've gotten out of there after the first time."

Clay ran his thumb soothingly over her fingers. "I can't imagine what you went through. It must've been hell."

"Accurate description. Three years, Clay."

He put his arm around her and drew her to his side. "Why are you telling me this?"

"Because I want you to know who I am. All my stupid decisions."

"Why? What's the point?"

"My point is that if this changes the way you feel about me, I want to know now. I *need* to know."

"Why would it change anything?"

"It's just...hard to really know a person," she said.

"And you want me to know you."

"Yes."

"How come?"

She held up her necklace. "I lost my necklace the last night I was with Trevor. It must've broken when we were fighting. I got the tattoo on my back to replace it. To remind me, permanently, that I can live the way I want to." She turned to face him. "Clay, I love you. I...trust you. Which is kind of a big deal for me."

He took both of her hands in his and the warmth in his eyes told her everything. "I understand that."

She opened her knapsack and took out the gun. As he watched, she unloaded it. Dropping the ammo back in her bag, she held out the gun to him.

"I won't need this anymore. I want to live my life with you. And Payton. If you'll still have me after everything I just told you."

Clay took the gun and tucked it into the back of his jeans. "I love you, too, Andie Tyler. And I'll do better than just *have* you. If you think you're up for it, I'll give you the ride of your life."

"That sounds good on so many—"

"Daddy?" Payton cut in. Andie hadn't heard her come outside. "Is Miss Andie going to marry you now?"

Andie and Clay laughed.

"I'll leave that up to Miss Andie herself." He stood, pulling Andie up with him, their hands still entwined. "What do you say, Miss Andie. Will you marry us?"

Her eyes filled with tears. "That depends," she said, trying to keep a straight face. "Can we all ride together?"

Clay looked down at his daughter. "What do you think, girly? Can that be arranged?"

"Yes!" Payton jumped up and down, which was exactly what Andie felt like doing. So she did. She took Payton's hands in hers and joined her. Then she went back to Clay's arms.

"Yes. I'll marry you. And your daughter and your used Harley and everything else about you."

Clay kissed Andie slowly, thoroughly, until Payton thumped both of them on their legs.

"Hey! You two are gonna have to cut that out sometimes."

Laughing, Clay picked his daughter up. She put

one arm around Clay's neck and one around Andie's. "It's the middle of the afternoon, so we can't ride into the sunset together," Clay joked, "but we could celebrate at Lamberts."

Andie touched her forehead to his. "We could. Since it's a special occasion and all. But after that, for the first time in my life, I plan to stay in as much as possible."

Clay kissed her tenderly. "Welcome home, biker girl."

* * * * *

HARLEQUIN *Super Romance*

COMING NEXT MONTH

Available October 12, 2010

HARLEQUIN®

A *Romance*

FOR EVERY MOOD™

Spotlight on

Inspirational

Wholesome romances
that touch the heart and soul.

See the next page
to enjoy a sneak peek from
the Love Inspired® inspirational series.

*See below for a sneak peek at
our inspirational line, Love Inspired®.
Introducing HIS HOLIDAY BRIDE
by bestselling author Jillian Hart*

Autumn Granger gave her horse rein to slide toward the town's new sheriff.

"Hey, there." The man in a brand-new Stetson, black T-shirt, jeans and riding boots held up a hand in greeting. He stepped away from his four-wheel drive with "Sheriff" in black on the doors and waded through the grasses. "I'm new around here."

"I'm Autumn Granger."

"Nice to meet you, Miss Granger. I'm Ford Sherman, from Chicago." He knuckled back his hat, revealing the most handsome face she'd ever seen. Big blue eyes contrasted with his sun-tanned complexion.

"I'm guessing you haven't seen much open land. Out here, you've got to keep an eye on cows or they're going to tear your vehicle apart."

"What?" He whipped around. Sure enough, mammoth black-and-white creatures had started to gnaw on his four-wheel drive. They clustered like a mob, mouths and tongues and teeth bent on destruction. One cow tried to pry the wiper off the windshield, another chewed on the side mirror. Several leaned through the open window, licking the seats.

"Move along, little dogie." He didn't know the first thing about cattle.

The entire herd swiveled their heads to study him curiously. Not a single hoof shifted. The animals soon returned to chewing, licking, digging through his possessions.

Autumn laughed, a warm and wonderful sound. "Thanks,

I needed that." She then pulled a bag from behind her saddle and waved it at the cows. "Look what I have, guys. Cookies."

Cows swung in her direction, and dozens of liquid brown eyes brightened with cookie hopes. As she circled the car, the cattle bounded after her. The earth shook with the force of their powerful hooves.

"Next time, you're on your own, city boy." She tipped her hat. The cowgirl stayed on his mind, the sweetest thing he had ever seen.

*Will Ford be able to stick it out in the country
to find out more about Autumn?
Find out in HIS HOLIDAY BRIDE
by bestselling author Jillian Hart,
available in October 2010
only from Love Inspired®.*

Rivales en las sombras
Katherine Garbera

HARLEQUIN™

Editado por Harlequin Ibérica.
Una división de HarperCollins Ibérica, S.A.
Núñez de Balboa, 56
28001 Madrid

I.S.B.N.: 978-84-9188-244-2
Depósito legal: M-16120-2018
Impresión en CPI (Barcelona)
Fecha impresion para Argentina: 15.1.19
Distribuidor exclusivo para España: LOGISTA
Distribuidor para México: Distibuidora Intermex, S.A. de C.V.
Distribuidores para Argentina: Interior, DGP, S.A. Alvarado 2118.
Cap. Fed./Buenos Aires y Gran Buenos Aires, VACCARO HNOS.

Harlequin® Historical
Historical Romantic Adventure!

THE MISTLETOE WAGER

Christine Merrill

Harry Pennyngton, Earl of Anneslea,
is surprised when his estranged wife,
Helena, arrives home for Christmas.
Especially when she's intent on
divorce! A festive house party
is in full swing when the guests
are snowed in, and Harry and
Helena find they are together
under the mistletoe....

*Available December 2008
wherever books are sold.*

www.eHarlequin.com   HH29525

REQUEST YOUR FREE BOOKS!

2 FREE NOVELS PLUS 2 FREE GIFTS!

◆ HARLEQUIN®

INTRIGUE®

Breathtaking Romantic Suspense

YES! Please send me 2 FREE Harlequin Intrigue® novels and my 2 FREE gifts (gifts are worth about $10). After receiving them, if I don't wish to receive any more books, I can return the shipping statement marked "cancel." If I don't cancel, I will receive 6 brand-new novels every month and be billed just $4.24 per book in the U.S. or $4.99 per book in Canada, plus 25¢ shipping and handling per book and applicable taxes, if any*. That's a savings of close to 15% off the cover price! I understand that accepting the 2 free books and gifts places me under no obligation to buy anything. I can always return a shipment and cancel at any time. Even if I never buy another book from Harlequin, the two free books and gifts are mine to keep forever.

182 HDN EEZ7 382 HDN EEZK

Name	(PLEASE PRINT)	
Address		Apt. #
City	State/Prov.	Zip/Postal Code

Signature (if under 18, a parent or guardian must sign)

Mail to the **Harlequin Reader Service:**
IN U.S.A.: P.O. Box 1867, Buffalo, NY 14240-1867
IN CANADA: P.O. Box 609, Fort Erie, Ontario L2A 5X3

Not valid to current subscribers of Harlequin Intrigue books.

**Want to try two free books from another line?
Call 1-800-873-8635 or visit www.morefreebooks.com.**

* Terms and prices subject to change without notice. N.Y. residents add applicable sales tax. Canadian residents will be charged applicable provincial taxes and GST. Offer not valid in Quebec. This offer is limited to one order per household. All orders subject to approval. Credit or debit balances in a customer's account(s) may be offset by any other outstanding balance owed by or to the customer. Please allow 4 to 6 weeks for delivery. Offer available while quantities last.

Your Privacy: Harlequin is committed to protecting your privacy. Our Privacy Policy is available online at www.eHarlequin.com or upon request from the Reader Service. From time to time we make our lists of customers available to reputable third parties who may have a product or service of interest to you. If you would prefer we not share your name and address, please check here. ☐

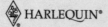 **HARLEQUIN®**

INTRIGUE

COMING NEXT MONTH

#1101 CHRISTMAS DELIVERY by Patricia Rosemoor
A Holiday Mystery at Jenkins Cove
Lexie Thornton gave up on romance after the love of her life was killed at an early age. But when Simon Shea mysteriously returned, Lexie's world turned upside down. Could Simon help Lexie unlock the secrets surrounding their pasts?

#1102 CHRISTMAS CRIME IN COLORADO by Cassie Miles
When Brooke Johnson found herself the target of a serial killer, it was up to police detective Michael Shaw to protect her. But then their professional relationship turned personal, and Michael knew survival depended on Brooke escaping the memories of her tragic past.

#1103 HIGH SCHOOL REUNION by Mallory Kane
Once Ultimate Agent Laurel Gillespie uncovered a ten-year-old clue that a former classmate's suicide may have been murder, her high school reunion turned deadly. With the help of former crush police chief Cade Dupree, Laurel was determined to solve the case, even if it meant losing Cade's affection—or her life.

#1104 THE MISSING MILLIONAIRE by Dani Sinclair
Harrison Trent's life was abruptly interrupted when beautiful Jamie Bellman claimed to be his bodyguard. To protect Harrison from the strange attacks, Jamie would risk everything—even losing her heart.

#1105 TALL, DARK AND LETHAL by Dana Marton
Thriller
With dangerous men hot on his trail, the last thing Cade Palmer needed was attractive Bailey Preston seeking his help to escape from attackers of her own. Could Cade tame the free-spirited Bailey as they fled both their enemies and the law?

#1106 A BODYGUARD FOR CHRISTMAS by Donna Young
The clues to Jordan Beck's hunt for his father's killers lay in the mind of beautiful bookseller Regina Menlow. With time running out, would Jordan and Regina be able to expose the terrorist who planned to wreak nuclear havoc on Christmas day?

Si se lo hubiera confiado a sus hermanas, no tendría que lidiar con Dec en aquel momento.

La larga mesa de juntas era de madera oscura y las sillas que la rodeaban de cuero. Se concentró en los detalles de la sala en vez de en el hombre que estaba de pie junto a la ventana. Apenas había cambiado en el año y medio que hacía que no lo veía.

Por detrás, reparó en que llevaba su pelo castaño rojizo más largo, pero seguía ondulándose al llegar al cuello de la camisa. Ancho de hombros y esbelto de cintura, seguía teniendo el cuerpo imponente que recordaba entrelazado al suyo. Un escalofrío la recorrió.

«No, no pienses en eso. Concéntrate en la adquisición. Cada cosa a su tiempo», se dijo.

—Dec, no pensé que volvería a verte.

Había pronunciado su nombre. Su voz había sonado decidida, lo que le agradó a pesar de que estaba temblando por dentro.

—Espero que sea una agradable sorpresa —replicó él, y sonrió con ironía.

Luego, se apartó de la ventana y se acercó a ella hasta quedarse a apenas a un palmo de distancia.

El aroma familiar de su loción para el afeitado la envolvió y cerró los ojos al recordar la intensidad de aquel olor en la base de su cuello. Se obligó a recuperar la compostura, se cruzó de brazos y se recordó que estaba allí por negocios. Unos golpes en la puerta le sirvieron de distracción.

—Adelante —dijo ella.

Ally, su secretaria, apareció con dos tazas con el logotipo de Infinity Games, y le dio una a cada

Capítulo Uno

Cari Chandler se detuvo bajo el umbral de la puerta de la sala de conferencias. En la pared del fondo había un retrato de su abuelo, de joven, con expresión decidida. Ahora se daba cuenta de que apenas sonreía. En aquel momento no estaría muy contento, puesto que el nieto de su enemigo más odiado estaba en sus dominios.

Desde finales de los años setenta, los Chandler y los Montrose habían estado enfrentados, tratando de sacarse mutuamente del mercado de los videojuegos. Su abuelo había ganado aquella trifulca hacía mucho tiempo, llegando a un acuerdo con una compañía japonesa y dejando fuera a Thomas Montrose. Pero nada de eso importaba ya, puesto que los herederos Montrose y su empresa Playtone Games habían dado el golpe de gracia con la adquisición hostil de Infinity Games. A Cari y sus hermanas, Emma y Jessi, solo les quedaba recoger los restos e intentar alcanzar algún tipo de acuerdo para salvar sus trabajos y su legado.

Cari, en su calidad de directora de gestión, había sido la elegida para tratar con Declan Montrose. Tenía sentido, puesto que se encargaba de las negociaciones, pero el secreto que llevaba tanto tiempo ocultando de repente se le hacía asfixiante.

uno. Cari rodeó la mesa hasta la cabecera. Se sentía más segura sentándose al otro lado de él. Ally le preguntó a Dec cómo le gustaba el café y le contestó que lo tomaba solo. Luego, se fue.

—Por favor, toma asiento.

—No te recordaba tan formal —replicó él, apartando una silla para sentarse.

Cari ignoró su comentario. ¿Qué podía decir? Desde la primera vez que lo había visto, se había sentido atraída por él. Incluso después de enterarse de que era un Montrose y, por ende, enemigo de su familia, había seguido deseándolo.

—Asumo que estás aquí para analizar los activos de mi compañía.

Él asintió.

—Me dedicaré las próximas seis semanas a evaluar los activos de la compañía sobre el terreno. Tengo entendido que tenéis tres divisiones de juego diferentes.

Debería habérselo imaginado. Había dejado a un lado las emociones para dedicarse a los negocios. Le gustaría poder hacer lo mismo, pero no se le daba bien ocultar sus sentimientos. Cíborg, había oído que lo llamaban, un apodo le hacía justicia.

La miró y en aquel instante se dio cuenta de que se había quedado estudiándolo fijamente. Aquello no iba a funcionar. En cuanto se fuera, llamaría a Emma, su hermana mayor y directora general de Infinity, y le pediría que ella o Jessi trataran con Dec.

—¿Cari?

—Lo siento. Sí, tenemos juegos para consola, móvil y en línea. Superviso las tres áreas.

–Necesito reunirme con todos los empleados y evaluarlos a cada uno. Luego redactaré un informe para la junta directiva con mis recomendaciones.

–Claro, sin problemas. Emma ya me había avisado de que querrías conocer a los empleados. ¿Qué vendrás, uno o dos días por semana? –preguntó, cruzando los dedos.

–No, quiero tener un despacho aquí para poder estar en el meollo –dijo echándose hacia delante–. ¿Acaso va a ser un problema?

–En absoluto –replicó Cari con la mejor sonrisa que pudo esbozar.

Al verlo reír, supo que su sonrisa había quedado demasiado forzada.

–Nunca se te ha dado bien ocultar tus sentimientos –observó él.

Cari sacudió la cabeza. Habían tenido una aventura de una noche, no una relación.

–No digas eso. No me conoces. Lo único que tuvimos fue una cita y una noche juntos.

–Creo que me hice una idea de cómo eres.

–¿De veras? –dijo ella–. Entonces, ¿por qué me dejaste sola en aquella habitación de hotel?

Dec se recostó en su asiento y dio un largo sorbo a su café antes de levantarse y acercarse hasta ella. Luego se apoyó en la mesa y se quedó mirándola desde arriba. Cari se sintió tentada a levantarse, pero no quería que creyera que la intimidaba.

–No soy hombre de compromisos –dijo por fin–. Y, aunque creas que no te conozco, Cari Chandler, tendría que estar ciego para no darme cuenta de que las cosas te afectan demasiado.

Quería negarlo, pero lo cierto era que tenía un corazón generoso, como el resto de la familia Chandler. Trabajaba como voluntaria en varias causas, donando su tiempo y su dinero, y en más de una ocasión se había sentido conmovida por alguna historia en el trabajo. Al principio Emma se había enfadado, hasta que se había dado cuenta de que así se ganaba la lealtad de los empleados porque sentían que los directivos se preocupaban.

—No esperarías que me aferrara a ti y te profesara amor eterno, Dec.

Apenas lo conocía a pesar de que habían compartido una noche de sexo. Tal vez le habría gustado volver a verlo y conocerlo mejor, pero había descubierto todo lo que necesitaba saber después de que se fuera.

—Fue solo una noche —añadió.

—Una noche fabulosa, Cari —dijo, y tomando el respaldo de la silla, la hizo girar para que lo mirara—. Quizá debería recordarte lo bien que lo pasamos juntos.

Ella empujó la silla hacia atrás y se levantó. Había llegado el momento de tomar el control de aquella reunión.

—No es necesario. Aunque me acuerde de los detalles de aquella noche, lo que se me quedó grabado fue la mañana de después.

—Por eso me marché. No se me da bien lidiar con las secuelas.

—¿Las secuelas?

—Ya sabes, las mujeres os ponéis muy sentimentales y decís cosas empalagosas.

Cari sacudió la cabeza. Estaba claro que para Dec no era más que una aventura pasajera. Con su secreto en mente, sabía que debía comentar algo de la noche que habían compartido, pero de momento no iba a hacerlo. Se concentraría en los negocios y en encontrar la manera de salvar el legado de su familia sin que fuera desmantelado y destruido.

Tenía que admitir que oír a Dec la ponía triste porque quería algo mejor para ella. Le habría gustado que le dijera que no había querido irse y que había pensado en ella cada día. Probablemente, aquellos eran los comentarios que él consideraba empalagosos.

–¿Decepcionada?

–Supongo que es por eso por lo que un codiciado multimillonario como tú sigue soltero.

Trató de disimular lo desencantada que se sentía porque fuera exactamente como había pensado que era. Había tenido esperanzas de haberlo conocido en un mal día.

–Quizá es que no he encontrado a la mujer adecuada que me haga cambiar –comentó con una medio sonrisa pretenciosa.

–No pareces un hombre al que se pueda hacer cambiar.

–*Touché*. Estoy contento con mi vida, pero eso no significa que no sepa valorar a una mujer como tú cuando se cruza en mi camino.

Quería seguir enfadada con él, pero estaba siendo sincero y no podía culparlo. Aunque le habría gustado tener algo más con Dec, había sabido desde el momento en que habían salido a cenar que lo único que buscaba era una aventura.

–Creo que tendría más suerte encontrando una aguja en un pajar.

–Cena conmigo y averígualo.

–¿Estarías dispuesto a considerar que Playtone Games sea socio sin voto en Infinity?

Dec rio.

–Imposible.

–Entonces no hay cena.

Necesitaba poner distancia y pensar antes de cometer alguna estupidez con él.

–Tenemos que trabajar codo con codo y no creo que pasar tiempo juntos fuera de la oficina sea apropiado –dijo ella por fin.

Antes era más impulsiva, pero después de la noche que había pasado con aquel hombre había aprendido que actuar sin pensar traía consecuencias.

–La Cari que conozco no toma decisiones solo con la cabeza.

–He cambiado –afirmó con rotundidad.

–Eso me gusta.

Cari era consciente de que tenía que asumir que el hombre con el que había tenía una aventura de una noche había vuelto. Cada vez tenía más claro que la compra de la compañía era el menor de sus problemas. Iba a tener que hablarle de su hijo, del hijo de ambos.

Pero no tenía ni idea de cómo hacerlo.

***

Cari había cambiado. Era evidente incluso para alguien como él, que solo había pasado una noche con ella. Dec sabía que las cosas entre ellos siempre serían complicadas, y mucho más en aquel momento. Sus familias eran enemigas y su primo, Keller Montrose, el presidente de Playtone Games, no iba a estar contento hasta que no quedara nada de Infinity y del legado de Gregory Chandler.

Aquella preciosa rubia que tenía ante él no iba a ser más que otro daño colateral.

Dec nunca la había considerado una enemiga. Desde el primer momento en que la había visto, había deseado conocerla mejor y no con el fin de usar esa información para arrebatarle su compañía.

Al ser adoptado, nunca se había sentido un verdadero Montrose, y siempre se había tenido que esforzarse en demostrar que era tan leal como Kell y su otro primo, Allan McKinney.

De vuelta en California y teniendo por oponente a Cari, era la ocasión de demostrar su valía ante la familia Montrose, además de volver a encontrarse con la mujer a la que no había olvidado. Con su cabello rubio cayendo en suaves ondas por sus hombros y sus bonitos ojos azules, lo había hechizado. No había podido olvidar su mirada mientras la había tenido entre sus brazos.

Fijándose con más atención, se daba cuenta de que el año y medio que había transcurrido desde que se separaron le había aportado una mayor confianza en sí misma. Fue subiendo la mirada desde sus zapatos marrones de cinco centímetros de tacón. Seguía teniendo los tobillos finos, pero sus gemelos parecían más musculosos. Aunque la falda le impedía ver mejor sus piernas, parecía haber ensanchado de caderas. La chaqueta evidenciaba que su cintura seguía siendo estrecha, pero sus pechos… Vaya, sus pechos eran bastante más generosos.

–Mírame aquí –dijo ella, señalándose los ojos azules.

Él se encogió de hombros y sonrió.

–Veo que has cambiado mucho en el último año. Has ganado curvas y eso me gusta.

Caminó hacia ella con pasos largos y lánguidos, y Cari fue retrocediendo hasta que no tuvo dónde meterse. Levantó el brazo para detenerlo, manteniéndolo apartado. Él permaneció allí, mirándola a los ojos, y tuvo que admitir que había cambiado. Había algo diferente en sus ojos. Lo estaba observando con más atención de lo que nunca antes lo había hecho.

Parecía cansada, aunque era normal teniendo en cuenta que Playtone por fin se había hecho con Infinity Games, y seguramente estaría preocupada por su puesto de trabajo.

Dec se apartó de ella.

–Lo siento. No pretendía avasallarte. Estoy seguro de que perder la compañía y que quede bajo nuestro control tiene que ser muy duro.

–No exageres.

Aquel comentario le provocó una sonrisa.

–Todavía no me he acostumbrado a la diferencia horaria.

–¿Diferencia horaria? No sabía que la hubiera

entre la sede de Infinity Games y las oficinas de Playtone.

Era muy ingeniosa. Dec se preguntó cómo no se había dado cuenta de esa característica de Cari año y medio antes. Claro que en aquel momento se había dejado llevar por el placer y había perdido el control.

–He pasado un año en Australia ocupado con la adquisición de Kanga Games.

–Esa compañía la habéis mantenido tal cual.

–Ellos no fastidiaban a nuestro abuelo.

–Mis hermanas y yo tampoco. Siempre os hemos tratado con respeto a ti y a tus primos.

–Me temo que eso no cuenta cuando se trata de venganzas –dijo él.

–Pero seguro que los beneficios sí.

–Claro.

Cari asintió, regresó a su silla y tomó asiento después de que lo hiciera él. Luego, entrelazó los dedos y Dec reparó en el anillo de la mano derecha que antes no llevaba. Era una sortija de platino con una fila de diamantes en el centro, el clásico regalo de un enamorado. Tal vez, mantenía una relación con alguien.

Quizá esa fuera la explicación de aquella seguridad en sí misma. Tenía un amante. Debería alegrarse por ella, aunque lo lamentaba si eso suponía no volver a besarla nunca más.

–¿Cuándo regresaste de Australia? –preguntó Cari jugueteando con el anillo.

Aquel simple gesto evidenciaba su nerviosismo.

–El sábado, pero todavía no me he acostumbrado al cambio de hora. Además, me he sorprendido al verte –admitió.

Se agachó para tomar el maletín que había dejado junto a su silla y lo puso en la mesa. Dentro tenía el ordenador y los informes que había empezado a preparar para la toma de posesión.

–¿Por qué te has sorprendido? Sabía que eras tú el que iba a venir. ¿Acaso no sabías que ibas a tener que tratar conmigo?

–Sí, Emma me lo dijo en un correo electrónico –respondió.

Lo que no iba a decirle era que no esperaba que su presencia le afectara tanto. Había pensado que después de haberse acostado con ella, la química entre ellos habría desaparecido. Pero se había equivocado.

Su cuerpo no tenía misterio para él. No había ni un solo centímetro que no recordara, aunque, teniéndola delante en carne y hueso, todos aquellos recuerdos que tenía de ella palidecían ante la mujer real.

Quería tener la oportunidad de explorar sus curvas y, no solo eso, sino de descubrir los secretos que guardaba en su interior. Si se entretenía con ella, tal vez consiguiera dejar de hacer tanta introspección.

De hecho, cuanto más pensaba en ello, más le parecía que Cari era la distracción perfecta para lo que fuera que le estaba afectando últimamente.

Necesitaba una distracción, y *voilà*, el destino había puesto en su camino a la única mujer a la que no había podido olvidar. Recordó que tenía seis semanas para completar la toma de posesión. Seguro que sería tiempo más que suficiente para satisfacer la curiosidad que sentía por ella, aunque aquella adquisición hostil no iba a facilitar la seducción. De hecho, si fuera prudente, lo mejor que podía hacer era olvidarse de los asuntos personales y concentrarse en los negocios. Pero se trataba de Cari, la mujer cuyo recuerdo lo había perseguido durante los últimos dieciocho meses, y tenía la oportunidad de averiguar por qué. ¿Sería porque solo había pasado una noche con ella? ¿Había algo más entre ellos?

–Entonces, ¿cuál es el problema? –preguntó ella con una medio sonrisa, y se echó hacia delante.

–No hay ningún problema.

Ella se levantó y puso los brazos en jarras. Aquella postura tensó la chaqueta sobre sus pechos generosos. Parecía estar flirteando y eso le gustaba, aunque presentía que era algo forzado.

–¿Estás seguro? ¿No será porque nuestras familias son enemigos acérrimos?

Le habría gustado responder que sí, pero sospechaba que el problema estaba en él. Apenas había dejado de viajar desde la última vez que la había visto y echaba de menos estar en casa. Nunca había tenido un sitio que considerara su hogar, ni el yate que tenía amarrado en el puerto de Marina del Rey y que había bautizado como *Big Spender,* en el que vivía, ni tampoco la mansión de Beverly Hills que había heredado de sus padres.

El deseo de tener algo permanente le había asaltado tres meses antes, y sabía que tenía que superarlo. Eso no iba con él. Había sido maravilloso ser adoptado por la familia Montrose, pero después de que sus padres lo usaran como títere en su divorcio, había descubierto que prefería estar solo. Más tarde, a la edad de veinticinco, había perdido a su padre en un trágico accidente de esquí, y dos años más tarde, a su madre le había fallado el hígado después de todo el alcohol que había ingerido para sobrellevar su vida.

Apartó aquellos pensamientos de su cabeza para contestar a la pregunta de Cari. ¿Le molestaba aquel enfrentamiento? Era algo con lo que había crecido, algo que formaba parte de su familia, y no podía ignorarlo.

–Tal vez –contestó.

Aunque iba a ser imparcial en su informe, sabía que Kell pretendía despedir a las tres hermanas Chandler en venganza por lo que su familia le había hecho a su abuelo en el pasado.

Era una tontería mantener una relación con Cari en aquel momento, y él no era un estúpido. Iba a tener que esforzarse en recordarlo porque, tal y como le estaba sonriendo en aquel momento, empezaba a creer que la relación funcionaría.

–Quiero tener la oportunidad de demostrarte que Infinity debería mantenerse íntegramente –dijo ella.

Estaba siendo sincera. Maldijo porque aquella afirmación le daba la excusa para volver a invitarla a salir. Claro que siempre podía convencerse de que iba a salir con ella por negocios y no porque estuviera deseando volver a besarla.

15

—Cena conmigo esta noche —le dijo.

Cari palideció, se mordió el labio inferior y apartó la mirada.

—No creo que eso sea una buena idea. Las próximas semanas van a ser muy complicadas.

No era precisamente un no, pensó Dec.

—Cierto, pero eso no es motivo para que no podamos ser civilizados. No estoy diciendo que nos vayamos a mi casa después de cenar…

—Ni hablar. Ahora soy mucho más prudente.

—¿Ves? Eso es lo que quiero que me expliques. Vamos a estar muy ocupados en el trabajo.

Quería saber más de ella. No había tenido suficiente con el tiempo que habían compartido hacía año y medio. Aquel podía ser un buen momento, mientras analizaba su empresa, para conocerla mejor.

—Estoy de acuerdo —dijo ella con una sonrisa traviesa que le hizo desear acercarse y besarla.

—Estupendo. ¿A qué hora te recojo?

—Me refería a que estaba de acuerdo con tu comentario.

Cari suspiró, apartó la silla de la mesa y se quedó mirándolo como si buscara algo. Después, pareció haber tomado una decisión y asintió.

—Dime dónde y me reuniré contigo a las siete. Ahora voy a pedirle a Ally que te busque un despacho y, hasta en tanto haya uno disponible, puedes trabajar en esta sala de juntas.

Dec dejó que se sintiera al mando de la situación y la observó caminar hasta la puerta, balanceando las caderas. La siguió unos pasos. Era su manera de despedirlo y, para Dec, eso era inaceptable.

A pesar de lo que Cari creyera, era él el que estaba al mando de aquella situación, tanto en la vertiente empresarial como personal. Lo había despedido como a un sirviente, algo que no toleraba de ninguna manera y menos aún estando aturdido por la diferencia horaria.

Cari se volvió y jadeó al ver lo cerca que estaba de ella. Luego se chupó los labios y Dec se percató de que era su manera de recuperar la compostura.

No había podido olvidar su sabor ni la sensación de sus labios junto a los suyos y, en aquel momento, lo que más deseaba era unir sus bocas. Siempre había conseguido todo lo que había querido y, hasta que no la había visto aparecer en la sala de juntas tan serena y segura de sí misma, no se había dado cuenta de lo mucho que la deseaba.

—¿Querías algo más?

—Solo esto —contestó él.

Luego bajó la cabeza y le robó el beso que tanto había deseado desde que la vio entrar en aquella sala, arrepintiéndose por haberla dejado tantos meses atrás.

Capítulo Dos

Cari no tenía planeado aquello. En absoluto. No esperaba sentir sus labios junto a los suyos ni deleitarse con su sabor tan familiar. Cuánto había echado de menos aquello. Entonces, se corrigió. No, no había echado de menos nada. Dec solo había sido la aventura de una noche. Aunque le habría gustado que fuera algo más, a él solo le había interesado de ella el sexo.

No quería mostrarse apasionada entre sus brazos, pero llevaba tiempo sintiéndose sola, más preocupada por su instinto maternal que femenino. Dec estaba despertando algo en ella que pensaba que había desaparecido. Una oleada de deseo la recorrió. La sangre parecía hervirle en las venas.

Lo rodeó con los brazos por los hombros, estaba decidida a disfrutar de cada segundo. Ladeó la cabeza, acopló su boca a la suya y lamió su lengua. Él gimió y, por primera vez desde que había vuelto a aparecer en su vida, sintió cierto control.

Pero ese control fue efímero. Cuando la tomó de las caderas y la atrajo hacia él para que sintiera su erección, sus pechos reaccionaron.

Sorprendida y temiendo que se diera cuenta, Cari alzó la cabeza y lo miró a la cara. Tenía los ojos cerrados y había un rubor de deseo en su piel.

Era un hombre impetuoso, pero sus labios siempre se habían movido con suavidad sobre los suyos. Subió la mano y le acarició el labio inferior con el pulgar. Se detuvo un momento, confiando en poder resolver el conflicto que se debatía en su interior. Pero entonces, Dec se aferró a sus caderas y supo que aquello solo le traería más complicaciones.

Dejó caer los brazos y se cerró la chaqueta para asegurarse de que no viera la humedad y adivinara que tenía un bebé.

Suspiró. No estaba preparada para que Dec volviera a su vida. Se había creado una rutina con su trabajo y su hijo, y de pronto Playtone Games y Dec lo estaban poniendo todo patas arriba. Deseó tomar a DJ y esconderse en el sótano hasta que aquello hubiera pasado, pero no podía salir huyendo. Estaba al cargo de la gestión del día a día y ella era la persona más indicada para informar a Dec del personal. Tenía que persuadirlo para que mantuviera al mayor número de empleados posible.

Él rio.

—¿Tan malo ha sido mi beso?

—Todo lo contrario, ha estado bien —dijo ella, decidida a ser sincera.

Nunca se le había dado bien mentir, algo de lo que se habían dado cuenta sus hermanas desde el primer momento en que se había negado a darles el nombre del padre de DJ. Pero se había empeñado en mantener el secreto dada la mala relación entre la familia de Dec y la suya.

—Entonces, ¿por qué suspiras? —preguntó atrayéndola hacia él.

Cari colocó la mano entre ellos para mantener la distancia y la sensación de control, porque era evidente que no había estado al mando de nada desde el momento en que había entrado en la sala de juntas. Retrocedió un paso y se topó con la puerta.

Él fue a agarrarla, pero Cari sacudió la cabeza.

—No puedo hacer esto, Dec. Tenemos que hablar y hay cosas que…

—No estoy haciendo esto por venganza.

—¿Cómo?

Ni siquiera se le había pasado por la cabeza, pero al oírselo mencionar, no le sorprendió la idea de que uno de los nietos de Thomas Montrose pretendiera vengarse sexualmente de la nieta de su enemigo.

—Solo quiero que sepas que lo que hay entre nosotros no tiene nada que ver con los negocios ni con nuestras familias. Esto es entre tú y yo, solo entre nosotros —dijo él.

—Me gustaría que así fuera.

No pudo evitar pensar en su hijo y en sus hermanas, y en el hecho de que a pesar de lo que él quisiera creer, lo cierto era que no vivían en una isla. Nunca estarían solos.

—Es mi opinión. No permito que mis primos gobiernen mi vida personal —dijo, apartándole un mechón de pelo y colocándoselo detrás de una oreja—. Tenía la impresión de que tú también tomabas tus propias decisiones.

—Por supuesto. Deja ya de… ¿Qué es exactamente lo que quieres de mí?

Estaba asustada y nerviosa, pero no por él sino por ella. Le sería fácil rendirse y darle lo que quería, una relación pasajera. Pero ella no era así. Dec Montrose era peligroso, se dijo, y no podía olvidarlo.

–Quiero una oportunidad. No que me juzgues por mis primos ni por esta compraventa. Nada de eso tiene que ver con lo que hay entre nosotros.

–Ya te he dicho que cenaré contigo.

Nada le gustaría más que creer lo que decía. Si fuera ingenua, se lo creería a pies juntillas, pero no lo era. ¿O acaso sí?

Se cruzó de brazos sin importarle que pensara que se estaba poniendo a la defensiva. Tenía que decidir cómo comportarse con Dec. Nunca se le había dado bien manipular a las personas. Prefería ayudarlas a encontrar la felicidad. Y lo que Dec quería eran dos cosas que no la dejarían en buena posición. Por un lado, su compañía y, por otro, estaba segura de que una vez que supiera de DJ, querría quedarse con su hijo.

–Quiero más que una cena.

–Eso es evidente –replicó ella.

–Nunca he sido sutil. Kell dice que con esta cara no puedo serlo –dijo señalándosela.

No era el clásico guapo, pero tenía una barbilla prominente y unos ojos marrones que le habían hecho imposible apartar la vista de él en el pasado, y también en aquel momento.

–Sabes sacar provecho de ella.

Él se encogió de hombros.

–Supongo que tuve que aprender desde pequeño a aprovecharme de mis puntos fuertes.

–Yo también. Nunca fui tan enérgica como Emma ni tan rebelde como Jessi. Tuve que encontrar mi propio camino.

–No te ha ido mal, por lo que parece. Todos con los que he hablado dicen que eres el alma de Infinity Games.

Cerró los ojos. Prefería que los empleados hubieran dicho que era la más arisca de la compañía. Eso lo haría todo más sencillo en aquella negociación. ¿Qué podía decir? Siempre se había preocupado por su personal y porque rindieran al máximo.

–Tú, sin embargo, eres el brazo ejecutor de Playtone Games.

–Así que soy un hombre de piedra que no tiene corazón. ¿Es así como me ves?

Cari se quedó sin respiración al ver un destello de dolor en sus ojos. Pero rápidamente desapareció y volvió a aparecer el galán seductor. Todavía no sabía muy bien qué quería de ella, pero estaba decidida a conocer mejor a aquel hombre. Tenía tiempo hasta la cena para pensar en cómo contarle lo de DJ y en encontrar la manera de convencerlo de que no despidiera a los empleados. También tenía que decidir hasta dónde pensaba llegar con él.

Tenía la desagradable sensación de que lo último iba a ser lo más difícil de todo.

Dec siempre había tenido la sensación de que era diferente a todos los demás. Ya de adulto, se había dado cuenta de que aquello tenía que ver con el hecho de ser adoptado. Su madre había insistido en que fuera tratado como el resto de los herederos Montrose, pero en su interior, Dec siempre había sabido que no era un heredero auténtico, y eso le había afectado.

Normalmente, un comentario así no le habría importado. Sabía que lo consideraban un tiburón, alguien frío y despiadado, un hombre sin escrúpulos a la hora de despedir a los empleados. Así eran los negocios. Por lo general, los que lo decían, eran aquellos a los que despedía. Pero oírle decir a Cari que no tenía corazón, le había dado que pensar.

–Así que un hombre de piedra, ¿eh, Cari? –repitió al ver que no respondía a su pregunta.

–No lo decía en ese sentido.

Pero reparó en que se mordía el labio inferior. Lo había dicho de corazón.

–No estoy aquí para hacerte daño a ti o a tu compañía. De hecho, como accionista, creo que deberías estar contenta por la compra. A pesar de la enemistad entre nuestras familias, vas a ser una mujer muy rica cuando esta operación termine.

–¿El dinero es lo más importante para ti, verdad?

–No soy un hombre sin sentimientos.

–Lo siento, no era mi intención ser descortés –dijo sin dejar de morderse el labio–. Bueno, quizá un poco sí. Es solo que me gustaría entenderte mejor.

Se adivinaba en su tono que estaba escondiendo algo, o quizá solo se lo estaba ocultando a él. Tal vez acababa de darse cuenta de que un simple beso no iba a ser suficiente. Por su parte, estaba deseando volver a abrazarla.

–Pues te deseo buena suerte –dijo él–. Tengo dinero suficiente para llevar una vida cómoda y no tenerme que preocupar. Aunque no es mal objetivo en la vida. La mayoría de la gente siempre quiere más.

–Cierto. ¿Es esa la razón por la que nuestros socios os vendieron sus participaciones?

–No fui yo el que trató con ellos, así que no lo sé. Pero cuando decidieron invertir en Infinity Games, buscaban ganancias.

–Lo sé. Es solo que odio los cambios.

A él, siempre le habían dado igual los cambios. Era consciente de que la vida era un continuo cambio. La gente que se volvía cómoda, acababa… Bueno, como Cari en aquel momento.

–No soy despiadado con el personal. ¿Es eso lo que te preocupa?

Ella sacudió la cabeza y jugueteó con el anillo de su mano derecha.

–Contigo hay que andarse siempre con cuidado, Dec. Esta mañana estaba decidida a mostrarme fría y distante y, sin embargo, he dejado que me besaras.

–Me gusta cómo eres –dijo él.

Ella esbozó aquella medio sonrisa que había llamado su atención en la convención de Atlanta. Era dulce y tentadora, e incitaba a un hombre a hacer todo lo necesario para que no se le borrara de los labios.

–Me alegro porque soy demasiado mayor para cambiar.

Él rio. A pesar de que formaba parte de la estirpe que más odiaba su familia, Cari no tenía malicia.

–Si tú eres mayor, yo debo de parecer un anciano.

Cari se atusó el pelo y dejó caer los brazos antes de quedarse fijamente mirándolo.

–Por ti no pasan los años. Sé que tienes trabajo que hacer. Si necesitas algo, pídeselo a mi secretaria, a menos que quieras que venga alguien a asistirte.

–No, no necesito secretaria. Además, una manera de reducir costes es aprovechar el personal en plantilla.

–¿Reducir costes? ¿Es eso en lo único que piensas cuando haces negocios? –preguntó ella.

Por su tono, no parecía compartir su criterio. Si le hubiera preguntado algo así sobre su vida personal, entonces sí se habría molestado. En los negocios, no había sitio para las emociones. Si por algún sitio se perdía dinero, había que atajarlo, y en Infinity Games se habían tomado demasiadas decisiones malas, quizá llevados por el corazón y no por la cartera. Eso los había llevado a una pérdida de control, y Dec estaba allí para poner orden.

–¿Qué otra cosa podría importarme? Al final, lo único que importan son las cifras. Por eso es por lo que hemos podido hacernos con tu compañía.

–A mí no me mueven los números, a mí me gusta que mis empleados trabajen y sean productivos.

–Quizá deberías haber estado más atenta a los números.

No había dicho nada cuando se había referido a ella como el alma de la compañía. Por experiencia, sabía que eso significaba que era una persona emocional. Tenía la sensación de que no sabía decir que no a sus empleados. Le gustaría estar equivocado, pero rara vez lo estaba. Eso significaba que iban a estar en desacuerdo en muchos aspectos.

Lo que quería de Cari no tenía nada que ver con los negocios. Haría su trabajo e intentaría conocerla mejor. Podía hacer ambas cosas a la vez sin que interfirieran.

–Bueno, claro que sé que los resultados son importantes, pero también pienso en la gente que hay detrás. Creo que tienen que sentirse seguros en el trabajo para dar lo mejor de sí mismos.

–Será interesante trabajar juntos. Tengo la sensación de que no te conozco, Cari.

–Es que no me conoces –replicó ella–. La mayoría de los hombres ven lo que quieren de las mujeres.

–Interesante razonamiento. ¿Crees que me conoces bien?

Ella se sonrojó.

–Lo siento. Es solo que odio la idea de que con tan solo mirar un papel puedas decir que necesitamos recortar personal, cuando detrás hay muchas personas con sus vidas.

–No voy a reducir el número de empleados así, a la ligera. Necesitamos ver por dónde estáis perdiendo dinero, Cari. Espero que seas consciente de que vuestra compañía no da tantos beneficios como podría.

–Sí, lo sé. Como dijiste, tenemos que trabajar juntos para que vuelva a ser rentable –dijo ella.

Luego, tomó el pomo de la puerta y Dec tuvo la sensación de que quería huir de él. ¿Cómo culparla? Ya le había dado dos cosas en que pensar.

–Lo siento –dijo él suavemente.

No tenía intención de aparecer en su vida de aquella manera. Lo cierto era que no tenía intención de aparecer en su vida de ninguna manera. No era el tipo de mujer con la que tendría una aventura, ni aunque no hubiera existido aquella enemistad entre sus familias.

No solo era el alma de aquella compañía de juegos, también era cariñosa y compasiva, cualidades desconocidas para el hijo de Beau y Helene Montrose. Por él se habían enfrentado y, al final, cuando su madre se había quedado sin argumentos, se lo había tenido que entregar a Thomas Montrose para usarlo como arma en aquella guerra contra los Chandler.

–Es imposible que esto salga bien –dijo ella.

–¿A qué te refieres?

–Te marchaste sin volver la vista atrás y seguramente pensaste que nuestros caminos no volverían a cruzarse. Ahora tenemos que trabajar juntos, y mientras que yo quiero salvar nuestra compañía, tú…

–Haré lo que mejor se me da –la interrumpió.

–¿Y eso qué es?

–Hacer que Playtone Games sea rentable y convencerte de que, a pesar de todo, no soy de piedra.

Cari entró en su despacho y descolgó el teléfono para llamar a Emma, pero enseguida volvió a colgarlo. Ya había pasado la época de recurrir a su hermana mayor. Ahora era madre y tomaba decisiones ella sola. En el trabajo, no necesitaba de los consejos de Emma, y también había aprendido a no depender de nadie en su vida privada. No podía dar marcha atrás ahora.

Pero no podía evitarlo. Estaba asustada solo de pensar que Dec estaba al otro extremo del pasillo y DJ en la guardería de abajo. Eran los dos hombres que más influencia tenían en su vida. Uno, porque así lo había decidido y el otro porque… ¿así lo había querido el destino?

Sacudió la cabeza. No podía pensar en eso en aquel momento, y le mandó un mensaje a su secretaria.

Ally llamó a la puerta y asomó la cabeza.

–¿Querías verme?

–Sí. Quiero que redactes un memorando al personal de parte de mis hermanas y mía comunicando que Playtone Games ha adquirido nuestra compañía y que la fusión se llevará a cabo en las próximas seis semanas.

–Muy bien, ¿algo más?

Ally lo dijo sin sorpresa ni preocupación. Su secretaria tenía treinta y dos años, se había casado el verano pasado, y Cari sabía que acababa de firmar la hipoteca de su casa. Debería estar preocupada.

–Diles que Dec Montrose va a estar controlándolos. Si trabajan al máximo, no tienen de qué preocuparse.

–De acuerdo, redactaré un correo electrónico y te lo mandaré para que le des el visto bueno.

–Gracias. ¿Podrías pedir que me manden a alguien para trabajar como mi asistente?

–¿Por qué?

–Ally, estoy pensando en mandarte a financiero. Estás capacitada para llevar cuentas y, de esa manera, no estarás vinculada a mí.

No estaba segura de cuánto sabrían los empleados de la mala relación entre su familia y la de Dec, y no quería correr el riesgo de que Ally se viera afectada por aquella vieja enemistad.

–No hace falta.

–Puede ser arriesgado seguir vinculada a este despacho –le advirtió.

–Como siempre dices, mientras haga mi trabajo, estaré bien. Además, no voy a abandonarte –dijo Ally con una sonrisa.

–Gracias. En ese caso, Dec y yo vamos a compartirte como secretaria. Tómatelo como dos relaciones independientes.

–De acuerdo.

Nada más irse su secretaria, Cari se recostó en su asiento y se volvió para mirar por las ventanas que daban al océano Pacífico. Respiró hondo y pensó que, si no ordenaba sus ideas, Dec la pisotearía. No podía dejar que eso pasara.

La puerta de su despacho se abrió bruscamente y, al volverse, se encontró con Jessi. Llevaba la melena oscura suelta sobre los hombros, y un denso flequillo le cubría la frente. En el lado izquierdo, tenía un llamativo mechón morado que le daba una presencia imponente.

–Bueno, ¿cómo te ha ido? –preguntó, dejando

una taza de café delante de Cari antes de sentarse en una de las butacas.

Llevaba unos pantalones estrechos negros, con un llamativo top y una chaqueta de esmoquin. A Cari le encantaba el estilo atrevido de su hermana.

–Gracias por el café –dijo antes de dar un sorbo.

–Supuse que te vendría bien. ¿Qué te ha dicho?

–Dec ha venido buscando sangre. Más o menos ha venido a decirme que va a hacer recortes y a averiguar cómo podemos ser más rentables.

Jessi apoyó un pie en la otra rodilla y se echó hacia atrás, a la vez que daba un sorbo a su chocolate.

–Era de imaginar. ¿Crees que puedes hacerle cambiar de opinión? ¿Tienes algo en mente?

–Eh…

Era una pregunta con segundas intenciones. Con Dec allí y estando su familia al mando del negocio, Cari se dio cuenta de que sus hermanas estarían en desventaja en cuanto se supiera quién era el padre de DJ.

–¿Te ha amenazado? –preguntó Jessi, poniéndose de pie al instante–. Ya he lidiado con el clan Montrose antes.

–¿Ah, sí?

–Por desgracia. Allan McKinney fue el padrino en la boda de John y Patti McCoy.

Cari recordó que Jessi había sido la dama de honor en la boda de su amiga Patti, celebrada en Las Vegas hacía dos años, aunque no recordaba que le hubiera hablado de ningún Allan.

–No lo sabía.

–Bueno, teniendo en cuenta nuestra enemistad

con esa gente, no me pareció oportuno hablar de ello. Además, Allan fue un completo imbécil en varios aspectos. Entiendo por qué hay tan mala relación entre nuestras familias. De todas formas, pasé el fin de semana más largo de mi vida en Las Vegas gracias a él. Si hace falta que entre ahí y…

—No, no necesitas hacer nada por mí, Jessi. Va todo bien con Dec. De hecho, hemos quedado para cenar esta noche.

Tenía que ir preparando el terreno para soltar la bomba de que Dec era el padre de DJ.

—¿Ah, sí? Entonces es que no se parece en nada a Allan, un tipo insoportable.

Cari rio y, por primera vez en la mañana, pensó que quizá no fuera el fin del mundo. Pasara lo que pasase en Infinity Games, sus hermanas y ella estarían bien.

Capítulo Tres

Dec se frotó la nuca mientras Ally escoltaba al jefe de programación del equipo IOS fuera de la sala de juntas. Necesitaba un buen trago y una noche en la que no tuviera que pensar en reducciones de personal. No le cabía ninguna duda de que parte del problema de Infinity Games era el hecho de que Cari daba demasiada libertad a sus empleados. Pero en aquel momento no importaba. Eran casi las seis y tenía una cita por primera vez en casi seis meses, así que se dispuso a marcharse.

–Que pase buena noche, señor Montrose –le dijo el guarda de seguridad al salir del ascensor.

El vestíbulo de Infinity Games era buena muestra de su historia. En una pared en letras grandes había un listado de los logros que la compañía había cosechado desde su creación a comienzos de los años setenta. Dec reparó en el primero, junto al que aparecían los nombres de Gregory Chandler y Thomas Montrose. El siguiente logro era la asociación con el gigante japonés del videojuego Mishukoshi, a raíz del cual el nombre de Thomas desaparecía. Ahí empezaba la enemistad entre las familias.

–Buenas noches. ¿Cómo me dijo que se llamaba? –le preguntó al vigilante.

Kell pensaba prescindir de aquel edificio, por lo que no habría necesidad de tener dos equipos de seguridad. Además, aquel hombre parecía un buen candidato para una jubilación anticipada.

–Frank Jones –contestó el vigilante.

Estaba impecable con su uniforme azul y, a pesar de su edad, Frank estaba en buena forma física.

–Yo soy Declan Montrose –dijo extendiendo su mano.

Intercambiaron un apretón firme. Aunque tuviera algunas canas, no era tan mayor como le había parecido desde el otro lado del vestíbulo.

–¿Quién le contrató?

–La señorita Cari. Me dijo que necesitaba a alguien que se tomara el trabajo en serio y que comprendiera que la seguridad era una parte muy importante –respondió Frank.

–¿Y con eso lo convenció para que aceptara el puesto? –preguntó Dec.

–Bueno, con eso y con su sonrisa. Cuando sonríe, hace que uno se sienta único para el puesto y quiera dar lo mejor de sí mismo –dijo Frank.

–Sí, es cierto que tiene esa cualidad –convino Dec.

De repente, comprendió por qué Cari era tan apreciada por su equipo. Sabía muy bien cómo hacer sentir a todos importante.

Mientras iba conduciendo su Maserati descapotable, sonó el teléfono. Todavía no estaba preparado para darle información a Kell, pero teniendo en cuenta que no solo era su primo sino su jefe, no podía ignorar la llamada.

–Aquí Montrose.

–Aquí, también –dijo Kell–. ¿Tan mal como nos temíamos?

–Peor. El personal es completamente leal. Si nos deshacemos de las Chandler, creo que podríamos tener un motín. No he parado en todo el día de oír lo maravillosas que son.

–Eso no me importa –dijo Kell–. Ya sabíamos que la toma de control iba a ser un desastre.

–Y estoy mitigando el desastre, pero va a llevar un tiempo.

Kell maldijo para sus adentros.

–Dijiste seis semanas.

–Y ese es el tiempo que necesito. Llamarme y darme la lata no va a hacer que tarde menos.

–Lo sé. Quería saber qué tal es esa Chandler. Se llama Cari, ¿no?

Era nerviosa, sexy y dulce. Pero su primo no tenía por qué saberlo. Y si había algo que Dec había aprendido de su famosa madre, era a guardarse información.

–Oculta algo.

–¿El qué? No hay ningún otro inversor entre bastidores –dijo Kell con plena certeza.

–Averiguaré lo que pueda, pero no me cabe ninguna duda de que esconde algo. Quizá se trate de alguna de sus hermanas. Por lo que tengo entendido, la mayor, Emma, es un tiburón de los negocios. Los empleados dicen de ella lo mismo que los nuestros de ti.

–Trataré de averiguar qué esconden. Tú sigue tratando de sacarle algo a Cari. Creo que el mejor amigo de Allan está casado con la mejor amiga de la mediana de las Chandler.

–¿Cómo lo sabes? –preguntó Dec.

A Kell no le importaban los asuntos personales, y menos aún si no tenían que ver con Playtone Games.

–Tuve la mala suerte de salir de copas con nuestro primo el pasado fin de semana y me contó todo sobre esa chica.

Así que Allan conocía a la hermana mediana y, a menos que estuviera equivocado, cosa que rara vez pasaba, él iba a conocer íntimamente a la hermana pequeña. Una vez más. Y esta vez iba a… ¿A qué? Él era el hijo adoptado de la dinastía Montrose. Había sido abandonado, adoptado y abandonado de nuevo a su suerte. No era hombre de compromisos. ¿Qué otra cosa podía tener con Cari aparte de una aventura pasajera?

De hecho, el único compromiso que tenía en su vida era con sus primos y con la compañía familiar, Playtone Games.

Con veinte años había intentado montar una empresa por su cuenta, pero Kell lo había llamado y no había podido dejar pasar la oportunidad de formar parte de aquella nueva generación de Montrose. Pero todavía tenía que demostrar su valía.

–¿Sigues ahí? –preguntó Kell.

–Sí, pero tengo que colgar. Tengo una cena de negocios esta noche.

–¿Con quién?

Dec oyó de fondo el programa de noticias económicas que Kell veía religiosamente todas las tardes. Era un genio para la bolsa, lo que explicaba en buena parte su éxito en los negocios.

A Dec siempre le había maravillado que tanto sus primos Kell y Allan como él aportaban algo único a la combinación. Formaban un buen triunvirato y, aunque era consciente de que no era un Montrose de sangre, era una parte insustituible en Playtone Games.

–Con Cari –dijo Dec por fin–, voy a cenar con Cari.

–Bien. Supongo que aprovecharás para averiguar qué oculta.

Tenía intención de descubrir todos sus secretos, pensó después de colgar la llamada con su primo.

Llegó al aparcamiento del club de yates Marina del Rey y aparcó su coche. Las oficinas de Playtone estaban en Santa Mónica, a pocos kilómetros de la sede de Infinity Games. Era algo que había hecho su abuelo Thomas deliberadamente para que cada día, cuando Gregory Chandler fuera a trabajar, tuvieran que pasar por delante de la competencia.

Esa noche quería comprobar que lo que había entre Cari y él era real. Tenía que haber otra razón además de la venganza para que hubiera vuelto a aparecer en su vida. Era consciente de que quería que Cari pasara de ser rival a amante. Pero esa noche, estaba decidido a ignorar todo aquello y disfrutar.

Cari estaba en el vestíbulo de su casa, con el teléfono en una mano y su hijo en la otra. Estaba intentando convencerse de que cancelar la cena no era una huida cuando DJ tiró con su manita del cuello de la camisa de su madre.

–*Mamamama*.

–Vaya.

Cari dejó el teléfono en la mesa del recibidor y volvió a la cocina. Sentó a DJ en su trona y se apoyó en un armario.

–No sé qué hacer.

El pequeño se quedó mirándola fijamente mientras le dejaba una galleta en la bandeja de la trona. Tenía los mismos ojos marrones que Dec. Sabía que si cancelaba la cena sería solo por cobardía. Estaba más asustada en aquel momento de lo que lo había estado por la mañana. Una cosa había sido ver a Dec en su despacho, donde tenía un cierto poder, y otra, cenar con él. Su cuerpo había estado a punto de revelar su secreto. Sabía que debía decírselo antes de que lo descubriera.

Se acarició los labios y recordó la sensación de su cuerpo junto al suyo.

«Esto es una locura. Llámale y cancela la cena», se dijo.

Tenía que hablarle de DJ. Había cosas que, una vez hechas, no tenían remedio. Eso era lo que su abuela solía decirle cada vez que llevaba un perro o un gato a casa. Su abuela siempre le recordaba que cuando la vida de otros entraba a formar parte de la ecuación, todo cambiaba.

Se miró una última vez al espejo.

–Díselo esta noche.

Sabía que no iba a ser fácil.

Aunque nunca había sido tan mandona como Emma ni tan rebelde como Jessi, no era cobarde. No era su estilo salir huyendo. Además, Dec tenía derecho a saber de su hijo y, hasta que no se lo dijera, se sentiría culpable.

–Voy a ir –afirmó sonriendo a DJ.

El pequeño dio unas palmadas y le devolvió la sonrisa. Era el niño más adorable del mundo. Volvió a tomarlo en brazos y se fue decidida a su habitación. Puso una manta en medio de su cama y unas almohadas alrededor para que no se cayera, y lo dejó allí sentado mordisqueando la galleta. Luego, se dispuso a prepararse para su cita, a la espera de que llegara Emma junto con su hijo Sam para hacerse cargo de DJ.

Sonó el timbre de la puerta y desde el monitor de seguridad vio que además de Emma y Sam, también había ido Jessi. No estaba preparada para soportar a sus dos hermanas a la vez. Se sentía tan insegura y asustada que estaba tentada de contarle su secreto a Emma. Entonces Emma la justificaría y…

«Déjalo ya».

Odiaba que hubiera momentos en los que todavía deseaba que alguien tomara decisiones por ella. Era una mujer hecha y derecha, madre de un niño. No podía dejar que otra persona controlara su vida. Tenía que dar un paso al frente.

–Pasad –dijo apretando el botón del intercomunicador–. Estoy en mi habitación vistiéndome.

Corrió al armario y sacó un vestido de cóctel de estilo retro que había comprado en rebajas. Aunque no le faltaba el dinero, su madre le había enseñado que estaba mejor en su bolsillo que en el de otro, y siempre había sido austera.

–A ver qué llevas puesto –dijo Jessi, ignorando a DJ y dirigiéndose directamente al vestidor.

Su hermana tenía aversión a los bebés y reconocía abiertamente que no le gustaban los niños hasta que no eran capaces de valerse por sí solos.

Cari se volvió para que Jessi la viera. El vestido le favorecía y el color morado contrastaba con la palidez de su piel. El corpiño era ajustado, con tirantes finos y un lazo de terciopelo que resaltaba su fina cintura. Se había puesto un collar de perlas negras que su padre había regalado a su madre en un cumpleaños y que ella había heredado tras la muerte de sus padres en un accidente de barco, pero en el último momento cambió de opinión y se puso el colgante que solía llevar.

–Estás preciosa, cariño. ¿Estás segura de que es solo una cena de negocios? –preguntó Jessi.

–Sí –respondió, y sintió que se sonrojaba–. ¿Qué otra cosa podría ser? Es un Montrose.

–Pues que no se te olvides –replicó Jessi mientras volvían al dormitorio.

Emma le dio el visto bueno.

–Estás muy guapa. ¿Qué es lo que no tienes que olvidar?

–Que Dec es el enemigo.

–¿Dec?

–Así se llama.

–Su nombre es Declan, Cari. Lo dices como si…

Emma la observó con atención.

Cari no quiso invitarla a que terminara la frase. Sabía muy bien cómo había dicho su nombre, como si fuera su salvación a la vez que su perdición.

Hasta el momento, le había dejado estar al mando de la situación en el despacho, pero por su propio bien y el de DJ, no podía permitir que pasara lo mismo aquella noche. Era ella la que tenía que tener el control.

Miró a sus hermanas mientras se ponía perfume. Parecían preocupadas y las sonrió mientras se atusaba la coleta y se alisaba el flequillo.

Esa noche iba a ser ángel y demonio a la vez. Dejaría a Declan Montrose impresionado y saldría victoriosa.

Cuando llegó al restaurante Chart House en Marina del Rey, Dec la estaba esperando en la barra. Estaba muy sexy y sofisticado todo vestido de negro: pantalones, corbata, camisa y chaqueta. No era una persona alegre, y aquel atuendo oscuro así lo reflejaba. Pero también le hacía parecer muy guapo. Las mujeres lo miraban de reojo. Suspiró y se preguntó si estaba lista para aquello. Desde que había descubierto que estaba embarazada, no había dejado de repetirse que tenía que ser valiente. Todavía seguía haciéndolo, así que enderezó los hombros y se dirigió hacia él.

Dec se volvió justo cuando se acercaba.

–Te he visto por el espejo –le explicó, ofreciéndole una bebida–. Recuerdo que te gustaba el *gin tonic*.

–Y me sigue gustando. Pero teniendo en cuenta

40

que debo mantener la cabeza despejada esta noche, creo que tomaré solo la tónica.

Él sonrió.

–Te pediré otra cosa.

Al momento volvió con otra copa, decorada con una cáscara de lima. Cari dio un sorbo a aquella bebida refrescante y decidió dejar de preocuparse. Ya encontraría la manera de decirle que tenía un hijo.

–¿Qué tal te ha ido hoy? –preguntó ella.

–No quiero hablar de trabajo esta noche. Quiero que nos pongamos al día. Tienes quince minutos hasta que nuestra mesa esté lista.

La condujo hasta un rincón más íntimo y le indicó con un gesto que tomara asiento. Después de sentarse, dedicó largos segundos a alisarse el vestido sobre las piernas.

–Te pongo nerviosa –dijo él cuando alzó la vista para mirarlo.

–Sí –admitió ella–, como cuando nos conocimos.

–¿Por qué? ¿Porque soy un Montrose?

Se quedó pensativa, aunque sabía la respuesta. Había pensado en Dec Montrose muchas veces.

–Es algo que tienes. Se te ve tan seguro y confiado, que una mujer tiene que andarse con ojo.

–No parece que lo estés haciendo.

–Hay una o dos maneras de conseguir que te distraigas –dijo ella–. Pero no siempre puede ser besándote.

Su risa la hizo sonreír. Dec solía estar serio la mayor parte del tiempo, así que cuando reía o sonreía, era una especie de regalo.

41

—Estoy deseando que lo intentes.

—Ya me lo imagino. Háblame de Australia.

—Eso son negocios —dijo él sacudiendo la cabeza.

—¿No has hecho nada más que trabajar en este año y medio? —preguntó ella—. No me lo creo. Te veo cambiado.

Él se encogió de hombros y dio un trago a su whisky.

—Quizá sea el hecho de que después de diez años de duro trabajo, Playtone Games ha conseguido por fin su objetivo.

—¿Hacerse con Infinity Games?

—Sí —respondió Dec—. Supongo que no querrás hablar de eso.

—No, claro que no. Debería habérmelo pensado mejor antes de irme a la cama con alguien que lleva décadas considerándome su enemiga.

—No te considero mi enemiga.

—¿De verdad?

—Ya no, he ganado la batalla. Ahora, es solo cuestión de poner orden a este desastre y pasar página. Ya no hay conflicto de intereses entre nosotros.

Claro que había un gran conflicto de intereses entre ellos y, por primera vez desde que naciera DJ, se dio cuenta de que su hijo era la pieza que necesitaba para conseguir que Dec hiciera lo que ella quería. En cuanto aquella idea se le pasó por la cabeza, le resultó repugnante y la desechó. Nunca utilizaría a su hijo para aprovecharse. Eso sería despreciable.

Al igual que lo era no haberle hablado de él, aunque estaba convencida de que sus motivos eran legítimos. No parecía la clase de hombre que desearía tener una familia o un hijo. Pero debía darle la oportunidad de decidirlo por sí mismo, ahora que había vuelto a aparecer en su vida.

–Hay algo que debería decirte –dijo Cari sin saber muy bien cómo comenzar aquella conversación.

–¿Se trata de un secreto?

–Algo así.

–Kell me ha pedido que averigüe qué estás ocultando –dijo Dec.

–¿Cómo?

¿Cómo sabía su primo que ocultaba algo? ¿Acaso sabría que había tenido un hijo de Dec?

–Le dije que el día había ido bien, salvo porque tenía la sensación de que había algo que no me estabas contando.

–Vaya.

Así que sospechaba que tenía que ver con la toma de control de su compañía. ¿Por qué iba a ser de otra manera? Habían tenido una aventura de una noche, no una relación. Nunca adivinaría lo que le ocultaba porque nunca caería en la cuenta.

–Pues se va a llevar una decepción, porque no guardo ningún secreto empresarial –dijo ella.

–Creo que sí. El vigilante me ha contado que consigues cualquier cosa de los empleados con tan solo una sonrisa.

Cari se sonrojó. Debía de haber estado hablando con Frank, quien era como un tío para ella.

–Frank exagera. Además, ¿qué podría hacer que hicieran?

–Amotinarse.

–Tú no eres el capitán del barco.

–Claro que sí. Soy yo el que va a conducirles por las aguas infectadas de tiburones.

–Pensé que eras tú el tiburón.

–Solo a tus ojos.

Pero a sus ojos no era un tiburón. Lo tomó de la mano y se la estrechó.

–El traspaso de control no va a ser fácil, pero no te culpo por lo que tengas que hacer.

–Entonces, ¿de qué me culpas? –preguntó él.

–De dejarme –respondió.

Aunque lo había dicho sin pararse a pensar, era la verdad.

–Ahora he vuelto.

–Así es, aunque no acabo de entender por qué estás aquí conmigo. Tu curiosidad hacia mí ya quedó satisfecha, ¿no?

–Ni mucho menos. Deseo más y estoy dispuesto a conseguirlo.

Capítulo Cuatro

Dec no podía relajarse. Solo podía mirar fijamente a Cari y preguntarse cómo no había visto aquella faceta suya dieciocho meses antes. Mostraba una seguridad en sí misma de la que antes carecía. Ahora flirteaba y sabía insistir para hacer valer su punto de vista. Antes, le había dejado llevar la iniciativa y marcar el ritmo.

Si se hubiera mostrado así en aquel hotel de Atlanta, le habría resultado más difícil dejarla.

—¿Por qué me miras así? —preguntó ella.

—Eres una mujer muy guapa. Seguro que estás acostumbrada a que los hombres te miren así.

Ella sacudió la cabeza y apartó la mirada.

—Hace tiempo que no. He estado ocupada.

—¿Ocupada con el trabajo?

Teniendo en cuenta el estado en el que estaba Infinity Games, lo dudaba.

—No solo con el trabajo. Mi vida es una locura ahora.

—¿A qué te dedicas fuera del trabajo, a obras benéficas?

—No te burles, no hay nada malo en las obras benéficas.

—Lo sé, pero las mujeres que hacen voluntariado, apenas dedican tiempo a sus familias.

–¿Te refieres a tu madre?

–Sí. Precisamente es así como le gustaba que la llamara, madre y no mamá.

–¿De veras? No sé nada de tu pasado.

–¿Por qué ibas a saber algo?

–Somos enemigos a muerte. He buscado información sobre ti en Google –dijo, y tomó otro sorbo del agua que había pedido para acompañar la comida–. Pero en internet solo encontré artículos relacionados con los negocios, así que cuéntame más, Dec. Quiero conocer tu punto débil.

–¿Quién dice que tengo un punto débil?

–Todo el mundo tiene uno.

–¿Incluso las rubias encantadoras?

–No sé otras rubias, pero yo desde luego que sí.

–Venga, dime de qué se trata.

–Olvídalo, amigo. Estamos hablando de ti –dijo ella.

Hablarle de su pasado no desvelaría ninguna debilidad. De hecho, dudaba de que tuviera alguna. Solo si algo le preocupara de verdad o temiera perder algo, sería vulnerable. Por tanto, no tenía nada que perder.

–Bueno, mis padres eran personas muy ocupadas. Mi madre hacía sus obras de caridad y mi padre trataba de agradar a mi abuelo con su ansia de venganza hacia tu familia.

–Deberían haberte dedicado más tiempo.

Si no tenía cuidado, aquello iba a convertirse en una historia triste y una mujer tan sensible como Cari se lo creería. Por un segundo, consideró aprovecharse de su faceta sentimental, pero enseguida descartó la idea. No necesitaba engañarla ni aprovecharse de sus buenos sentimientos para salir victorioso.

–Teníamos la típica relación familiar, pero cada uno vivía su vida. Nos fue bien. Siento si te ha parecido que me desagradan las obras de caridad.

–No te preocupes. Doy dinero a algunas organizaciones, pero no colaboro como voluntaria. Paso la mayor parte de mi tiempo libre en casa o comprando por internet.

–¿De verdad? Pensé que te gustaba más la vida social.

–Y así era, pero últimamente, contigo y con tus primos buscando haceros con nuestro negocio, he tenido que concentrarme en otras cosas.

–No voy a decir que lo sienta.

–¿Te refieres a la oportunidad de conseguir lo que tanto deseaba tu abuelo?

Algo así, aunque para él, era más una cuestión de vencer que de cobrarse una vieja deuda.

–En absoluto. Me alegro de que lo hayamos conseguido. Así puedo pasar más tiempo contigo.

Cari puso los ojos en blanco.

–¿Por qué este repentino interés en mí?

Era la única pregunta para la que no tenía respuesta. Solo podía decir que después de pasar tanto tiempo en Australia, lejos de todo, se había dado cuenta de que ya no tenía las mismas prioridades que antes.

–Quizá porque me interesas.

–Sí, claro. Tendrás que perdonarme, pero no me lo creo.

–Bueno, esta noche sí. Tenía intención de sonsacarte cierta información que...

–Mentiroso. Has dicho que nada de negocios.

–Esa era mi intención al principio. Pero cuando te he visto llegar, solo he podido pensar en la noche que pasamos juntos y me arrepiento de no haberme quedado.

Cari se pasó un mechón de pelo por detrás de la oreja, se mordió el labio inferior y suspiró.

–Habría sido complicado.

–Se me dan muy bien las complicaciones.

–Creo que esta habría sido demasiado incluso para ti –dijo ella.

–¿A qué te refieres?

A veces tenía la sensación de que mantenían dos conversaciones diferentes. Podía achacarlo al hecho de que ella fuera una mujer y él un hombre, y se comunicaran de manera diferente. Pero había algo más que eso. Tal vez sus secretos...

–A que hubiéramos seguido juntos después de aquella noche –respondió ella–. ¿No era eso de lo que estabas hablando?

–Sí, pero lo decía porque mis primos no lo habrían entendido.

–¿Confraternizar con el enemigo? –dijo, y suspiró–. Eso siempre suena muy romántico hasta que llega la hora de dar respuestas a tus hermanas.

Él rio.

–Sí, habría sido difícil. Tal vez nos hice un favor marchándome.

–No hables como si hubiera algo entre nosotros. Esto es una cena, no una cita romántica.

–Ese beso en la sala de juntas no dice lo mismo.

–Hace tiempo que no besaba a un hombre. No te sientas especial.

Demasiado tarde. Precisamente era así como se sentía. Había algo en ella, en su sonrisa y en sus besos que lo hacían sentirse como el único hombre de la tierra.

–Me rompes el corazón.

–Ja, ja –dijo ella antes de dar otro sorbo a su vino–. No creo que un simple comentario pueda herir tu ego.

–¿Por qué piensas así?

–Has irrumpido en mis oficinas como si nada hubiera ocurrido entre nosotros. Me cuentas que vas a prescindir de mi plantilla, me dejas impresionada y luego me dices que vamos a cenar juntos. ¿No te parece que eso es una demostración de un ego colosal?

Dec dio un trago a su vino para evitar que lo viera sonreír. Su padre siempre le decía que tenía más seguridad en sí mismo que inteligencia.

–Supongo que no todo se debe al ego. Al fin y al cabo, estás aquí conmigo esta noche.

–Ahí has acertado –convino ella.

–Difícil no sentirse especial.

No pretendía tener una relación formal con Cari. Se conocía bien como para saber que solo se sentía cómodo viviendo el presente. No le gustaba recrearse en el pasado ni soñar con el futuro.

**

Después de cenar, Cari se disculpó para ir al aseo y llamó a su hermana para ver cómo estaba DJ. Sabía que Jessi ya se habría ido y que Emma estaría a solas con Sammy y DJ. Eran las ocho y media, la hora en que solía sentarse en el sofá con su iPad y hacer compras por internet mientras el bebé dormía en sus brazos.

–¿Qué tal está?

–Inquieto, no deja de llamarte –respondió Emma–. Pensé que esta era su hora de irse a la cama.

–Me gusta tenerlo en brazos hasta que se queda dormido.

–Eso era lo que me temía. Sam ha puesto unos cojines en la habitación del bebé y le está leyendo un cuento.

–No sabía que Sam supiera leer.

Su sobrino tenía tres años.

–Bueno, todo lo que hace es pasar páginas e inventarse historias según los dibujos.

Cari rio y lamentó no estar en aquel momento con su hijo y su sobrino.

–Sammy es un encanto con DJ.

–Lleva tiempo queriendo tener un hermanito –dijo Emma–. Habíamos pensado dárselo este año.

–Lo siento –dijo Cari.

Nadie imaginaba que Helio moriría tan joven. Su muerte había sido inesperada para todos y Emma se había volcado en el trabajo. Lo cierto era que la única persona que sacaba el lado tierno de su hermana era Sam.

–Está bien. ¿Qué tal la cena? ¿Te ha contado algo?

–La cena bien. Ahora vamos a tomar algo al puerto. ¿Puedes quedarte un rato más?

–Sí, de hecho, creo que me voy a llevar a DJ a mi casa. Tal vez se quede dormido en el coche. Si te apetece, ven a recogerlo o, si no, puedo llevarlo mañana a la guardería de Infinity Games.

–De acuerdo, le echaré de menos esta noche.

–Relájate y trata de sacarle información a Dec de lo que están planeando.

–Haré lo que pueda. Quizá pase por tu casa más tarde.

–Como quieras. Cuídate.

–Tú también.

Después de colgar, se retocó la pintura de los labios y se atusó el pelo antes de volver a la mesa.

Mientras se acercaba, reparó en que Dec estaba hablando por teléfono y dudó, pero enseguida se acordó de lo que Emma le acababa de decir. Tenía que averiguar qué iba a hacer con la compañía. Pero lo cierto era que no tenía ningún interés en hacerlo. Nada más llegar a la mesa, Dec se despidió y colgó, así que no pudo obtener ninguna información.

–¿Lista para irnos? –preguntó.

Cari asintió mientras él se ponía de pie. Luego la tomó de la cintura y la acompañó entre las mesas hasta la puerta del restaurante. Era evidente que podía haber atravesado sola el salón, pero tenía que reconocer que le gustaba sentir el calor de su mano a través de la tela del vestido.

No pudo evitar estremecerse al sentir sus dedos rozándole la cremallera de la espalda.

–¿Tienes frío?

Negó con la cabeza, aunque enseguida se dio cuenta de que debería haber dicho que sí.

–Echo de menos acariciarte –susurró, acercándose a su oído para que nadie más pudiera oírlo.

Ella también lo echaba de menos. Se detuvo en seco y se apartó de él.

–Pues no tenías por qué.

–Ya me he disculpado.

–Lo sé, pero eso no te da derecho. Creo que debería irme.

–Pensé que querías hablar –dijo él.

–Así es, pero no puedo si vas a estar tocándome.

–Pretendía ser cortés.

Cari era consciente de que estaba siendo exagerada y no solo por culpa de Dec. Hacía mucho tiempo que un hombre no la acariciaba y lo estaba deseando. No sabía si por culpa de sus hormonas o de Dec.

–Lo sé.

Dec le dio las llaves al aparcacoches.

–¿Te parece bien si vamos en mi coche al puerto y luego volvemos a recoger el tuyo?

–De acuerdo.

Confiaba en ser capaz de hablarle de DJ mientras tomaban una copa. Pero todavía no sabía muy bien cómo contárselo. En parte, no quería hacerlo. No estaba segura de que estuviera preparado para ser padre.

–Aquí está mi coche.

–¿Un Maserati?

–Sí, me gustan los coches veloces y deportivos.

–¿Por qué no me sorprende? ¿Has pensado alguna vez qué harás cuando tengas una familia?

–No tengo pensado tener familia.

Al encontrarse con sus ojos marrones, Cari se dio cuenta de que hablaba en serio. Había querido averiguar más de él, y lo único que había descubierto era que su madre participaba en obras benéficas y apenas le había dedicado tiempo. Quizá eso explicara por qué no quería tener familia.

–¡Vaya! –exclamó sin saber muy bien qué decir.

–Soy un solitario.

«Allá vamos», se dijo Cari al subirse al coche.

No sabía qué hacer. A pesar de lo que él pretendiera o de lo que ella deseara, Dec tenía un hijo y ella era la madre. Tenía que decírselo.

La fantasía de que cayera de rodillas y le hiciera una promesa de amor eterno acababa de desvanecerse. Aquello era la vida real.

–¿Estás bien? –preguntó Dec.

–Sí –respondió.

Luego, se acomodó en el asiento y se dejó llevar por la suave música que sonaba en el coche. Aunque no amaba a Dec, no pudo evitar sentirse triste. Era la primera vez que se daba cuenta de que los sueños podían romperse con la misma facilidad que los corazones.

Dec sintió que le cambiaba el humor al llegar al puerto. Se sentía parte de aquel lugar porque vivía en un yate que estaba allí amarrado. Hacía tiempo que había decidido que no quería vivir en una casa grande, probablemente para distinguirse de sus padres. Le gustaba fingir que todo lo que podía comprar no significaba nada para él. Dudaba de que Cari accediera a tomar una copa en su yate, el *Big Spender*. Su primo Allan lo había bautizado por él, en clara referencia a que le gustaban las cosas caras.

Dec se abrió paso por el club de socios hasta una mesa ubicada en un balcón, lejos del resto de clientes. A aquella hora de la noche, el sitio estaba tranquilo. Le hizo una señal al camarero y, cuando se acercó, ambos pidieron un café descafeinado.

–Parece que he dicho algo que te ha molestado –dijo él.

–Tengo algo que decirte.

–Adelante.

–No es tan fácil como había imaginado.

Estaba empezando a preocuparlo. ¿Qué querría decirle que tan difícil le resultaba?

–¿Estás casada?

–No, no habría venido a cenar contigo si tuviera una relación con otro hombre. Para mí, los compromisos son importantes.

–Para mí también –dijo él–. Por eso los evito.

–¿De veras? ¿Es por algo que te ocurrió en el pasado?

–Sí.

–Cuéntamelo.

Les llevaron los cafés y, aunque el camarero se había marchado, Dec no dijo nada. No le gustaba pensar en el pasado. No le gustaba contar que era huérfano y que el matrimonio de sus padres adoptivos había sido una farsa. Él era una pieza más en la imagen de familia ideal, pero nada de aquello había sido real.

–No me gusta hablar del pasado –dijo Dec al cabo de un rato.

–Sin el pasado no tenemos manera de saber hacia dónde vamos.

–Me gusta vivir el presente.

–Pero tienes que planear el futuro. Es necesario aunque solo sea para lograr tus metas empresariales.

Él se encogió de hombros.

–El trabajo me motiva, aunque solo sea por no fracasar.

Cari sacudió la cabeza.

–No sé qué más decir o cómo decir esto. Aquella noche que compartimos…

–¿No la has olvidado? Yo no he podido quitármela de la cabeza.

–En cierto modo –respondió acariciando el colgante que llevaba al cuello.

Dec se fijó en el colgante y reparó en que tenía dos iniciales: DJ.

Estaba empezando a unir las piezas, pero no le veía sentido a la conclusión a la que estaba llegando. Eso que tanto le estaba costando contarle, no podía ser lo que estaba rondándole en la cabeza.

No habría esperado tanto tiempo para decírselo.

–¿Qué estás intentando decirme?

Cari dio otro sorbo a su café. Dec percibía la tensión de su cuerpo y el nerviosismo de su mirada. Trató de mantener la calma al igual que hacía cuando tenía que despedir a alguien.

–Puede que parezca… Después de que te fueras… Maldita sea, no hay forma de decir esto. Me quedé embarazada. Tuve un bebé hace nueve meses, un niño –dijo, y se sintió incapaz de dejar de hablar–. Sé que debería haberte llamado, pero al principio no podía creer que estuviera embarazada. Entonces,… Bueno, tu compañía estaba planeando hacerse con el control de la mía y…

–¿Tengo un hijo?

–Sí, tiene nueve meses –dijo mientras rebuscaba en el bolso y sacaba el teléfono móvil.

Dec la ignoró mientras su cabeza no dejaba de dar vueltas. Cari estaba diciendo algo, pero era incapaz de escuchar sus palabras. Solo podía pensar en que los planes que había hecho para su vida acababan de desvanecerse. Tenía que asimilar aquello. Un hijo, su hijo.

Cari le tendió el teléfono. Miró la pantalla y vio a su hijo por primera vez. Tenía los ojos de su mismo color marrón. No había dientes en su sonrisa y sus ojos eran grandes. Parecía un niño feliz. Dec sintió que se le paraba el corazón y que el estómago le daba un vuelco. Aquello lo cambiaba todo. Era una complicación que ni siquiera él sabía cómo asumir.

Se levantó tirando la silla y, al volverse, vio su reflejo en el espejo. Nunca había tenido un vínculo con nadie y Cari acababa de decirle que tenía un hijo. Era el primer familiar consanguíneo que conocía.

–Tengo un hijo…

Capítulo Cinco

Cari sabía que podía haberle dado la noticia de una forma mejor, pero al menos ya lo había hecho y se sentía aliviada. Siempre se había dicho que Dec había hecho su elección al marcharse, y ella había tomado la mejor decisión, tener aquel hijo sola. Se sentía mal por habérselo ocultado a Dec, pero no había tenido otra opción.

Dec estaba callado y la expresión de sus cálidos ojos marrones era fría y distante. Sabía que lo había dejado impactado, y estaba deseando acabar aquella conversación y marcharse del bar del puerto. Nunca se había sentido tan insegura en su vida, excepto en el momento en que había tomado en brazos a su hijo por primera vez y había deseado poner el mundo a sus pies, sin saber cómo hacerlo.

—Teniendo en cuenta que decías que no querías formar una familia…

—Eso fue antes de que supiera que tenía un hijo —dijo sin apartar la vista de la foto del teléfono—. Tiene mis ojos.

Había una nota de sobrecogimiento y cierto nerviosismo en su voz. Nunca antes lo había visto así. Aquello le había impresionado.

Por fin dejó el teléfono sobre la mesa y la miró. Aparte de alguna sonrisa ocasional, aquella era la primera vez que veía emoción en él. Parecía enfadado y tenía que reconocer que eso la asustaba. Se sentía culpable por la manera en que le había dado la noticia a Dec. Parecía realmente impresionado. Cuando volvió a sentarse, Cari fue a tomarlo de la mano, pero él la apartó rápidamente sin dejar de mirarla.

–Sé que tiene tus ojos –reconoció ella por fin–. Escucha, tenemos que hablar –añadió, tomando la iniciativa.

Una vez más, quiso dar la impresión de saber lo que estaba haciendo, tal y como había hecho desde el día en que había nacido su hijo. Era importante que Dec no dudara de ella, porque si se daba cuenta de que le estaba abandonando la seguridad en sí misma, se haría con el control de la situación.

–No intenté ponerme en contacto contigo porque antes de descubrir que estaba embarazada, no supe nada de ti. Era como si hubieras pasado página y te hubieras olvidado de todo, así que yo tenía que hacer lo mismo.

–Aun así, deberías…

–¿Qué? Fíjate, ni siquiera hoy estás siendo amable y cariñoso, a menos que cuentes ese beso en la sala de juntas. No puedo darme el lujo de esperar para comprobar si has cambiado. Ahora soy madre, Dec, tengo alguien más en quien pensar.

Se quedó mirándola como si no la hubiera visto antes. Tenía razón en lo que decía. Nadie, ni siquiera aquel hombre, iba a proteger a su hijo como lo estaba haciendo. Tenía que tenerlo presente, pensó sentada frente a él.

Dec suspiró y se atusó el pelo. Las manos le temblaban al tomar la taza y Cari se preguntó qué se le estaría pasando por la cabeza. Nunca se le había dado bien adivinar las intenciones de otras personas.

–Está bien, vamos a dejar este juego de buscar culpables –dijo él–. Me he comportado… Bueno, no importa. Recuerdo que usé un preservativo.

Cari había pensado en eso un millón de veces. Habían usado protección y, aunque por entonces no tomaba la píldora, había creído que estarían a salvo. Había sido seis semanas más tarde cuando había empezado a sentirse mal y a vomitar que había empezado a pensar… Había intentado convencerse de que podía ser un problema de estómago por pasar tantos meses viajando por conferencias. Pero cuando el vientre le había empezado a crecer, le había resultado imposible negar el hecho de que aquella noche que habían pasado juntos habían engendrado un bebé.

–Lo sé. Supongo que debió de romperse. Créeme, he repasado cada detalle de aquella noche un millón de veces. Durante una temporada, antes de que DJ naciera, deseé que no hubiera ocurrido. Nunca he sido tan impulsiva.

–¿DJ? –preguntó echándose hacia delante.

No quería darle demasiado tiempo para pensar porque le venía mejor que Dec tuviera la guardia baja.

–Sí, le puse de nombre Declan Junior, pero siempre lo llamo DJ para que nadie de la familia sospeche quién es el padre. Como nació en California, no tuve que poner el nombre del padre en el certificado de nacimiento y, para mis hermanas, DJ es el resultado de una aventura de una noche, alguien cuyo apellido desconocía.

–Supongo que caerán en la cuenta cuando empiece a…

–Te estoy hablando de él porque estás aquí y tal vez algún día DJ quiera conocerte.

Sabía que tenía derechos sobre su hijo, pero había visto a muchos padres arruinando la vida de sus hijos, como por ejemplo el suyo. No estaba dispuesta a correr el riesgo de que DJ se encariñara con Dec para luego verlo marchar cuando terminara con la fusión de las compañías.

No tenía motivos para pensar que haría algo diferente. Dec era prácticamente un desconocido para ella.

–Quiero conocer a mi hijo –dijo él por fin, mirándola a los ojos–. Quiero conocerlo y tener la oportunidad de ser un padre para él.

–No hace ni media hora decías que no querías tener una familia –le recordó.

Nada le gustaría más que creerlo. No se le había borrado de la cabeza la imagen de familia feliz. Quería tener un compañero con el que criar a DJ, pero todavía no estaba segura de que Declan Montrose pudiera ser ese hombre.

Dec estaba aturdido. Aquella era la mayor sorpresa que se había llevado jamás. Nunca había pensado en tener hijos porque sabía lo frágil que era la vida y lo difícil que era ser un buen padre. Siendo niño, se había sentido abandonado a su suerte en dos ocasiones. La primera, cuando sus padres biológicos lo habían entregado en adopción y luego, al irse a vivir con Helene y Beau Montrose a su mansión de Beverly Hills. Ambos llevaban una vida muy ajetreada y solo se preocupaban de él para las fotos de familia, olvidándose de él como si fuera una mascota en vez de un niño.

Tener un hijo, que alguien dependiera de él fuera del trabajo, era algo para lo que no estaba preparado. Había tratado de seducir a Cari, pero de repente, aquel deseo había pasado a un segundo plano. Tenía que pensar muy bien qué iba a hacer y decir en aquella situación. Todavía la deseaba y la idea de un hijo con ella no le asustaba tanto como habría sido de esperar.

Siempre había sido una persona solitaria y se conocía lo suficientemente bien como para saber que seguía siendo el mismo hombre de siempre. Sin embargo, por primera vez desde que dejara la casa de sus padres, tenía un objetivo, aunque no sabía muy bien cuál era.

Un hijo. La idea seguía haciendo que le temblaran las manos. Se olvidó de los nervios, apoyó las manos en la mesa y se echó hacia delante.

–Quiero ver a mi hijo –repitió.

No iba a dejar de hacerlo hasta que tuviera al pequeño entre sus brazos. Le resultaba increíble que tuviera un hijo.

Ella asintió.

–Será más fácil si esto queda entre tú y yo. Una

vez se enteren nuestras familias, todo se complicará.

Cari no tenía ni idea de cuánto se complicaría, pensó Dec, sobre todo cuando se enterara Kell. Su primo estaba obsesionado con la familia Chandler y, teniendo en cuenta que había crecido con su abuelo, Kell había concentrado toda su energía en vengarse. Siempre estaba pensando la manera de hacer caer a los Chandler, por lo que usaría a DJ como arma arrojadiza. No le cabía ninguna duda de que intentaría convencerlo de que se hiciera con la custodia del niño para criarlo en el odio hacia los Chandler al igual que le había pasado a él.

En su cabeza, trató de ordenar todo lo que había pasado. El orden y la planificación siempre habían regido su vida y, a pesar del hecho de que Cari estaba sentada frente a él, mirándolo con aquellos enormes ojos azules suyos y una expresión resuelta, estaba decidido a hacerse con el control. Al final, se lo agradecería.

—Mañana iré a tu casa a conocer a nuestro hijo.

—Llámalo DJ.

—¿Por qué? Es mi hijo y puedo referirme a él así.

—Sí, pero todavía no estás listo para ser un padre.

La miró arqueando una ceja, preparado para rebatirle el hecho de que podía ser un padre excelente. Pero entonces pensó en su Maserati y en que un bebé no podía vivir en un yate. Había muchas cosas que tendrían que cambiar.

—Estoy deseando intentarlo.

Cari se mordió el labio inferior y ladeó la cabeza sin dejar de observarlo. Parecía estar buscando algo y trató de no mostrarse desesperado, pero no podía obviar que por primera vez desde que lo incluyeran en la familia Montrose, tenía a alguien de su misma sangre. Sus primos y él estaban unidos por un propósito, pero tanto ellos como él sabían que no era un verdadero Montrose. Ahora tenía un hijo, alguien que le pertenecía.

La importancia del momento lo sacudió en su interior y se aferró a la mesa para alargar ese instante. Ya no estaba solo y aquella mujer era la llave para acceder a su hijo. Lo único que sabía de ella eran los sonidos que emitía cuando la tenía entre sus brazos.

–Es bueno intentarlo –dijo ella.

Dec no tenía ni idea de qué estaba hablando, solo sabía que estaba dispuesta a darle una oportunidad y eso era lo único que necesitaba.

–¿Te parece bien que me pase por tu casa mañana por la mañana?

–A primera hora tengo que recogerlo de casa de Emma y luego podemos quedar en la playa.

–¿Por qué en la playa?

–A DJ le gusta mucho. Además, mi asistenta estará en casa y es la hermana de la asistenta de Emma. Quiero que de momento esto quede entre tú y yo. No quiero que DJ se convierta en parte de lo que ha habido entre nuestras familias.

–De acuerdo –convino él–. Cuando te dije que nunca iba a tener familia, lo hice solo porque no quería que supieras que te deseaba.

–Sí, claro. Era tu forma de advertirme de que esta vez tampoco planeabas quedarte.

Así había sido exactamente, y se alegraba de que no pretendiera que fuera alguien que no podía ser. Por un lado, estaba molesto con ella por no imaginárselo formando parte de su pequeña familia, pero por otro, se sentía aliviada. Quizá pudiera ser el tío favorito de DJ.

Pero sabía que no se sentiría satisfecho. Saber que tenía un hijo le hacía pensar en cosas que nunca antes habían considerado importantes o que nunca había pensado que le serían aplicables a él. De pronto, sentía el deseo de visitar la mansión de Beverly Hills que había heredado de sus padres cuando su madre había muerto ocho años atrás. Quería estrechar a su hijo entre sus brazos y enseñarle a ser fuerte. Quería que aquel niño al que solo había visto en el teléfono de Cari creciera sin los problemas y temores que habían dominado su vida.

—Lo siento, Cari. Seguramente hiciste lo correcto al guardar el secreto de nuestro hijo.

—Hice lo único que podía hacer.

—Ahora que sé que tengo un hijo, podré ayudarte a tomar decisiones.

—No necesito ayuda —replicó ella.

—¿Qué necesitas? —preguntó.

Era consciente de que tenía que mostrarse colaborador y tratar de convencerla de que poseía todas aquellas cualidades que ella consideraba necesarias para ser el padre de su hijo. Porque cuanto más pensaba en DJ, más se daba cuenta de que por primera vez desde que se fuera de su casa y empezara a trabajar con Kell en la compra y escisión de empresas, quería hacer algo por sí mismo. Quería construir algo que le quedara a su hijo. Quería construir una familia.

Cari no estaba segura de lo que quería, más allá de irse a casa y alejarse de Dec. Sabía que se estaba esforzando y era una de las cosas más tiernas que había visto en él. Bueno, la más tierna. Dec no era un hombre que pidiera nada. Estaba acostumbrado a conseguir todo lo que quería.

La noticia que le acababa de dar lo había pillado desprevenido. Pero su reacción también había sido una sorpresa para ella. Había pensado que se negaría a creer que tuviera un hijo y lo rechazaría. Había temido que se encogiera de hombros y se diera media vuelta. Pero aquella reacción era la que en secreto había deseado.

En su cabeza, podía imaginarse a Jessi sacudiendo la cabeza y diciéndole a Cari que espabilara, que no se dejara engañar. Dec seguía siendo el mismo que antes. Al fin y al cabo, la gente no cambiaba en un rato.

Dec era un hombre acostumbrado a destruir cosas. Era el brazo ejecutor de Playtone Games y probablemente habría cientos de personas cuyas vidas se habrían visto alteradas por la frialdad de sus decisiones. Era una tontería pensar que no iba a aplicar aquellos mismos principios en su vida personal.

—Creo que debería irme —anunció Cari—. Si no te apetece llevarme de vuelta al restaurante, puedo tomar un taxi.

–¿Por qué dices eso?

–Supongo que necesitas tiempo para asimilar lo que te he contado.

–Por supuesto, pero no hace falta que tomes un taxi. Tenemos que empezar a conocernos.

Cari asintió.

–Por eso acepté cenar contigo.

–Por eso y porque te sentías culpable.

No pudo evitar sonreír ante su comentario.

–Tal vez.

No había sido consciente de la tensión emocional que había sido mantener en secreto a DJ, pero por primera vez aquella noche, se sentía capaz de respirar sin sentir un nudo en el estómago.

–Bueno, cuéntame cómo te sentiste cuando te enteraste –dijo Dec–. Debió de ser toda una sorpresa.

Cari se recostó en su asiento y recordó cómo había acudido a aquella clínica en Las Vegas, adonde había asistido a una feria de videojuegos. La noticia que le había dado el médico había sido la confirmación de sus sospechas.

–Al instante decidí que no iba contar quién era el padre.

–¿Por qué no? –preguntó él–. ¿Te llevas bien con tus hermanas, no?

–Estamos bastante unidas. Cuando vivían nuestros padres, papá estaba siempre ocupado trabajando y mamá no siempre estaba disponible. Así que Emma y Jessi cuidaban de mí. Quise contárselo, sobre todo teniendo en cuenta que Emma ya tenía un hijo, pero tuve miedo.

Estuvo a punto de llevarse la mano al vientre al recordar el instante en el que había decidido ocultar el nombre del padre a sus hermanas.

–Sabía que tenía que protegerlo y mantenerlo a salvo. Desde aquel momento, él se convirtió en mi prioridad.

La estaba mirando de una manera diferente, y no podía culparlo. No había que ser muy lista para darse cuenta de que le habría gustado que la noche fuera de otra manera.

–¿No hay nada que te desconcierte?

–Esto sí –admitió él–. Siempre he sido cuidadoso y nunca había pensado en tener un hijo.

Ella sonrió.

–DJ ha sido una sorpresa para ambos. Le dije algo parecido a Jessi cuando estaba preparando la habitación del bebé unas semanas antes de que naciera y me dijo que tal vez el destino tenía preparado un plan diferente para mí.

–¿Eso piensas? –preguntó él.

–Ya veo que tú no. Pero a una parte de mí le gustaría creer que lo que pasó entre tú y yo fue algo más que una revolución de hormonas, que aunque solo quisieras pasar una noche conmigo, hubo algo más entre nosotros. Sé que parezco una romántica empedernida.

–Yo no soy un tipo romántico. Creo que el preservativo se rompió y que por eso tenemos un hijo. Pero también creo que lo que hagamos con él, cómo lo criemos, cómo nos tratemos, esas son las cosas que tendrán un mayor efecto en él.

–Estoy de acuerdo, y es por eso por lo que hasta

que decida lo contrario, vamos a mantener en secreto que eres el padre de DJ.

No parecía muy contento con aquella decisión, pero le daba igual. No quería arriesgarse a enamorarse de un hombre acostumbrado a salir huyendo, que siempre tenía un pie en la puerta.

–De acuerdo, pero tú y yo vamos a salir juntos.

–¿Por qué? ¿Para qué?

–Es la única manera de que nuestras familias se acostumbren a vernos juntos. Y con el tiempo, se enterarán de lo que nos une a DJ y a mí. ¿No te parece mucho mejor que antes me conozcan?

Tenía razón.

–No sé, creo que es mejor que esto quede entre nosotros.

Sus hermanas iban a someterla al tercer grado. Aun así, estaba cansada de mantener en secreto la identidad del padre de DJ. Tal vez pudiera tener la oportunidad de tener la familia que siempre había deseado con el único hombre que al besarla le había hecho olvidar todo, excepto lo agradable que era estar entre sus brazos.

Capítulo Seis

Dec quería que salieran juntos y Cari se había limitado a asentir con la cabeza, pero había sido prudente de no aceptar nada en firme. Era imposible que sus familias los aceptaran como pareja. Emma y Jessi tendrían mucho que decir cuando se enteraran de que estaba saliendo con un Montrose.

Sobre todo teniendo en cuenta que Dec se estaba ocupando de evaluar y fragmentar la compañía que había sido de su familia durante generaciones. Daba igual cómo lo calificara, todos sabían que estaba allí para destruir la empresa y vengarse así en nombre de Thomas Montrose por haber sido apartado de Infinity por Gregory Chandler, el abuelo de Cari.

Se frotó los ojos mientras miraba el reloj. Eran las tres y media y seguramente a Emma no le agradaría que apareciera en su casa a aquella hora para recoger a DJ. Pero necesitaba tener a su hijo en brazos. No había hecho bien permitiendo que su hermana se lo llevara. Necesitaba abrazar su cálido y pequeño cuerpo y aspirar su olor de bebé para recordarse que debía ser fuerte. Sin embargo, estaba tumbada en su cama, pensando en Dec. ¿Acaso le sorprendía?

No había olvidado la noche que habían pasado

juntos. Desde entonces, ningún otro hombre le había interesado. ¿Estaría interesada en Dec?

¿Se sentía atraída por él? Desde luego que sí. ¿Sentía algo más que deseo? No lo conocía lo suficiente como para estar segura. Por lo que sabía de él, era un hombre que sabía pasárselo bien cuando quería y serio en los negocios, pero poco más podía decir de él.

Quizá su idea de salir juntos era una buena idea. Así tendría la oportunidad de conocerlo y comprobar si podía ser un buen padre para DJ. Daba igual que fuera suyo el esperma. De alguna manera, era como si hubiera acudido a un banco de esperma. ¿Por qué no se le había ocurrido decirle eso a sus hermanas?

Jessi sospechaba que el padre de DJ era alguien conocido. Siempre estaba haciendo preguntas capciosas para sacarle el nombre. Si Cari no estuviera tan convencida de mantener el secreto, haría tiempo que le habría contado que era Dec.

Se dio la vuelta y ahuecó la almohada, antes de abrazarla y cerrar los ojos. En su debilidad, no pudo evitar imaginarse que estaba acurrucada junto a Dec.

Ni siquiera fingió estar pensando en otro hombre. Estaba sola en su habitación y no iba a engañarse. Era débil en lo referente a él, y tuvo que recordarse que era un hombre, con sus defectos.

Dec tenía fobia al compromiso. A veces se sentía frustrada por no hacer las cosas de manera más sencilla. Habría sido mucho mejor enamorarse de Jacob, de la empresa que auditaba la contabilidad todos los años. Siempre la estaba invitando a salir y, según le había dicho en numerosas ocasiones, estaba deseando formar una familia.

Pero no se sentía atraída por Jacob. Era un tipo serio y algo aburrido. Siendo justos, se parecía bastante a ella, y siempre había soñado con alguien un poco más atrevido. Pero en aquel momento, tumbada en su cama, no le resultaba divertido ni emocionante correr riesgos, y se preguntó cómo dejar de hacerse ilusiones de que Dec era como ella quería que fuera.

Incluso cuando esa noche le había dicho que tenían que dejar aquel juego de buscar culpables, había percibido un brillo de culpabilidad en sus ojos e incluso de dolor. Pero mientras conducía su Maserati y le decía que no quería una familia, tal vez no se había parado a pensar en cuánto le habría gustado conocer antes a su hijo para haber podido estar con ellos.

Se frotó la frente y volvió a darse la vuelta una vez más. No podía dejar de dar vueltas a aquellos pensamientos, así que se levantó de la cama y se fue al estudio. Encendió la lámpara de la mesa y se sentó en el diván antes de tomar su iPad y una manta. Una buena terapia de compras le vendría bien. Nada le aclaraba más las ideas que comprar. En aquel momento, necesitaba dejar la mente en blanco.

Pero al encender el iPad, vio el rostro sonriente de DJ. Aquellos grandes ojos marrones la miraban y se preguntó cómo mantener a Dec apartado de la vida de DJ si cabía la mínima posibilidad de que fuera el padre que deseaba que fuera.

Acarició el rostro de su hijo en la pantalla y pensó que, por encima de todo, tenía que protegerlo. Lo mejor que podía hacer respecto a Dec y a aquella idea suya de salir juntos era mantener una relación platónica.

Claro que eso no iba a ser fácil. No había tardado en sentir cómo la sangre le corría más rápido por las venas y sus pechos se hinchaban. Deseaba a Dec. Sentía su cuerpo vacío y ansioso. Deseaba acostarse con él, pero no era estúpida. La vez anterior, las consecuencias habían cambiado su vida y, en esta ocasión, podían ser incluso más peligrosas.

Tenía que mantener la cabeza fría. Abrió el navegador y vio que todavía tenía abierta la página de inscripción de unas clases de natación para ella y DJ. Recostó la cabeza en la pared y cerró los ojos.

Si alguien le hubiera dicho que aquel hombre iba a tener tanta influencia en su vida, no lo habría creído. Pero aunque no era su novio y hacía año y medio que no lo veía, Declan Montrose estaba influyendo en cada decisión que estaba tomando.

Dec esperaba a la entrada del muelle de Santa Mónica, donde habían quedado. Había pasado muchas tardes de sábado allí con su niñera hasta que al cumplir diez años su madre había decidido que ya era mayor para aquellas distracciones.

Mientras esperaba bajo el sol de mediados de agosto a conocer a su hijo, se preguntó si debería darle a Cari un cheque por los gastos de crianza del niño y marcharse.

Su madre habría hecho eso. Nunca había sido una mujer cariñosa y, cuando le había preguntado por qué habían adoptado un niño, se había limitado a contestar que lo habían hecho para que Thomas Montrose no pusiera las manos en su fortuna. Estaba amargada porque el dinero había sido la razón de su matrimonio. Sacudió la cabeza y se frotó la nuca.

–¿Dec?

Se dio media vuelta y vio a Cari a unos metros de él. Iba vestida para trabajar, con unos pantalones negros estrechos a juego con una fina blusa de manga larga. Se adivinaba el sujetador debajo. Pero sus ojos se fijaron en el bebé que llevaba en brazos.

No sabía qué hacer, y se subió las gafas de sol a la cabeza y sonrió.

–Sabía que llegarías pronto.

Parecía nerviosa y recordó al niño que había sido y que nunca había estado a gusto con sus padres. Nunca se había sentido querido ni deseado. Miró al niño que Cari tenía en brazos y sintió una oleada de ternura.

–Este es DJ –dijo Cari cuando Dec se acercó a ella.

Se quedó mirando a su hijo y de nuevo sintió un arrebato de emoción. Los ojos se le llenaron de lágrimas y mantuvo la cabeza gacha para que Cari no lo viera. Nunca había sentido nada tan intenso.

–¿Puedo tomarlo en brazos?

–Claro –contestó.

Volvió al bebé en sus brazos y se lo tendió.

Dec vaciló. Se sentía inseguro e incómodo, y el bebé gimoteó al cambiar de brazos.

–Tranquilo, DJ.

–*Mamamama*.

El pequeño alzó las manos y Cari tomó las gafas de sol de Dec un segundo antes de que lo hiciera DJ.

–Lo siento, tiene obsesión por las gafas y no creo que te quieras quedar sin ellas.

–No importa –dijo él.

Estaba asimilando el hecho de que aquel niño era hijo suyo. De todo lo que había conseguido en la vida, aquello era lo más inesperado.

–¿Quieres que demos un paseo por el muelle? –dijo Cari.

–Claro.

–¿Estás bien? –preguntó ella al echar a andar.

Dec asintió. No estaba preparado para hablar de sus sentimientos.

DJ llevaba un pelele de algodón y olía a colonia de bebé. Sus pequeñas manos no dejaban de moverse por los hombros de Dec. Al final, tuvo que pararse para mirar al niño, que no dejaba de emitir sonidos.

Tenía un hijo.

Aunque se había enterado la noche anterior, tenerlo en brazos lo hacía real. Hasta aquel momento, había podido pensar en el futuro y hacer sus propios planes, pero a partir de aquel momento debía tener en cuenta a aquel niño para asegurarse de que no le faltara nada. Mirándolo a los ojos, sentía la necesidad de ser mejor persona.

Nunca le habían importado los comentarios de otras personas. Desde muy joven había aprendido que no podía agradar a todo el mundo y no se había preocupado de nadie más. Sin embargo, en aquel momento, quería ser un héroe a los ojos de DJ.

El bebé se quedó mirándolo fijamente y acarició la cara de Dec, que no podía apartar la vista de su hijo. Los ojos eran suyos, y la nariz y el pelo rubio, de Cari.

Se volvió y la vio a unos metros, haciendo una fotografía con el teléfono móvil.

–*Mamama*…

Dec se giró hacia Cari.

–Le gusta hacer esos sonidos.

–¿Qué más cosas hace?

–Le gusta morderse la mano. A veces se vuelve irritable, pero acabo de darle de comer y de cambiarle para que estuviera tranquilo –explicó Cari, volviendo junto a ellos–. Quería que estuviera muy guapo cuando te conociera. ¿Qué piensas?

–Lo has hecho muy bien, Cari.

–Me dieron muchos analgésicos durante el parto.

–¿De veras? Quiero saberlo todo.

–¿Ahora?

Él sacudió la cabeza.

–Vamos a desayunar. Así podremos hablar de lo que vamos a hacer. No sé qué piensas, pero me gustaría formar parte de su vida.

–Muy bien, vayamos a hablar.

No le preocupaba que los vieran sus hermanas. Estaban paseando por la mañana un día de diario.

Se dirigieron hasta una cafetería con mesas al aire libre, y dejó a DJ con Cari mientras iba a buscar los cafés y unos pastelillos. Desde dentro, la observó a través de las cristaleras y se dio cuenta de que otros hombres se fijaban en ella. Era muy atractiva, y ni siquiera tener a un bebé en brazos los frenaba. Por vez primera en su vida, sintió celos.

Deseó salir y reivindicarlos como suyos. Eso lo asustaba, porque no estaba del todo seguro que pudiera tenerlos o qué sería de ellos a largo plazo. Sabía que debía encontrar una respuesta cuanto antes.

Cari había visto un lado diferente de Dec al tomar a DJ por primera vez en brazos. No quería olvidar que lo que él pretendía en aquel momento era que aquello funcionara, pero una vez que todo volviera a la normalidad, quizá no quisiera una relación seria. Tenía treinta y cinco años, edad suficiente para haber sentado la cabeza ya, aunque no había encontrado razón para hacerlo. Seguía soltero y sabía que era, tal y como él mismo había reconocido, porque era un hombre solitario.

–Un descafeinado con leche –dijo él, dándole la taza.

Luego se sentó frente a ella en una de aquellas pequeñas mesas que se habían puesto de moda en todas las terrazas y que le obligaba a estirar las piernas a cada lado de las de ella.

Resultaba imposible sentarse y estar cómodo para un hombre tan grande como Dec. Medía casi dos metros. Cari se preguntó si algún día DJ llegaría a ser así de alto.

–Gracias.

–De nada –respondió Dec antes de dar un sorbo a su café solo–. Tengo las ideas bastante claras en esto. Quiero empezar a salir contigo y que nos conozcamos. También quiero pasar ratos a solas con DJ para que se vaya acostumbrando a mí.

Ella lo miró entornando los ojos. Tenía que mostrarse firme, al fin y al cabo, era la madre de DJ. No podía ceder como a veces hacía en cuestiones de trabajo.

–¿Sabes algo de niños?

–No, pero aprendo rápido.

–Creo que lo mejor será que vengas a casa para estar con DJ. De esa manera, estaré cerca por si algo no va bien. ¿Te parece?

–Para empezar sí, pero quiero que se acostumbre a estar en mi casa.

–¿Dónde vives? –preguntó ella–. Mi casa está en Malibú.

–Ahora mismo me estoy quedando en la mansión de mis padres en Beverly Hills, pero me gusta vivir en mi yate.

–No estoy segura de…

–Sé que un yate no es el hogar ideal para un bebé. He quedado con un agente inmobiliario después del trabajo para que me enseñe varios pisos.

Ya había empezado a cambiar, pensó Cari. Pero un bebé era imprevisible. Había momentos en los que DJ empezaba a llorar y nada lo calmaba. ¿Cómo reaccionaría Dec en una situación así?

–Bueno, ya iremos improvisando.

–Muy bien. Pero quiero que sepas que en algún momento querré llevármelo a mi casa.

Ella asintió. Cuando DJ tuviera treinta años, podría ir donde quisiera.

–En relación a salir juntos –continuó Dec–, no quiero que esto sea una relación forzada.

–Ya veo que te has preparado una lista.

Él la miró frunciendo el ceño.

–Lo cierto es que sí. Yo… Esta es la primera vez que tengo a alguien de mi propia sangre. No quiero estropearlo.

Cari sintió que se derretía. Quería ser prudente y volver a verlo como un hombre frío, pero era difícil, viéndolo tan serio.

–¿Qué es lo siguiente que tienes en tu lista?

–Quiero conocerte.

–Yo también a ti –admitió ella.

–Bien. Una cosa más… Todavía te deseo.

Alargó la mano y le acarició la mejilla, provocándole un escalofrío.

–Ya me lo había imaginado. Yo también te deseo, pero no sé si es solo porque eres la fruta prohibida.

–¿Prohibida?

–Personificas al enemigo de mi familia –aclaró Cari.

–¿Es por eso que aceptaste aquella cita?

–No. No supe quién eras hasta casi el final de la cena.

–¿Cómo es posible que no me conocieras?

–Siempre que me hablaban de tu familia, pensaba en Thomas Montrose. Tenemos su retrato en el edificio.

–Y una vez que supiste que era yo, el enemigo a muerte, ¿qué pensaste?

–Espero que lo que te voy a decir no se te suba a la cabeza. Eres encantador cuando quieres algo.

–Lo sé –replicó él con aquella sonrisa arrogante suya–. Empezaremos a salir y ya veremos adónde nos lleva esta relación.

–¿Y si no funciona? –preguntó ella–. ¿Seguirás viendo a DJ?

–Sí. No sé qué clase de padre puedo ser, pero quiero ser el mejor para él. Quiero que crezca sabiendo que su padre le quiere.

–¿Sentirse querido es importante para ti?

–¿Sabes que soy adoptado, verdad?

Ella asintió. Nunca habían hablado de ello y se preguntó si se sentiría incómodo.

–Siempre supe que mis padres biológicos no me quisieron –añadió Dec.

–Pero tus padres adoptivos te eligieron.

–Lo sé, pero siempre tengo esa duda de si soy lo suficientemente bueno porque mis padres biológicos me abandonaron.

Cari asintió. Aquello explicaba por qué Dec trabajaba tanto y cómo siempre estaba persiguiendo nuevos objetivos. Sabía que podía ser un buen padre si evitaba que DJ se sintiera así. Claro que eso no era suficiente. Iba a tener que demostrárselo con hechos antes de poder confiar en él.

–De acuerdo. Y esto de las citas, ¿cómo va a funcionar? –preguntó ella.

–Como sabes, tenemos mucho trabajo esta semana. Tengo entendido que te van a entregar un nuevo juego.

–Sí. Quizá deberíamos esperar hasta la semana que viene.

–No, podemos quedar a cenar esta misma noche. Me pasaré por tu casa cuando acabe de trabajar para que me cuentes cómo te ha ido el día.

El hecho de que estuviera dispuesto a buscarle un hueco en su horario le gustó.

–Eso estaría bien.

–¿Dónde dejas a DJ por el día?

–En la guardería de Infinity. Por la tarde, lo subo a mi despacho y mientras acabo de trabajar.

–Podría recogerlo yo.

–No, mis hermanas se enterarían y empezarían a hacerse preguntas. Emma tiene un hijo de tres años que también va a la guardería.

–Entonces, llevaré algo de comida y cenaremos juntos en tu despacho.

No lograba entender cómo lo hacía, pero Dec siempre acababa saliéndose con la suya. En cuanto desplegaba su encanto, ella sucumbía. En el futuro, iba a tener que ser más prudente. No quería ponerle las cosas fáciles.

Aunque era la primera en reconocer que un hijo le cambiaba la vida a cualquiera, todavía no confiaba en Dec.

Tendría que estar atenta para no perder el rumbo más de lo que ya lo había perdido, algo que le resultaría mucho más sencillo si no le gustara.

Capítulo Siete

De vuelta en su despacho, Cari trató de concentrarse en el trabajo, pero las continuas interrupciones de los empleados se lo impedía. Todos le preguntaban por Dec, por el futuro y por lo que Cari pensaba que iba a pasar con sus puestos de trabajo, pero no tenía respuestas. Le pidió a Ally que se ocupara de las llamadas y subió a la planta ejecutiva en la que estaba el despacho de Emma.

Cuando había sido nombrada directora de gestión, había tomado la decisión de tener su despacho en la planta de oficinas. Quería estar donde los empleados pudieran verla a diario para así estar al tanto de en qué estaban trabajando. Aquel gesto había dado sus frutos y se llevaba muy bien con la plantilla.

–Parece que vas con prisa –dijo Emma al verla salir del ascensor.

Su hermana vestía un impecable traje de chaqueta y llevaba su melena oscura recogida en un moño. Era su habitual ropa de trabajo. Siendo la primogénita, la responsabilidad de dirigir Infinity había recaído sobre ella.

–Así es. ¿Te vas? –le preguntó a Emma.

–Sí, tengo una comida de trabajo al otro lado de la ciudad –respondió Emma mirando la hora en su reloj–. ¿Me necesitas, quieres que la cancele?

Cari recordó cuando tenía siete años. En las noches en que tenía miedo, recorría el largo y oscuro pasillo hasta la habitación de Emma y se quedaba al lado de su cama susurrando su nombre hasta que apartaba las sábanas y la invitaba a acostarse con ella. Siempre que había tenido problemas, había recurrido a Emma.

Le resultaba muy difícil no contarle todo, especialmente después de que Dec hubiera vuelto a aparecer en su vida. Quería confiar en alguien y liberarse de aquella carga. Pero sabía que no podía hacerlo. Sonrió a su hermana, aunque suspiró para sus adentros.

–Siempre necesito a mi hermana mayor, pero no quiero que canceles los planes que tienes para la comida. Tenemos a toda la plantilla asustada. Solo necesitaba escapar un rato donde nadie pudiera encontrarme –dijo, lo cual era cierto en parte.

No podía trabajar con tanta gente entrando y saliendo de su despacho, haciéndole preguntas cada cinco minutos.

Siempre había llevado una política de puertas abiertas. Había aprendido de su paso por los distintos departamentos que a los empleados les gustaba ser escuchados.

–Puedes quedarte en mi despacho. Estaré fuera hasta las dos –dijo Emma–. Sam me ha pedido que te dijera que puede cuidar de DJ cuando quieras.

–¿De veras?

–Sí. Quiere enseñarle a decir «¿qué pasa, perro?».

–¿Para qué?

–Porque cree que te hará mucha gracia –respondió Emma–. Me contó que estuvisteis bailando mientras veíais no sé qué programa.

–Se supone que eso era secreto –replicó Cari.

No pudo evitar sonreír al recordar lo bien que se lo había pasado con su sobrino viendo aquel concurso de cantantes, y pensó en todo por lo que había tenido que pasar Emma desde que murió su marido. Si Emma había conseguido salir adelante, ella también podría. Los Chandler no se caracterizaban por esconder la cabeza. A pesar de lo mucho que deseaba tomar distancia, no podía huir de Dec.

–Gracias, Emma.

–De nada, cariño. ¿Estás segura de que no me necesitas?

Cari reunió todas sus fuerzas y se irguió. Era una mujer adulta, una ejecutiva, y ya no dependía de su hermana. No podía seguir huyendo ni esconderse cada vez que le ocurriera algo.

–Por supuesto, muchas gracias, hermanita. Creo que solo necesitaba un descanso. Bajaré contigo en el ascensor.

Aunque el trayecto de bajada fue breve, Cari se sintió una mujer cambiada. Tenía la sensación de que desde que Dec había llegado, había perdido el control no solo en la empresa sino en su vida personal también. Tenía que recordarse que seguía siendo la mujer segura en la que se había convertido desde el nacimiento de su hijo. El que Dec estuviera allí, al final del pasillo, no cambiaba nada.

–Pensé que te habías ido –dijo Ally al verla regresar a su despacho.

–Necesitaba un respiro, pero he cambiado de opinión. Creo que deberíamos convocar una reunión para los empleados. Envía un correo electrónico a todos para que estén a las dos en el comedor. Y que nos preparen galletas y refrescos. Voy a presentar a Dec y a explicar la fusión. Contestaré preguntas, pero solo de temas generales.

–¿Estás segura de que quieres hacerlo? La gente parece que se ha vuelto loca.

–Lo sé, por eso tenemos que hacerlo. Creo que si lo dejamos todo claro será lo mejor.

–¿Todo claro? ¿A qué te refieres?

–A que habrá reducción de personal y que la mejor manera de salvar sus puestos es trabajando y no viniendo a verme a mí –dijo Cari–. Voy a ir a hablar con Dec.

–Creo que el señor McKinney está con él.

–¿Su primo? ¿Qué está haciendo aquí?

–No lo sé –respondió Ally–. Creo que deberíamos poner micrófonos en la sala de juntas –añadió arqueando una ceja.

–No creo que eso sea una solución.

–Así sería más fácil saber qué cabezas van a cortar.

–También es ilegal.

–Qué puntillosa –bromeó Ally.

Cari sonrió a su secretaria antes de entrar en su despacho. Tenía que aclararse las ideas antes de ir a hablar con Dec. Anotó algunas preguntas sobre los objetivos de reducción y las fechas límite para llevarlos a cabo. Pero mientras escribía, se dio cuenta de que tenía otras preguntas. Quizá por eso se sentía tan impaciente.

Quería saber qué esperaba por salir con ella y si la volvería a besar otra vez. En cuanto identificó sus verdaderas preocupaciones, se sintió mejor. Lo deseaba y aquella mañana, al verlo con DJ en brazos, le había resultado aún más atractivo. No parecía un solitario ni un hombre que la abandonaría por segunda vez.

Y esos eran pensamientos muy peligrosos.

Dec se recostó en el respaldo del sillón de cuero que había hecho traer de Playtone y miró a su primo, tratando de averiguar por qué había venido hasta allí. Allan tenía treinta y cinco años, como él, y era unos centímetros más bajo. Tenía el aire de la familia Montrose, con su denso pelo oscuro y sus ojos grises. Le gustaba pasar tiempo al aire libre y siempre estaba bronceado, algo que no era difícil en California.

—¿A qué has venido? —preguntó Dec después de comentar el último partido de los Lakers—. Dudo que hayas venido para hablar de baloncesto.

—Kell piensa que has vuelto cansado de Australia y que por eso no estás centrado —comentó Allan.

—¿Por qué piensa eso? No he dejado de mandarle informes desde que llegué. Está ansioso y actúa como un maníaco.

—Estoy de acuerdo, pero le dije que me pasaría por aquí para comprobar que todo estuviera bien.

—Bueno, ya lo has hecho, así que supongo que ya hemos acabado.

—Todavía no. La secretaria de la directora de gestión me ha fulminado con la mirada.

–La plantilla no parece muy contenta de que hayamos comprado la compañía. Algunos se muestran muy beligerantes, pero podré soportarlo. Es lo que suele pasar en la mayoría de las empresas que compramos –dijo Dec.

–Kell se lo está tomando de manera muy personal –observó Allan.

–Lo sé –convino Dec, y empujó hacia atrás su asiento–. ¿Y tú? Sé que no estoy tan implicado en la rivalidad como vosotros. Quiero decir que a mi madre le daba igual lo que pasara con Gregory. Ella se escudaba en su dinero. Para ella era la solución.

–Era una solución, pero no la que el abuelo quería –observó Allan–. Creo que tu padre también estaba harto de la rivalidad. Por eso es que…

–Se casó con una heredera –dijo concluyendo la frase de su primo–. Lo sé. Solía decirlo cuando bebía. ¿Por qué no podía olvidarlo el viejo?

–Porque él no era así. Tampoco Kell.

–Bueno, en esto va a tener que ceder un poco. Ya no se llevan las adquisiciones hostiles ni eso de despedir a todo el mundo. Sobre todo en nuestra industria. Acabaríamos perdiendo mucho talento –explicó Dec–. Entre los empleados hay gente que nos interesa mantener para que sigan diseñando juegos para nosotros.

–Lo entiendo –dijo Allan–. No envidio tu trabajo. ¿Por qué lo haces?

–¿Qué quieres decir?

–Ambos sabemos que no te hace falta trabajar.

Dec no sabía cómo explicarlo. Lo cierto era que ser parte de la compañía le hacía sentirse como un verdadero Montrose. Quería ayudar a sus primos a conseguir su objetivo de vengarse de los Chandler. Siempre había estado al margen hasta aquel día en que, a sus veintitrés años, Kell lo había llamado para preguntarle si quería trabajar con ellos en la empresa familiar y ayudarlos para hundir Infinity.

—Soy un Montrose.

—Cierto —afirmó Allan con una sonrisa—. ¿Qué tal te va con la Chandler con la que estás tratando?

No estaba dispuesto a revelarle a Allan sus verdaderos sentimientos hacia Cari, especialmente cuando ni él mismo sabía cómo controlarlos. Como directiva estaba haciendo un gran trabajo dándole el espacio que necesitaba para evaluar al personal.

—Es buena.

—Conozco a Jessi, la hermana mediana.

—¿Ah, sí? ¿Desde cuándo?

Recordaba que Kell le había comentado algo sobre Allan y la hermana mediana.

—Desde hace un par de años. Su mejor amiga está casada con mi mejor amigo. Cada vez que celebran algo, ahí está para fastidiarme.

—¿Tan en serio se toma la rivalidad? —preguntó Dec.

Por lo que veía en Cari, a ella no parecía importarle demasiado.

—Le gusta incordiar —contestó Allan—. Hizo que investigaran a John antes de la boda.

—¿Estás de broma, no? Su familia es una de las más ricas del país.

—Sí, lo sé. Pero según ella, el dinero no convierte a nadie en una buena persona.

–Quizá lo hizo para fastidiarte.

–Seguramente. Esa mujer me altera.

–Te entiendo perfectamente –murmuró Dec.

–¿Acaso tienes problemas con las mujeres? No sabía que estuvieras saliendo con alguien –dijo Allan.

–Algo así –anunció justo en el momento en que la puerta se abría.

Alzó la mirada y vio a Cari. Llevaba el pelo como de costumbre recogido en una coleta, con el flequillo cubriéndole la frente. Sus ojos azules tenían una expresión burlona.

–Siento interrumpir, pero necesito hablar contigo sobre una reunión con los empleados.

–Me alegro por la interrupción. ¿Conoces a mi primo Allan?

–No –respondió, acercándose para estrecharle la mano a Allan.

–Pareces menos guerrera que tu hermana.

–Lo intento. Ella tampoco tiene una buena opinión de ti.

–Ya me he dado cuenta, por la manera en que me mira cada vez que coincidimos en la misma habitación –dijo Allan, soltándole la mano–. No te pareces a tus hermanas.

–Lo sé. Cuando era pequeña, solían decirme que era adoptada.

–Yo lo soy –intervino Dec–. Tenemos mucho en común –añadió bromeando.

–Interesante –dijo su primo, mirándolos alternativamente a él y a Cari.

–¿Qué es interesante? –preguntó Cari un poco confusa.

–Nada –respondió Allan.

Dec se volvió hacia su primo.

–Allan, ¿no tenías que marcharte?

–Todavía no. He venido a observar, ¿recuerdas?

La situación era incómoda para Dec. No quería que su primo los observara a él y a Cari juntos. Pero sabía que no había forma de sacar a Allan de allí salvo que lo echara.

A pesar de que Cari no tenía interés en ver al primo de Dec, le había servido para recordarle que había otros jugadores en aquella partida. Era difícil no tomarse toda aquella situación como un juego. Allan era un adversario al que debía convencer para unirse a su equipo o para destruirlo.

En su cabeza, se había vestido con una armadura y un escudo antes de acudir a la sala de juntas, y se alegraba de haberlo hecho. Se dio cuenta de que debía mantener un férreo control sobre sus citas. Había algo en Dec y en todo aquel asunto que le hacía desear que el momento hubiera sido otro.

¿Habría sido capaz de salvar Infinity si hubiera buscado a Dec nada más enterarse de que estaba embarazada en vez de quedarse esperando? Probablemente no. La enemistad entre familias no se acababa con matrimonios ni herederos. La Primera Guerra Mundial había sido buena prueba de ello.

–¿En qué te puedo ayudar? –preguntó Dec a Cari, sacándola de sus pensamientos.

–Los empleados están muy nerviosos. Los he

convocado esta tarde para una reunión y quisiera darles información para tranquilizarlos.

—¿Qué ideas tienes?

—Me gustaría darles algún detalle en concreto sobre el recorte de personal, que sepan de qué tanto por ciento estamos hablando, y que cabe la posibilidad de que, si se esfuerzan, estarán a salvo.

Allan se echó hacia delante y la miró.

—Siéntate, Cari.

Tomó asiento al otro lado de la mesa.

—¿De veras crees que si lo saben se quedarán más tranquilos? —añadió Allan.

—Sí. Mi equipo es muy bueno cumpliendo objetivos económicos. Todos sabemos que hay que hacer recortes, y en el pasado, recurriendo a la plantilla y pidiéndoles ciertos sacrificios, lo hemos conseguido. Quiero que la transición sea fácil para ellos. Todos están preocupados.

—Bueno, todavía no tenemos unas cifras concretas para los recortes. Todavía estoy recogiendo información para que la analice Allan.

—Soy el director financiero —aclaró Allan.

—Lo sé —dijo Cari—. Nos gusta conocer al enemigo. Y según Jessi, tienes pezuñas y cola.

—Yo creo que la diabólica es ella —afirmó Allan.

Cari se mordió el labio para evitar sonreír. Era más que evidente que Allan y su hermana no se llevaban bien.

—En tu opinión, ¿qué recortes crees que serían necesarios?

Dec miró a Allan. Los primos parecían comunicarse sin necesidad de palabras. Cari se echó hacia atrás en su asiento y los observó. Dec era el más atractivo de los dos. Allan también era guapo, pero no le atraía tanto como Dec. Mientras lo miraba fijamente, reparó en que tenía una pequeña cicatriz debajo del ojo izquierdo que no había visto hasta aquel momento.

Y su boca... Había pensando mucho en aquellos labios y en la manera en que habían presionado los suyos mientras la buscaba con su lengua. Desde el primer beso, había disfrutado de su buen sabor.

—¿Crees que puede funcionar, Cari?

Había estado soñando despierta y se había perdido algo importante. Tenía que fingir que estaba de acuerdo con lo que acabaran de decir o reconocer que no estaba prestando atención.

—Explicadme qué planes tenéis.

Dec asintió y le pasó el cuaderno en el que Allan y él tenían algunas cifras anotadas. En su área, preveían un incremento del margen de beneficio del veinte por ciento, por lo que no se prescindiría de ningún empleado.

—Creo que es factible.

Supondría más horas de trabajo y adelantar la producción de juegos. De hecho, mientras estudiaba los números, se le ocurrió una idea con la que conseguir algo más que salvar puestos de empleo. Tal vez le diera un motivo a Playtone de mantener Infinity en funcionamiento.

—Me alegro de oírlo. Es un objetivo muy ambicioso —dijo Allan—. Pocos departamentos de compañías de videojuegos conozco que pudieran hacerlo.

Dec tomó la palabra antes de que Cari pudiera decir nada.

—Bueno, no has visto a Cari en acción. Llevo dos días escuchando a los empleados decir que es la mejor jefa que han tenido nunca. Creo que estarían dispuestos a matar por agradarla.

Cari puso los ojos en blanco.

—No exageres. Es solo que soy una persona empática.

—Es más que eso —terció Dec—. Tienes algo especial.

Cari sintió que le ardían las mejillas y sacudió la cabeza. Había un brillo en los ojos de Dec que no tenía nada que ver con su visión empresarial y sí con el vínculo que había entre ellos. Y durara o no, sabía que siempre habría aquella fuerte atracción entre ellos.

—Bueno, eso no lo sé. Pero intentaré hacerlo lo mejor posible —dijo ella, poniéndose de pie dispuesta para marcharse.

—Te veré en la cena —se despidió Dec.

—Lo estoy deseando —reconoció, y sonrió antes de darse media vuelta y marcharse.

Confiaba en que Allan la viera como una mujer segura y decidida, y no como un manojo de nervios. Incluso la armadura imaginaria que llevaba puesta empezaba a tener resquicios. Iba a ser difícil mantener separada su vida personal de la laboral, porque no sabía prescindir de sus emociones cuando tomaba una decisión. Y Dec era un hombre que la hacía sentir muy emocional.

Capítulo Ocho

Dec encargó a su restaurante favorito que les llevara la cena a las siete. Desde la primera vez que cenó con Cari en su despacho dos semanas atrás, aquel se había convertido en su momento favorito del día. Aquella tarde, muchos de los empleados seguían trabajando y, al llegar al despacho, reparó en que su secretaria se había ido. Se detuvo junto a la puerta y la observó sentada en el suelo con DJ.

El pequeño enseguida lo vio y gateó hacia él.

–Ah, hola, Dec.

–¿Qué estás enseñándole?

Dec dejó la comida en la mesa y se agachó para tomar a DJ en brazos. Volvió a sentir que se le encogía al corazón al pensar que era su hijo. Abrazó al bebé y el niño le sonrió mientras intentaba agarrarle la nariz.

–*Mamama*.

–No, yo soy papá.

–*Mamama* –repitió DJ.

–Es muy cabezota, supongo que le viene de…

–Cuidado con lo que dices –dijo Cari, poniéndose de pie.

–Iba a decir lo mismo –terció Dec–. ¿Lo dejo sentado aquí mientras comemos? –preguntó acercándose al portabebés que estaba junto al escritorio.

–Sí, tengo un yogur para él en la nevera. ¿Sabes cómo ponerlo?

–Claro.

Aunque fuera nuevo en aquello de ser padre, con Cari cerca se sentía seguro. Además, pocas cosas había en su vida que no hubiera sido capaz de resolver. Aquello no era diferente. Cuando había montado negocios por su cuenta, se había dejado guiar por su intuición y se había negado a aceptar el dinero que sus padres le habían querido dar, para demostrar su valía. Y le había ido muy bien.

–¿Necesitas ayuda? –preguntó Cari volviendo con el yogur.

Dec se había quedado mirando el portabebés en vez de colocar al bebé en él. Lo sentó y le abrochó las sujeciones antes de ocuparse de la comida que había llevado para cenar.

–¿Te importa si cierro la puerta?

–En absoluto.

Cari empezó a dar cucharadas de yogur a DJ, que no parecía muy convencido.

–¿Estás segura de que es bueno? Es un niño.

Cari puso los ojos en blanco y lo miró.

–Sé muy bien lo que necesita mi hijo.

Dec levantó las manos en señal de rendición y siguió preparando la mesa para cenar.

–Supongo que estoy celoso del vínculo que tienes con nuestro hijo, cuando yo apenas lo conozco. Ni siquiera sabía que le gustara el yogur.

–Bueno, y el pollo le encanta. Te queda mucho para ponerte al día. ¿De veras quieres hacer el esfuerzo?

Dec la miró y se preguntó qué habría querido decir. Sintió un arrebato de ira, pero al mirarla, vio miedo en sus ojos. No podía olvidar que había sido él el que la había abandonado después de una noche.

–¿En qué estás pensando? –preguntó ella.

–En que me habría gustado que me hablaras de él antes de que naciera –respondió Dec sin disimular la emoción que sentía–. Me siento engañado.

–Lo sé, pero ni siquiera ahora puedo decir que lo habría hecho de otra manera. Teniendo en cuenta que fue una aventura de una noche y que no era fácil dar contigo… Era como si el destino quisiera que tuviera a DJ yo sola.

–Puedo entenderlo.

Eso explicaba en parte por qué se sentía tan confuso. También era consciente de que estaba completamente justificado que dudara de él.

–Y quiero hacerlo –continuó Dec–. No sé si estoy cambiando y tienes todo el derecho a cuestionarme, porque cada vez que lo haces, refuerza el deseo de estar con mi hijo.

–Bien, es lo que pretendo.

Cari le limpió la cara a DJ y luego volvió a la nevera. Después de calentar leche en el microondas, volvió con un biberón.

–¿Toma leche de fórmula?

–No, es leche materna –explicó–. Me resulta más fácil extraerla para poder compatibilizar la lactancia con la jornada laboral.

Le dio el biberón a DJ y enseguida se lo tomó. Al cabo de unos minutos, los ojos empezaron a cerrársele.

–Es como un reloj. En cuanto acaba de comer, le da sueño.

–Supongo que eso nos viene bien para cenar. Ya está todo listo –anunció Dec.

–Voy a dejar el portabebés en el suelo, así lo veré mejor mientras comemos.

Dec la observó dejar un peluche junto a su hijo antes de taparlo con una manta.

–No me gusta dejarlo en el portabebés, pero cuando me quedo a trabajar hasta tarde, prefiero que esté durmiendo.

–¿Sueles quedarte trabajando hasta tarde? –preguntó Dec.

–Bueno, no quiero hacerte sentir culpable, pero desde que supimos de la compra, no hemos parado de trabajar.

–Siento que haya sido así. Tenía que haberte advertido de que nada iba a detener a Kell de conseguir su objetivo.

–No me sorprende. La tenacidad parece que es una característica de los Montrose.

–Solo soy Montrose de apellido.

–Pero te criaron ellos, Dec. ¿Por qué te empeñas en decir que eres diferente?

–Siempre me he sentido diferente. No es algo que alguien me haya dicho, es solo que tengo la sensación de que tengo que esforzarme continuamente para demostrar mi valía.

–¿Por qué? He buscado información sobre tu familia y, sin el dinero de tu madre, Thomas Montrose no habría podido mantener su imperio de videojuegos.

Dec se quedó mirándola. Se sentía desconcertado. Era como si Cari lo estuviera defendiendo a él y a su derecho de ser un Montrose. No había dicho nada que no supiera ya, pero oírselo decir a otra persona marcaba la diferencia.

–Es cierto, pero nunca he sentido que encajara.

–Lo siento –dijo ella–. No te hablé de DJ no porque no encajaras en mi idea de lo que debía ser un padre. Es solo que no estaba segura de querer complicarlo todo aún más.

Él asintió. Era evidente. Era una buena madre y quería mucho a DJ. Esperaba que algún día pudiera formar parte de ese círculo de personas a las que quería.

Durante la cena, Cari descubrió mucho sobre Dec. Había dejado a DJ en la guardería, donde el personal estaba haciendo horas extra. Tenían cunas y DJ estaba mucho más cómodo durmiendo allí que en el portabebés. Además quería aprovechar para tener a Dec para ella sola y pensar en qué iba a hacer con él.

Parecía su primera cita. Aunque Dec no quiso seguir hablando de su pasado, sentía que estaban en la misma línea.

Seguía habiendo una fuerte atracción entre ellos. Cada vez que lo miraba y lo pillaba observándola, sentía que la sangre le ardía en las venas. Y cuando sus manos se rozaban, un cosquilleo le subía por el brazo, provocando un delicioso estremecimiento por todo su cuerpo. Pero la noche no iba solo de sexo, sino de conocerse mejor. Quizá fuera capricho del destino que hicieran las cosas en otro orden.

–¿En qué estás pensando? –preguntó Dec, sacándola de sus pensamientos.

–En que por fin te estoy conociendo.

–Eso no es cierto. Ya me has visto desnudo. Me conoces muy bien.

Cari negó con la cabeza.

–Te equivocas. Hoy he visto esto por vez primera –dijo alargando la mano y acariciando la cicatriz de debajo de su ojo izquierdo–. ¿Cómo te lo hiciste?

Dec tomó su mano y se la llevó a los labios para besarla.

–Tengo esa cicatriz desde los nueve años. Había ido por primera vez a hacer camping con mi abuelo, Kell y Allan. Mis primos llevaban yendo desde los seis años, pero mi madre y mi abuelo habían tenido sus peleas, así que no había podido ir hasta ese verano.

–¿Por qué peleaban?

Parecía que el viejo Thomas tenía problemas con todo el mundo.

–Por el dinero de mi madre –contestó Dec–. Así que cuando llegamos a Bear…

–¿Big Bear? Mis abuelos maternos tenían una casa allí arriba.

–Sí, Big Bear –dijo él–. ¿Quieres que acabe de contarte la historia?

–Claro –respondió Cari sonriendo.

–Así que llegamos y mis primos eran unos expertos con las tablas de *snowboard*, pero yo nunca me había subido a una. Sabía esquiar porque mi madre había insistido en que aprendiera cuando estuvimos el invierno anterior en St. Motriz. Pero Kell dijo que el esquí era para peleles, así que me subí a una tabla de *snowboard*, perdí el control y me di contra un árbol. Me lleve un buen golpe en el lado izquierdo de la cara y me quedó esta cicatriz.

Cari no esperaba aquello. Lo tomó de la mano y le acarició los nudillos, sintiendo lástima de aquel niño desesperado por demostrar su valía ante los Montrose y ocupar su sitio.

—¿Aprendiste a hacer *snowboard*?

—No. Solo sé esquiar y me da igual lo que piense Kell. Se sintió mal porque me obligó.

—Erais solo unos niños. Tu abuelo debería haber intervenido.

—Él pensaba que esa clase de cosas nos venían bien. Decía que siempre debíamos quedarnos con hambre.

—No estoy de acuerdo. No quiero criar a DJ de esa manera.

—No me quejo del modo en que me criaron, pero quiero que DJ tenga una infancia mejor que la que yo tuve.

—¿Es por eso que quieres tener una relación conmigo?

—En parte sí. No quiero que piense nunca que no le quise. Sé cómo me sentía sabiendo que mis padres biológicos… Bueno, eso ya es agua pasada. ¿Qué me dices de ti? ¿Tienes alguna cicatriz?

No quería que cambiara de tema de conversación. Quería saber más de Dec y de su forma de ser, pero era evidente que no quería seguir hablando del pasado.

–Tengo una cicatriz y si averiguas dónde está…

–Me dejarás besarla.

–¿Para qué ibas a hacer eso?

–¿Está en algún sitio interesante?

–No –respondió ella, sacudiendo la cabeza.

–Vaya. ¿Pero me dejarás besarla si lo adivino?

–Claro.

Era imposible que lo adivinara.

–Ponte de pie –le pidió Dec.

–¿Por qué?

–Para examinarte. ¿Cómo voy a tomar una decisión si no dispongo de toda la información?

Cari puso los ojos en blanco. Era evidente que Dec no quería que pasara nada entre ellos esa noche. No parecía tan serio y preocupado como de costumbre, así que dio una vuelta para él. Se estaba mostrando cordial, pero no la estaba permitiendo conocer su verdadero yo.

Ella estaba mostrándose tan abierta como de costumbre. Tal vez, si no abriera tanto su corazón…

–Detrás de la rodilla.

Cari abrió los ojos como platos y lo miró con el ceño fruncido.

–Sí. ¿Cómo lo has adivinado?

–Ha sido casualidad.

–Imposible –dijo mirándose los pantalones–. Confiesa.

–Supongo que te niegas al beso.

–No, hemos hecho un trato. Solo quiero saber cómo lo has sabido.

–Te vi desnuda, Cari, y he revivido aquella noche en mi cabeza muchas veces. Tengo memorizado cada centímetro de tu cuerpo, desde la cicatriz de detrás de tu rodilla hasta la mancha de nacimiento que tienes al final de la espalda.

Sintió que se derretía. El que recordara aquellos detalles… No, no significaba nada. Solo que era un amante muy observador, cosa que ya sabía.

Lo miró y sintió un nudo en el estómago mientras luchaba contra algo que no debía hacer. Alzó la mano y le hizo un gesto con el dedo.

Dec se levantó y lentamente caminó hasta ella. Cari lo detuvo a escasos centímetros de ella, poniéndole una mano en el pecho.

–No sé si eres un seductor, un amante serio o el mayor error de mi vida.

–Soy un seductor que muy seriamente está dispuesto a amarte. Respecto a lo otro, esto no me parece un error –dijo y, atrayéndola entre sus brazos, la besó.

La manera en que sus labios se movían sobre los suyos era firme y decidida. La sujetó con firmeza por la nuca y se adueñó de su boca, tomando lo que quería de ella y dándole aquello que no sabía que ansiaba hasta ese mismo momento. Cada uno de los movimientos de Dec la empujaba a olvidarse de sus reservas y a dejarse llevar por sus deseos. Su lengua jugueteó con la suya antes de metérsela en la boca. Sus manos se deslizaron por su espalda hasta llegar a la cintura y atraerla hacia él.

Cari sintió la fuerza de su pecho musculoso bajo el tejido de la camisa. Sintió la tensión de sus dedos al clavarse en su cintura y levantarla del suelo para estrecharla contra su cuerpo. Sintió su potente erección y supo que el juego se había acabado.

No cabían juegos con aquel deseo, y tampoco los quería. Ya le había contado que tenían un hijo y estaban buscando la manera de que sus empresas se fusionaran. Además, hacía año y medio que no tenía sexo, que no sentía las manos de un hombre acariciando su cuerpo. Y no cualquier hombre, sino aquel.

Lo rodeó por los hombros y le acarició el pelo. Él ladeó la cabeza hacia la izquierda y el beso se volvió más profundo. Cari deseaba más. Olía a hombre, a deseo y a Dec. Era un olor que pensaba que no volvería a percibir y, aunque había intentado no darle importancia, se alegraba de que hubiera vuelto a su vida.

Separó la boca de la suya y alzó la vista para mirarlo a los ojos. Tenía la piel sonrojada por la excitación y el brillo de su mirada era tan intenso que no pudo evitar estremecerse. Dec volvió a unir su boca a la suya y esta vez el beso fue más lento, sensual y profundo.

Cari dejó de pensar y cedió a la pasión que la arrastraba. Él volvió a levantarla del suelo, sujetándola por el trasero mientras movía las caderas para presionar su erección contra su entrepierna. Al rozarla en el lugar preciso, ella dejó caer la cabeza hacia atrás mientras él le besaba el cuello.

—Rodéame la cintura con las piernas —susurró junto a su piel, haciéndola estremecerse.

Cari obedeció y Dec atravesó el despacho hasta colocarla sobre el escritorio. Sin que dejara de rodearlo por la cintura con las piernas, la levantó por las caderas para que sintiera su erección.

Luego apoyó las manos en el escritorio a cada lado de ella.

–Échate hacia atrás.

Ella vaciló.

–Hazlo.

Cari hizo lo que le pedía y se apoyó sobre los codos, mientras él empezaba a desabrocharle lentamente los botones de la blusa. Se detuvo al dejar a la vista el sujetador y besó la piel que acababa de descubrir.

–Recuerdo que la última vez llevabas encaje –dijo él.

–Mis pechos son más grandes ahora.

–Ya lo veo –dijo tomando su pecho izquierdo con la mano y pellizcándole el pezón.

Sentía los pechos llenos y unas gotas de leche humedecieron el sujetador. Dec se frotó los dedos y deslizó la mano por debajo.

Cari se preguntó si aquello echaría a perder la magia del momento. A ella no le afectaba en absoluto porque ardía por él y lo deseaba en aquel instante. Lo miró a los ojos y comprobó que seguía teniendo aquella mirada de deseo, combinada con una dulce expresión que nunca antes había visto en su rostro.

–No resulta muy sexy, ¿no?

–Tal vez para otro hombre, pero para mí es un recordatorio de lo que compartimos.

Quería preguntarle más sobre aquello, pero él se inclinó y la besó. Esta vez no fue un beso tan impetuoso, pero sí igual de intenso. Se sentía sobrecogida por aquel arrebato de ternura, mientras seguía estrechándola contra él y besándola profundamente.

–Lo siento –dijo ella, sin saber muy bien cómo evitar que su pecho siguiera haciendo eso.

–No te disculpes –replicó Dec mientras seguía desabrochándole la blusa.

Cari se aferró a sus hombros y trató de atraerlo hacia ella, pero él mantuvo la distancia.

–¿Todavía me deseas? –preguntó él, mirándola a los ojos.

–Sí –respondió, sabiendo que no podía ocultarle nada a aquel hombre–. Sí.

Capítulo Nueve

Aquella era la respuesta que esperaba escuchar.

Dec deslizó la mano entre ellos y le abrió el botón y la cremallera de los pantalones. Cari arqueó las caderas mientras sentía su mano introducirse por la apertura. Luego, su boca volvió junto a la suya.

Todo en Cari le resultaba más intenso. Su perfume embriagaba sus sentidos con cada inspiración. Su piel parecía más suave que nunca y, después de tener a DJ, sus curvas eran más generosas. Estaba disfrutando con todo lo que estaba descubriendo de ella.

A pesar de que pensaba que la conocía, se estaba dando cuenta de que no sabía nada de ella. Tal y como se sentía en aquel momento, como si estuviera a punto de explotar si no se hundía en ella, le hacía arrepentirse de haber antepuesto los negocios a todo. Debería haberse quedado en sus brazos.

Metió la mano por debajo de sus bragas, acariciando con un dedo la húmeda calidez de su apertura. Ella suspiró su nombre entre jadeos y él la miró sonriente. Cari se movió contra él y su mano encontró primero su muslo y luego la dureza de su miembro erecto. Lo acarició de arriba abajo por encima de los pantalones, aferrándose a él y jugueteando con la punta.

Luego buscó su cremallera, pero él se adelantó y liberó su pene. A continuación, deslizó los dedos por su entrepierna y ella lo atrajo hacia sí, rodeando su miembro con la mano. Dec aprovechó su brazo libre para levantarla del escritorio.

–Quítate los pantalones.

Ella hizo lo que le pedía y, cuando los tenía por los muslos, volvió a dejarla sobre la mesa y tiró de ellos y de las bragas hasta dejarlos en el suelo, quitándole los zapatos a la vez. Luego le hizo separar las piernas y se inclinó sobre ella. Inhaló su esencia femenina y empezó a darle besos por el interior del muslo, subiendo hasta mordisquearle la cadera.

Cari se revolvió y le puso una mano en la cabeza a Dec y otra en el vientre. Él reparó en que ya no tenía el vientre tan liso como antes y había algunas estrías. Toda señal de que había tenido un hijo suyo lo excitaba cada vez más. Estaba deseando volver a hacerla suya.

Su hijo había dejado huella en ella y él también quería hacerlo. Bajó la cabeza para morderle el interior del muslo, y luego la lamió y besó en el mismo sitio, antes de volver la cabeza hacia el centro. No había olvidado el sabor de su intimidad y estaba deseando volver a disfrutarlo.

Le separó aún más las piernas y le acarició el clítoris con la lengua. Luego, siguió explorándola suavemente con la boca. Cari se revolvió, pero él la sujetó para que se quedara quieta y poder seguir disfrutando de su rincón más íntimo. Luego, la penetró con la punta de un dedo y ella lo buscó con las caderas tratando de sentirlo completamente en su interior.

Dec bajó la cabeza un poco más y hundió la lengua en ella. Cari tomó su cabeza entre las manos y se acercó aún más a él. Sabía que estaba al límite. Podía sentirlo por la forma en que su cuerpo lo buscaba. Dec se apartó e introdujo su dedo hasta dar con su punto G.

Ella emitió un sonido agudo y Dec sintió que su cuerpo se tensaba alrededor de su dedo. Mantuvo la mano donde la tenía hasta que Cari se desplomó, y permaneció mirándola, sonriendo.

—Gracias —dijo ella.

—Ha sido un placer.

—No, el placer ha sido mío. Hace siglos que no sentía algo así.

—¿Cuánto exactamente?

—Año y medio —respondió observándolo con sus ojos azules—. He estado ocupada y a la mayoría de los hombres no les interesa una mujer que acaba de ser madre.

—Me alegro.

No quería ningún otro hombre en escena. Se sentía dueño de ella y de DJ. Ambos eran suyos.

Sí, decidió. Era suya y no sabía qué hacer con ella más allá del sexo, pero no estaba dispuesto a dejar que se marchara. Le daba igual que fuera demasiado inocente para un hombre como él.

Cari buscó su miembro, que seguía erecto, y lo acarició. Al inclinarse sobre él, Dec sintió su aliento y el roce de su lengua. Luego, un escalofrío lo recorrió, y no pudo evitar sentir que una gota de su esencia escapaba a su control. Ella la chupó antes de introducirse el pene en la boca, mientras él ponía una mano en su cabeza y le acariciaba la melena rubia.

Deseaba disfrutar de cada segundo de aquello. Trató de apartarla para advertirle de que tenía que parar, pero ella le puso las manos en la espalda para seguir como estaban. No dejó de recorrerlo hasta que sus caderas comenzaron a sacudirse por los espasmos del orgasmo.

Cari siguió chupándolo con fuerza hasta que se quedó completamente extenuado. Cuando se apartó, Dec no supo qué decir, aunque Cari tampoco le dio la oportunidad de hablar. Se limitó a sentarse, lo rodeó con sus brazos y apoyó la cabeza junto a su corazón. Él la abrazó y la preocupación de si era el hombre adecuado para ella desapareció. Al menos por esa noche solo quería disfrutar de estar entre sus brazos.

Cari no tenía palabras ni encontraba la manera de fingir que aquello solo era sexo. Temía que Dec la dejara al igual que había hecho la vez anterior. Hasta aquel momento, no se había dado cuenta de que aquel temor seguía dentro de ella, oculto bajo una seguridad que no era más que superficial.

Giró la cabeza y apartó la vista, confiando en ocultarle a Dec sus emociones. Se fijó en el portabebés de DJ y recordó que la última vez que había estado en los brazos de aquel hombre, su vida había cambiado. Y aunque tomaba la píldora, no estaba dispuesta a correr riesgos de nuevo.

Se apartó de él y se levantó del escritorio. Luego, recogió su ropa interior con toda la dignidad que pudo reunir.

–Voy al baño. Enseguida vuelvo –dijo, y se fue antes de que Dec dijera algo.

Cerró la puerta de su cuarto de baño privado y se sentó en el inodoro. Un torbellino de emociones la invadió. El placer todavía inundaba cada rincón de su cuerpo y tuvo que parpadear para evitar que las lágrimas que ardían en sus ojos se le escaparan.

Quería que aquello fuera real, no solo el sexo sino la cena y la conversación. Lo deseaba tanto que le preocupaba que lo estuviera convirtiendo en algo que no era.

¿Y si cuando volviera a su despacho él se mostraba indiferente con lo que acababa de pasar? ¿Cómo se comportaría? No sabía mostrarse fría ni distante con él. Con cualquier otro hombre… Qué demonios, con otro hombre no se habría sentido como con él. Poco a poco se estaba dando cuenta de que quería más de él de lo que nunca conseguiría, a pesar de que lo estaba intentando.

Pero para ella, no era suficiente con que lo estuviera intentando. Necesitaba que fuera alguien que estaba segura que nunca podría llegar a ser. Tenía la sensación de que se iba a llevar una gran desilusión.

De repente, sonaron unos golpes en la puerta.

–¿Estás bien? –preguntó Dec desde el otro lado.

–Sí, lo siento. Solo necesito unos minutos más.

–Tengo que limpiarme. Luego, iré a buscar a DJ a la guardería, así podrás tener unos minutos para ti sola.

–De acuerdo.

Necesitaba tiempo e intimidad. Se levantó, consciente de que no podía esconderse allí para siempre. Después de asearse, volvió a vestirse. Tenía el pelo revuelto, así que se soltó la coleta y volvió a hacérsela mirándose al espejo.

Cuanto más lo intentaba, más temía que aquella noche hubiera sido un error. Era demasiado pronto para que hubiera una relación sexual entre ellos. Él todavía estaba asimilando que tenía un hijo y ella tenía que hacerse a la idea de que había vuelto a su vida.

Abrió la puerta y se encontró el despacho vacío. Retiró los platos de la cena y reparó en que Dec se había dejado el portabebés. Su teléfono sonó y, al mirar la pantalla, vio que era Emma.

–Hola, Emma.

–Hola, ¿interrumpo algo importante?

–No, he tenido una cena y me iba a casa. ¿Alguna novedad?

–No dejo de dar vueltas a la idea del correo electrónico que me mandaste esta tarde, a lo de sacar un segundo juego este trimestre para aumentar los beneficios y cumplir los objetivos económicos de Allan.

–Yo también he estado pensando en eso.

Había pasado a un segundo plano mientras había estado con Dec aquella tarde. La llamada de Emma era justo lo que necesitaba para volver a la realidad.

–Bueno, ¿qué te parece si llamas a Fiona? Sabes que estuvo el año pasado en ese programa casamentero con Alex Cannon. ¿Sigues siendo amiga de ella, verdad?

No precisamente, pensó Cari. Había conocido a Fiona en un campamento de verano con dieciséis años y durante tres habían mantenido amistad por correspondencia. Pero no tenían una relación como para llamar a su nuevo marido y pedirle que los salvara con el desarrollo de un nuevo juego.

—Veré lo que puedo hacer, pero yo no contaría con eso. Estaba pensando en que podíamos pedirle a nuestro equipo que desarrollara un juego a partir de alguno que ya tengamos para lanzarlo en Navidad para tabletas.

—¿En qué consistiría?

—La partida se desarrollaría en una casa o en un árbol, con una temática navideña. Es solo una primera idea, pero sería un juego navideño y es un mercado lucrativo.

—Me gusta. Voy a mandarte una convocatoria de reunión a ti y al comité de proyectos. Puede ser justo lo que necesitamos, usar nuestros recursos.

—El balance final mejorará, y aunque tiene que estudiarlo el departamento financiero, apuesto a que no necesitaremos vender muchos para empezar a ver beneficios.

—Bien pensado, estoy deseando que lo veamos mañana. Gracias, Cari.

Se despidió de su hermana y se recostó en el respaldo de su sillón, deseando poder resolver con tanta facilidad el asunto entre Dec y ella. Pero los videojuegos eran mucho más sencillos que la vida real, porque eran simplemente eso, juegos.

Esa noche, todo le sonreía, pensó Dec mientras Rita, la niñera, le entregaba a DJ en la guardería. Luego, lo llevó de vuelta al despacho de Cari. DJ no paraba de hacer sonidos alegres y Dec se sentía el rey del mundo. Pocas veces se había sentido tan… Bueno, ni siquiera sabía cómo llamarlo. Aunque no era un amargado, tampoco era feliz. Esa noche estaba empezando a vislumbrar cómo podía llegar a ser.

Aun así, cada vez que tenía a Cari entre sus brazos, sentía un profundo temor de que si la soltaba, desaparecería. Sabía que no era como él y que no se marcharía sin más, pero no podía evitar temer que lo hiciera. Le estaría bien empleado si lo hacía, pero estaba empeñado en mostrarle… ¿El qué?

Era evidente que quería de él algo más que sexo, y nunca se le había dado bien demostrar sus sentimientos. No le había mentido cuando le había dicho que aquella mañana se había marchado para evitar complicaciones. Sin embargo, allí estaba, deseando que… Había visto el miedo en los ojos de Cari cuando se había refugiado en el cuarto de baño. Con DJ en brazos y su mirada somnolienta clavada en él, Dec sintió la responsabilidad de sus actos.

No sabía si debía pedirle matrimonio. ¿Qué pasaría después? Casarse no era la solución a los problemas que todavía había entre ellos.

Tenía que encontrar las palabras apropiadas y el momento adecuado de decirlas. Entonces, tal vez pudieran salir adelante. Lo que realmente quería era llevarse a Cari y a DJ a su yate y navegar hasta el horizonte. Pero eso sería salir huyendo y dejarlo todo atrás, y no podía hacerlo cuando por fin se sentía parte del clan de los Montrose.

Ya no era el extraño que siempre había sido y Cari tampoco estaría dispuesta a separarse de sus hermanas.

Se detuvo en el pasillo que llevaba al despacho de Cari y se quedó mirando los premios y las fotos del personal que había en la pared. Se fijó en una foto y reconoció a Cari, Emma y Jessi con su abuelo. Su hijo descendía de aquella familia.

En aquel momento se dio cuenta de lo importante que era salvar las dos líneas hereditarias de su hijo, y no tenía ni idea de cómo hacerlo. Kell no estaría satisfecho si Infinity Games seguía existiendo, aunque solo fuera en parte, cuando se completara la absorción de la compañía.

Siguió avanzando por el pasillo. Al oír a Cari en el teléfono, se detuvo en la puerta. Llamó a la puerta antes de abrirla y la encontró sentada detrás de su escritorio, con los brazos cruzados.

—Supongo que ya estás deseando irte a casa.

—Sí, es tarde y tengo una reunión a primera hora —replicó Cari—. Además, DJ tiene que irse a la cama.

—Creo que la siesta le ha venido bien.

—Tienes razón —dijo ella extendiendo los brazos al niño.

Dec lo besó en la cabeza antes de dárselo.

Cari se colgó la funda del ordenador portátil y

la bolsa de pañales al hombro, y se colocó a DJ en la cadera mientras tomaba el portabebés.

–Deja que yo me ocupe. De hecho, deja que lleve también esos bolsos –dijo Dec y trató de quitárselos.

Pero Cari le apartó la mano.

–No te preocupes, estoy acostumbrada a hacerlo sola.

No pretendía molestarlo con aquellas palabras, pero él las sintió como un puñetazo en el estómago. Estaba acostumbrada a hacerlo sola porque la había abandonado. ¿Cómo podía tranquilizarla? Seguía deseándola y nunca antes se había sentido así. Si pudiera, se quedaría con ella para siempre.

–Creo que tenemos que hablar.

–Esta noche no –dijo ella.

–Sí, esta noche –insistió tomando las bolsas y dejándolas sobre la mesa–. No me gusta cómo te estás comportando.

–Siento que no te guste, pero no sé qué hacer para que no sea así.

–Yo sí –afirmó acercándose de nuevo a ella.

–Detente –dijo Cari levantando una mano–. El sexo no va a arreglar esto.

–Tampoco lo pensaba, solo quería darte un abrazo, Cari. Quiero que tengas la seguridad de que esto no va a ser como la última vez.

–Lo sé, Dec. Ahora, tenemos un hijo.

Capítulo Diez

–Así es, quiero hacerme un hueco en tu vida, pero no es suficiente, ¿verdad?

No tenía ni idea de cómo construir una relación. Era un experto dividiendo compañías y fraccionándolas en partes. Se le daba muy bien marcharse antes de que las cosas se pusieran feas, y allí estaba, tratando de convencer a la única mujer que mejor lo conocía de que quería cambiar.

Cari se encogió de hombros y Dec sintió como si una flecha atravesara su corazón. Sabía que no la estaba engañando y no le iba a resultar fácil persuadirla. Con medias verdades y grandes gestos no iba a ganársela. Iba a tener que esforzarse para convencerla de que estaba siendo sincero.

Cari se mordió el labio inferior y sacudió la cabeza.

–No lo sé. Esta noche ha estado bien y he disfrutado mucho hasta el momento en que…

No acababa de entender qué quería decirle. Renegó de sus padres adoptivos por haberlo abandonado cuando ni siquiera sabía hablar o caminar. Si hubiera crecido con ellos, habría aprendido algo viéndolos interactuar y ahora podría usarlo con Cari.

–¿Hasta que qué?

Nerviosa, Cari se colocó un mechón de pelo detrás de la oreja y luego se frotó la mejilla contra la cabeza de DJ. Abrazaba a su hijo como si sacara fuerzas al hacerlo.

–¿Cari?

Ella suspiró.

–Hasta el momento en que me di cuenta de que no estaba segura de que fueras a quedarte. O de que iba a ser como la otra vez. Sé que te dije que había cambiado y lo he hecho, pero tengo que admitir que siento algo por ti, Dec. No es amor ni nada parecido, es solo que eres el padre de mi hijo y eso es difícil de obviar.

Dec dio un paso atrás sin saber muy bien qué decir. Se frotó la nuca y maldijo para sus adentros por haber tenido una infancia que lo había dejado tan vacío que había acabado haciendo daño a aquella mujer. Estaba intentando ser el hombre que ella necesitaba, pero iba a tener que esforzarse mucho más para hacerla feliz.

–Pensaba que sabías que estoy intentando establecer un vínculo contigo.

No quería hablar de lo que él quería ni de cómo deseaba que ella llenara aquel vacío que lo había acompañado durante tanto tiempo.

–Lo único que sé es que no quería que te fueras, pero tampoco podía retenerte. No estoy segura de si estás fascinado con la idea de tener un hijo, el primer familiar de sangre que conoces, o si hay algo real entre nosotros.

Había dado en el clavo con aquel comentario y no debía sorprenderle. Era una mujer astuta y sus empleados se habían pasado toda la semana diciéndole que era una persona empática. Quería aliviar su sufrimiento poniéndoselo más fácil, pero a la vez tenía que mantenerse a la defensiva por ser quien era.

–Quiero establecer un vínculo contigo, Cari. No quiero hacerte promesas porque sé lo fácil que es romperlas. Pero lo estoy intentando. ¿Puede ser suficiente por ahora? –preguntó Dec.

Aunque nunca había esperado gran cosa de la vida, no soportaba el dolor ante la idea de perderla. Cuando estuviera a solas, tendría que analizar aquella nueva debilidad. Ese tipo de preocupación iba en detrimento del empresario que estaba llevando a cabo una importante operación mercantil. Aquel era el peor momento para que le provocara aquel torbellino de emociones.

Cari ladeó la cabeza y se quedó observándolo, cosa que solía hacer cuando sopesaba sus opciones. Dec confiaba en estar a la altura y parecerle sincero. En sus ojos le pareció reconocer dudas y cierta desilusión, y frunció el ceño.

–Pareces dispuesto a darme un puñetazo si no digo que sí –dijo ella por fin con una amarga sonrisa.

–Solo estaba siendo sincero.

Ni siquiera se le daba bien parecerlo. ¿Cómo demonios iba a asumir un compromiso con ella y su hijo? Iba a tener que admitir sus sentimientos y expresarlos. ¿Sería capaz? Su padre nunca lo había hecho y apenas había llegado a conocerlo. Siempre había deseado llevarse bien con él y tener una relación más estrecha.

Ella sacudió la cabeza y sonrió.

–No deberías poner esa expresión tan fiera si quieres que la gente piense que eres sincero.

–No puedo evitarlo. Desde que entraste en la sala de juntas nada me ha resultado indiferente. Desde el momento en que volviste a aparecer en mi vida, nada ha sido como antes.

–¿Debería darte las gracias?

–Te lo digo como cumplido, pero es evidente que no lo ves así. No se me da bien este tipo de conversación. ¿Debería marcharme?

Se acercó a él sosteniendo a DJ en la cadera y le puso la mano en el pecho, sobre el corazón, donde un rato antes había apoyado la cabeza. A pesar de que Dec no sabía lo que hacía, sentía que se estaba abriendo paso. Estaba haciendo lo que necesitaba para demostrarle que era muy importante para él.

–No te vayas. Tengo miedo de estar reconociéndote más mérito del que mereces. No quiero ser una estúpida y que vuelvas a defraudarme.

–Bueno, no voy a irme a ningún sitio.

–¿De veras?

–Sí –respondió él.

Cari dio unos pasos vacilantes hacia él y Dec la observó fingir que apenas la había hecho cambiar en su estimación.

A mediados de septiembre se celebraba el pícnic de los empleados de Infinity Games. Muchos no estaban contentos con Dec porque tenían que trabajar más que nunca. Pero, gracias a los datos que Cari les había enviado, todos estaban al tanto de que sus esfuerzos estaban dando sus frutos e iban a superar el objetivo de beneficios marcado. Así que el ambiente en la barbacoa era distendido.

—Davis me ha sonreído al recoger su plato —le dijo Dec con una sonrisa irónica, después de que el último grupo de empleados se alejara.

—No le caes bien, pero ayer me dijo que entendía que el resultado final era lo importante —replicó Cari.

Dec y ella se ocupaban del primer turno de comida caliente.

Habían pasado poco más de dos semanas desde su encuentro en la oficina de Cari, y habían tenido varias citas. Estaban aprovechando para conocerse mejor. Aunque todavía había momentos en los que Cari tenía la impresión de que Dec se mostraba muy reservado, estaba contenta de tenerlo en su vida. Emma y Jessi pensaban que estaba loca por salir con él, pero ambas habían dejado de hacer comentarios cuando les había dicho que era feliz, algo que por otra parte era cierto. A la vez se sentía asustada, paranoica y neurótica. No sabía por qué Dec tenía tanto miedo al compromiso, y estaba haciendo todo lo posible por mantenerse calmada. Pero cada día se sentía más enamorada de él y le costaba luchar contra sus propios sentimientos.

—Así que este es el famoso cíborg de Playtone Games.

Al oír la voz de su hermana, Cari alzó la vista y sintió que Dec se ponía rígido.

—Tú debes de ser Jessi Chandler —dijo Dec, volviéndose para saludar a su hermana.

Vestía una atrevida combinación de vestido corto con botas militares.

–Jessi, prefiere que lo llamen Dec –medió Cari, acercándose a su hermana para darle un abrazo–. Sé amable –le susurró junto al oído.

Jessi le guiñó un ojo.

–¿Así que tratando de mezclarte con los humanos?

–En efecto. ¿A qué viene eso? –preguntó Dec dirigiéndose a Jessi.

–Solo quería que te dieras cuenta de que los empleados son personas con vidas y trabajos que nada tienen que ver con lo que Gregory Chandler pudo hacerle a Thomas Montrose –replicó Jessi.

–Es un hombre justo, señorita Jessi –intervino Frank, acercándose en la fila para llenar su plato–. Buenas tardes, señor Montrose, señorita Cari.

–Hola, Frank –dijo Cari, y empezó a servirle la comida al vigilante de seguridad.

–¿De veras? –preguntó Jessi a Frank.

–Sí. Sé que muchos empleados estaban un poco asustados al principio, pero se han dado cuenta de que demuestra interés con sus preguntas y propone mejoras. Creo que a la mayoría les está empezando a caer bien.

Cari miró a Dec. Se había sonrojado y parecía incómodo. Jessi tampoco parecía muy contenta y le dirigió a su hermana una mirada dura que no supo interpretar.

–Gracias, Frank, disfruta de la comida.

–Esa es mi intención –dijo antes de marcharse.

–Quedáis relevados –anunció Jessi.

Junto con Marcel, su secretaria, se colocaron al otro lado de la mesa, ocupando los puestos de Cari y Dec.

—Disculpa a Jessi —dijo Cari una vez se distanciaron.

—Está bien. Kell me dice cosas peores. ¿Quieres aprovechar para comer algo antes de que tu hermana Emma traiga a DJ?

—Claro —contestó—. Se ve que has causado una buena impresión en Frank.

Dec se encogió de hombros.

—Hace seis meses le habría ofrecido la jubilación anticipada con un paquete de beneficios, pero hablando con él, me di cuenta de que todavía puede aportar algo aquí. Lo último que quiere es jubilarse.

—Lo mismo pienso. Es inteligente y está muy fuerte para su edad.

—¿Cómo lo sabes?

—Fue él el que subió mi nueva mesa Luis XIV. No sabes lo que pesaba.

—¿Por qué te gustan esos muebles tan rococós? No son muy funcionales.

—Claro que sí. Además, a la gente le gusta, tienen su personalidad. No me gusta ser otra aburrida mujer de negocios.

—No hace falta ver tu oficina para darse cuenta de eso —comentó Dec antes de mirar a su alrededor y robarle un beso—. Busquemos un sitio donde sentarnos.

Cari lo siguió por entre las mesas de pícnic y, al pasar, dos diseñadores de juegos los invitaron a sentarse con ellos. Sabía que Dec había estado hablando con el personal, pero, sentada allí a su lado, tuvo la sensación de que se estaba integrando en la empresa. No sabía si sería para que la fusión fuera más fluida o porque tenía otro propósito.

Mientras escuchaba la conversación, se dio cuenta de que formaba parte del grupo. Parecía un hombre diferente al que había conocido en aquel congreso de hacía año y medio. Se preguntó si sería un cambio permanente o si siempre se comportaba así cuando llevaba a cabo adquisiciones de compañías. No tenía forma de saberlo con seguridad, por lo que iba a tener que decidir si confiar en él o no.

Mientras la miraba sonriente, sintió su mano tocándole el muslo bajo la mesa y supo que ya confiaba en él. Lo veía como a un hombre que sabía encontrar su hueco, un hombre que comprendía que para tener un futuro exitoso tenía que construir algo y no echar abajo lo que ya existía, un hombre al que podía considerar suyo.

Dec buscó un rincón lejos del sol y de los demás asistentes al pícnic. La tarde estaba dando paso a la noche y, en cuanto oscureciera, una banda comenzaría a tocar y habría fuegos artificiales. Había pasado el día con los empleados de Infinity Games. Se había mostrado cordial con todos y lo habían hecho sentirse parte del equipo.

Pero sabía que no era así. En menos de dos semanas tenía que presentar su informe a la junta directiva e iba a tener que prescindir de algunos. El caso era que tenía la sensación de que ellos también lo sabían y, aunque nunca había imaginado que le importaría, se daba cuenta de que así era.

Las adquisiciones de compañías no ponían en una posición cómoda a alguien empático, pero debía vigilar los números. Nunca antes se había encontrado en una situación así y sabía que la culpa era de una rubia.

Cari seguía esperando que diera lo mejor de sí mismo y se esforzaba por estar a la altura. Había pasado el día charlado con unos y otros y había jugado al voleibol, y ya estaba cansado de tanta gente. No quería exponerse más de lo necesario. Siempre había tenido la cabeza fría en los negocios y nunca había dejado que nada lo afectara.

Pero Cari Chandler le estaba haciendo cambiar, y no solo en su vida personal.

–Ah, aquí estás –dijo Cari acercándose a él con DJ en brazos.

–*Mamamama* –balbuceó el bebé.

El niño vestía unos pantalones caqui y una camisa azul.

–Hola, pequeño –dijo Dec, ofreciéndole sus brazos.

El niño se echó hacia él y Cari se lo dio. Al abrazar a su hijo, se relajó.

–Necesitaba un respiro.

–Te entiendo. Estos días se hacen muy largos. Ya verás la fiesta de Navidad.

–Cari, quería hablarte de eso.

–Dime.

Se quedó mirándolo con sus enormes ojos azules y Dec sintió una punzada de dolor en sus entrañas ante lo que iba a decir.

–Cuando llegue Navidad, Infinity Games habrá cambiado.

–¿Qué quieres decir?

–Sabes que estoy aquí para cerrar la compra y fusión de vuestra compañía. Una de las cosas que estamos considerando es llevarnos a parte de vuestra plantilla a las oficinas de Playtone.

–Después de lo de hoy, ¿vas a seguir adelante con eso?

–Cari, es mi trabajo.

–Pensaba que te empezábamos a importar.

–Y así es. DJ y tú me importáis.

–Pero no su herencia.

Había dicho aquellas palabras sin pensar y sabía a qué se refería. En las últimas semanas se había establecido un vínculo entre ellos que no quería que se rompiera, pero sabía muy bien lo que tenía que hacer. Kell no iba a cejar en su empeño de venganza solo porque Dec hubiera empezado a sentir algo por una de las hermanas Chandler.

–Lo mismo podría decir de ti y de tus hermanas –señaló Dec–. La compañía estaba en peligro. No éramos los únicos interesados en compraros.

Ella sacudió la cabeza.

–Estábamos pasando un día muy agradable. ¿Por qué te pones así?

–Así, ¿cómo? Es a esto a lo que me dedico. No importa que me caigan bien tus empleados, vamos a tener que prescindir de algunos. Son negocios.

–Yo no pienso así.

–Esa es una de las cosas que más me gustan de ti. Pero eso no significa que deba dejar de lado mis obligaciones solo para agradarte.

Cari se cruzó de brazos y le dirigió una mirada dura.

–No puedo enfadarme contigo cuando lo que dices tiene sentido.

Dec puso los ojos en blanco. Era imposible que alguien pudiera enfadarse con ella.

–¿Por qué te has venido a este rincón? –continuó ella–. ¿Acaso te cuesta relacionarte con la gente a la que vas a tener que despedir?

Dec no tenía agallas para decirle que necesitaba aislarse de todas aquellas personas. Él no era como Cari y no le afectaría la reducción de personal que tenía que llevar a cabo.

–Algo así.

–Siento no haber sido más comprensiva –dijo Cari, y le dio un breve abrazo.

–No te preocupes. ¿Por qué me estabas buscando?

–Para ver si podías quedarte con DJ. Mis hermanas y yo tenemos que presentar el espectáculo y dar las gracias a los empleados por el trabajo que han hecho este año.

Dec se dio cuenta de que para ella, los empleados eran como de la familia. Se sintió mal. Sabía que los tres primeros nombres en la lista de despidos se apellidaban Chandler y, mientras observaba a aquella mujer por la que había empezado a sentir algo, pensó en el impacto que eso tendría en su vida.

—Me quedaré con él encantado, pero ¿no crees que la gente empezará a hacerse preguntas?

—Nadie se atreverá —respondió ella—. Pero si quieres seguir aquí escondido…

—No me estoy escondiendo, pero creo que lo más prudente es que me mantenga alejado de los empleados.

—A mí también me lo parece.

Cari se inclinó para besar a DJ en la cabeza antes de darse la vuelta y marcharse. Dec la observó abrirse paso entre la gente, saludando y parándose a charlar con unos y otros. Aunque eran muy diferentes y nunca le había costado despedir a nadie, Cari iba a pasarlo mal cuando supiera que ella era una de las personas de las que había que prescindir.

Cambió a DJ de brazo y se dio cuenta de que deseaba encontrar la manera de evitar que se fuera porque, al igual que Frank, estaba convencido de que no soportaría no ir cada día a Infinity Games.

Capítulo Once

–Ya hemos llegado –dijo Cari deteniendo el coche en la mansión de los Chandler.

Cari temía la comida dominical con sus hermanas. Sabía que era imposible que supieran lo que había pasado en la mesa de su despacho tres semanas antes. Tampoco sabían de las citas que Dec y ella habían tenido o de cómo, sin quererlo, se estaba enamorando de él. Pero ese día se sentía transparente. Se alisó la falda y se ajustó el cinturón después de salir del coche ante la casa de Emma.

En teoría, debían turnarse para organizar aquella comida semanal, pero por algún motivo siempre acababan en casa de Emma. A Cari le gustaba pensar que era porque la casa en la que vivía su hermana había sido la de sus abuelos y, también, porque tenía personal de servicio que se ocupaba de preparar la comida. Pero tenía la sensación de que era por algo más.

A Emma le gustaba ser la anfitriona. Le gustaba que todos recurrieran a ella. Era la mayor y la más mandona, así que siempre la dejaban salirse con la suya.

Miró a DJ, que estaba ocupado mordisqueando un barco de plástico. Lo sacó del coche y se dirigieron a la casa. De niña, había pasado allí los fines

127

de semana, corriendo por los suelos de mármol y jugando al escondite en los jardines.

Miró a su hijo y sonrió. En breve, él estaría haciendo lo mismo. Nada más entrar a la mansión, lo dejó con la señora Hawkins, la niñera.

Se preguntó cómo sería la casa en la que Dec se había criado. ¿Qué clase de recuerdos tendría de ella?

–Sam estará encantado de ver a este pequeño –dijo la señora Hawkins.

–DJ también. Le encanta jugar con su primo –asintió Cari, y se volvió hacia el pequeño–. Vas a ver al primo Sammy.

–*Mamamama* –balbuceó mirando a su madre con aquella gran sonrisa suya.

Se inclinó y besó al niño en la cabeza, antes de que la señora Hawkins se diera la vuelta para marcharse.

–¿Dónde están mis hermanas?

–En el estudio de su abuelo –contestó la niñera.

Daba igual que Gregory Chandler llevara muerto casi diez años o que aquella casa fuera en la actualidad la residencia de Emma, siempre sería su estudio.

Cari entró en la estancia de paneles de madera y se imaginó que todavía olía a los puros de su abuelo. A pesar de los grandes ventanales del fondo por los que entraba la luz del sol, era un lugar oscuro y muy masculino. De niña, pocas veces había entrado allí porque eran los dominios de su abuelo.

–Hola, chicas –dijo Cari–. Pensé que íbamos a comer.

–Sí, y lo haremos –repuso Emma–. Como Jessi está a cargo del marketing, quería comentarle tu idea del juego de Navidad.

–¿Ahora? No tengo datos aquí y es domingo, mi equipo está disfrutando del fin de semana.

–Está bien. Le daremos unas ideas generales. Lo mantendremos en secreto. No quiero que nadie de Playtone se entere hasta que tengamos el producto terminado.

–No sé si podremos –advirtió Cari–. Dec siempre está en las oficinas y ya le he explicado a Allan los objetivos financieros. Si no explicamos el plan y hacemos algunos progresos, creo que corremos el riesgo de perderlo todo.

–¿Por qué se lo has contado a Allan? –preguntó Jessi.

–Estaba en el despacho para ver a Dec –explicó Cari–. Por cierto, ¿qué pasó entre vosotros?

Jessi parecía incómoda, algo que no era propio en ella.

–Nada. Es solo que se enfadó mucho cuando se enteró de que había mandado investigar a John antes de casarse con Patti.

–¿Por qué lo hiciste?

–Se conocieron en Las Vegas. No sabía nada de él y Patti tiene un gran patrimonio. Podía ser un cazafortunas.

Cari le dio una palmada a su hermana en el hombro. Jessi no confiaba en nadie salvo en aquellos que le habían demostrado su lealtad. Aquello la entristecía, porque le hacía recordar a la niña dulce que había sido antes de que la vida la endureciera.

–¿Y lo era?

–¿Crees que habría dejado que se casara con él si lo hubiera sido? –preguntó Jessi, evidentemente disgustada–. Allan se puso muy gallito y estuvo muy desagradable conmigo.

–¿Solo porque encargaras a un detective que investigara su pasado?

–Bueno, quizá también porque le ofrecí un soborno para ver si lo aceptaba y se iba –contestó Jessi bajando la voz.

Cari sacudió la cabeza y no pudo evitar reírse.

–Supongo que no fue bien.

–John te perdonó, pero Allan no.

–Bueno, no importa –intervino Emma–. Quiero saber más de Cari y Dec. Sé que tuvisteis una cita la primera noche que se presentó en la oficina y hay rumores de que estáis saliendo. ¿Es así?

–Sí, así es. Acabamos hablando de todo un poco e hicimos buenas migas.

–¿Buenas migas? –repitió Jessi–. No pareces tú.

No le apetecía tener aquella conversación, pero era la oportunidad de hablarles de Dec y DJ.

–Pues sí, soy yo. Supongo que ha aparecido en el momento adecuado.

–No creo que sea una buena idea salir con él –observó Emma.

–Voy a encargar que lo investiguen –intervino Jessi–. Entonces decidiremos si puedes seguir saliendo con él.

–No –dijo Cari poniéndose de pie–. Lo siento, pero es mía la decisión. Voy a salir con él a pesar de la enemistad que hay entre nuestras familias.

–¿Tan poco significa para ti la familia? –preguntó Emma.

–No, no es eso. Pero los hombres como Dec...

–¿Los hombres como Dec? ¿Tan bien lo conoces?

–No tan bien como insinúas, pero me gusta. Tampoco he conocido a tantos hombres que me hayan interesado.

–No desde que te quedaste embarazada –puntualizó Emma.

–No quiero que os interpongáis. Sé muy bien lo que estoy haciendo.

–Eso espero, porque no creo que te anteponga a Playtone Games –dijo Emma–. A la vista de que la reunión de la junta directiva es mañana, creo que no hay nada que puedas hacer ahora. Solo espero que sepas lo que estás haciendo.

Cari no estaba segura. Era consciente de que estaba poniendo a Dec por delante de sus obligaciones en la compañía. Tenía que encontrar la manera de convencerlo para que dejara la empresa tal y como estaba, sin que saliera de su vida. No estaba dispuesta a conformarse con menos.

Cari pensaba que había sentado las bases para evitar que Infinity Games fuera engullida. Confiaba en que lo que Dec sentía por ella lo llevara a la conclusión de que tanto su empresa como sus hermanas y ella deberían permanecer intactas.

Cari se fue de casa de su hermana y tomó la autopista del Pacífico sin un destino en mente. Llevaba puesto un CD de música infantil que parecía estar haciendo las delicias de DJ.

No había razón para el nudo de nervios que sentía en el estómago. Estaba haciendo todo lo que podía para evitar que su plantilla perdiera el trabajo. Sus hermanas estaban bien y no tenían problemas. Y en aquel momento, estaba convencida de que Dec y ella acabarían juntos y felices para siempre.

Pero Jessi y Emma habían plantado una semilla de duda en su cabeza. No podía avanzar en su relación con Dec sin saber qué planes tenía en relación a ella y sus hermanas.

Sabía que cabía la posibilidad de que Dec recomendara que fueran despedidas. Todo el mundo sabía que no tenía sentido duplicar cargos cuando ambas compañías se dedicaban a lo mismo.

Pero durante semanas había albergado la esperanza de que hubiera una manera de que se pudieran fusionar ambas empresas. Sin embargo, en aquel momento, tenía que enfrentarse a la realidad. Los herederos Montrose no permitirían que las hermanas se quedaran.

Seguramente, eso era precisamente lo que Dec y sus primos pretendían. Detuvo el coche junto a un mirador y dejó el motor en marcha al comprender el origen de aquella angustia en su estómago. Tenía miedo de que incluso después de que destruyera el legado de su familia, siguiera amándolo.

No había querido reconocerlo, pero era la verdad: estaba enamorada de él.

Se volvió para mirar a DJ en su asiento y se dio

cuenta de que desde el momento en que Dec había vuelto a aparecer en su vida, lo había querido.

Pero también deseaba que salvara su compañía, se encariñara con su hijo y la amara. Quería que fuera un hombre completamente diferente al que había conocido.

No estaba siendo realista. No necesitaba que Jessi le dijera que Dec no tomaba decisiones empresariales con el corazón. Lo había llamado cíborg y realmente lo era cuando se trataba de escindir las compañías que Playtone adquiría.

También sabía que estaba entusiasmado con su hijo. Lo había visto tirado en el suelo, jugando con DJ, y también besándolo y abrazándolo cuando pensaba que no miraba. Por la expresión de sus ojos, era evidente lo mucho que le importaba su hijo.

Por otro lado, le gustaba y la hacía sentirse la única mujer en el mundo. Daba igual que para él aquello solo durara seis semanas.

Se frotó la nuca y decidió que iba a preguntarle abiertamente qué intenciones tenía. Ya no haría más conjeturas acerca de si la quería o si se quedaría con ella. Tomó su bolso, sacó el teléfono móvil y marcó su número.

—Montrose al habla —dijo Dec.

—Soy Cari. ¿Tienes un momento?

—Sí, he quedado con mis primos para jugar al voleibol y estoy de camino. ¿Qué pasa?

—Eh… me gustaría invitarte a cenar esta noche. ¿Te parece bien a eso de las seis y media, en mi casa?

—Me gusta la idea. Tengo unos temas que quisiera discutir contigo.

—Yo también —repuso ella.

—Y no se trata de negocios —añadió Dec.

—Perfecto, lo mío tampoco. Nos veremos luego.

—Lo estoy deseando —dijo él antes de colgar.

La tensión de su estómago desapareció y se sonrió en el espejo retrovisor. Necesitaba saber en qué punto se encontraban y, al parecer, él también buscaba respuestas a las mismas preguntas.

El amor que tanto temía reconocer empezaba a bullir en su interior y tardó un minuto más en poner el coche en marcha. Quería disfrutar de aquella sensación. Sus hermanas le habían advertido de lo imposible que era que sus sueños se hicieran realidad, de que no podía tenerlo todo con Dec. Pero en aquel momento decidió que al menos debía arriesgarse para conseguir que sus sueños se hicieran realidad y tener el futuro que tanto ansiaba, en el que siguieran estando su empresa y el padre de su hijo.

Dec no recordaba cómo había empezado aquella tradición pero los domingos por la tarde, si todos estaban en California, Kell, Allan y él, junto con John, el mejor amigo de Allan, quedaban a jugar al voleibol en el parque Clover de Santa Mónica. Se le daban muy bien los deportes. De niño, y por su exceso de energía, lo habían apuntado a muchas actividades para que su niñera no se volviera loca.

Kell ya estaba allí cuando Dec llegó en camiseta de tirantes y pantalones cortos, y lo saludó dándole la mano.

–¿Qué tal va todo?

–No puedo quejarme –contestó Dec–. Hace mucho tiempo que no juego.

–Deberíamos haber ido a Australia a verte –replicó Kell.

–No te preocupes –dijo Dec encogiéndose de hombros–. Estabas ocupando haciendo realidad el sueño del abuelo.

–No creo que estuviera satisfecho aún. Las Chandler siguen al mando de Infinity Games.

–Precisamente quería hablarte de eso.

Se había dado cuenta de que no iba a ser capaz de recomendar que despidieran a Cari. Formaba parte del día a día de la empresa y, sinceramente, quizá influido por sus sentimientos, pensaba que era una parte esencial para mantener el éxito de Infinity Games.

–Tú me dirás.

A pesar de que no se había quitado las gafas de sol, Dec podía sentir su gélida mirada.

–Creo que no va a ser tan fácil como pensábamos apartar a las Chandler de la compañía.

–Eres un genio en esta clase de operaciones. No te subestimes. Estoy seguro de que sabrás hacer lo que cualquier Montrose haría –dijo Kell.

Dec asintió. «Lo que cualquier Montrose haría». Aquellas palabras lo angustiaron. Sabía cómo demostrarle a Kell que era un Montrose, pero no podía olvidar que había sido adoptado y que era hijo de su madre. Ella había odiado a Thomas Montrose más que a nadie.

Kell sacó su teléfono móvil.

–Lo siento, tengo que contestar un correo electrónico.

Dec se apartó y dejó que su primo mayor hiciera lo que mejor se le daba, ocuparse de los negocios. Era evidente que no tenía ningún interés en olvidarse del pasado.

Había sido criado por su abuelo en aquella vieja casa de la que Thomas se había negado a marcharse. Su padre era el mediano y Dec siempre se había dado cuenta de que nunca había estado a la altura de lo que esperaba de él. El padre de Kell había muerto en la Tormenta del Desierto, la primera guerra en Irak. Había sido imposible para el padre de Dec competir con un muerto incluso después de casarse con una rica heredera que había aportado miles de millones a los cofres de la familia.

–¿Listos para que os pisoteemos esos traseros? –dijo Allan, mientras se dirigía hacia ellos acompañado de John.

–¿Has estado bebiendo? –preguntó Dec mientras estrechaba la mano de John.

–Tan engreído como de costumbre –dijo John–. Me alegro de que estés de vuelta.

–Gracias –replicó Dec–. Echaba de menos estos partidos de los domingos.

–Tampoco parece que hayas pasado mucho tiempo sentado –comentó Allan.

–Claro que no. En Australia, solía quedar con unos tipos de Kanga Games para jugar al *squash*.

–Me alegro –dijo Allan, dándole una palmada en el hombro–. John y yo hemos mejorado mucho nuestro juego. Ya casi somos una leyenda.

John rio y Kell guardó el teléfono y se unió a ellos.

—¿Listo?

—Claro —contestó Dec.

Lanzaron una moneda al aire y les tocó a Dec y Kell sacar primero. Después de un rato jugando, Dec no pudo evitar preguntarse por qué Allan era tan diferente a ellos. ¿Sería porque era Montrose por vía materna y porque el abuelo había tratado a la tía Becca como si fuera una princesa, sin enfrentarla a sus hermanos?

Pensó en su hijo y se dio cuenta de que quería que DJ se pareciera más a Allan que a él o a Kell. Quería que su hijo fuera feliz y que tuviera amigos con los que pasarlo bien. Quería una vida de felicidad y no de amargura para su hijo, y sabía que si despedía a Cari, no habría manera de que DJ no se viera afectado por ello algún día.

Nunca había estado tan cerca de sentirse plenamente integrado en la familia Montrose como en aquel momento y había aceptado el hecho de que para hacer feliz a su familia adoptiva iba a tener que sacrificar la felicidad de su hijo y de su propio futuro.

No se engañaba con la idea de que Cari seguiría con él si continuaba adelante con el plan que tanto agradaría a Kell. Pero, ¿qué pasaría si no lo hacía? ¿Mantendría su puesto en Playtone?

Tenía un número de acciones suficiente para pararle los pies a Kell si quería, gracias a que su madre las había comprado cuando la compañía había salido a bolsa, pero no quería hacer de aquello una lucha de poderes. Quería encontrar la manera de hacer que todas las partes se dieran cuenta de que para construir el futuro tenían que olvidarse de vengar las rencillas del pasado.

–¿Vas a sacar o piensas quedarte ahí mirando la pelota? –le preguntó Kell.

–Lo siento. Se me acaba de ocurrir algo sobre la compra de Infinity –respondió Dec.

–No me pidas disculpas por querer aplastar a los Chandler. Es lo único en lo que pienso –replicó su primo.

–¿Lo único?

–Bueno, y en dormir también.

Dec sintió un nudo en el estómago. Sus primos eran como sus hermanos. Era incapaz de hacer algo que pudiera molestarlos, pero tenía la sensación de que a Allan no le importaría tanto como a Kell que se quedara una de las hermanas en la empresa. Tenía que ser muy prudente para conseguirlo.

–Tenemos que encontrarte una afición –dijo Dec.

–¿Y cómo llamas a esto? –preguntó Kell.

–Ganar –respondió Dec.

Sacó la pelota una última vez y se hizo con el triunfo del juego.

–Buen partido –dijo Allan–. ¿Queréis venir a mi casa a tomar unas cervezas? Podemos ver las carreras.

–No puedo –contestó Dec–. Tengo una cita.

–¿Con quién? –preguntó Allan.

–Voy a salir con Cari.

–¿Cari Chandler? –dijo Kell.

–Sí, estamos saliendo.

–¿Y te parece sensato?

Dec dirigió una dura mirada a su primo.

—Mi vida personal es mía. No va a afectar a los negocios.

—A menos que dejes de tener claro cuáles son tus prioridades.

—Tranquilo –dijo Allan mientras John se apartaba unos pasos en dirección hacia la playa.

—Sé muy bien cuáles con mis prioridades –replicó Dec.

—Eso lo dices ahora, pero… Estamos a punto de hacer realidad lo que el abuelo tanto deseó. ¿Por qué arriesgarlo todo por una mujer?

—No es una mujer cualquiera.

Kell sintió como si la cabeza le fuera a explotar.

—A partir de mañana, me ocuparé personalmente de la fusión de las compañías.

—Tengo el informe terminado. Tengo que añadir algunos detalles, pero está listo para ser presentado mañana lunes. No tienes por qué apartarme de mi trabajo.

—¿Qué has averiguado?

—Prefiero esperar hasta mañana.

—Quiero saber que Gregory Chandler no nos ha puesto una trampa desde el más allá con una nieta seductora.

—Ella no es así.

—Ya lo veremos.

Dec se apartó antes de que Kell pudiera decir algo más, pero en el fondo sabía que iba a tener que elegir entre el pasado y el futuro. Para un hombre acostumbrado a vivir en el presente, se encontraba en una situación muy incómoda.

Capítulo Doce

Cari dejó a DJ en su cuna para que durmiera la siesta. Eran las cuatro de la tarde. Había intentado que se durmiera antes para que estuviera despierto cuando llegara Dec, pero el pequeño se había negado, así que se le había hecho tarde para preparar la cena. Se olvidó de su idea de preparar un asado y optó por pasta. Era más fácil y rápido. Ni que Dec fuera a darse cuenta de que estaba enamorada de él solo por prepararle la cena.

Había empezado a preparar un granizado de café de postre y, como solo había que añadir hielo picado cada treinta minutos, lo tenía todo bajo control. Al frotarse la nuca, cayó en la cuenta de que todavía no se había arreglado el pelo. Puso el temporizador y corrió a su habitación.

Eran las seis. Dedicó unos minutos más a peinarse y maquillarse, y luego se puso un sencillo vestido de verano que le dejaba al descubierto los brazos y disimulaba la barriga que le había quedado después de dar a luz. Contenta con su aspecto, se dispuso a volver a la cocina, pero el timbre de la puerta sonó antes de que llegara.

Respiró hondo y trató de relajarse. Ni que aquella noche fuera a cambiarle la vida, aunque lo deseara. Nunca había pensado que pudiera sentir aquello por Dec. El hombre que la había abandonado se estaba haciendo un hueco en su vida de una manera totalmente inesperada.

De camino a la puerta, se percató de que no había puesto música. Al abrir, se encontró a Dec con el pelo húmedo, vestido con unos pantalones cortos caquis y una camisa con el cuello abierto. Llevaba unas gafas de sol que se quitó nada más verla.

—Hola, preciosa. Parece que hace siglos que no te veía.

—Lo mismo digo –replicó ella sonrojándose.

Luego, se hizo a un lado para dejarlo pasar y Dec le entregó un gran ramo de flores multicolores.

—Gracias.

—No sé cuáles son tus flores preferidas, así que te he traído margaritas porque me han recordado a ti.

Cari se quedó mirando aquella mezcla de pétalos amarillos, rosas y naranjas.

—¿Por qué te recuerdan a mí?

—No sé, me hacen sonreír.

Sintió una intensa emoción. Quería ser prudente, ir despacio y no tomarse cada uno de sus comentarios como una declaración de amor. Pero era difícil. Sus sentimientos hacia él hacían que lo viera de una manera diferente.

—¿Por qué me sonríes de esa manera? –preguntó él.

—A veces puedes ser muy amable.

—Pensé que era amable todo el tiempo.

Ella negó con la cabeza y se acercó para besarlo. Solo pretendía que fuera un breve roce de labios a modo de agradecimiento, pero se convirtió en algo más. Lo rodeó por los hombros con su brazo y se puso de puntillas para besarlo.

–Vaya, si es así como reaccionas por un puñado de flores, voy a traerte un ramo cada día.

Cari se apartó. La idea de tenerlo con ella cada día le provocó aquella sensación efervescente. Nada podía estropear aquella noche. El temporizador sonó en la cocina y DJ empezó a llorar a la vez.

–¿DJ o la cocina? –preguntó Dec–. Dime de cuál prefieres que me ocupe.

–¿Te importa ir a por DJ?

Pensó que preferiría estar con su hijo que andar buscando qué hacer en la cocina. Además, quería que la cena y el postre fueran perfectos.

–En absoluto –dijo él con una sonrisa.

Últimamente, parecía sonreír más, y esperaba que fuera por ella.

–¿Tengo que hacerle algo a DJ?

–Eh… Cámbiale el pañal y ponle la ropa que le he dejado preparada. ¿Crees que podrás vestirlo?

–Me las arreglaré –respondió Dec, asintiendo.

Se fue por el pasillo y Cari se apresuró a volver a la cocina. Dejó las margaritas en la encimera y abrió el congelador para remover aquella mezcla helada. Luego sacó un jarrón para meter las flores, tratando de no darle importancia al hecho de que se las hubiera comprado.

El caso era que no solía recibir flores a menudo. Sus hermanas le habían mandado un ramo al dar a luz a DJ, pero antes de eso hacía años que nadie le había regalado uno. Recortó los tallos y metió las flores en el jarrón antes de dejarlo en medio de la isla de la cocina.

Luego, siguió haciendo la cena. Había decidido preparar una sencilla salsa de tomate, ajo y albahaca para acompañar la pasta. Llenó una cacerola de agua y la puso a hervir, y después se dispuso a preparar pan de ajo.

Estaba nerviosa por hacer la comida y poner la mesa, pero lo que de verdad quería era acabar de cenar cuanto antes y poder hablar con Dec. Le había dicho que tenía algo importante que decirle y, después de la manera en que la había saludado al llegar, esperaba que le dijera que sentía por ella lo mismo que ella por él.

Seis semanas antes, Dec se habría reído a la cara de cualquiera que le hubiera dicho que estaría cambiando pañales y deseando pasar una noche en casa. Nunca había sido muy hogareño. Pero esa noche, con aquel delicioso aroma a comida flotando en el ambiente y su hijo de diez meses riendo mientras le cambiaba de ropa, Dec sintió que aquel era el único sitio donde deseaba estar.

Aquella agradable sensación era lo que le había convencido de que no iba a abandonar a DJ y a Cari. Y eso era lo que lo asustaba, porque todavía no había pensando la manera de evitar que Cari perdiera su trabajo. Pero esa noche, no le preocupaban los juegos ni la enemistad de años. Solo quería disfrutar de la sensación de que por primera vez en su vida sentía que tenía un hogar.

Daba igual que técnicamente fuera la casa de Cari o que nunca hubiera estado allí antes. Parecía haber encontrado lo que siempre había estado buscando. Aquel vacío que durante tanto tiempo lo había acompañado ya no lo sentía tan frío.

Sentó a DJ y miró la ropa que le había puesto. Quería que Cari se diera cuenta de que formaba parte de sus vidas. Para él era importante establecer una relación con ellos antes de la junta directiva del día siguiente.

Levantó a DJ del cambiador y el pequeño trató de bajarse al suelo. La casa era de una sola planta, por lo que no había escaleras que pudieran suponer un peligro para él. Lo dejó en el suelo y lo siguió mientras gateaba hasta la cocina.

Pensó en Allan y Kell, y en cómo sus primos solo se preocupaban del trabajo, y se dio cuenta de que había cambiado. Sabía que iba a tener que tomar una difícil decisión en relación a Infinity y Playtone. Seis semanas atrás, habría sido fácil, pero ya no.

Al ver a DJ entrando en la cocina y a Cari tomándolo en brazos para darle un beso, Dec supo que la decisión estaba tomada.

–Qué bien te queda esta ropa, pequeño. Vas a juego con tu padre.

Lo miró con tanto cariño que Dec se asustó. Se dio la vuelta y se frotó las manos. Cari parecía muy vulnerable y seguramente no era consciente de ello.

–He traído vino y me lo he dejado en el coche. Enseguida vuelvo.

Se apresuró a salir de la casa y, una vez fuera, se detuvo a medio camino del coche. Se quedó mirando su Maserati. Por un lado, deseaba subirse al coche y alejarse de aquella situación.

Si se iba, Kell encontraría la manera de vengarse y, con el tiempo, Cari acabaría por pasar página. No tendría que elegir entre su primo y el objetivo que había perseguido toda su vida, y Cari y DJ, que eran su futuro. No era un cobarde. Le costaba creer que hubiera abandonado a Cari en aquella habitación de hotel dieciocho meses atrás.

Una suave brisa se levantó en aquel viejo barrio en el que Cari vivía.

Había cambiado, pensó, y era como si no acabara de aceptarlo. Tenía miedo porque había encontrado algo que no quería perder. Tenía a Cari y a DJ. Nunca había pensado que pudiera sentirse tan vulnerable, pero así era.

Tomó la botella de vino y volvió a la casa. Encontró a Cari bailando con DJ en la cocina y al verlo, se paró en seco. Sabía que pasara lo que pasase al día siguiente, nunca olvidaría esa noche.

–¿Quieres bailar conmigo? –preguntó ella.

Dec dejó la botella en la encimera y tomó entre sus brazos a la mujer y al bebé, y bailó con ellos alrededor de la cocina al ritmo de la música que sonaba de fondo. DJ rio y Cari canturreó la letra de la canción.

Todo parecía sencillo. Tenían que estar juntos. Era la solución a la que había estado dándole vueltas toda la tarde y que su pequeño hijo parecía ver con claridad.

No sabía cómo iba a hacerlo, pero cuando las aguas se calmaran después de la reunión del día siguiente, se marcharía con el respeto de sus primos, junto a Cari.

Apenas habían tenido la oportunidad de hablar de nada serio durante la cena con DJ acompañándolos y ensimismado mirándolo. Pero en cuanto lo puso a dormir y volvió para sentarse con Dec en el patio trasero para contemplar el anochecer, Cari supo que había llegado el momento de hablar.

Dejó el monitor del bebé en la mesa y se sentó a su lado en una tumbona doble.

–Gracias –dijo él tomándola de la mano.

–¿Por qué? –preguntó ella con expresión interrogante–. Ya me las has dado en la cena.

–Gracias por mi hijo. No me había dado cuenta hasta esta noche del regalo que es. Podías haber tomado otra decisión, teniendo en cuenta que no estaba a tu lado. Y no te habría culpado, claro que tampoco me habría dado cuenta de lo que me estaba perdiendo.

Cari sintió un nudo en la garganta y sus ojos se llenaron de lágrimas. Nunca sabría lo difícil que había sido tomar la decisión, teniendo en cuenta que estaba sola y que él era enemigo declarado de su familia.

–No sé qué decir.

–No tienes nada que decir.

La atrajo entre sus brazos y le hizo apoyar la cabeza en su hombro. Luego se colocó a su lado hasta quedar frente a frente.

Deslizó las manos por su costado hasta llegar a la cadera y se aferró a sus nalgas. Ella se acercó más a él.

–¿Confías en mí? –preguntó él.

Su voz sonaba suave en la oscuridad.

–Sí, Dec.

–¿Puedo hacerte el amor? Desde que estuvimos juntos en tu despacho, no hemos pasado de besarnos al despedirnos, pero no puedo esperar más.

A continuación acercó las caderas a las de ella para que sintiera su erección.

–Yo tampoco.

Era consciente de la frontera que había levantado entre ellos desde aquella noche en su oficina, pero todo había cambiado. Deseaba estar entre sus brazos. No había pensado en otra cosa en las últimas semanas. A pesar de que no estaba del todo segura de que pudiera confiar en él, seguía deseándolo. Después de las señales que había visto aquella tarde, nada le haría más feliz que hacerle el amor.

Dec acercó la boca a la suya, y se fundieron en un beso dulce y apasionado. Bajo la luz de la luna y rodeados de la fragancia de las flores del jardín, Cari se sentía en el paraíso.

Deslizó las manos entre ellos y comenzó a desabrocharle la camisa hasta que sintió el vello de su pecho bajos sus manos. Luego, empezó a acariciarle sus fuertes pectorales y siguió bajando hacia su vientre. Dec metió el ombligo y tomó su mano para detenerla.

Cari apartó la boca de la suya y buscó sus ojos, pero Dec hundió el rostro en su cuello y fue besándola mientras le subía la falda. Con suaves movimientos arriba y abajo comenzó a acariciarle el muslo, haciéndola estremecerse.

Ella le desabrochó el cinturón y buscó el botón del pantalón a la vez que él deslizaba la mano bajo las bragas.

Dec le hizo separar aún más los muslos y se detuvo ante su entrada, rozándola con tan solo la punta de su miembro. Ella se revolvió, buscando que la penetrara, pero él no accedió.

Cari lo miró a los ojos y él unió sus labios a los suyos con fuerza metiéndole la lengua en la boca a la vez que la penetraba. Una oleada de placer la sacudió mientras se hundía completamente en ella. Lo rodeó por la cintura con las piernas y lo urgió a moverse más deprisa, apretándole con los talones en el final de la espalda.

Luego, con la lengua entrelazada a la suya, Cari sintió las primeras sacudidas del orgasmo. Apartó los labios de los suyos y gritó su nombre mientras él la embestía una y otra vez hasta que se corrió y todo su cuerpo se estremeció.

Cari sacudió las caderas una última vez y Dec se desplomó sobre ella. Estaba encantada de sentir todo su cuerpo encima, y lo abrazó con brazos y piernas con toda su fuerza. Luego, lo besó suavemente y, cuando alzó la vista, la estaba mirando con una ternura que nunca antes había visto en sus ojos.

Dec los hizo rodar de costado, la estrechó entre sus brazos y le acarició la espalda. Ella trató de cambiar de postura, temiendo estarle aplastando el brazo con su peso, pero él la obligó a quedarse como estaba y a apoyar la cabeza en su pecho, justo encima de su corazón.

Cari cerró los ojos, deleitándose con la calma que le transmitían sus latidos. Estando en sus brazos, no tenía que preocuparse de los problemas que Emma había comentado aquella tarde. Emma no conocía a Dec como ella. Un hombre que la abrazaba con tanta ternura no podía ser capaz de hacerle daño.

Capítulo Trece

Dec la estrechó entre sus brazos mientras caía la noche. Quería hacerle el amor de nuevo, pero esta vez en una cama y no en una tumbona al aire libre. Aun así no se arrepentía. Había esperado mucho tiempo para volver a tenerla así abrazada. Habría reventado si no se hubiera hundido en ella.

Si quería tenerla y mantener contentos a sus primos Montrose, tenía que decidir qué iba a hacer a continuación. Le costaba pensar teniendo a Cari en sus brazos. Se abrochó los pantalones, recogió las bragas de Cari y se las guardó en el bolsillo para que no se quedaran allí. Luego se levantó y la tomó en brazos.

Ella se revolvió y le sonrió.

—Tengo sueño.

—Sí, lo sé —dijo él—. Yo también y estoy deseando dormir abrazado a ti. ¿Te importa que me quede a pasar la noche?

—Estaba deseando que lo hicieras. Pero prométeme que seguirás aquí cuando me despierte.

Dec se sintió dolido por aquella pregunta. No podía culparla. Iba a tener que demostrarle con hechos que quería quedarse.

—Sí, te lo prometo.

Antes de que la llevara al interior de la casa,

Cari tomó el monitor del bebé. Luego, Dec enfiló hacia su dormitorio.

—¿Cómo sabías dónde estaba mi habitación?

—Lo he visto antes.

La dejó en el suelo y Cari puso el monitor sobre la mesilla.

—Necesito usar el baño antes de meterme en la cama.

—Adelante. Yo usaré el baño del pasillo y nos encontraremos aquí.

Cari se fue al baño y Dec aprovechó que se había quedado solo en la habitación para mirar a su alrededor. Había muchas fotos del bebé sobre la cómoda. Toda la vida de su hijo estaba allí documentada. Se fijó en las fotos de los nueve meses en los que había estado ausente de sus vidas y se dio cuenta de que DJ no tenía por qué enterarse si jugaba bien sus cartas en los siguientes días.

También sabía que iba a tener que ofrecerle a Cari lo que quería de él. Sexo y compañía durante las cenas no iban a ser suficiente. Se pasó las manos por el pelo y se fue al baño para asearse.

Después, cuando volvió al dormitorio, se encontró a Cari metida en la cama. Estaba recostaba sobre unas almohadas y, al verla, se quedó inmóvil en el umbral sin saber muy bien qué hacer. Por supuesto que se había acostado antes con mujeres, pero siempre había sido algo espontáneo y con sexo de por medio. Esta vez era diferente.

Estaba allí porque quería y no pudo evitar sentirse vulnerable ante aquella situación. Le recordaba su primera noche en la mansión de sus padres y cuánto había deseado quedarse allí para siempre. Su deseo se había cumplido, pero no había resultado como esperaba.

–Ven a la cama –dijo ella retirando las sábanas e invitándolo a entrar en la habitación.

Había dejado encendida la luz de la mesilla de noche y un suave y cálido resplandor iluminaba la habitación. Quería creer que su sitio estaba allí, con ella, pero sabía que no. Él era la oscuridad y ella la luz.

Quería resistirse. A pesar de lo que llevaba todo el día pensando, su instinto le decía que se diera media vuelta y se marchara. ¿Acaso no había aprendido que la vida era más fácil cuando no dependía de nadie? ¿Qué clase de padre sería si seguía temiendo permanecer en un lugar?

Claro que eso no cambiaba sus sentimientos por DJ. Sentía mucho amor por su hijo y quería lo mejor para él, pero seguía dudando si era lo mejor para DJ y Cari.

A pesar de que ella había llenado ese vacío en su interior, todavía no sabía qué podía ofrecerle. Todavía no había descartado la idea de subirse a su Maserati y poner rumbo a Canadá.

–¿Dec?

Notó un temblor en su voz y supo que estaría imaginándose lo que sentía. Las dudas de todas aquellas semanas, había alcanzado su grado máximo. Una vez que había llegado hasta donde estaba y había conseguido lo que quería, la aterrorizaba aferrarse a ello.

Cari era muy diferente a cualquier persona que

hubiera conocido y no podía estar más claro en aquel momento. Dio un paso hacia ella y, a pesar de que le sonrió, vio una sombra de tristeza en sus ojos. Tenía tanto miedo que dudaba que fuera el hombre que ella necesitaba.

No solo aquellos sentimientos le eran desconocidos, sino que le resultaba imposible encontrar el equilibrio entre lo que siempre había deseado, la aceptación de los Montrose, y la única cosa sin la que no podría sobrevivir, el amor de Cari.

El amor era efímero y siempre había estado fuera de su alcance. Aunque en aquel momento lo estuviera mirando con tanto amor, ¿cuánto tiempo duraría? ¿Seguiría sintiéndolo cuando sus hermanas se quedaran sin trabajo y se viniera abajo el legado de su familia?

Lo dudaba. ¿Cómo iba a hacerla feliz él solo? ¿Cómo iba a ser el único que le diera esperanza cuando sabía que no era digno de ser amado y que nunca había sido suficiente para nadie?

Cari se despertó tan pronto como de costumbre y se volvió para mirar a Dec durmiendo a su lado. La había despertado en mitad de la noche para hacerle el amor y había disfrutado de tenerlo con ella. No había tenido la oportunidad de decirle lo que sentía porque veía que estaba confuso.

Si tuviera que adivinar, diría que no estaba seguro de cómo manejar sus propios sentimientos. Por lo que sabía de su infancia, había crecido en un hogar sin amor y, en parte, quería compensarle aquella carencia. Pero sabía que no podía. Se inclinó y le acarició la incipiente barba de su mejilla.

Dormido, no parecía tan duro y dispuesto a comerse el mundo. Recordó la ternura de su expresión después de que le hiciera el amor fuera.

Aunque le resultaba difícil reconocerlo, había una vulnerabilidad en Dec que nunca antes había visto. Se dio la vuelta antes de hacer alguna estupidez, como dibujar corazones en su pecho y despertarlo para hacer el amor otra vez.

Quería ver cómo estaría esa mañana, si la apuesta que estaba haciendo obtendría su recompensa o si terminaría con el corazón roto y sola de nuevo.

Sacudió la cabeza al levantarse de la cama, tomó su bata y salió de la habitación. Había una importante reunión de la junta directiva esa mañana en el edificio de oficinas de Playtone Games, donde Dec presentaría su informe ante sus hermanas y ella, además de al comité ejecutivo de Playtone. Por su parte, tenía una simulación del juego que querían lanzar en Navidad lista para enseñarles con el que esperaban que se mantuviera viva la marca Infinity.

Fue a ver a DJ, que estaba despierto y jugando con un peluche en su cuna.

–Buenos días, pequeñín.

Lo sacó de la cuna, le cambió el pañal y lo vistió antes de ir a la cocina para darle de comer. Oyó la ducha de su baño y supo que Dec se había levantado. Trató de convencerse de que era una tontería estar nerviosa, pero cuanto más tiempo permanecía allí sentada esperándolo, más aumentaba aquella sensación. Terminó con DJ, lo tomó en brazos y regresó al dormitorio con una taza de café. DJ se retorció para bajar y ella lo dejó en el suelo antes de ir al vestidor a buscar su ropa. Entonces, oyó que se abría la puerta del baño.

–Papa –balbuceó DJ.

Cari salió del vestidor y miró a Dec.

En aquel momento, parecían una familia de verdad excepto por la manera en que la miraba. No parecía estar ilusionado No pudo evitar sentir cierta desazón. Lo amaba y seguramente él sentía lo mismo por ella. ¿Por qué se habría quedado a pasar la noche si no fuera así?

No tenía respuestas y, por primera vez, se dio cuenta de que el amor la hacía vulnerable. Necesitaba algo de Dec que quizá no fuera capaz de darle y tampoco tenía derecho a pedírselo. El amor no era esa emoción mágica que había imaginado. Claro que teniendo en cuenta la forma en que su relación con Dec se había desarrollado, no era una sorpresa.

–Buenos días –dijo él con voz ronca de recién levantado–. He usado tu maquinilla para afeitarme. Espero que no te importe.

–No, claro que no. Eh… ¿vas a venir a nuestras oficinas esta mañana o vas directamente a Playtone?

–Tengo que pasar primero por casa para cambiarme. Luego iré a Playtone –contestó–. Hoy va a ser un día largo.

Se adivinaba en él la tensión ante el día que tenían por delante. Cari respiró hondo.

–Sí, va a ser difícil para todos. Pero he estado

trabajando en los objetivos financieros que Allan fijó. Creo que vas a sorprenderte con algunas de las cosas que voy a mostraros.

Dec esbozó una medio sonrisa.

—Eso estará bien. ¿Necesitas algo de mí para tu presentación?

—No, ¿por qué?

—Kell es un hueso duro de roer, cariño. Espero que lo que presentes sea contundente y puedas respaldarlo con documentación.

—Por supuesto —dijo ella— ¿Crees que va a haber malas noticias?

—Va a haber algunos recortes —contestó—. Pero no pudo contarte nada más.

Cari sintió un nudo de nervios en el estómago. Aquello no sonaba bien para Infinity, pero tenía que ser realista.

Desde el principio había tenido la sensación de que su puesto y el de sus hermanas corrían peligro. Confiaba en que el nuevo juego y el flujo de ingresos que generaría fuera suficiente para conseguir ganar tiempo.

—No te preocupes por eso. Sé que estás haciendo tu trabajo.

—¿Quieres que cuide de DJ mientras te duchas?

—¿Tienes tiempo?

—Claro —respondió Dec.

Cari enfiló hacia el baño, pero de repente se detuvo y se volvió hacia él.

—Cuánto me gustaría hacer desaparecer al resto del mundo.

—A mí también, pero creo que ambos hemos

sabido desde el principio que eso no era posible. Lo que ocurra entre nosotros va a estar influido por tus hermanas, mis primos y la enemistad que surgió con nuestros abuelos.

–Lo sé, es solo que me gustaría que todo fuera mucho más sencillo. Cuando pase todo este revuelo de la reunión, quiero hablar contigo. Tenía pensado hacerlo anoche, pero algo me distrajo.

–¿No sería por mi culpa? –bromeó él–. ¿Quieres distraerte otra vez?

–Me encantaría, pero quiero ser puntual y causar buena impresión a la junta directiva de Playtone.

–Lo entiendo. Estate relajada y demuéstrales lo mucho que te importa tu empresa. Y presume de lo que vales.

–¿Eso cómo se hace? –preguntó ella.

–Siendo tú misma.

–Lo intentaré.

–Lo harás muy bien, lo sé –dijo, y la besó antes de dejar que se marchara al baño.

Después de ducharse, Dec se marchó a su casa para cambiarse y ella a las oficinas de Infinity Games. Tenía la sensación de que, a pesar de que había pasado la noche con ella, estaba guardando las distancias.

Después de pasar por su yate y cambiarse de ropa, Dec no se dirigió directamente a las oficinas de Playtone. Antes, se fue a la mansión de Beverly Hills en la que se había criado. Mientras buscaba en la guantera el mando a distancia para abrir la verja, recordó el primer día que había llegado allí.

Por entonces tenía cuatro años, así que sus recuerdos eran borrosos. Solo sabía que lo esperaba una nueva familia y que le habían dicho que eran ricos, así que se había imaginado una casa impresionante. Los portones de hierro con las iniciales de su madre seguían abriéndose con tanta lentitud como lo habían hecho aquella primera vez. Mientras aceleraba el Maserati y enfilaba el camino de acceso, pensó que, independientemente de lo que ocurriera ese día, nada iba a hacerlo cambiar.

Nunca se había sentido un Montrose, en parte porque había sido adoptado, pensó mientras salía del coche y se dirigía a la puerta principal. Pero la otra razón era su madre.

En una ocasión, cuando tenía dieciséis años, después de oírla refunfuñar por haberse casado con su padre, le había preguntado por qué lo había hecho. Helene le había contestado que se había dejado engañar por amor.

Abrió la puerta. Tan solo se oía el ligero zumbido del aire acondicionado y olía a limones. Aunque nadie vivía allí, tenía contratado un servicio de limpieza semanal.

Con las palabras de su madre resonando en su cabeza, recorrió la enorme casa en la que había crecido. De repente, una idea lo asaltó. Tal vez Cari estaba jugando con él.

Había percibido un cierto tono de desesperación cuando le había preguntado por la reunión que iban a tener ese día. Ambos sabían que Infinity

Games era historia y que en breve quedaría muy poco de la compañía que había fundado Gregory Chandler.

Pero, aparte de eso, ¿había algo más que un hijo entre ellos? ¿De dónde venía ese deseo de olvidarse de toda lógica empresarial y dejarse llevar por su intuición para salvar el trabajo de Cari? ¿Sería amor? No lo sabía. Su madre no había querido o había sido incapaz de describirle lo que era el amor. Lo único que tenía claro era que no quería sentir lo mismo que su madre. Había acabado dándose a la bebida cuando se había dado cuenta de que su padre se había casado con ella por su dinero.

¿Y si todo lo que había hecho Cari había sido con la intención de conseguir que traicionara a sus primos para salvarse ella y sus hermanas?

Se frotó la nuca y supo que no podía buscar respuestas en el pasado. Tenía que tomar una decisión ese mismo día. Tenía que confiar en Cari y en la nueva vida que quería construir con él.

Ese futuro no debería asustarlo tanto, pero no sabía cómo construir una vida con ella ni con nadie. No se sentía tranquilo con la idea de tener a Cari a su lado porque sabía lo frágil que era su vínculo con ella. No sabía cómo permanecer a su lado. Una cosa eran seis semanas y otra toda una vida. ¿Sería capaz?

Además, ¿lo querría ella para siempre? Le incomodaba no saberlo, y eso era lo peor. No tenía ni idea de lo que ella sentía. Tal vez, lo único que buscaba era un padre para su hijo.

Le había dicho que quería hablar con él esa noche. ¿Para qué? Después de la reunión, si lograba salvar su puesto en la empresa, ¿le contaría Cari sus verdaderos sentimientos o seguiría adelante con su vida?

Sacudió la cabeza. No estaba dispuesto a cambiar de opinión ni a alterar los planes que tenía para Infinity por ella. Solo esperaba que fuera lo suficientemente perspicaz como para darse cuenta de que aunque quisiera compartir su vida con ella, no podía tomar decisiones empresariales a la ligera.

Salió de la casa, confiando en no seguir los pasos de sus padres. Habían sido unos desgraciados que no habían sido capaces de encontrar la verdadera felicidad. En aquel momento se dio cuenta de que llevaba toda la vida huyendo para no encontrarse en la situación en la que estaba.

Amaba a Cari Chandler y no tenía ninguna duda de que iba a causarle una gran desilusión. Esperaba que fuera solo por esa vez, pero no podía estar seguro. Nunca se le habían dado bien las relaciones y estaba convencido de que sus hermanas no lo aceptarían nunca.

Sabía que eso podía poner mucha tensión en una pareja. Había crecido en un hogar en el que dos familias habían estado en conflicto. Mientras conducía hacía las oficinas de Playtone Games pensó en Thomas Montrose El hijo de aquel hijo que nunca había pensado que estaría a la altura iba a darle lo que el resto de los Montrose no había podido darle: la venganza que tanto había ansiado. Iba a hacer que una Chandler se doblegara no solo en la sala de juntas sino en la vida.

Lo sabía porque iba a sacrificar la posibilidad de tener un futuro feliz para salvar a Cari de él. Estaba convencido de que no era el hombre adecuado para ella y aquella mañana había tenido la oportunidad de darse cuenta de que había cambiado, pero no de decirle que la amaba. Ella se merecía un hombre que pudiera repetírselo todos los días de su vida.

Capítulo Catorce

Emma y Jessi dependían de la impresión que Cari causara a la junta directiva de Playtone Games durante la reunión, por lo que no podía evitar sentirse nerviosa mientras esperaban en la sala de juntas.

–¿Te ha contado Dec lo que ha puesto en su informe? –preguntó Emma.

–No, eso no lo haría nunca –respondió Cari a sus hermanas–. Es muy leal con sus primos como yo lo soy con vosotras.

–Es comprensible –dijo Jessi–. Por cierto, ¿vais en serio? Patti me ha dicho que Kell no está muy contento de que Dec esté saliendo contigo.

–¿Cómo lo sabe Patti? –preguntó Cari.

Confiaba en que Dec hubiera encontrado la manera de salvar todos los puestos de trabajo de Infinity, pero sabía que era un sueño estúpido. A pesar de que diera con una nueva forma de aumentar los beneficios, habría despidos.

–John está aquí de visita. Estuvo jugando al voleibol con Dec, Kell y Allan, y parece ser que hablaron de ti.

Cari se preguntó si les habría hablado a sus primos de DJ. Sabía que Allan ya se había enterado de que estaban saliendo por aquella conversación en su sala de juntas.

No tuvo tiempo de hablar nada más con sus hermanas porque se abrió la puerta y Kell Montrose entró. Lo primero que llamó la atención de Cari fue su mirada fría y dura. Miró a las tres con tanto desdén que no pudo evitar estremecerse. En aquel instante supo que aquello no iba a ir como esperaba.

Allan entró a continuación, con gesto serio y pensativo, y luego apareció Dec, que evitó mirarla. Cari dejó en la mesa, delante de ella, su presentación.

Jessi le dio unos golpecitos en el muslo bajo la mesa para animarla, y luego le apretó la mano antes de que hablara.

—Antes de que empecemos, quisiera comentaros algunas variaciones en nuestra fuente de ingresos —comenzó Cari—. Si me lo permitís…

—No esperábamos esto —dijo Kell—. Llegados a este punto no creo que nada de lo que puedas decir hará cambiar nuestros planes.

—Esto puede suponer un importante incremento de los beneficios, y supera el objetivo que fijamos hace seis semanas —explicó Cari.

Podía ser muy blanda con sus empleados, pero también sabía sacar las uñas cuando era necesario para protegerlos.

Kell se volvió hacia Allan.

—¿Le dijiste cuál era el objetivo?

—Sí. Era un objetivo muy ambicioso y Cari quería encontrar una manera de ahorrar para aportar su granito de arena.

—Esto no lo habíamos hablado —replicó Kell.

Cari se alegró de no ser Allan, porque Kell fulminó a su primo con la mirada.

–Sin ánimo de ofender, Cari, no pensaba que fueras capaz de alcanzarlo. Estoy deseando saber cómo piensas conseguirlo.

Cari le hizo una señal con la cabeza a Jessi, que enseguida se puso a repartir la documentación con la información financiera que habían preparado. Cari fue explicándoles las cifras, deteniéndose en el significativo aumento del veinticinco por ciento en las ganancias que el lanzamiento del nuevo juego conllevaría.

–Pero todo eso es una hipótesis –recalcó Kell.

–No, es una realidad –replicó Cari–. Tengo la demo del juego en mi iPad, por si quieres jugar.

–¿Una demo de un juego? –preguntó Dec–. ¿Cómo es posible que hayas tenido tiempo para desarrollarlo?

–Usamos como punto de partida un juego que ya teníamos y le añadimos una temática navideña. Se ha encargado el equipo que iba a desarrollar un nuevo juego en el segundo trimestre del año que viene. Han trabajado muy duro en esto.

Le pasó el iPad a Kell y los tres hombres se turnaron para jugar antes de devolvérselo a Cari.

–Estoy impresionado. Estas son las ideas innovadoras que valoramos en Playtone –comentó Kell.

–Me alegra oírlo –dijo Cari.

–Pásale a Dec una lista con el nombre de todos los que han participado en este proyecto –le pidió Kell.

Cari asintió y Dec le sonrió. Estaba satisfecha con la presentación que había hecho, y esperaba que fuera suficiente para que Kell se diera cuenta de la valía de aquella generación de Chandler.

–¿Qué tal si volvemos a reunirnos dentro de unas semanas? –preguntó Emma–. Ya has visto de lo que somos capaces.

Kell negó con la cabeza.

–No, esto no cambia nuestros planes. Dec, por favor, comienza con tu presentación.

Emma palideció y Cari tuvo un mal presentimiento al ver a Dec levantarse.

–Os daré una copia de mi informe después la reunión.

–¿Por qué no ahora? –preguntó Jessi.

–No quiero que lo leáis antes de que tenga la oportunidad de explicarlo. Añadiré la nueva fuente de ingresos, pero como Kell acaba de decir, realmente no cambia mucho de lo que ya habíamos planeado. Cuando llegué a Infinity Games lo primero en lo que reparé es en que hay duplicidad entre lo que hacemos en Playtone y lo que hacéis aquí. Por ejemplo, no necesitamos dos directores de desarrollo técnico, así que recomiendo que prescindamos de uno.

Cari sintió que hervía de ira mientras Dec continuaba hablando de todas las áreas en las que pensaba que debía haber recortes. Según él, tres cuartas partes del personal debían mantenerse porque eran buenos trabajadores y poseían lo que denominó como «conocimientos de diseño de vanguardia». Al menos la mayoría de sus empleados iban a conservar sus empleos.

–Por último, estoy seguro de que no es ninguna sorpresa que recomiende reducir los puestos directivos de Infinity Games –dijo Dec con tono neutral–. Aunque Cari, Jessi y Emma dedican muchas horas a la compañía y cumplen sus funciones, creo no hay necesidad de mantenerlas. En un principio, iba a recomendar prescindir de las tres, pero en las últimas seis semanas he visto cuánto depende el personal de Infinity de Cari. Ella es su motor, su animadora, y todos trabajan más cuando ella se lo pide. Teniendo en cuenta que mantendremos a la mayoría del personal de Infinity, creo que debería quedarse y continuar como directora de gestión.

Jessi se levantó de un salto y comenzó a hablar, pero Cari no prestó atención a su hermana. Solo tenía oídos para Dec. ¿Había recomendando mantenerla en su puesto por su relación? No podía quedarse si Emma y Jessi eran despedidas.

Se levantó, señaló a Dec y le indicó que se acercara a un rincón de la habitación. Sus hermanas estaban teniendo una acalorada discusión con Kell y Allan, pero a Cari solo le interesaba una persona.

–¿De qué se iba todo eso? –susurró cuando se hubieron apartado de la mesa.

–¿Qué quieres decir?

–¿Por qué me quedo yo y no Jessi o Emma? Las tres somos vitales para la supervivencia de Infinity Games.

–Porque siempre estás en las trincheras con el personal. Pero las otras…

–Basta, Dec. Las otras son mis hermanas. No podemos construir una vida en común si piensas despedir a mis hermanas.

–No estamos construyendo una vida en común –dijo Dec.

–Entonces, ¿qué hemos estado haciendo?

–Demonios, no quise decir eso –farfulló Dec–. No puedo salvar a las tres, Cari. A Kell no le gustó la idea de que te quedaras, pero le dije que era la única alternativa que aceptaría.

–Te lo agradezco, pero no tienes ni idea de la situación en la que me colocas.

–Era difícil de todas formas. No puedo darle la espalda a mi familia –dijo él después de que pasaran largos segundos.

–Tampoco te lo estoy pidiendo. Lo único que te pido es que pienses en nuestro hijo.

–Lo hago pensando en él, así que no intentes chantajearme con eso. Lo tengo presente tanto como tú.

–Sí, pero tu familia sale victoriosa. ¿Crees que podemos ser felices estando mis hermanas tan enfadadas? Yo también estoy enfadada.

–Sé realista. Es mejor de lo que esperabas.

–No –replicó ella–. Te he demostrado cómo podemos seguir trabajando como lo hemos venido haciendo hasta ahora y que Infinity Games puede quedarse como está. Te he enseñado todo lo que tenía y parece que eso no significa nada para ti.

–Ya no tomas decisiones en Infinity Games porque ya no eres dueña. Tienes suerte de que estemos considerando mantener a la mayoría de la plantilla.

Cari sacudió con la cabeza cuando la ira y el dolor se fundieron en su interior.

–Tenía que haber imaginado que dirías algo así. No eres capaz de quedarte y ver la devastación que dejas a tu paso.

–Esta vez no voy a salir huyendo –replicó Dec.

–Quizá sí.

–Deja de actuar así. Son negocios, no el fin del mundo. No puedes dirigir una empresa guiándote por los sentimientos.

–Tú sí porque no tienes corazón. Pero yo no soy como tú, Dec. Te quiero, pero apuesto a que ni siquiera te importa. No entiendes cómo el amor lo cambia todo, cómo te hace preocuparte de las personas que te rodean y de las consecuencias de tus actos. Dijiste que esto no me afectaría a mí ni a DJ, pero claro que lo hará –explotó Cari–. He sido una tonta por creer que podrías cambiar. Pensé que te quedarías y construirías un futuro conmigo y con nuestro hijo, pero ahora veo que no era eso lo que te interesaba. Y aunque te agradezco que quieras mantenerme en mi puesto, no voy a quedarme.

Se volvió para alejarse de él y se encontró con que los demás los estaban mirando. Al ver la cara de sus hermanas, supo que los habían oído. Tenías los ojos como platos y se habían quedado boquiabiertas.

Cari respiró hondo antes de hablar.

–Sí, habéis oído bien, Dec y yo tenemos un hijo en común. A pesar de que nos abandonó, lo recibí de nuevo en nuestras vidas pensando que había cambiado, aunque ahora veo que todavía está obsesionado por esa vieja disputa familiar que no tiene nada que ver con el presente.

–Lo sabía –dijo Jessi.

–¿Lo sabías? ¿Por qué no dijiste nada? –le preguntó Allan.

–Acabo de recibir esta mañana el informe del investigador privado. Debería haber dicho que lo sospechaba –puntualizó, y se volvió hacia Kell–. No puedes despedir a las tías de tu propio sobrino.

–El bebé no cambia nada –sentenció Kell.

–Lo cambia todo –intervino Emma–. Ahora somos familia y no podemos seguir tratando de aniquilarnos. Es hora de poner punto final a esta guerra.

–No –dijo Kell–. No me rendiré solo porque Dec y Cari hayan tenido una aventura. Eso no ha sido una relación, ha sido un error.

Cari se encogió ante su comentario.

–¿Fue un error, Dec? –preguntó.

Dec la miró, y la expresión de sus ojos le recordó a la de un animal atrapado en una trampa. Luego le dio la espalda y se volvió hacia su primo.

–Kell, ya está bien de tonterías.

–No son tonterías. Se llama olfato para los negocios –replicó Kell.

–Pues el buen sentido empresarial no se basa en venganzas –dijo Emma, caminando hacia Cari y rodeándola con su brazo.

Mientras sus hermanas la sacaban de la sala de juntas, Cari miró a Dec. Parecía de piedra, como si no sintiera nada, muy diferente del hombre en cuyos brazos había dormido la noche anterior. Sintió que se le rompía el corazón en mil pedazos y pensó que aquel era el peor momento de su vida.

Mientras avanzaban por los pasillos de Playtone Games hacia el ascensor, rompió a llorar y ya no pudo parar. Jessi le dio unas palmaditas en el hombro y trató de calmarse, pero le resultó imposible. Se había dejado engañar por Declan Montrose una vez más. Después de pasar semanas fingiendo que sentía algo por ella, dándole esperanzas de que lo suyo podía prosperar… Era todo tan cruel y la afectaba tanto que no creía posible que alguna vez pudiera recuperarse.

Cuando llegaron al aparcamiento, bajo la luz deslumbrante del sol, se detuvo, incapaz de seguir caminando. Sus hermanas la abrazaron, y lloró. Todas sus esperanzas y sueños se habían esfumado y no sabía cómo iba a recoger los pedazos rotos de su corazón y continuar con su vida. Quería para DJ más de lo que en aquel momento podía ofrecerle, pero tenía que reconocer que un hombre como Dec nunca podría ser un padre para su hijo, porque no era el hombre que ella necesitaba como compañero y amante.

Dec se quedó conmocionado ante las palabras de Cari, aunque no debería sorprenderse. Sabía que lo amaba. Nunca se habría acostado con él de no ser así, y lo había sabido desde el principio.

Pero le había dolido cuando le había dicho que no tenía corazón y que seguía anclado en el pasado. Había intentado mantenerse en la fina línea que separaba lo que le debía a su familia y lo que quería para él.

—¿Tienes un hijo? —preguntó Allan, acercándose a él.

—Sí, pero no lo he sabido hasta que volví a encontrarme con Cari.

–Deberías habérnoslo contado –dijo Kell.

–¿Para qué? No habría cambiado nada.

–Tienes razón. No habría cambiado nada, pero no te habría pedido que te ocuparas de la compraventa.

Dec se quedó mirando unos segundos a su primo antes de hablar.

–No estoy de acuerdo con todo lo que ha dicho Cari, pero tiene razón en que no podemos seguir obsesionados con el pasado. Para mí, todo esto no tiene nada que ver con el abuelo. Ya sabes que nunca estuvimos muy unidos.

–Entonces, ¿de qué se trata? –preguntó Kell.

–Me gustan los desafíos y vosotros sois mi familia. Solo nos tenemos a nosotros, o bueno, en mi caso, lo que tenía hasta que supe de mi hijo.

–¿Tú también piensas lo mismo, Allan?

–No estoy en esto por venganza –respondió Allan–. Quiero decir que tal vez el abuelo tenía su carácter y…

–Tal vez –le interrumpió Kell–, ninguno de los dos os acordáis de que Gregory Chandler apartó a Thomas de los negocios buscando su propio beneficio.

Era evidente que Kell no estaba siendo razonable y recurría a los argumentos de siempre. Dec no tenía ningún interés en volver a hablar del tema una vez más, así que enfiló hacia la puerta.

–Mi madre nunca quiso formar parte de esto y ahora entiendo por qué. No sé qué va a pasar entre Cari y yo, pero no quiero perderla. Es la primera persona que amo en mi vida –dijo y, al pasar junto a la puerta, dio un puñetazo al marco–. Maldita sea, os lo he dicho a vosotros antes que a ella.

–Ve tras ella –dijo Allan, señalando hacia fuera–. Kell y yo vamos a buscar la manera de que esto sea una fusión y no la destrucción de Infinity Games.

–Habla por ti, Allan –explotó Kell sin poder disimular su ira.

Nunca haría las paces con la familia Chandler.

Por su parte, Dec no quería seguir siendo un Montrose y vivir bajo aquel manto de odio bajo el que se habían criado. En aquel momento entendía a su madre mejor que nunca. Desde la puerta, vio cómo Allan se levantaba y rodeaba la mesa hasta Kell.

–Ya no somos unos críos –dijo Allan en tono suave–. Eres el presidente porque te hemos votado, pero no te olvides de quién posee la mayoría de las acciones. O reculas en esto y buscamos una fórmula mejor para todos o quizá acabes perdiendo tu puesto en la siguiente reunión.

Kell maldijo entre dientes, apretó los puños y dio un puñetazo en la mesa.

–Ahora mismo no puedo –farfulló, y salió a toda prisa de la sala de reuniones.

Dec miró a Allan.

–¿Por qué me estás apoyando? No somos de la misma sangre.

Allan se acercó y le dio un apretón en el hombro.

–Claro que sí, siempre lo has sido. En cuanto Kell se tranquilice, se dará cuenta de que tu hijo es el futuro de ambas compañías. Eso importa más

172

que el que Thomas se apunte un tanto sobre Gregory. Al fin y al cabo, su nieto es un Montrose.

Allan tenía razón, pero a Dec le daba igual. Tenía pensado hablar con Cari después de la reunión, pero después de lo que le había dicho, no iba a ser fácil reconquistarla.

Allan salió de la sala de reuniones en busca de Kell para calmarlo y Dec se desplomó sobre un asiento pensando en lo mucho que quería a Cari. Los negocios, el dinero y los Montrose no significaban nada para él si no la tenía a su lado.

Sacó el teléfono móvil y vio en la pantalla la foto que Cari le había hecho con DJ. Le había dado mucho más de lo que nunca le podría agradecer y se merecía más de él, algo que le demostrara que de verdad había cambiado.

Pero lo suyo no eran los grandes gestos. Aunque fuera capaz de cambiar, no sabía cómo enamorar a alguien. Confiaba en que confesarle su amor fuera un comienzo, pero también tenía otras ideas.

Le llevaría un tiempo poner en marcha su plan, pero no le importaba. No quería dejar nada al azar. La noche anterior, cuando se le había ocurrido un plan para salvar el puesto de Cari mientras la rodeaba con sus brazos, se había dado cuenta de que había sido muy estrecho de miras. Cari y él eran parte de algo mucho más grande, y tenía que ganarse a sus hermanas antes de ir tras ella y recuperarla.

Capítulo Quince

–Siento haberme venido abajo –dijo Cari más tarde, sentada en el salón de Emma.

DJ y Sam estaban jugando en el suelo, y ya estaba más calmada después de haberse tomado medio litro de helado.

–Estabas en tu derecho. Si Dec me lo hubiera hecho a mí, se habría llevado un puñetazo.

Cari esbozó una medio sonrisa, pero no le pareció divertido.

–No quiero hablar de Dec. Deberíamos pensar un plan para que las tres sigamos formando parte de la plantilla. Estoy segura de que el departamento financiero podrá recalcular las cifras y…

–No quiero hablar de trabajo –la interrumpió Jessi–. Todos te hemos oído decir que amas a Dec. ¿Qué piensas hacer ahora?

–No lo sé –contestó–. Pensé que actuaría de otra forma. Creía que… Bueno, da igual lo que creyera, no puedo hacer que cambie. Ahora entiendo por qué son tan importantes para él la compra de Infinity y los Montrose.

–Sí, es adoptado.

–¿Cómo lo sabes?

–He encargado que lo investiguen. También sospechaba que era el padre de DJ.

Cari debería haberse imaginado que Jessi lo averiguaría.

–Se me pasó por la cabeza que Dec podía ser el padre de DJ cuando empezaste a salir con él –añadió Emma–. Últimamente, no querías saber nada de hombres.

–No pensaba contarle nada de DJ.

–¿Y qué pasó? Nunca has hablado del tema –observó Jessi.

–Simplemente nos sentimos atraídos y acabamos en la cama. A la mañana siguiente, había desaparecido y me sentía como una estúpida, así que ni intenté ponerme en contacto con él. Al principio, no sabía que era un Montrose.

–¿Qué pasó cuando supiste que te habías quedado embarazada? –preguntó Emma.

Sus hermanas la observaban atentamente.

–Había pasado tanto tiempo que no quería saber nada de él. Fue una sensación abrumadora.

–Deberías habérnoslo contado, Cari. Si lo hubiera sabido, habría intentado localizar a Dec.

–No habrías podido protegerme de esto, Emma. A pesar de la enemistad de nuestras familias, una vez que averigüé quién era, supe que tenía que hablarle de DJ.

–¿Por qué? –preguntó Jessi–. Renunció a sus derechos cuando se fue.

–Porque es el padre de DJ y todos queremos a nuestros padres a pesar de todo. ¿Os acordáis cómo papá siempre quería agradar al abuelo a pesar de que nunca le decía nada agradable?

–Por supuesto que sí –contestó Jessi–. A ver, entiendo tu punto de vista, pero deberías haberme dejado volver ahí dentro y darle un puñetazo. Hoy se ha comportado como un perfecto imbécil.

–Sus primos querían deshacerse de nosotras y estaba entre la espada y la pared. No debería haber sido tan dura con él.

–Por supuesto que sí –dijo Emma–. Debería haber hablado contigo antes de entrar ahí y hacer su propuesta. Están muy preocupados con los resultados y no estoy diciendo que tenía que haber hecho las cosas de otra manera en cuanto a prescindir de Jessi y de mí, pero no debería habértelo soltado de esa forma.

No era una sorpresa que Emma tuviera argumentos a favor tanto de Dec como de ella. Siempre había sido muy ecuánime y sabía muy bien cómo funcionaban los negocios. Todas lo sabían.

–Supongo que estaba dolida, y la ira de Kell era aterradora. No quiero que mi hijo tenga relación con ellos. Son muy peculiares.

–Estoy de acuerdo –dijo Jessi–. Allan no es tan desagradable como Kell, pero es evidente que están muy unidos.

Cari suspiró.

–Estoy algo enfadada con el abuelo por la manera en que apartó a Thomas Montrose de la empresa. Me pregunto por qué lo hizo.

–Nunca lo sabremos. Pero tendrás una buena historia que contarle a DJ cuando sea mayor de por qué no nos llevamos bien con la familia de su padre.

Aquello entristeció a Cari. Sabía que se había dejado llevar por la furia y deseó no haberlo hecho. Debería haberse preocupado solo por sacar adelante su trabajo cuando Dec había entrado en escena. Nunca iba a poder mostrarse indiferente teniéndolo cerca.

–Debería haberme mantenido al margen.

–Ya es demasiado tarde. Tenemos que seguir adelante –terció Emma–. Creo que los empleados se vendrían con nosotras si fundamos una nueva compañía.

Cari sacudió la cabeza. No quería un nuevo enfrentamiento con los primos Montrose en el que sus hermanas y ella partían con desventaja. Había sacrificado demasiado por una vieja enemistad y ya estaba harta.

–¿Crees que no lo harían? –preguntó Emma–. Pensaba que eran leales.

–Puede que sí, pero entonces Playtone nos buscaría de nuevo. No quiero seguir luchando en la misma batalla –dijo Cari.

Miró a su hijo y decidió que había llegado la hora de irse a casa. Quería abrazar a DJ y olvidarse de que se había desnudado emocionalmente ante la impasibilidad de Dec.

–Estoy cansada, chicas. Creo que me voy a ir a casa. Podemos vernos mañana para pensar qué pasos dar a partir de ahora.

–¿Estás bien para conducir? –preguntó Jessi.

Había una nota de preocupación en su voz y Cari se preguntó si su hermana sabría que un corazón roto dolía más que cualquier otro sufrimiento. Luego recordó que, a pesar de su aparente dureza, Jessi tenía un corazón blando.

–Sí, estoy bien.

Tomó a DJ en brazos y se despidió de su sobrino. Una vez en el coche, de camino a su casa, decidió que no quería pasar la noche allí. No quería dormir en una cama que olía a Dec ni recorrer una casa que ahora contenía recuerdos de él.

Se fue al hotel Ritz Carlton y pidió una habitación. Tumbada en la cama, pensó en la última vez en que Dec la había dejado y el tiempo que le había costado olvidarse de él. Esta vez iba a ser mucho peor.

Llenó la bañera y se metió en el agua con su hijo. Su pequeño mundo no había cambiado. Lo envidiaba porque, a pesar del pasado o de lo que había sucedido ese día, nunca lo recordaría.

Allan y Dec tardaron toda la tarde en convencer a Kell de que aceptara darles una oportunidad a Jessi y Emma para que demostraran su valía.

–No me gusta la mediocridad.

–Me da igual mientras les des una oportunidad de demostrar lo que valen –dijo Dec–. Es lo único que podemos hacer llegados a este punto.

Miró a sus primos y dejó escapar un suspiro.

–Voy a necesitar unos días para intentar recuperar a Cari –añadió.

–Dijo que te quería. No creo que lo tengas tan difícil –dijo Allan.

–Dijo que se sentía como una estúpida por amarme –puntualizó Dec–. No debería haber dejado que se fuera.

Kell se levantó, se acercó a él y le dio una palmada en el hombro.

—La recuperaras. ¿Qué podemos hacer para ayudar?

—¿Ya no te importa que sea una Chandler?

—Como dijiste antes, tienes un hijo, Dec, y eso lo cambia todo.

Dec se alegraba de oírlo. Kell podía ser muy testarudo, pero sabía reconocer cuando algo estaba bien.

—Quiero que DJ se sienta como un verdadero Montrose.

—¿Qué significa eso? —preguntó Allan.

—Nunca me he sentido un verdadero Montrose —respondió Dec—. Siempre tuve presente que era adoptado.

—Para nosotros, siempre has sido un Montrose. No quiero volverte a oír eso —intervino Kell.

Le alegraba que sus primos le dijeran eso. Siempre había buscado sentirse integrado y por fin lo había conseguido. Ahora, tenía que ganarse a Cari de nuevo y luego ya podría relajarse. Solo había una manera de hacerlo: tenía que demostrarle que tenía raíces.

Pensó en su gran mansión vacía de Beverly Hills y supo lo que debía hacer.

—Tengo que dejar el Maserati y buscar otro coche. ¿Podéis hacerme un favor?

¿Por qué vas a cambiar el Maserati?

—No es un coche para niños.

Después, les explicó a sus primos cómo podían ayudarlo, y se mostraron entusiasmados de poder aportar su granito de arena. Tenía la sensación de que Kell seguía sintiéndose mal por su arrebato de ira. Dec no estaba seguro de que fueran a tener éxito en lo que les había pedido, pero los dejó para poner en marcha su plan.

Se fue al concesionario de Porsche y cambió el Maserati por un Cayenne antes de ir a casa de Cari. Cuando llegó, el sol se estaba poniendo y se encontró la casa vacía. Llamó a su teléfono, pero le saltó el buzón de voz. Quería poner fin a aquel distanciamiento cuanto antes.

Ahora que sabía que la amaba, quería que su vida con ella comenzara en aquel mismo instante. Se le ocurrió llamar a Allan y le pidió que llamara a la esposa de John y le pidiera el teléfono de Jessi. Treinta minutos más tarde lo había conseguido. Eran poco más de las nueve, algo tarde, aunque no demasiado teniendo en cuenta que su futuro estaba en juego.

—Soy Dec —dijo cuando Jessi contestó—. ¿Podría hablar con Cari?

—No está aquí. Se ha ido a casa, pero no creo que le apetezca verte.

—Estoy en su casa y aquí no hay nadie —replicó Dec, comenzando a sentir pánico.

¿Y si había tenido un accidente?

—¿Cómo? ¿Estás seguro de que no se está escondiendo de ti?

—Completamente seguro. Aquí no hay nadie y tampoco veo su coche aparcado —explicó Dec.

Se quedó mirando la casa y pensó en cómo había puesto su vida patas arriba. Quizá debería respetar sus deseos y dejar que se ocultara de él. Pero esta vez no podía hacerlo, esta vez la amaba y quería tenerla a su lado.

–Voy a ver qué puedo averiguar –dijo Jessi después de largos segundos–. Si te ayudo en esto, estarás en deuda conmigo.

–De acuerdo, te deberé una, pero no puedo hacer nada para parar la compra.

–No pasa nada. Pensaré en algo que puedas hacer por mí. Te llamaré.

–Estaré esperando.

Dec permaneció cuarenta y cinco minutos sentado en la entrada de la casa de Cari antes de que su teléfono finalmente sonara.

–Dime.

–Está en un hotel. Dice que no soporta la idea de dormir en una cama que ha compartido contigo –dijo Jessi.

Aquellas palabras cortaban como un cuchillo.

–¿Dónde está?

–¿Por qué quieres saberlo?

–¿A ti qué te parece?

–Quieres recuperarla, te has dado cuenta de que lo has estropeado todo. Pero quiero oírtelo decir.

–Lo he estropeado todo –admitió–. Ahora, dime dónde está.

–En el Ritz Carlton de Marina del Rey. Se registró hace dos horas, así que debió de ir directamente desde casa de Emma.

–Gracias –dijo Dec antes de colgar.

Estaba a poco más de un kilómetro de donde estaba anclado el yate en el que vivía. Se alegró de que estuviera tan cerca. Era tarde para ir, pero por la mañana, cuando se despertara, le demostraría lo mucho que significaba para ella.

Condujo hasta el hotel y se fue a la recepción. No quisieron darle el número de habitación, pero aceptaron entregarle un sobre. Se fue al yate, pero no pudo dormir entre la excitación de verla por la mañana y el temor de que no aceptara su invitación ni sus disculpas.

El sobre que se encontró en la puerta de su suite era blanco y tenía el membrete del Ritz Carlton, pero al mirar el anverso reconoció la letra de Dec. Lentamente lo abrió y sacó la tarjeta que había dentro.

Por favor, ven a desayunar conmigo al Big Spender, en el muelle siete del club de yates de Marina del Rey. Quiero disculparme.

Dec

Aunque apenas explicaba nada en la nota, estaba deseando verlo y escuchar lo que tenía que decirle. Había pasado mala noche y se enfrentaba a una vida llena de noches solitarias sin Dec. Si lo que pretendía era disculparse, quería oír lo que tenía que decirle.

Pidió que les subieran ropa de las tiendas y vistió a DJ antes de hacerlo ella. Luego, se fueron en coche hasta el puerto. No necesitó pedir indicaciones para dar con el yate de Dec ya que se encontró un rastro de corazones con su nombre escrito en ellos que llevaba hasta el muelle en el que estaba atracado. La pasarela estaba bajada y había un camino de pétalos de rosas que llevaban hasta la cubierta, en donde formaban un gran corazón.

–¿Hola? –dijo al subir a bordo.

–Hola –contestó Dec, subiendo los escalones.

Parecía cansado, como si no hubiera pegado ojo en toda la noche. Se acercó a ella y la tomó en sus brazos. Besó a DJ en la cabeza y luego a Cari en los labios.

–Te quiero –le dijo.

Las palabras se quedaron flotando y se sintió desvalido.

Cari fue a decir algo, pero él se lo impidió poniéndole un dedo en los labios. No quería que le dijera todas las razones por las que no lo amaba. Sabía que lo había estropeado todo y le iba a llevar toda una eternidad recuperarla. Pero estaba dispuesto a asumirlo.

–Ayer por la mañana, cuando salimos de tu casa, sabía que iba a ser un día difícil. También sabía que no iba a poder despedirte y que te pediría que te casaras conmigo. Eso era lo que quería, no sé cómo las cosas se descontrolaron tanto.

–Creo que fue por tu primo. Quería nuestras cabezas –dijo Cari–. Pero también tuvimos algo que ver. Quería que dejaras de pensar como un empresario e hicieras lo que yo quería, así que me tomé la reunión como una gran prueba.

–Bueno, puede que Kell quisiera vuestras cabezas, pero también es cierto que dije cosas que no debería haber dicho. Mi vida cambió cuando me enteré de que tenía un hijo y me dio miedo admitirlo.

Cari ladeó la cabeza y se quedó mirándolo. Dec vio lágrimas en sus ojos.

–Yo también te quiero. Quiero que formemos una familia, pero no sé cómo podemos hacerlo si mantenemos esta disputa.

–Estoy de acuerdo –convino él, tomando su rostro entre las manos y secándole las lágrimas con los dedos–. Antes de nada, deja de preocuparte por los negocios. Kell, Allan y yo hemos acordado dar a tus hermanas una oportunidad para demostrar por qué debemos mantenerlas en sus puestos. No es ninguna garantía, pero es mejor que nada. Ah, y Kell ha accedido a ser más amable a partir de ahora.

–Es un comienzo –dijo Cari, rodeándolo por la cintura y apoyando la cabeza en su pecho–. ¿Hablabas en serio cuando dijiste que me amabas? –preguntó en voz baja.

Dec empezó a tener esperanzas de que podía recuperarla.

–Sí. Sé que dijiste que no tenía corazón, y no te equivocabas. Mi corazón no es mío porque te pertenece a ti.

–Yo también te quiero, Dec. Todos esos corazones que conducían hasta ti… Nadie había hecho nada tan bonito por mí. Me haces sentir especial.

Agachó la cabeza y la besó.

–Eres muy especial para mí. Me da miedo decirte lo mucho que significas –las lágrimas volvieron a asomar a los ojos de Cari y lo abrazó con fuerza–. Quiero que seas mi esposa –continuó Dec–. Que nos casemos y formemos una verdadera familia.

–Yo también lo deseo –admitió ella–. No he dejado de desearlo desde aquella primera cena después de que volvieras. No quería creer que fueras el hombre de mis sueños, pero eres eso y mucho más.

–Espero poder estar a la altura, Cari. Voy a esforzarme mucho por ser ese hombre. De hecho, voy a enseñarte una sorpresa después de que desayunemos.

–¿Otra?

–Y unas cuantas más –dijo él con una sonrisa.

La llevó hasta la mesa dispuesta con el desayuno y, cuando acabaron, bajaron del yate para enseñarles el Cayenne.

–Este es mi nuevo coche –dijo, señalando el vehículo con el asiento del bebé en el asiento trasero–. Hablo muy en serio cuando digo que quiero compartir mi vida contigo.

Le creía. Estaba aprendiendo algo más sobre el hombre al que amaba: cuando se proponía algo, no paraba hasta conseguirlo.

Luego, condujeron hasta Beverly Hills sin que Dec le dijera adónde iban. Se detuvo para enviar un mensaje de texto y permanecieron sentados de la mano a la espera de que le contestaran. Cuando finalmente recibió respuesta, puso el coche en marcha.

–Cierra los ojos –le pidió.

Cuando Cari los hubo cerrado, Dec tomó una calle y al cabo de unos minutos paró el coche. Lo oyó salir y sacar a DJ antes de abrirle la puerta a ella y ayudarla a salir.

–Me llevo a DJ. Tú quédate aquí un momento.

Se quedó allí parada bajo el sol del mediodía.

Dec volvió junto a ella, solo, y la tomó en brazos. Luego la besó lenta y apasionadamente y cuando se apartó, le dijo que abriera los ojos.

Al hacerlo, Cari vio una gran mansión con un lazo en la fachada. Había una gran pancarta que decía: *Cari, ayúdame a llenar esta casa de amor y convirtámosla en nuestro hogar.*

Se fundió en un abrazo con él y hundió el rostro en su cuello.

–Sí, claro que sí –dijo ella.

–Estupendo. Para empezar, he invitado a nuestra familia.

Sorprendida, abrió los ojos de par en par. Al cruzar el umbral vio a Kell, Allan, Emma, Sam y Jessi con su hijo. No parecían amigos íntimos, pero estaban siendo civilizados.

DJ empezó a dar palmas.

–Mama, papa.

Dec dejó a Cari en el suelo y el pequeño gateó hasta ellos. Cari se agachó para tomar a su hijo en brazos, satisfecha de haber conseguido todo lo que siempre había deseado del amor y de la vida.

No te pierdas, *Cautivos del detino,*
de Katherine Garbera,
el próximo libro de la serie
Amantes y enemigos.
Aquí tienes un adelanto…

Allan McKinney parecía un actor de Hollywood con su cuerpo esbelto, hecho para el pecado, el estiloso corte de su pelo castaño oscuro y sus penetrantes ojos grises, capaces de hacer que una mujer se olvidara de pensar. Pero Jessi sabía que era el demonio disfrazado.

Era un mal tipo y siempre lo había sido. Conociéndolo como lo conocía, no se imaginaba que se hubiera acercado a su mesa de Little Bar, en la zona de Wilshire/La Brea de los Ángeles, por otra razón que no fuera pavonearse de su última victoria.

Solo habían pasado tres semanas desde que él, junto a sus vengativos primos de Playtone Games, se hubieran hecho con la compañía de su familia, como colofón a la rivalidad de toda una vida.

Acababan de salir de una reunión en Playtone Games en la que había hecho una propuesta para salvar su puesto. Lo más humillante de aquella fusión empresarial era arrastrarse a los pies de Allan. Era una buena directora de marketing, pero en vez de poder continuar en su puesto y sacar adelante el trabajo, tenía que ir una vez en semana a la ciudad desde Malibú y demostrarle a los Montrose que se estaba ganando su sueldo.

Allan se sentó en el taburete de al lado rozando con sus largas piernas las suyas. Se comportaba como si fuera el dueño no solo de aquel lugar, sino del mundo entero.

Eran las cinco de la tarde y el bar empezaba a llenarse de gente que acababa de salir de trabajo. Allí era una persona anónima y podía relajarse, pero con Allan a su lado interrumpiendo su momento de paz iba a ser imposible.

–¿Has venido para restregármelo por las narices? –preguntó ella.

Era lo que se esperaba del hombre que pretendía ser y con el que se había enzarzado en una competición desde el momento en que se habían conocido.

–Es algo muy de los Montrose McKinney.

Su padre siempre había advertido a sus hijas que evitaran a los nietos de Thomas Montrose debido a las malas relaciones entre ambas familias. Había seguido su consejo, pero antes incluso de la compra de la compañía, no le había quedado más remedio que tratar con Allan cuando su mejor amiga, Patti, se había enamorado y luego casado con el mejor amigo de él.

–No exactamente. He venido a hacerte una oferta –dijo.

Luego, le hizo una seña a la camarera y le pidió un whisky.

–Gracias, pero no necesito tu ayuda.

Allan se pasó la mano por el pelo, entornó los ojos y le dirigió una mirada que la obligó a enderezarse en su asiento.

–¿Te diviertes provocándome?

Bianca

¿Estaba listo para enfrentarse a la verdad que ella le estaba haciendo ver?

SUTIL SEDUCCIÓN

SUSAN STEPHENS

Luca Tebaldi se había pasado toda la vida tratando de distanciarse del imperio familiar. Por ello, se sintió furioso cuando una cazafortunas se hizo con todas las propiedades de su fallecido hermano y le obligó a regresar.

Decidido a conseguir que Jen Sanderson confesara cómo había logrado engañar a su hermano, y renunciara a todo lo que este le había dejado, se la llevó a su isla siciliana.

Sin embargo, Luca descubrió que Jen era inocente en más de un aspecto. La sensual mujer lo desafiaba y enardecía sus sentidos.

Bianca

Vendida a un multimillonario

UN JUEGO DE VENGANZA

CLARE CONNELLY

La aristocrática Marnie Kenington se hundió en la desesperación cuando sus padres la obligaron a abandonar a Nikos Kyriazis; pero no lo olvidó, y tampoco olvidó su sensualidad. Por eso, cuando años más tarde insistió en reunirse con ella, el corazón de Marnie se llenó de esperanza… hasta que Nikos se lo aplastó bajo el peso de una fría e implacable amenaza: si no se casaba con él, no daría a su padre el dinero que necesitaba para salvarse de la bancarrota.

La traición juvenil de Marnie había empujado a Nikos a convertirse en un tiburón de las finanzas, y ahora estaba a punto de vengarse de los Kenington. Además, el famoso aplomo de Marnie no funcionaba en el dormitorio, y él sabía que podría ajustar cuentas de la forma más tórrida.

¡YA EN TU PUNTO DE VENTA!

Deseo

*Iba a poner toda el alma y el corazón
para que siguiera siendo suya*

RECUPERAR SU AMOR
CAT SCHIELD

La cantante Melody Caldwell le había dado varios meses al empresario Kyle Tailor para formalizar su relación, pero el destino había intervenido antes de que tomasen una decisión: Melody estaba embarazada.

Celos, miedo, ilusión. Kyle no sabía qué sentir al recibir la noticia de Melody. Había intentado proteger su corazón, pero entonces un admirador misterioso empezó a interesarse demasiado por ella y él se dio cuenta de que quería que Melody siguiese siendo suya y, para ello, tenía que tomar medidas…

She laughed, and the sound—well, it caused a powerful and wholly unexpected shift inside him. Scared the hell out of him and, paradoxically, made him yearn to hear it again.

* * * * *

Discover how this rugged rancher's wanderlust
is tamed in time for a merry Christmas, in
A STONE CREEK CHRISTMAS.
In stores December 2008.

Silhouette®

SPECIAL EDITION™

FROM *NEW YORK TIMES* BESTSELLING AUTHOR

LINDA LAEL MILLER

A STONE CREEK CHRISTMAS

Veterinarian Olivia O'Ballivan finds the animals in Stone Creek playing Cupid between her and Tanner Quinn. Even Tanner's daughter, Sophie, is eager to play matchmaker. With everyone conspiring against them and the holiday season fast approaching, Tanner and Olivia may just get everything they want for Christmas after all!

Available December 2008
wherever books are sold.